CHALLENGES OF HONOR

GODDESS'S HONOR
BOOK THREE

JOYCE REYNOLDS-WARD

HOT SUMMER NIGHT

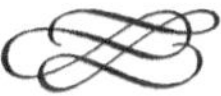

Katerin ea Miteal poured cold berry tea for herself and her unexpected visitor, Orlanden en Selail, into the metal-framed glass mugs she had brought back from her last trip to Medvara. They were a precious, prized find that she stored carefully between uses during the traveling summer camps of the Three Leaders of the Two Nations of Clenda and Keldara. An indulgence, one of the few she allowed to remind herself that she was no longer a wandering circuit healer and could find room for such a small luxury.

She took her time straining the tea into the mugs through the metal filter that came with the cups, feeling the pressure of Orlanden's gaze on her back. At the same time she kept one eye on the fading dusk outside, waiting for the first sliver of the moon that meant it was time to speak with Rekaré.

Why are they here so soon? What has gone wrong?

"What tea is that?" Orlanden asked.

So he was observing formalities, and would not talk about anything of significance until they had both had tea.

"Huckleberry, from Wickmasa," Katerin said, glancing past the rolled-up sides of her lodge to check for moonrise as the dusk deepened. "Fresh from this year's harvest, with a hint of sage. My own blend."

"I have always liked your blends," Orlanden said.

"Thank you." Katerin glanced toward the great ridge toward their east. No sign of the full moon edging over the trees yet.

She finished pouring the tea, grateful that Orlanden and his beloved, Haran en Mershaunten, brother to the current ruler of the neighboring nation of Larij, hadn't arrived earlier in the afternoon. Itchy, sore and sweaty from her day's work of gathering roots, brush, grass, berries, and seeds for her winter potion-making, she had gone down to the spring-fed pond that served the camp to wash and change. Now she wore a loose-fitting undyed non-magical linen tunic and trousers, her sweaty work clothing airing out on a line strung between the young redbark pines near her outside hearth.

Why are they here early?

Her thoughts continued to spin as she focused on straining the tea. Haran and Orlanden were at least half a moon cycle early for the traditional late-summer trip that Alicira, one of the Three Leaders, made to the hot springs at Wixtnal, on the border between Larij and Keldara. As hot as it had been this summer, none of them had been looking for Haran and Orlanden to come for at least another cycle.

Katerin heaved a sigh, wondering if it was Katerin Healer or Katerin ea Miteal that Orlanden sought an audience with.

Too much of Katerin ea Miteal these days.

Best to get this discussion over with. She walked to the small wooden table and chairs where Orlanden sat, fixing her with that owl-like gaze he had when serious subjects came up. Katerin made every move even and deliberate, giving herself time to prepare for this talk. She set the mugs down on the table before easing herself down in the hide and twig camp chair, wincing at muscles aching from the day's work. She had gathered half a season's worth of supplies. The Gods had been generous—but now she ached from toiling through the heat.

"I'm surprised you're here this soon. Isn't it still hot in the flatlands? Or are you in need of my services?"

Orlanden's skin had the yellowish underlay of hardened pitch instead of the healthier, pink-shaded brown it should be at this stage of summer.

Does he want Katerin Healer, then?

Or was it simply aging? They were all getting older, and even though she was the younger, she could feel age creeping up on her as well, especially after a long days working.

But even as she asked, she knew it wasn't the answer. She didn't let herself glance next door where Haran and Alicira, spoke in low, intense voices. Wixtnal, Haran's holding, had its own healers because of the hot springs.

No. This was something political. Something that required Alicira's touch—and possibly Katerin's input as Alicira's cousin, given the shape Alicira was in.

"It has been a hot summer." Orlanden blinked quickly, reminding her even more of the great gray owl who lingered near camp.

"Perhaps you should take some tea along when you and Haran escort Alicira to the hot springs," she said. "For yourself, not just for her."

Orlanden smiled, but it faded quickly. "I appreciate your concern, Katerin, and I would love to have some of your tea for myself. But—" he exhaled deeply. "While I have a slight touch of liver problems, I have also needed to devote many hours to meetings and negotiations down in Medvare-the-city rather than my usual duties on the high plateaus of Larij. Most of my spring and summer has been spent indoors this year."

Apprehension tightened Katerin's gut.

Political. He is speaking to Katerin ea Miteal, then.

Gods.

Of course, she had suspected this.

Worse, Alicira's fading health meant Katerin, as one of her surviving relatives, had to take a more dominant position in politics. She had noticed the quick stricken expressions on Haran and Orlanden's faces at Alicira's condition. Her cousin had aged dramatically over the summer, in spite of Katerin's best treatments. And if Orlanden had been in Medvare-the-city—then that meant he had been speaking to Katerin's other cousin, Rekaré ea Miteal, the Leader of Medvara. Rekaré, Alicira's daughter.

"Rekaré has not advised me of any problems in Medvara." She stared into her tea.

"This is an issue involving magic." Orlanden set his tea down. She looked up to meet that steady, unblinking gaze. "And given the Lady Alicira's current ailments, it is a matter of significant urgency." He reached into his vest and extracted an envelope from an inner pocket. "The Lady Rekaré wishes you to open this after you speak with her tonight." He laid it on the table.

Katerin studied the blue-sealed envelope without touching it. The silver-edged stamp was clearly her cousin's. A tiny blue and silver vortex swirled over it then faded in a shimmer of silver sparkles. Locked, and not in a pattern keyed to her for easy access. Rekaré would have to give her that key during tonight's conversation.

Cold washed over Katerin despite the warm wind blowing through the lodge.

A matter of the House of Miteal.

More than that, the meaning of the silver locking shimmer suggested a more significant concern.

Daran has remembered us.

The threat from the distant Empire-over-Sea that Rekaré's— and Katerin's—people originated from was the only issue she could think of that would require such a secure lock.

She coughed to clear her throat. "Did my cousin give you indication of what the situation is?"

"As you have already surmised from the lock, it involves the Empire-over-Sea." Orlanden picked up his tea. "I am not privy to all of Rekaré's concerns. But I can tell you that there is unrest, and both the Mershaunten and Rekaré have been approached by interests from Daran."

Interests from Daran.

Katerin's hand remained steady as she lifted her teacup, despite her inner nerves.

"What kind of interests?" she asked. She craned her head to peer outside for the first sign of moonrise.

"Mercantile. Trade. Not political, at least not to Larij," Orlanden said. "I do not know for certain about those who approach Rekaré."

Was that the silver curve of the first edge of the moon glowing over the trees? Yes.

Katerin set her tea down, relief flooding through her. "I need to prepare for my conversation with Rekaré."

Orlanden rose with her. "The other factor is the Lady Alicira's health." His voice dropped lower. "Rekaré wishes for her presence and advice as soon as possible. Can Alicira safely travel by sternwheeler to Medvare-the-city?"

He left *in her condition* unsaid but she could tell he was thinking it.

"Sternwheeler, yes." Katerin knelt by her woven reed travel chest and removed the lid. She picked up the palm-sized blue and silver wool square with clear crystal shards embedded in it that sat in the top tray and slipped it into one of the two leather bags that hung from her belt. "Horseback, no. Do you know what condition the Keldara River is in? Is the water too low for an easy transit to Katlinq port, where the Keldara meets the Chellana?"

"I checked before we left Wixtnal. The canoe men are still running the Keldara."

"Good." Katerin rose. "I need to speak with Rekaré now." She reached for the envelope, only to stop when the blue shimmer flashed red. *Guarded, then, and keyed to Orlanden until Rekaré gives me the key. But Witmara might be able to work around it—her magic is strong enough.* "Will you safeguard the message until I return? Or will it protect itself?"

Her daughter Witmara was a curious almost eleven-year-old, after all.

Orlanden raised a brow at her. "You are worried about security in *this* camp?"

"Witmara."

Orlanden relaxed, a smile spreading across his face. "I look forward to seeing her."

Katerin chuckled in spite of her worry about the conversation ahead of her. "She will be happy to see her guest uncle."

"And I have a birthday present for my guest niece," Orlanden said. "As does Haran. Do you think she'll be here soon?"

Katerin shrugged. "The kidpack will be dancing with the moon tonight. She may dart in to grab a shawl once things cool. I will probably be back by then, but—one never knows with a child in summer camp. They come and go as they please."

"All right. I'll wait for her."

"I will be back soon." Katerin slipped out the door.

Her strides quickened as she marched away from the camp. Two hundred paces from the outer ring of lodges, her daranval Rainin trotted up, her current foal capering around them. Rainin nudged Katerin. She scratched around the mare's ears while sending her a mental picture of their destination. Rainin nuzzled her side, then angled herself so that Katerin could jump up on her back without any tack. She buckled her knees slightly as Katerin grabbed her mane and swung up with the ease of long practice.

They cantered away, following a faint track across the wide flat on top of the ridge. Rainin's colt, blood bay with the silver forelock and silver streaks in his mane and tail that marked him as a daranval, one of the magic-gifted horse breed, thundered ahead of his dam. The silver in his stubby mane and short tail gleamed in the last rays of sunset, the moon not yet high enough to spread its own glow. He paused as the flat ended, angling down sharply over a rocky slope to a smaller, narrower, meadow sprinkled with the great redbark pines common to this part of the Clendan high ridges.

Rainin nickered at her colt and dropped to a walk. He followed as Rainin picked her way through the rocks to the lower meadow. They walked for twenty paces, until they reached a square formed by four big fallen trees. Katerin slid off and climbed over the trees. Rainin snorted at her colt and jumped the tree. The colt nickered a protest but obeyed his dam's command. She followed Katerin to the small stone shrine formed of four thin slabs enclosing carved stone figures of the Seven Crowned Gods. Her breath blew hot on the back of Katerin's hand.

Katerin halted, Rainin on her right side, and knelt before the shrine.

"Lady Dovré, once again I call upon your aid to speak with my cousin Rekaré." She reached into her pouch and brought out the crystal-embedded wool square, placing it in front of the figure that represented her patron Goddess. Next, she brought out an oatcake she'd made just that day and put it on the square.

Rainin rested her muzzle against her back. Once again the bond between human and daranval stirred.

RaininandKaterin,

Rainin thought at her.

> KaterinandRainin,

she thought back, joy running through her. Even after their eleven years as bondmates, the thrill of joining with her daranval in thought never changed.

> My blessing upon you.

Blue light flashed around them, growing in intensity as the Goddess's presence joined them.

> I would speak to my cousin Rekaré,

Katerin mindspoke to the Goddess.

> Granted.

The crystals within the weaving shone brightly as the oatcake disappeared. Then a wavering form grew over the patch, solidifying into Rekaré's shape. Katerin sat upright, knowing that Rekaré saw her in a similar manner.

"A good summer's evening to you, cousin," Rekaré said.

"And to you as well," Katerin responded. "Haran and Orlanden arrived in camp today, to take your mother to Wixtnal."

"I did not expect them to get there so quickly," Rekaré said. "Has Orlanden talked to you yet?"

"He has shown me the letter, yes, and told me I need your token to open it."

Rekaré sighed. "Then you know I need my mother to come here as soon as she can. I have—news."

"You should know the Old One does not fare well," Katerin warned. "She is fading fast. I do not know if she will survive the winter."

If she even lasts that long.

"That bad?"

"Yes."

"I—" Rekaré's voice caught. "Would it be better that she spend several days at Wixtnal before coming here? We are quite hot and humid, and if a few days soaking at Wixtnal will make a difference in her strength…." Her voice trailed off.

Katerin shook her head. "It will not change her status. She's going to Wixtnal for comfort and farewells, not healing. What is your need?"

"I can't speak openly. You'll understand why when you read my missive. But it is a matter of Daran, and one of great concern." Rekaré swallowed hard. "Share it with my Heartfather Heinmyets and Secondmother Inharise as well as my mother. It is something which will affect both the Two Nations and Medvara."

"I will do that."

"And Katerin? If my mother needs the time to say farewell, then take it. But please. If it is not needed—do not linger. Do not dawdle. I have need of both of you, as soon as you can get here." Rekaré looked down at the great gold signet on her left hand that, along with the citrine in her necklace called the Light of Medvara, marked her position as Medvara's Leader. "If Inharise and Heinmyets could come as well?"

Katerin shook her head, apprehension raising a deeper chill within her.

"Not with this year's harvest, not until they can seal the enchantments on this year's crop. This spring's shearing did not contain much magic, and they need to be present for the Coos berry harvest to ensure we are strong for the upcoming winter. We are hoping that the berries will hold the land's magic the wool lost." She omitted any mention of the magic in Rainin's colt.

Witmara would not forgive me if I draw attention to him.

"I remember your magic production report from last month," Rekaré said. "I wish it were not so. The news that came to me means we need every shred of sorcery we can harvest, between the Two Nations and Medvara." She glanced off to the side. "One moment, Melarae!" She snapped her fingers, sending a spellflare that flashed brighter than Katerin expected. "You can't come over here without breaking the link! I still need to speak to your cousin Katerin."

She didn't hear Melarae's response.

Perhaps Melarae needs time with a sorceress of her own age and family.

"Should I bring Witmara?" she asked, also concerned about the intensity of that magic flare.

Does Melarae need that much restraint?

Worrisome, if so.

"Yes. It may be a succession matter." Those words added to her worry, but before she could respond, Rekaré held something out to Katerin. "Here is the token to unlock that seal."

She took the smooth disc. Her fingers passed through Rekaré's. The silver disc tingled in her fingers as she placed it in her bag.

"I will see you soon, then, cousin?" Rekaré asked, uneasiness edging her voice.

"As soon as we can safely get your mother to the stern-wheeler port," Katerin answered, keeping her voice steady and reassuring.

"Thank you. Thank you, and all praise to our Goddess." Something didn't sound right in Rekaré's voice, not just disquiet but something Katerin couldn't quite identify.

Melarae? A succession matter? Does that mean Witmara—no. Melarae is not Rekaré's only child. She still has Linyet.

"All praise to our Goddess," Katerin echoed.

Rekaré's form disappeared. Rainin gave Katerin's back a gentle push with her nose, then stepped away. Katerin got up, bowing to the Dovré statue and mechanically tucking the communication patch into her pouch. She followed Rainin out of the sacred square before swinging up. The colt scampered over to them and thrust his head underneath his dam's belly to nurse as Katerin settled on her back. He squealed an objection as Rainin walked off, then galloped up the hill in front of them, flagging his tail as he ran. At the top he capered and bucked, a moonbeam catching the silver in his mane and tail.

The great gray owl swooped over the colt. Katerin caught her breath.

What does that mean?

The colt snorted and chased after the owl as it flew back into the trees, Rainin nickering after him. He reared and struck at the tree the owl took refuge in, then thundered back to Rainin's side, once again trying to nurse.

Normally his antics would be enough to make Katerin laugh. But dread enhanced by the owl's flight filled her thoughts. What would happen to the colt if he turned out to be the greatest expression of the land's magic this season? She had promised this colt to Witmara once he came into his name. The two were as bonded as girl and daranval could be before the colt's weaning and naming.

If the land's need comes first—if we have to do the Sacrifice—

Gods, she hoped that wouldn't be the case. She had never experienced the Sacrifice but had only heard stories about it.

Nonetheless, the magic harvests were poor this year. But the Two Nations and Medvara had enough resources to survive one summer like this.

Not enough for two years, however.

Next year will be better.

It had always been this way.

But the combination of magic's failure in this summer harvest and what Rekaré *hadn't* said about Melarae did not bode well.

MOTHERS AND DAUGHTERS

"MAMA, WHY DO WE HAVE TO DO THIS STUPID MAGIC OUTSIDE? It's hot!" Melarae whimpered from behind her.

Not even a moment to recover from that spell!

Rekaré bit back the angry retort she wanted to snap at her daughter, fingers tightening on the long, twisted strands of the dry grass of the interior courtyard. One clump came up by the roots and she guiltily tucked it back into the ground, expecting a complaint from the land.

Nothing. No sting on her fingertips. Perhaps the land understood her frustration.

She's just young and summer heat does not agree with her.

And she hadn't moderated the bite of the spellflare she had flicked toward Melarae to silence her.

She has to learn. Interrupting magic has consequences.

Better Melarae experience the short sharp pain of a tempered jolt from her mother to teach this lesson, instead of an uncontrolled lash from someone not inclined to tolerate a child's lack of control.

I should be more patient. I put my mother through the same flares of uncontrolled magic. Why can't I be as patient with Melarae as Mother was with me?

She didn't want to think about Katerin's other news, but she couldn't avoid fretting.

Another worry to add to her concerns about Melarae. About Medvara's sluggish, sullen response to her magic ever since the rains came sparsely this past spring. She should be feeling the land pulsing against her bare feet and hands. But—nothing. That wasn't right.

And now Katerin's words echoed through her thoughts, tightening Rekaré's insides in a dread she hadn't expected from this conversation with her cousin.

No. It couldn't be. Her mother was too young to die. Wasn't she?

I do not know if Alicira will survive the winter.

Her cousin would know—she had been her mother's healer for eleven years.

Oh Gods.

Guilt tugged at Rekaré. If it had not been for her—or the choices she had made before challenging her father Zauril for the leadership of Medvara—her mother might be in better health.

I need to be a better mother to Melarae than I was a daughter to Alicira.

"I'll be with you in a moment, Melarae," she said, struggling to keep her voice even, fatigue expended from working magic pulling at her.

Melarae wasn't the only one who didn't like the summer heat in Medvare-the-city. Oh, if only they could be up in the mountains with the herds! Not down in this muggy hot valley where the Saktrin and Medvara rivers met before flowing into the great Chellana. Not in this carefully crafted garden without a blade of grass out of place, dry as it was. If only the land's magic pulsed against her knees and hands to rejuvenate her after a working like this, instead of remaining mute.

You have a responsibility to the land even when it is silent. And you are only cranky because Melarae tried to get too close when you passed that key to Katerin. Just the use of magic, nothing more.

Rekaré gathered herself and stood. She picked up her communication patch and brushed the few stems of dry grass off of it, then tucked it into the fine-threaded wool bag that hung from her belt. She bowed to the shrine with the porcelain figures of the Gods, feeling inadequate. Then she took a deep breath before turning to face her daughter, feeling guilty as she saw how Melarae lay curled around herself.

Did I use too much of a sting to reprimand her? Maybe I shouldn't have brought her out here—but she has to learn how to use this magic someday.

"We can go inside now." She kept her voice soft as she reached down to take her daughter's hand.

Melarae squealed and jumped up, snatching her hand away. "I don't need your help!" She marched toward the door, arms wrapped protectively around herself.

Relief and annoyance warred within Rekaré as she followed her daughter to the stone patio in front of the House's garden entrance. Melarae grasped the elaborate metal handle to pull the door open.

"Ow!" She jumped back from the door and tucked her hands under her armpits.

"Let me see," Rekaré said, voice half-commanding, half-reassuring.

Melarae blinked hard, face scrunching up to hold back tears. Rekaré knelt in front of her daughter, extending her own hands.

"Please. Let me see," she repeated. "I didn't mean my spell-flare to bite you that hard. You can't interrupt me when I speak to Katerin through the weave. Understand? The magic has its own force, and I was working with strong flows."

If you don't understand this, my dearest daughter, how will you ever control your own magic?

Melarae's lower lip protruded slightly as she frowned. "There was a bee, and I was *afraid*. Things didn't feel right!"

"It was the magic," Rekaré said, doing her best to keep a soothing tone in her voice. "It can have a buzzing sensation like that of a bee."

Melarae shook her head. "It *was* a bee. Big and black, with purple and gold on it. It kept flying right at me and wouldn't go away! I couldn't make it stop, so I wanted your help."

"That's not—" Rekaré stopped herself before she said more, dread mixed with guilt flowing into her.

Not a bee. That means that the reddest of red Goddesses—I should have listened to Melarae when she called to me, even if it meant breaking the tie.

Rekaré was *his* daughter, which meant that Melarae was *his* granddaughter as well. And her father Zauril had been beloved of Nitel, who preferred to manifest as a purple wraith.

You are seeing ghosts.

Still, she would feel better once her mother and cousin were here to observe Melarae's behavior for themselves. To issue their own verdicts about how much strangeness she saw in her daughter, and for them to tell Rekaré that she was just being a silly and overprotective mother, seeing shadows that didn't exist.

Shadows in her daughter. Shadows in this damned house.

Something is wrong with my daughter. I've failed her. Failed everyone.

"Mama?" The fear in Melarae's voice brought Rekaré's thoughts back to the current situation. "Your face looks scary."

"I didn't mean it to be, dear one. Can you show me that bee?"

Melarae shook her head. "It disappeared after you flicked that magic at me. Can I learn how to do that?"

"First you need to learn how to control your magic," Rekaré

said, working to keep her voice steady. "For now, let's heal those palms, shall we? Did you try to stop my spellflare with your hands?"

"No." The pout faded from Melarae's lips. "I—I was swatting at the bee. It was *this close*—" she showed about a palm's width distance between her two hands. "—when your sorcery hit it. The bee disappeared."

The fear tightened even more firmly within Rekaré.

"Let me see your hands," she repeated. "I'm sorry. When the spellflare hit the bee, it must have splashed over onto you. I'm sorry."

"Why?" Melarae asked, finally extending her hands.

Relief flooded through Rekaré as she saw that Melarae's hands were not blistered, just bright red, as if she had fallen hard on them.

She must have used magic of her own to protect herself.

"The bee may have been a sorcerous artifact," she said. "You will need to watch for them. With our land's magic fading this year, that lack of renewed sorcery may open us up to predators from outside Medvara." *And within this house.* "Now let me teach you the charm that will help you ease such things yourself, without my help."

Gods, she hoped this incident had happened just because magic levels were low this year, and not because she'd been feeling a malign presence lurking around the Leader's House. Zauril? Or his patron goddess Nitel? Or just worry because of the challenges of this summer?

If the bee had been any other color....

Perhaps she needed to call her husband Cenarth and son Linyet back from their surveys of the herds—no, in a year like this, his survey of the sheep herds and magic in the lambs' fleeces was more important than ever. But she could use the steady strength of her beloved to quiet her fears.

What happens if I lose him like I am losing Melarae?

Rekaré pressed her lips firmly together and refocused on her daughter.

I choose not to lose either one of them.

Melarae traced the signs Rekaré showed her upon each palm, whispering the invocation to Dovré. The red faded.

At least that spell works for Melarae.

Maybe things were not as dire with her daughter's ability to work magic as they seemed. Magic did come late to some users.

"Come." Rekaré reached out again for Melarae's hand. "Let's go to dinner."

"Will I be able to talk to my cousin Witmara like you do to Katerin someday?" Melarae asked.

"I hope so." They entered the House. However, as they progressed toward the family wing, Rekaré felt as if a malevolent gaze bored through her back.

Perform an exorcism and purification ritual when Katerin gets here.

Hopefully that would be the only thing needed to make things right.

But after Melarae went to bed, she would check all the wards in the Leader's House yet again. Just because it had been eleven years since she'd killed her blood father Zauril didn't mean that he was completely gone from this place.

Especially if he seeks to bring me down through his granddaughter.

Gods, she shouldn't be feeling this way about her own child!

She wanted her mother. She wanted her cousin. She wanted them to tell her that she was just imagining things.

ORLANDEN STILL SAT IN HIS CHAIR, READING A SCROLL, WHEN Katerin returned to her lodge. "Witmara is with Haran and Alicira," he said, rewrapping the scroll. "I told her I would give her my guest uncle present when you were ready. It is something you will want to see as well. She will need your help with it."

"I'm glad she's with them right now. After talking to Rekaré—I don't want Witmara around when I read this."

Katerin extracted the silver disc and placed it on the blue and silver seal. The shimmering blue and silver vortex swirled solid blue, then silver, then faded along with the disc. Katerin picked up the envelope and slid the paper out.

> *Please share this information with the Leaders as well as Haran and Orlanden, then destroy it. Chiral, rebel heiress of a sub-family within the Ralsem seeks Medvara's aid in escaping Emperor Chatain in Daran. My spy Detaluna vouches for Chiral's origins, but not for her motives. Sorcerer-Captain Vered concurs with Deta. Chiral seeks asylum and invokes the Miteal Agreement.*

"Oh dear," Katerin groaned, letting the letter fall to her lap. No wonder Rekaré did not want to mention specifics.

Even speaking through the Goddess might not be entirely safe over this long a distance. Chatain was more magically powerful than his grandfather Etikar and father Dunaran had been. Etikar and Dunaran had mostly ignored their relatives who had fled Daran. But ever since Rekaré had become the Leader, Chatain's agents had periodically sought to disrupt Medvara.

She shook her head. Orlanden raised a brow at her.

"Politics of Empire," she explained.

She picked the letter up again.

> *I need you and my mother to be here when Chiral arrives for the good of Medvara, to help me protect the*

land. Deta and Vered will be suppressing her magic while voyaging over Sea. Vered believes the voyage upriver will not affect her ability to keep Chiral under protection while they travel on water. But once they arrive at Medvare-the-city, she offers no further guarantees. They will be here before the half-moon. How soon before I am unsure.

Please. Make haste. Other things are happening. Chatain remembers his exiled relatives, and from what Deta says, he would do his best to strip the land of all magic. I dare not mention his name when you and I speak through the weave for concern it might draw his attention, even with the Goddess's protection.

Dovré feels so far away from me, cousin. There are others who whisper things to me. I would have at least you and Mother here to help me banish those presences, especially in this time of sorcerous drought and Chatain's growing threat. I have need of the Banisher of Shadows.

R.

"Banisher of Shadows," Katerin whispered. "No. Not that."

"May I read it?" Orlanden asked.

"Yes, yes," Katerin said absently.

She shivered even though the evening breeze still held a whisper of summer warmth. This news made her want to return to the shrine—not to speak to Rekaré, but to her late beloved, Metkyi, an acolyte and now assistant of the God Staul.

I do not want to reawaken the Banisher of Shadows.

She almost thought she could hear her mother's shade chortling from the Other Side. A quick flare of anger washed through Katerin.

I will not follow Terani-the-God-Killer's path! I will not!

"Mama?" Witmara stood in the doorway. "I saw you were back. Uncle Haran suggested I show you his guest uncle present."

Katerin shook off her worries as Orlanden gave the note back to her. She quickly tucked it back into the envelope.

"Of course. What did your guest uncle give you?"

"This," Witmara said. She held out a folder made of soft white doeskin. Katerin unwrapped the thong that held it closed. Inside was a journal with covers made from the same white doeskin, brushes, several goose quills, and a small box that contained assorted inks. "Isn't it wonderful? Now I can keep my own journal just like you!"

Katerin swallowed hard. *My daughter is growing up.*

"This is a powerful gift," she said. "Very valuable. You will need to be careful with it. Did Uncle Haran explain to you what this means?"

Witmara nodded. "Larijian journal sets are *the best*, he says. And since I am going to be eleven in a few days, I need a journal worthy of the sorceress we hope I will be."

Katerin smiled ruefully at her daughter, recognizing her own words in Witmara's voice. She gently cupped her daughter's chin in her hand, stroking Witmara's cheek with her thumb.

"Now I know why your uncle asked me not to order a journal set for your birthday." This set was one that she had seen Witmara admiring last year when they had visited Wixtnal, before going to Medvare-the-city for their annual fall visit with Rekaré. Had Haran been with them? No, but Orlanden had. "You may want to thank your uncle Orlanden for telling Haran what you wanted."

The price for this set was much more than she could afford.

"Thank you Uncle Orlanden!" Witmara bustled over to Orlanden and gave him a big hug.

Orlanden chuckled as Katerin carefully repacked the journal set. "Your Uncle Haran knows that I'm the one who notices such things." He winked at Katerin. "Trust me, he still would not know the difference between parchment and paper, or types of inks."

She set the folder down on the set of shelves that held Witmara's summer goods.

We will need to be packing them tonight.

"Thank you, Orlanden," she said.

"Always a pleasure. And now. Your mother is here, so it is time for *me* to give you my guest uncle present." Orlanden gestured toward the other chair. "Sit down, and close your eyes."

Witmara threw herself into the chair and squinched her eyes tightly shut. Orlanden reached into his vest and pulled out a blue velvet bag.

Katerin gulped as she recognized the design on the jeweler's bag. Jeral was the premier designer of magic-friendly jewelry in Wixtnal.

Orlanden carefully extracted a necklace and fastened it around Witmara's neck. It had two engraved silver center plates with a blue stone shot through with silver threads set between the two plates. Except for the stone, it was nearly a match for the necklace Katerin wore underneath her shirt. Orlanden brought out a silver cuff bracelet with the same type of stone set into it and slipped it onto Witmara's wrist.

Witmara gasped.

"Is it—is it?" She opened her eyes and stared at the stone in her bracelet. Then she reached up to feel the necklace. "Is it like yours, Mama?"

Katerin picked up her hand mirror set in a redbark pine wood frame and held it toward her daughter. "See for yourself."

"Oh," Witmara breathed as she studied herself in the mirror, delicately touching the stone.

Katerin admired the lapis stone against her daughter's sun-darkened skin. Both she and Witmara were fairer than most of the camp, the shade of dry brown earth instead of the redbark pine or damp brown earth colors common amongst the peoples of Keldara and Clenda. But the summer sun darkened Witmara's skin to a light shade of redbark. Only their thin, narrow faces with high foreheads and thin brows marked the Aireii bloodlines that identified their cousinship to Alicira and Rekaré and their status as members of the Miteal family.

"You will need to activate the protective spell in it," Orlanden said to Katerin. "I thought it best to get her a necklace and bracelet, not bracelet and ring."

"A ring is best given from a potential mate, not a guest uncle," Katerin agreed.

"Plus she is still growing and a bracelet will fit her better over time. Do you like it, Witmara?"

"It's beautiful. Mama, it's just like yours except for the stone!"

Katerin extracted her necklace with the white and black-flecked purple stone from under her tunic, along with the ring that matched the necklace.

"Your father Metkyi gave this one to me, along with my ring." She didn't wear the ring on her hand all of the time—far too fragile given Katerin's everyday life, especially in summer—but the necklace was a frequent reminder that Metkyi still watched over Katerin and Witmara from the Other Side.

"Will *he* be a part of my blessing?" Witmara asked, her voice very soft now.

"You know he watches over us," Katerin said. "But yes, I will ask him through Staul to guard you." She glanced at Orlanden. "This too is a valuable gift."

"Jeral pointed it out to me when I was last in his Wixtnal shop," Orlanden said. "He asked how old Metkyi's daughter was, then told me that this was one of his favored stones. Apparently

Metkyi appeared to him in a vision and told him that this necklace and bracelet were for Witmara."

Katerin forced a chuckle. "Was there ever a magical stone that Metkyi didn't like?"

"I do not know."

"Thank you, Orlanden," Witmara whispered. "Thank you so much."

"Sometimes the Gods tell me what is needful," Orlanden said. He moved toward the door. "I will join Haran, and not be in the way."

"You are never in the way!" Katerin protested. But she knew what he meant. "Besides, I think we should go to the shrine for this blessing," she added. "Not here. You can stay if you like."

Orlanden shrugged. "I want to spend some time with Alicira as well," he said quietly. This time when he looked at Katerin, the deep pain and sympathy he had kept hidden made his face sag into sadness.

He knows that she has less than a year left. Maybe this trip to Medvara might extend her life for another season.

She hoped so, for all of them.

AN UNEXPECTED GOD SPEAKS

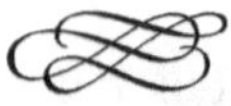

THE NEXT MORNING, REKARÉ ROSE AFTER A RESTLESS NIGHT'S half-sleep, unsettled by her dreams and the heat. Even though every window had been wide open all night, the Leader's House was stuffy and sweltering.

She walked to the Great Hall without carrying a light, knowing the passage well enough not to need it. A distant robin's cry heralded the gradual fading of the night. Sweat rolled down her neck even with the light summer shift she wore, though how much of that was due to the weather and how much to her nerves, she wasn't sure.

She kicked off her sandals at the Great Hall's doorway, its windows also thrown wide open to catch the slightest breeze. Heat still radiated from the rugs as she walked across them to the polished wood floor in front of the Great Tapestry. She had woven it with Cenarth's help eleven years ago, after their marriage and her investiture as Leader of Medvara.

To rule you must weave.

That had been the law in Varen even before the arrival of the Miteal exiles from Daran. The Great Tapestries reflected the magics of the nations of Varen, and each Leader needed to form their own.

The Tapestry shimmered with its own light. Rekaré knelt at the edge of the wood floor in front of it. She lit a smudge of sagebrush from Keldara mixed with Medvaran lavender and Clendan juniper to purify herself and her thoughts, then dropped it into the waiting blue glass bowl instead of fixing it in the holder. She pulled the Light of Medvara from under her shift. It glowed in the presence of the Tapestry, the two major artifacts of the Leaders of Medvara greeting each other.

Rekaré studied the Tapestry as the smudge smoke rose, assessing the magical status of the land through the changing colors of the fabric. It depicted the great Medvaran Valley and the Arteldinnei that formed part of Medvara's eastern boundary. To the south, a dark splotch marked Cooscol and the formerly failed original home of the magical Coos berry bushes, a slight sparkle of sorcery from the bushes glowing so faintly it was hard to see on the Tapestry. A faint green shimmer identified the high mountain pastures of the Stardance breed of sheep that carried the most magic in their fleeces. This year the Tapestry showed the land in the pale sick yellow-green of a shallow lake with too much algae instead of the deep rich green of spring grass, reflecting the sorcerous drought that plagued Medvara and the Two Nations.

A deep orange dot glowed by the Saktrin River, near Medvare-the-city. Rekaré's hands flew to her mouth in surprise.

Cenarth and Linyet will be home soon!

She hadn't expected their return to be this swift. Part of her wanted to sink back on her heels in relief but another part of her fretted at this sudden, unheralded change. Combined with that sick yellow-green of the pastures, did their early return portend even further issues with the renewal of magic in Medvara this summer?

Perhaps Cenarth senses my concerns.

She *had* wished for him to be at her side after speaking to Katerin yesterday. Her mother's fading, the news from Vered and Detaluna, and Melarae's experience with the bee yesterday—all of that together fretted her.

She wanted those dear to her nearby. Close where she could watch and protect them. Her fingers clenched tightly. Even after eleven years she did not trust the land of Medvara, still felt trapped by a fate spun for her by her mother in conjunction with the Gods. A doom she dared not spurn after the years of sacrifice that brought Alicira to the state Katerin now reported.

And last night's dreams still haunted her.

Images of a strange city lying in ruins about Rekaré as she battled an unseen foe had remained with her as she woke, still vividly lingering with her now, not banished by the Tapestry as she had hoped.

More concerning was her vision of a thin, pale man's face capped with silver-threaded bright red hair and framed with orange-red beard. Dark blue eyes pierced into her deepest self even as she sought to wrap shadows around herself to hide from his gaze.

Chatain.

You cannot evade me forever, Rekaré. You will fight me and die. Like our ancestor Elithtra did with Etikar, like your great-grandfather Alexran did with Zauril. The house of Miteal will fall completely and I will make it happen. Sooner or later I will break your wards in Medvara.

She wasn't certain if her dreams spoke truth. *Could* Chatain actually project his voice within her thoughts? Or did the dreams just reflect her fears?

I am sick of hiding—but what about Medvara? What about my children?

She had spent so much time restoring Medvara. She couldn't walk away from it—or Cenarth. Too much depended on her remaining responsible and tied down here instead of following her deepest urges to wander free.

But what happens if these dreams are the truth?

Rekaré inhaled deeply, letting the smudge calm her thoughts. Sagebrush, lavender, and juniper. The Two Nations and Medvara. All three lands her home, all three lands tied to her.

Lady Dovré, I ask for your wisdom,

she asked the Goddess.

Were my dreams truth or were they simply my fears running away from me?

No answer came.

Rekaré bowed low, repeating her words.

No response. No sense of presence from that Goddess.

There was a distant pressure, filled with gray and darkness.

Rekaré shivered.

Lord Staul?

The presence drew nearer, projecting foreboding and unrest. Rekaré bit her lower lip, vowing to herself that she would not mention *that Goddess* by name. But it was gray and dark, not purple and magenta, so no, it had to be Staul, not *her*.

Lord Staul, what would you do with me?

The God with Two Faces was one of her patrons but a lesser one, present in his persona as Staul the Balancer, not Staul the Destroyer. This manifestation did not feel like the Balancer that Rekaré was familiar with. She had only glimpsed Staul as Destroyer from a distance, when she had battled her father for control of Medvara and its magic. Staul had struck at Zauril through Rekaré in his rage at the death of his priest, Metkyi.

A cold finger ran along her cheek.

Ah, Rekaré, Rekaré. Lady of Sorrow.

She steeled herself to stare straight ahead at the Tapestry and not wince away from the skeletal form that sidled next to her, wrapping a bony arm around her shoulders.

Lord Staul. I do not know you in this form.

The cold, bony fingertip lifted her chin and turned her head to face the grinning skeletal skull of Staul the Destroyer.

The answer you seek will not come from my sisters or my other self.

Rekaré swallowed hard but met the black glow from Staul's eyes directly, without flinching.

Did you send me that dream last night?

He laughed, a high and whispery cackle that sent dread down through her body and into her toes.

Oh Rekaré, oh child of my heart, oh daughter of she who was bold enough to dice with me for your future. What you saw was but one truth. One future.

What city did I see and why did I see it if it is not my Medvare?

Waykemin, Dera, Adalane, Fenras, Medvare,
Nere...what does it matter? You saw one path
you may take—sooner, rather than later. Best
you be prepared. Choices lie before you.

What choice must I make, Lord Staul?

I cannot advise. I can only warn. Choose wisely
and well, little one. A war greater than you can
imagine lies within your grasp.

A war? With whom?

A war greater than you can imagine,

Staul repeated, now sounding impatient.

One choice leads to success. The other leads
to failure. Be alert. Be wise.

Lord Staul, how will I know which choice is
which?

The god snorted, not unlike the sound Rekaré's daranval mare Basnen made when irritated.

Be alert. Do not let the choice sneak up on you.
I will be your ally—but only if you choose
rightly. War is coming.

With Chatain?

Chatain? He is but a bit of cottonwood fluff in
the wind. Sea foam is greater than he! Be alert.
Be aware. The Balancer sleeps as the
Destroyer grows great. Change comes to Varen
and Daran alike. Be ready when it happens.
Listen to the Banisher of Shadows.

And then Staul was gone, leaving only that chill from his touch on her jaw. A single bony fingertip segment lay on the polished wood floor in front of her, next to the bowl that held the smudge. Rekaré picked it up.

Remember,

Staul's dry, dusty voice whispered yet again in her thoughts as her hand clenched the bone.

The Balancer sleeps as the Destroyer grows great. Remember the Banisher of Shadows.

But it was only the God's voice, and not his presence, in this token.

Yet.

It was not wise to disdain the gifts of Staul, whether as Balancer or Destroyer.

I will remember,

she promised the God, and tucked the bone into the bag at her belt where she carried her most important magical tokens.

The clatter of hooves on cobblestones just outside the Great Hall's windows announced the arrival of riders. Than Cenarth's voice calling to the stable hands.

Relief flooded over her. She bowed to the Tapestry, extinguished the smudge, then rose, slipping on her sandals and hurrying out of the hall. She rushed through the House toward the yard, eager to see her spouse and her son.

Cenarth had just lifted a sleepy-eyed Linyet from his pony when she reached them. Her beloved smiled when he saw her, his dark brown eyes lighting up with the joy she so cherished in him. Enough of her encounter with Staul still possessed her that she sensed Cenarth's aura. Its orange-gold warmth made her realize how cold inside she had been while he was gone.

He balanced Linyet in one arm and wrapped his other arm around Rekaré, bringing her into a hug with him and their son. She buried her nose deep into his neck, absorbing the musky scent mixed with horse and sheep, then raised her head to meet his thick brown lips—*so warm. So warm.* It was hard to be warm inside when Cenarth was gone, even in the heat of summer.

Linyet squirmed between them and she pulled back, laughing for no reason except to see Cenarth's wide smile. She ran her fingers through Cenarth's curly hair and pulled Linyet closer.

"I am happy to see you, but back so soon?"

Linyet wiggled from her grip, wrapping his arms around her legs in his own hug after he reached the ground.

"It was time," Cenarth said simply. "I had the sense I was needed here."

"All is well?" she asked, stepping back. She untangled Linyet from her legs and bent down to kiss his head. "Perhaps you would like Mama to lead you on Sark to the stables to put him away?"

Linyet nodded. She helped him back onto the pony and took Sark's reins from Cenarth.

"As well as can be," Cenarth said, following his riders toward the barn and leading his daranval, Quartel.

"The sheep?"

"Magic is there. Not as much in each individual lamb as there has been in past years—but there are more triplets than in past years, so the total magic is the same," Cenarth said, taking his hand in hers as they led horse and pony toward the barn. "Things are better than we feared."

"And that is very good news," Rekaré said, not wanting to say more until they were alone.

Cenarth caught her eye and made a quick sign to indicate that he had more to share. His quick smile as she frowned dispelled her sudden worry that he was covering up for a greater problem.

With that they were in the stable, and it was time to curry horses. She helped Linyet unsaddle Sark, then supervised as he groomed the pony. By the time they were finished, Linyet was tired enough not to object when Rekaré picked him up.

She walked back inside the Leader's House, holding Cenarth's hand, for the moment free of worry. One faint regret pulled at her as they entered the House.

If only Melarae were here too—

"Where Melarae?" Linyet demanded, as if he read Rekaré's mind.

"Still sleeping," Rekaré answered.

"I go see her. I want sleep too." He squirmed until she put him down, and he trotted off toward the nursery.

Cenarth rested his hand on Rekaré's shoulder and pulled her close. "He didn't get a lot of rest. We left camp in the middle of the night."

"What's wrong?" she asked, turning within his arms to face him.

He kissed her again. "Artel appeared to me."

Rekaré frowned. *The Gods are moving—why?* Artel was Cenarth's patron, true, but Artel the Judge rarely spoke unsolicited to his followers.

"Did you ask for his advice?"

Cenarth shook his head. "At first I thought it was a dream, but I woke and he was still there. He said I needed to return to Medvare. Since the shepherds don't require me to be there, now that the summer count is done, and Artel was quite insistent—I woke Linyet and our escort, left our excuses with the night guard, and rode for Medvare. At times I thought I should take Linyet in the saddle in front of me, but he's a tough kid. Mother will be pleased with her grandson. He rides like a true Tauri, just like he'd been raised in Clenda instead of Medvara."

"He rides like his father," Rekaré said softly, stroking Cenarth's cheek.

"*And* his mother," Cenarth said archly. "Who was it that rode Elantai to victory in the Chellni Challenge instead of Father's chosen rider?"

Rekaré laughed and leaned against Cenarth. "True, very true. And it was worth every bit of scolding and punishment that Mother and Heartfather and Secondmother gave me for doing it!"

She nuzzled her head into his chest and they stood quietly together for a moment, Cenarth holding her close. Then he eased his grip on her.

"Artel was most insistent that my place was here," he said, taking her hand and moving toward their suite. "But you had not sent messages, so I was unsure. I thought if there was an emergency you would have called to me. So I was not certain if this is an upcoming danger or a current danger."

"Things are—brewing," Rekaré said. They held hands as they walked down the hallway.

Quanyits, the head worker on morning duty, hurried toward them before Rekaré could say more.

"My Leader," she said, bobbing her head in quick respect before continuing. "Bring breakfast to your quarters or to the dining hall?"

"Quarters, please," Rekaré said. "Linyet went to the nursery with Melarae, but they may both be asleep."

"We shall see about that," Quanyits said wryly. "He may wake her up."

"He has been riding long and hard," Cenarth said. "Tell Tlikset that, please."

"Melarae may want to spend time with her brother instead of in lessons," Rekaré added. "But if Linyet sleeps longer than

Melarae, Tlikset can bring her to us. I will take charge of her instruction today. Tlikset can stay with Linyet."

"I will tell her so." Quanyits dipped her head again, and scurried off.

Cenarth raised a brow at Rekaré. "So what is happening with Melarae?" They continued walking and reached their suite. Cenarth opened the door and they went inside.

Rekaré sighed and sank down on a couch next to the window, breathing deeply of the sweet early morning fragrance from the dark blue cirelen blooming directly underneath the sill. "Several things have happened while you were gone. Detaluna and Vered are bringing a refugee from Chatain to Medvare from Adalane, a scion from a rebel branch of the Ralsem."

"Why here?" Cenarth sat next to her and reached for a bootjack. He fitted it to one boot and began to lever his foot out of it. "Why not one of the Old Countries? Why bring her across sea? That only draws Chatain's attention to us." The boot yielded and he switched the bootjack to the other foot.

"She has asked for refuge per the Miteal Agreement," Rekaré answered. "And both Deta and Vered confirm that she does in fact conform to it."

"That Agreement will cause us more trouble than it is worth," Cenarth grumbled as he worked on his second boot. "Bringing a refugee from Chatain here is dangerous business."

"Agreed, but—at this moment we cannot yet renounce it. Not unless I can replace the wards on Medvara to reflect that treaty change, and I can't do that yet. Not until the children are older. They're too young to contribute to the wards but too old for me to represent them to the land." She paused. "And as for Melarae—a bee was buzzing around her while I spoke to Katerin last night. At dusk. While the moon was rising. A big black bee with purple and gold on it that kept flying at Melarae, until she interrupted me. She tried to get my help but didn't tell me why. I tossed a spellflare at her so she wouldn't break my link with Katerin. The enchantment struck the bee when it was between Melarae's hands and it disappeared. Melarae's hands were reddened but not burned."

"And yet you won't renounce the Agreement?" Cenarth heaved a deep breath and stripped his socks off. He set them aside. "If you have that sort of spying happening while you are speaking with Katerin, then Chatain is too close of a threat for my comfort."

"I do not think this bee was of Chatain or of Daran," Rekaré said, her voice dropping. "Those colors—they remind me of Zauril's patroness."

"I thought your mother and Katerin drove that Goddess out of Medvara."

"That's the other thing." Rekaré choked, finding it hard to continue. "Katerin says that Mother is failing. That—" she gulped. "That she may not survive the winter. If she is dying, then those safeguards for our land may be inadequate as well. We need to renew the wards, take Mother out of the link and replace her with Katerin. Adding a further change to the Agreement may be too much sorcery for the land to accept. Especially given the state of the land's magic. I dare not ask more of it, not with my mother also being sick."

"Alicira's health is that poor?"

Rekaré nodded.

Cenarth shook his head, blinking hard, and took both her hands. Alicira had been as close a Secondmother to him as his mother Inharise had been a Secondmother to Rekaré.

"What is to be done?"

"Katerin is bringing her here by sternwheeler, as quickly as possible." Rekaré drew a deep, shuddering breath. "I had sent Haran and Orlanden to escort them here before that Ralsem refugee—Chiral is her name—arrived, to help provide us a defense against any danger she might present. I sent a private message with Orlanden telling Katerin my concerns so I did not need to speak openly through the enchantment. I felt that having the Banisher of Shadows here would be best."

Cenarth nodded. "I see. I am glad you thought of that."

"Yes. After Melarae told me about the bee, I was even gladder of my precautions. And then this morning—I woke from a dream of death and destruction that I had caused. An unknown city. As I woke, Chatain threatened me with the complete destruction of all the Miteal. I did not know in truth if it were him or my fears speaking." She looked out the window to the garden outside, as a faint breeze riffled through the cirelen bushes. *Maybe some relief from this heat at last?* But as it grew stronger and warmer she sagged slightly. Another day of the hot wind from the east. "So I consulted the Tapestry. I had just finished when you arrived."

"What did Dovré say?"

"Dovré did not speak to me." Rekaré continued to stare out the window. "Staul the Destroyer did." She glanced back at Cenarth as he inhaled sharply, hissing. "Yes. The Destroyer told me that what I saw was but one possible future." She pressed her lips together firmly for a moment, then continued. "He said that war is coming, one greater than any we might have with Chatain. That choices lie ahead of me, one successful, one not. Change is coming to Varen and Daran, and the Balancer sleeps as the Destroyer grows great. That I am to listen to the Banisher of Shadows."

Cenarth's hands tightened on hers. "Artel said something similar to me last night. But a greater war than with Chatain? That would mean the Gods themselves ride to battle, but with whom?"

"*When the Destroyer wakes, Gods and humans alike tremble,*" Rekaré quoted from the Romance of Staul and Dovré.

Cenarth tsked. He slipped his hands free from hers and stretched.

"All right, then. It is wise to listen to Staul the Destroyer. If war is coming, then we need to be ready, both physically and magically. I will check our battle readiness. After breakfast I will review our troop strength on the eastern borders with the Saubral. If the Destroyer indeed is waking, then the Saubral and their Shadowwalkers will be bolder in their trespasses. I'll also send out messages to Nere and Cooscol to warn them about possible Saubral depredations. What about Larij?"

"I had thought to send Haran and Orlanden to alert the Mershaunten," Rekaré said. "But I think I will send messages up the river both to catch Katerin on their way down, and to warn Larijian ports along the Chellana. My mother may prefer to keep Haran and Orlanden by her side in her illness, especially since Heinmyets and Inharise are not free to come here."

"Oh dearest. I thought once we ruled in Medvara we would be at peace." Cenarth pulled her close to him again. "I thought that Daran would not seek more trouble here."

"We *were* at peace—for a few years," Rekaré said. "I suppose this means that Chatain sees me as a real threat."

Cenarth kissed the top of her head. "He would be a fool *not* to see you as a threat, in spite of your open vows to seek no power beyond Medvara. But I had hoped for a longer respite, that our children would be older once Daran remembered us."

"I did as well, dear one. But the gods—" Someone knocked on the door. Rekaré extended her awareness and sensed Quanyits's presence. "Come in," Rekaré said.

Quanyits pushed a cart loaded with platters of bread, fruit, breakfast steak, and eggs into the room. "The children are both asleep. Tlikset said that Linyet came into the nursery and crawled onto his sister's bed. He remembered to take off his boots first."

"Good, good," Cenarth said. "At least he has learned to shed his boots before bedtime on this trip."

Rekaré rolled her eyes. When the children were younger, it had been Melarae who climbed into bed to cuddle with her younger brother, and removing muddy boots had not always been a priority for either child. Still, when one had been away on a trip, the child who returned climbed in with the other. Though their paths were starting to diverge, at least they were close in that respect.

It is not siblings that the Miteal war with.

Historically, that role fell to cousins, if not between parents and children.

Now she wondered if that could also be the war that Staul had referred to. She and Katerin had vowed years ago to be allies and support for each other as part of the Miteal Agreement, so—

No. Not Witmara against Melarae and Linyet. No!

Gods. She hadn't thought of that prospect until now. She'd almost prefer the possibility that the Gods were referring to the arguments between herself and Melarae instead.

Almost.

THE HEAT OF THE DAY WAS HARD ON ALICIRA. KATERIN CALLED A halt in a cluster of redbark pine along the main road and supervised the quick raising of a cloth canopy to provide more shade for Alicira. After that, Haran and Orlanden helped Alicira off of the travois and underneath the awning. She sank gratefully against the padded tripod backrest Katerin set up for her, leaning her head back and closing her eyes.

"Everything hurts," she groaned. "I wish I was strong enough to sit a horse. It couldn't be as rough as that travois!"

"Soon enough we'll reach the wagon road," Katerin said soothingly. She sorted through her traveling medication bag for more pain medication, and poured a spoonful. She was careful to keep her back to Alicira as she enchanted the dark green liquid to increase its effectiveness as much as she dared. Alicira would know she had done it, but this way she wouldn't have Katerin's manipulations staring her in the face.

Relieve the pain in her joints without knocking her out.

Alicira started coughing with a dry, harsh hack, wheezing between spasms. Katerin pressed her lips together in annoyance.

Damn cough.

She couldn't combine the magically strengthened pain potion with the powders she used to stop her cousin's cough. Perhaps together the plain potions without magic might ease her pain—the coughing had to be dealt with first, though. She reluctantly poured the syrup onto the ground and reached for another bottle in the protective case, pouring a small amount of red syrup into the spoon.

Alicira made a face as Katerin held the spoon to her lips.

"Cough or pain?" she rasped, voice hoarse.

"Cough first. You don't want to strain your back muscles any more than they already are."

"Bleh." She swallowed the red syrup, making a face at its bitter flavor.

"Give her some water, Witmara. Pain potion is next." Katerin turned back to her case and poured more of the pain syrup into the spoon. She studied it, calculating. Perhaps she could risk a milder spell with the potions in combination? "How bad do you hurt?"

"Bad enough that I don't think even the combination of the cough potion with the pain potion will ease it. I have shooting pains through my spine and hips." Alicira cleared her throat and coughed once, but it was moist-sounding now. She turned her head to spit out mucus.

"I don't want to knock you out while traveling."

"The pain is getting worse."

"I know." Katerin studied the dark green syrup. She whispered a spell that was less intense than the previous one.

I hope this is enough.

Alicira settled back after the second dose, closing her eyes.

"Stay with Alicira," Katerin ordered Witmara.

She tucked the spoon into her belt, and slipped Rainin's bridle off, hanging it from the saddle horn, then loosened Rainin's cinch before turning her free to graze and drink from a nearby spring.

Katerin followed Rainin and the other equines down into the trees to the spring and joined the riders easing their way to the water amongst the horses. At last she could rinse the spoon, get a fresh drink, and splash the dust and sweat off of her face.

That done, she slipped her spoon back into her bag and climbed back up the hillside to where Alicira's shelter sat amongst the trees on top of the ridge, calculating.

Another day and they would be at a wagon road. Heinmyets had sent riders ahead to prepare a wagon to take them the rest of the way into Dera. So they had two and a half more days of road travel before Dera, then a day's canoe travel down the Keldara River to the Chellana—and from there three days on a sternwheeler, stopping at night so that magicians and daranvelii alike could recover from the ill effects of water on those possessing sorcery.

Can Alicira tolerate that much road travel without resting for a few days?

Katerin's steps dragged as she approached the shelter. After Rekaré's words, she didn't want to dawdle. But how best to travel without overtaxing the Old One?

Witmara sat next to Alicira, holding a water bag. Alicira spoke to Haran and Orlanden, but Katerin was too far away to hear what they said.

She studied her cousin, assessing her strength. Alicira was thin, had been thin since the middle of last winter when the winter's sickness had struck her hard. The cough had not gone away with the spring, unlike past years. Her already pale skin was pastier than ever, lacking the faint rosy glow she had when healthy. Her silver hair hung limply, without her normal gold highlights. Katerin saw the outline of Alicira's arm bones easily, and moments like helping Alicira rise from the travois only demonstrated how much weight she had lost.

And yet—Alicira's blue eyes were still clear and bright, now that the pain potion was starting to work. She focused on Haran and Orlanden, then gestured to Witmara for water. Her hands shook when she tried to take the water bag, but Witmara held its weight while Alicira drank. As she lowered the bag, Alicira said something to Haran and Orlanden. Witmara knelt next to Alicira, bowing her head slightly. Alicira placed her hand on Witmara's new necklace.

Haran and Orlanden got up. Haran stopped Katerin before she went any closer.

"She wants to speak to Witmara alone," he said softly. "Something to do with blessing Orlanden's gift."

"Then I don't want to interfere." Katerin followed them to where the other riders lingered near the shelter.

When she had done her part in activating the spell in Witmara's necklace last night, she had sensed some deeper elements within it. Not magic she was familiar with—but if her cousin felt strong enough to work with that type of sorcery, then who was she to meddle? Alicira was more experienced in magic than Katerin, and *should* know her limits.

Best that she keep trying as long as she can.

She sat on the ground next to Haran. Abeyets, the patrol chief in charge of Alicira's guard, handed Katerin a travel cake made with pounded dried venison, dried huckleberries, and enough pine nut flour mixed with fat to hold it together. After she took it, he squatted next to her.

"Leaving Clenda is hard on her," Abeyets said quietly. He

leaned in closer. "She will not want others to know, but she was in tears after we left camp. And again before we stopped. I do not think it was all pain."

"No. It wouldn't be," Katerin said. "But the pain *is* getting worse."

"Witmara's presence seems to help her." Abeyets straightened up.

"Thank you, Abeyets," Katerin said.

"Mama?" Witmara said behind her. "Alicira would like to talk to you."

Katerin got up, wincing at the stiffness of her new leather riding trousers.

"Is she all right?" She studied Witmara's new necklace.

Did that stone glow with a new light? The green flecks amongst the blue seemed to shine more brightly, along with faint traces of black and gray within the matrix.

Katerin's chest tightened.

Staul. Staul's magic.

The black and gray were his colors.

She had known it was possible that Staul could become Witmara's patron. Metkyi had been a powerful priest of Staul—but it still hadn't stopped him from being killed in that last battle against Zauril. Katerin had hoped that Witmara would follow her affinity with Dovré and not Metkyi's links to Staul. But Witmara showed little interest in healing, or the other things of Dovré.

Everything except that colt of Rainin's.

"Just tired." Witmara dropped into Katerin's place next to Haran.

Katerin stepped away from the group, walking toward Alicira. Her gut tightened as she noticed that Alicira's eyes were closed. Had this little bit of travel been too much for her cousin?

"I'm just feeling the pain potion," Alicira said as Katerin came up. "Between it and the cough syrup, I'm a little bit floaty."

"That's better than feeling pain." Katerin lowered herself to the ground.

"It interferes with me doing too much magic." Alicira opened her eyes. "I was barely able to complete that last spell. I'd almost say you *wanted* to keep me from doing magic." A wry smile softened the thrust of her words.

"Magic draws your strength down. You need to rest while we're traveling. Let me deal with the sorcery."

Alicira flicked one hand at Katerin. "But what about your work as Banisher of Shadows?"

"Banisher of Shadows was only needed to help Rekaré defeat Zauril. She's better off sleeping."

"Goddess's golden tits," Alicira growled. "Katerin, the magic you inherited from your father has many more possibilities than you allow it. What are you going to do if something happens—Gods forbid—to Rekaré? The children are too young to defend the Miteal, and it will fall to you. You need to be prepared."

"*If* that time comes, I will deal with it," Katerin said.

"It may not be a matter of *if*, but *when*," Alicira warned. "Especially with the power that Witmara possesses. Once she comes into her magic in a couple of years, you will need to be ready. I was not prepared for the strength that Rekaré showed. You are even less prepared than I was. Witmara may even come into her magic sooner than you expect. She will be very strong."

"I know that," Katerin said softly. "I dread that likelihood. But I am called to be a healer. To be both healer and Banisher of Shadows does not work. I also fear calling up the shade of Terani-the-God-Killer."

Alicira grasped Katerin's hand in a tight grip. "Do not let your mother's ghost keep you from what is yours by right. Terani did not understand what she controlled, and it destroyed her. Unlike your mother, you know what you can wield. When you banished the Gods Karnoi and Cirdel from Keldara, even though you let the other Gods work through you, you did not go into the dreamless sleep. Not like Terani did when she banished Nitel from Waykemin."

"Right."

"Then. Do. Not. Let. That fear shape your magical actions." Alicira emphasized her words with a shake of Katerin's hand. "Claim your heritage. I would see you strong and whole in the magical world before I die, to be a true heir of your-father-my-uncle's strength and power. We need your strength, Katerin. Now more than ever. Rekaré needs it. Witmara will need it."

"I will try," Katerin said. "But enough of that. Witmara. I could not unlock the deepest levels of that stone, but from what I saw as she joined us—Staul is strong in her."

Alicira smiled sadly. "She is her father's child as much as she is yours. Does it help that the Balancer sits strongly in her, not the Destroyer?"

"That is good news. But is Dovré in Witmara at all? There are days when I wonder if that is possible."

"The Goddess is buried deep in her. Once she bonds with a daranval, especially if it is that colt—" Alicira nodded to where Rainin grazed, her colt now nursing. "—it will bring out Dovré's aspect in her. Because the Balancer is also strong in her, that may mean Witmara will be able to balance both Dovré and Staul. Alas, I do not think she is drawn to healing, my dear."

"No. She is not. I had hoped that Staul would not call her to be a priest like her father."

"Time will tell. Not all those dedicated to Staul are priests or destroyers. Not all called to Dovré are healers. She could end up becoming a Leader or Leader's advisor."

"Not a Leader in Keldara or Clenda. And Rekaré has two children."

"Leadership does not always come to the sons and daughters of the previous Leader." Alicira exhaled a long and slow breath. "There are three potential heirs to Medvara, and it could be argued that Witmara as Metkyi's daughter is of Keldara and could replace Heinmyets—may that day be long away."

"I would hope that any Leadership does not come to Witmara. I dread the possibility for myself."

"Oh Katerin, Katerin." Alicira squeezed her hand again and closed her eyes. "I am feeling sleepy."

"Then rest, and don't worry about matters of sorcery and state."

Alicira's eyes popped open again. "At this point in time, my dear cousin, I cannot avoid thinking about matters of sorcery and state. Sometimes the Gods whisper things to me while I sleep. We sit on the edge of a great upheaval. Times are changing. Choices need to be made. My time remaining here is short, and I would see that my descendants and family are safe." She looked away from Katerin, moisture welling up in her eyes. "I worry about this magical drought. I fear that I will no longer see my spouses in this life because of the necessities caused by this sorcerous drought. I have spent so much of my life with Heinmyets and Inharise that I feel bereft even though their blessings ride with me. And yet I wish to see Rekaré, and do what is needed as a result of this Ralsem rebel in Daran. I dread that I will not have the strength I need to do what is necessary."

Her eyelids drifted shut again.

Katerin rose to her knees and kissed Alicira's forehead. "Rest, dear cousin. May Dovré grant you a peaceful sleep. You cannot solve all the problems of the world, whether they are of sorcery or of state."

"I would try," Alicira grumbled.

"And I will do my best to support you. For now, sleep. We will travel again when you are ready."

"If only I could ride instead of be dragged along in a travois," Alicira murmured. "But I don't think I have the strength."

Katerin squeezed Alicira's hand. She knelt next to her cousin until Alicira's breathing fell into the smooth pattern of light sleep. Then she kissed her hand and laid it on her chest. Alicira stirred and mumbled something. Katerin gently stroked her brow.

"Sleep untroubled," she whispered.

"*Delian,*" Alicira breathed sleepily. "It's not time to join you. Not yet, brother. I have too many things to do. Give me more time. No. Don't bring Alame. Don't bring Metkyi. *Not yet.*"

Katerin froze. Then she pushed herself up, wobbling over to Rainin. Her daranval raised her head and gently nuzzled Katerin, then wrapped her head and neck around her. She buried her head in Rainin's neck, fighting back the sobs that threatened to overcome her.

I need to speak to Metkyi soon. About Witmara, and about the ghosts around Alicira.

She did not think Alicira's brother Delian would be her escort to the Other Side.

But Metkyi might be—or Witmara. Before his death, she had seen her beloved Metkyi guide the dying to the next life. Would his daughter have the same power?

Oh Gods and Goddesses. I would not choose this path.

What she wanted might not matter to the Gods.

PORTENTIOUS REUNIONS

Six days later Katerin was happy to see Nixyin, the last port before Medvare. It wasn't the most pleasant harbor on the river, but it was the *last port*.

Nixyin had a tough reputation as a town of brawlers and scoundrels. It always seemed like the hottest place in summer and the coldest in winter. Strong winds continually pummeled it so that the Larij-operated ferries across the great Chellana River required deft hands in order to dock safely. It was part-Saubral, part-Larijian by treaty, the strongest Saubral presence on the river. Her nose wrinkled as the stench from the Saubral tannery wafted over them, mingled with the stink from the massive stock pens and slaughterhouses.

Gods, I hope the smell doesn't make Alicira sicker.

Tomorrow was a shorter journey, and its end. Katerin didn't travel well on any sort of water, but traveling downriver in the heat of summer had been excruciating for Alicira. She had chosen to lie on deck under a canopy during the day with Haran and Orlanden at her side, refusing to eat until they stopped to spend the night on land. Katerin split her time between fussing over Alicira and comforting Rainin and her foal in the hold, alternating duties with Witmara. Both of them felt nauseous, but *someone* had to deal with suffering magicians and magical creatures.

Water travel is not friendly to sorcerers or daranvelii.

In the past three years they had made this passage by sternwheeler, once Rekaré's technologists had mastered the art of combining magic and wood to fuel the boilers that powered the ship. On those previous trips her cousin had been able to manage her illness with a stomach powder.

This time, Katerin mixed yet another syrup to dose Alicira morning, noon, and night. It worked more quickly and responded better to magical amplification than the powders did, though Alicira was reluctant to test its strength by eating while she faced water travel. Katerin and Witmara took the powders for relief, and she fed Rainin moistened grain with the anti-nausea powder in it. It helped, but Rainin's foal suffered from the new sensation.

Still, nothing could ease the sorrow hanging over their party. Haran and Orlanden kept Alicira company, taking turns reading to her. Alicira slumped in her chair, silent except when she pointed out landmarks to Witmara. Katerin noted her own landmarks but did not share them. This trip revived memories of the desperate ride with Rekaré and Cenarth to challenge Zauril, as she and Metkyi had grown closer. Those remembrances were engraved in bitter characters on her heart.

Rekaré's messenger met them at the port, coming on board to find Katerin and Haran before they disembarked.

The messenger handed letters to Haran, Alicira, and Katerin. She noted they were sealed with a simple spell, one she could counter with her own ring. After Katerin opened the seal and gave Alicira and Haran their letters, she opened her own.

Staul the Destroyer has come to me in a vision. He warns me of a war with a foe greater than Chatain, and advises me to look to the Banisher of Shadows. Cousin, I know you are reluctant to take that role onto yourself, but—Medvara has need. The Two Nations have need. Be prepared.

Haran looked up from his letter. He handed it to Orlanden, then gestured to the messenger.

"Can you route messages to the Larijian express for me, or do I need to make my own arrangements?"

"I can arrange safe and secure mail delivery to your brother the Mershaunten," the messenger said.

"Good. Come with me." Haran bowed to Katerin and Alicira. "Orlanden, I will write a cover for that letter to send to the Mershaunten. If you could stay and help the others get settled?"

"I can do so," Orlanden said.

Haran took the letter from Orlanden and left.

Alicira sighed. "Nixyin stinks as much as ever."

"Will you be all right?" Katerin asked.

"Depends on the wind. Where are we staying?"

"I sent a message to the Residence to be ready for us two days ago," Haran said. "Further away, but it will be more pleasant in this heat than hiring a closer lodging. The wind usually blows the stench away from it."

"Let us hope it remains so. Witmara. Before they take my small trunk off the boat for this evening, could you retrieve my journal so we can review it? I forgot to pull it out of the trunk this morning." Alicira handed Witmara a disc. "The lock is a lesser magic. You know how to work it."

"Yes," Witmara said. "Your black journal?"

"The very one. It should be on top."

"I'll get it now." Witmara rushed away.

While Witmara fetched Alicira's journal, Katerin and Abeyets got Rainin and her foal out of the hold. The foal staggered down the ramp after his dam. She steadied him at the bottom until one of Abeyets's men took over, and watched them lead the daranvelii down the dock and onto land, then down the street. The colt ventured a quick caper, staggering slightly.

It's good that we have only one more day on the water. It's starting to bother him.

Then she went back on the ship to help Alicira.

Orlanden and Katerin eased Alicira out of her hammock and into the woven willow steel-wheeled chair. He took over guiding the chair down the ramp, holding it back so that it didn't rush down. Witmara joined them once they were on the dock, followed by Haran and the messenger.

They loaded Alicira into the waiting wagon from the Residence, easing her onto a mattress that cushioned her ride. She lay on her side, facing out, holding the side of the wagon tightly against the jostling as dockhands loaded the small trunks they took ashore for the evening. Haran and Orlanden joined her in the wagon bed while Katerin and the others led the daranvelii and horses behind them.

The Residence was in the upper village, located on a small bluff overlooking the waterfront. It sat at the end of a long main street that contained most of Nixyin's businesses and nicer houses, above the stench of the lower village. Katerin gave Rainin's lead to Witmara and supervised the Residence staff as they unloaded Alicira. The envoy on site welcomed them, taking them around the back to a lovely small walled, sheltered garden with a cold supper waiting. Haran fixed himself a plate and then went inside with the envoy, to review the port's accounting.

They lingered outside after eating. The inside of the Residence was still hot and stuffy in spite of the gusty east wind.

The staff lit torches and glowlights, and they settled in for evening work. Alicira and Witmara reviewed one of Alicira's magical note journals. Katerin made her own notes, and reexamined the last volume of Metkyi's journals. She had wanted to consult with him before they left Keldara but there had been no time for her to do so. But thoughts of her dead beloved hovered about her. Nixyin was the first stop on the Chellana with a formal shrine for Staul, perhaps her best option to speak with Metkyi's spirit.

Take advantage of the opportunity.

Communication with Staul and Metkyi was best done closest to the middle of the night.

When both Witmara and Alicira had finally gone to bed, Katerin slipped out, taking only Abeyets with her.

Nixyin's shrine for Staul was near the waterfront. During the governance of Nixyin by the Shadowwalker Gegarth for the Saubral, the shrine had been dedicated solely to Staul the Destroyer. After Rekaré killed Gegarth, priests of Staul had come from Medvare-the-city to purify and balance Staul's shrine. Now images of Staul as Destroyer and as Balancer resided in Nixyin.

But still, the streets around the shrine reeked of the Destroyer, both magically and mundane. That was one reason Katerin was grateful for Abeyets's presence as she walked down the dark waterfront street. Abeyets rested one hand on the hilt of his sword and she did the same for her short sword. The gazers did nothing more than look, however, and let them pass peacefully.

When they reached the shrine, she turned to Abeyets. "Do you wish to come inside?"

Abeyets shook his head. "I will stand watch. Not that it is needed at Staul's shrine, but nonetheless, I'll wait out here."

She didn't blame him. Only those dedicated to Staul sought

out his places unless they had to do so. Every part of Dovré within Katerin screamed a warning as she rang the bell to request entrance. The door creaking open put her on edge, and the priest on duty, a Saubral who wore a necklace of teeth and finger joints, beckoned her inside. He pressed his hands together and bowed to Katerin.

"What brings the Banisher of Shadows to Staul's humble abode here in Nixyin?" he asked.

She returned his bow. "I have not taken up the mantle of Banisher of Shadows," she said.

At least not yet.

The priest raised one eyebrow sharply. "I see that role resting upon you, my lady of Dovré. What brings you to Staul this evening?"

Katerin dropped two silver pieces into his outstretched hand. "I would consult with one who was beloved of Staul the Balancer in his life."

"I doubt that you require this, Banisher of Shadows, but I must ask, by Staul's dictate. Do you need assistance to summon the one you seek?"

She shook her head. "I will speak to him using my own spirit and my own tokens. I do not need the help or protection of others."

The priest bowed again. "Then you should know that the shadow of Metkyi has been waiting for you, lady of Dovré. You will not need to fear the Destroyer tonight."

"I do not fear the Destroyer."

Not since Metkyi died.

Nonetheless, Katerin fought back an urge to seize the Eye of Dovré that lay concealed under her tunic.

The priest nodded. He walked away, gesturing for her to follow. They went down a hallway and into the main chamber, where votive candles burned before the back-to-back statues of the Balancer and the Destroyer, twice the height of a tall man.

The priest tapped on the shoulders of three shadowy figures who knelt before the statues.

"The Lady of Dovré has arrived, and seeks private audience with Lord Metkyi," he said after the third one rose to face him, all three wearing dark green cowls that marked them as novices dedicated to Staul.

"Does the Lady require our assistance?" The speaker was female, with a slight lisp that made Katerin suspect she was Saubral. But she could not see the woman's face due to the cowl. In any case, Nixyin was home to both Larijian and Saubral peoples, and had been for many years.

"She does not. She is the Banisher of Shadows and has earned the right to be alone with the God and those who serve him on the Other Side."

"Ah." The woman bowed to her, then led the other two out.

"When you are ready, Lady, knock and we will let you out," the chief priest said.

"Thank you," Katerin breathed.

She waited until they had left the chamber. The rasp of the doors locking behind her sent chills through her gut, but she reminded herself that it was for the protection of all nearby should the God choose to possess her.

The precautions had a purpose. Weaker persons maddened by Staul's presence had gone raging out of his temples to destroy any and all within their reach. She doubted she was at risk. But for safety's sake, she pulled the necklace Metkyi had given her out from under her tunic. The wire wrapping of the Eye of Dovré caught on her little finger and she hesitated, then brought it out as well.

It is who I am. Staul knows that.

She rubbed the stone in her silver ring, facing the statues of the God, then raised her left hand, palm facing her so that the stone was turned toward the statues.

"I wish to speak to a beloved of Staul," she said plainly.

A thick silence was her only answer, not that she expected any more. Others might choose to flatter the Destroyer and Balancer for fear of his power. Not Katerin. While she was limited in the number of times she could summon Metkyi per season, everything she had gone through made this God much less fearsome to her.

Her arms and legs grew heavier as the presence of the God loomed near. The air became thicker and more humid, cloying and sticky in her nose as she inhaled and exhaled. She wrapped her right hand around the stone in her necklace, and struggled to keep her left hand raised. A faint booming echoed around her and the golden threads within the clear crystal of the Eye of Dovré shone brightly through the darkness. Gray-green shadows shimmered between her and the statues. The votives flickered, their flames first diminishing almost to nothing before leaping high, as if they were torches.

Then the God Himself stood in front of Katerin, a robe covering his body, leaving only his forearms, hands and head visible. The pressure around her eased, as did the humidity. His face and bald head were that of the Balancer, but his exposed forearms and hands were the skeletal form of the Destroyer. He wore a necklace of human skulls.

The first time I've seen the Destroyer this dominant in the God.

She wondered what that meant.

"Banisher of Shadows," Staul said, his voice creaking and hissing, as if it came from a snake. "I see you are bold enough to wear my sister's token openly here."

"It is who I am," she answered. "And I have not yet taken up the title of Banisher of Shadows again."

"Beware your reluctance. The cycle turns. Things change."

"So my cousin Rekaré has told me, and so have I seen within the land." Katerin drew a steady, deep breath, not looking away from the God's scrutiny. "I wish to speak with my beloved, Lord Staul, if you are done with me."

"I am for now. We must talk before you leave. Have you the toll?"

"I do indeed." She dropped the hand from her necklace and fumbled in her pocket for the small bentwood cedar box. She held it out to Staul. "A small token, I fear. The land's magic is scarce this summer."

"So I am aware." Staul opened the box. A rare smile spread across the God's face as he studied the contents. "Honey and berries? You call this a small token?"

"Fresh huckleberry honey and berries from Clenda," Katerin said. "A slight thing—but very dear this summer."

"This is far from a slight thing, oh Banisher of Shadows." Staul closed the box and tucked it into his robes. "Trust the Lady of Dovré to know a God's small pleasures. My sister is blessed in your honor of her."

"She also advised me in my choice of your gift," Katerin added.

"She did well. My blessings upon you, Banisher of Shadows. Metkyi will be with you shortly. Choose your words wisely, as our time is limited, more so than before."

The God vanished. The votive flames continued to burn high. Then, from behind the statues, a wraith-like fog oozed into the chamber. It solidified and took shape, until Metkyi's form stood before her. She could still see the flames of the votives through the outline of his body, and her heart ached.

How much longer before he is so deep into the Shadows that I will not see him until I cross to the Other Side?

Her lost love had grown less substantial at first sight during their seasonal meetings. Katerin knew that this would happen, that it was the way things had to be—but her heart ached to see it.

She pulled the second bentwood box out of her left pocket.

"A gift for you, my dearest," she said, removing the lid and holding it out to Metkyi. "Berries and jerky."

Metkyi took the box with a bow. He scooped berries and jerky into his shadowy mouth. Four bites. With each bite he became more solid. By the last bite she no longer saw the flames through his translucent figure.

"Katerin. Beloved." Metkyi dropped the box and stepped forward to embrace her.

She let him touch her first, having learned over the years that if she gave in to her own yearning and made the first contact, her hands would only slide through his form. But if she waited for him to move first, his body was solid.

Pressure on her arms, first cold, then warm. Cold lips on her forehead that warmed as they rested there. She allowed herself now to take Metkyi in her arms and they stood together silently. She felt his body warm in contact with hers, but he did not breathe. At first his lack of breath had bothered her, but now she was used to it.

"Ah, Katerin, Katerin," Metkyi finally said. "I wish I were able to be beside you in these difficult times. It's hard to watch from the Other Side."

"I wish so as well."

He smiled at her and stroked a flyaway strand of dark hair behind her ear. "We have much to talk about and little time to do it in." He pulled away, still holding her left hand, and led her to an alcove with a bench.

"Isn't that always the case?" she countered. "The God warned me."

"Now more than ever. What troubles you?"

"Where do I start?" She heaved a trembling breath. "Witmara. Alicira. Rekaré. The Banisher of Shadows. The sorcery drought. Daran remembering the land of Varen."

"Quite a bit, and I'm sorry to say I can't help with all of it."

Katerin bit her lip, thinking about her priorities.

Our daughter, then the Banisher of Shadows.

"I worry about Witmara. It is looking more and more like

she will be of Staul—is she going to be the one who guides people to their deaths, like you used to?"

"Our daughter will not be a simple priest, my dear. Not like I was."

"I hardly think you were a *simple* priest. Not with what you did for Rekaré before she became Leader."

"There is much more in store for Witmara than priesthood," Metkyi said, stroking his chin. "But not even the Gods are certain of what lies ahead. Many elements are present that could change things quickly. Too many wild cards." His voice lowered. "Katerin, for your own protection, you must be ready to call up the Banisher of Shadows in yourself. Daran and Chatain are nothing compared to what is coming."

"What is coming?" Ice-cold talons tightened around her gut. At least he had brought up the Banisher first—but that he had done so was not a good omen.

A bleak expression crossed Metkyi 's face and he frowned. "The Gods themselves are readying for war. Both on the Other Side amongst each other and among humans. Chatain has wakened things he should not, but Chatain is not the only one to do so. Be ready, my love. Keep your Banisher self ready. When Alicira passes to the Other Side, things will happen quickly."

"She is so close now," Katerin breathed. "I fear she will not last long once she is in Medvara. Several days ago in her sleep she was telling Delian to wait, not yet. Not to bring Alame. Not to bring you. But then she rallies—" her voice trailed away.

"Her time is not as soon as you fear, dearest. At least under current circumstances. That can change."

"Who will escort her to the Other Side? You?"

"I do not know." Metkyi shook his head. "Perhaps Delian. Perhaps Alame. Maybe myself, but that is not likely. I do not know—I am not privy to this knowledge."

"I was afraid Witmara might be the one to guide Alicira to her death."

"No. As I have said, the choice of a simple priest will not be Witmara's. You have raised her to rule. From what I have seen— she will rule. Where, what, how, I do not know. But she will rule."

"I would not have cursed our daughter so."

Metkyi took her head in his hands. "You feel this way because of who you are and what happened with Terani. Beloved. You are Alame's daughter as well as Terani's. You may be called to rule."

"I would not wish it."

"You may not have a choice, dear heart." He kissed her forehead.

"What does that mean for Witmara?"

"Great opportunity—for good and for bad." He shook his head. "More I cannot say. I do not know all of it, and some of what I know—I am bound not to share. Be careful in these days to come, beloved. While I wait for you here, I would not have you cross to the Other Side prematurely. My heart tells me that you will need to become the Banisher of Shadows—and perhaps more. Your survival is key to our having a good outcome."

"More?" But even as she asked, the deep rumble announcing Staul's return throbbed through her.

"The forecasts are shadowed," Metkyi said. He stroked her cheek again, and kissed her. "Not even the Gods know what will happen next."

"Metkyi." The God was with them now. "It is time."

"I hear and obey, my lord Staul." Metkyi took Katerin's head in his hands. He kissed her forehead, her nose, and finally her lips one last time. "My blessing upon you and upon our daughter. I will watch over you as best I can, but be careful, my love."

"I will," she promised.

Metkyi backed away from her. The God touched him, and Metkyi faded away.

"My lady Katerin," Staul said.

She rose. "Yes?" she said through a tight throat, not wanting to show the tears she wanted to shed.

It was not a good idea to show weakness around this God.

"A token of my esteem for the times to come, and in return for a delightful gift." Staul held out his hand, something cupped in his palm.

One did not reject Staul's gifts. This God did not give much away. She extended her hand to his. He dropped a single bone disc into her palm, scored on one side, blank on the other.

"What is this for, my lord?"

"This is one of the chips Alicira tossed when she diced with me to determine the fate of her unborn daughter."

She studied the chip, turning it in her fingers. "I thank you."

"It is not much protection unless you take on the role of Banisher of Shadows," the God said. "But it is a tool that the Banisher may find of value."

"Why would you give this to me? Dovré is my patron."

Staul's bony fingertip stroked her cheek, bringing cold where Metkyi had left warmth.

"My sister is not the patron of the Banisher of Shadows. I would have the Banisher protected where my sister cannot do so. There will be days when you may need the Destroyer as well as the Balancer, and this chip keeps you safe from my redder side."

"Lord Staul, what is your game?" Something inside of her quailed at her boldness, but she shoved that feeling back. "If I am to become the Banisher of Shadows, I would know why."

"A gamble," the God said. "Survival. For all of us, Gods and humans alike."

He stroked her cheek again, then faded away.

Katerin exhaled deeply. She studied the disc again before

sliding it into her bag. Then she went to the door and knocked, her head spinning and her legs wobbly, overwhelmed by the magic she had expended. She managed the politenesses required as she left the chamber, barely able to see more than a few paces ahead. It took all of her willpower to not show her weakness to Staul's priest.

At last she stood on the step outside the shrine. Abeyets turned to her.

"Are you able to walk?" he asked in a low voice. "Or did the God ride you so hard that a carriage would be wiser?"

Katerin determinedly lifted her chin. "Unless you deem it safer to do otherwise, I can walk—if you lend me your arm for support."

Right now, she didn't trust any carriage driver in this Gods-forsaken place. Haran's people might have a foothold here as part of Larij's trade policies, but Nixyin was still predominately Saubral, and Gegarth's kin lurked in the shadows. They would not look favorably on the cousin of Gegarth's killer, no matter how Staul favored her.

One more day and we will be at Medvare.

Medvare posed its own challenges, but at least there she had more protections.

THE NEXT EVENING, REKARÉ AND HER FAMILY WAITED AT THE docks as the sternwheeler negotiated its way into the moorage. The last rays of the sun caught the white and gold paint of the smokestacks and made them shine brighter than ever.

Her hand tightened on Cenarth's, and he squeezed it back. She kept her other hand steady on Melarae's shoulder, careful not to pass her tension to her daughter.

The sternwheeler finally slipped into place. The crew

worked steadily to secure its moorings but not at a frantic pace to get the ramp down that would suggest trouble.

Rekaré pushed back her concern. All was well. All would be well.

At last they extended the ramp. The daranvelii were first off, Katerin leading Rainin. A bright blood bay colt with a silver forelock staggered down the ramp after Rainin, swaying as Witmara guided him and kept him from stumbling over the side of the ramp. He nickered plaintively and Rainin answered with a throaty, reassuring whicker. Rekaré caught her breath at the sight of the amount of silver in the colt's mane and tail, realizing why Katerin took the daranvelii off first. Katerin led Rainin toward them, looking frantic.

"Cenarth, can you get Rainin and her foal on the earth?" she asked. "The colt—he was having problems last night at Nixyin, and it has only gotten worse today. It's his first water trip."

"I've got them."

Cenarth took Rainin's lead. She whinnied worriedly. Katerin stopped and met Rainin's gaze. They studied each other. The mare nickered again, then nuzzled her colt as Witmara brought him up next to her. Linyet joined her, careful not to touch the colt.

"Should I stay with him?" Witmara asked Katerin, not stepping away from the colt.

She must be planning to bond with him at weaning.

Rekaré half-smiled, remembering those early days between daranval foals and the young humans making their first daranval-human link. She and Cenarth had bonded to Basnen and Quartel in the same manner, getting to know them as foals and connecting to the young daranvelii at weaning time.

"He'll be fine with Cenarth and Linyet," Katerin said. "I need your help with Alicira."

"Let Witmara go, cousin." Now Rekaré could move. "I'll help

you with my mother. Cenarth, go ahead. Linyet, you listen to Witmara about the foal."

Witmara smiled gratefully at Rekaré. Cenarth led Rainin away and Linyet helped Witmara, taking a position on the other side of the foal from her.

"Thank you, Rekaré," Katerin said. "Today's passage through the rapids was difficult. I don't know who had the spins worse, Alicira or the foal. Witmara's been beside herself."

"I remember those days bonding with a foal," Rekaré said. "It will be a good attachment between them, strong as that colt is."

"If we don't have to—" Katerin checked herself from saying more, glancing behind Rekaré.

Out of the corner of her eye Rekaré spotted Melarae hanging back, not saying anything.

"You could go with Witmara and Linyet," Rekaré said to her daughter.

Melarae shook her head, her lips pressed tightly together. She didn't say anything.

"I'm just worried about the magic drought in the Two Nations," Katerin said in a low voice. "It has been difficult this year."

She worries about the Sacrifice.

"Unlikely that things will progress that far," Rekaré said. "Cenarth tells me that the magic in this year's flocks here, at least, is not as diminished as we feared. Besides, given the tie that colt and Witmara already have—he would not be available for the Sacrifice. If things get that desperate because of the drought we'll have many more problems than this to deal with." She sighed. "So. Let's get Mother to the Leader's House."

She and Katerin started up the ramp, Melarae trailing behind them.

"I warn you, cousin, she's not looking well." Katerin contin-ued, speaking softly as they reached the top of the ramp. "I'm hoping she'll be better after a day or so on solid ground. She had a difficult night in Nixyin, and I don't know how much longer my potions can keep her pain at bay."

Rekaré didn't hear the rest of what Katerin said as she spotted her mother, between Haran and Orlanden. Alicira lay back in her willow wheelchair, eyes closed. But her face was as pale as cottonwood fluff, without the slightest trace of color in it. Rekaré reached out blindly to take Katerin's arm. Katerin stopped and faced her.

Rekaré leaned close to Katerin. "Is my mother that close to death?"

Katerin swallowed hard. "It will be soon, Rekaré, unless she rallies. Magic pulls heavily at her and she just doesn't seem to regain strength. Ever since we got your message and she parted from Heinmyets and Inharise, she has declined more quickly than I thought. I hope it's just the travel, but if you've seen—"

"You two don't need to whisper about my health," Alicira said, tiredness and exasperation both in her voice. She opened her eyes. "I know I look bad right now. I will be better once I'm off of water. And I *am* glad to see you, daughter."

Rekaré went to her knees in front of her mother's wheelchair. "I am glad to see you, Mother." She fought back an urge to bury her head in her mother's lap, choosing instead to rest her hands on Alicira's knees. "But seeing you like this makes me remember the price you paid over the years to keep me safe."

A faint smile tugged at her mother's lips. "Well worth the cost." She looked beyond Rekaré. "Is that Melarae? She's gotten so big over the past year!"

Rekaré turned her head. Melarae hung back behind Katerin. "Yes. Come forward to see your grandmother, Melarae." She turned back to Alicira. "Linyet is helping Witmara and Cenarth with Katerin's daranvelii. He's becoming quite the horseman."

"Good, good." Alicira sighed. "Now can we get onto solid ground?"

"We need to steady the wheelchair as it comes down the

ramp. This one's not bad. But the night before Nixyin, at the Lone Peak ferry?" Katerin shook her head. "Barely wide enough to roll the chair down, and I feared we'd lose her off the side."

"I'm going to have a discussion with my brother about that dock at Lone Peak," Haran said as they eased Alicira forward. "Honestly, I had no idea it was so difficult." He scowled. "It's not good for trade, either, to have such poorly maintained wharves."

"It's only been three years since regular sternwheeler traffic started," Alicira said. "Not every port is going to be in the best of shape, and Lone Peak has light use—Ouch!" She winced as they hit a rough spot in the ramp.

"Are you all right?"

Alicira nodded. Rekaré noticed, though, that her mother bit down hard on her lip.

Once on the dock they walked alongside her wheelchair to the carriage. Rekaré glanced at the coachwoman, Baseré.

"Did Cenarth continue on to the stable?" she asked.

"Yes," Baseré said. "Witmara and Linyet are with him." She opened the carriage door. "Perhaps we should get the lady Alicira in first. Then the wheelchair can be fastened to the back."

"It can come with the wagon," Rekaré said. "I have assistants from the Healing House waiting with another chair at the Leader's House." She looked over at Katerin. "The Medvaran Healing House has asked to place several apprentices with you."

"Apprentices?" Her cousin frowned. "I'm not sure—"

"Higher-level apprentices," Rekaré hurried to assure her. "Neinyet has worked a traveling circuit and Onadral has spent time as a village healer. Both want to study advanced methods with you. Erotrial the Head of the House assures me that both are capable of substituting for Katerin Healer when she has to be Katerin ea Miteal—and I have more need of you as Katerin ea Miteal than as Katerin Healer."

Katerin grimaced.

"I will be all right," Alicira reassured her. "House duties must be met."

"*Politics,*" Katerin grumbled. But she did not argue further.

It took Rekaré, Katerin, Orlanden, and Haran working together to move Alicira from the wheelchair to the coach. Katerin steadied Alicira's head and Rekaré guided her feet, while Orlanden and Haran slid their arms underneath Alicira. She clung to Orlanden and Haran as they carried her, lips pressed together so tightly that they paled. Once inside the coach, Katerin and Rekaré sat on either side of Alicira to hold her up.

Alicira leaned against Rekaré. She was shocked at how feather light her mother's weight was. Heat radiated from Alicira. Rekaré put her arm around her mother's shoulders and held her close. Her eyes met Katerin's.

Melarae sat across from them, solemnly staring at her grandmother.

She should have gone with the other children. I wonder why she didn't?

It wasn't as if her daughter had taken much interest in Alicira before now. Linyet had been more inclined to listen to his grandmother than his sister.

Alicira coughed. "Yes, child, this is what a seriously ill person looks like," she said archly to Melarae. "Go ahead and ask questions. I can see them in your eyes." Her voice softened on the last words.

"Does it hurt much?" Melarae blurted.

"Yes. I hurt constantly. I live for those moments when your cousin can give me more painkiller."

"Are you afraid to die?"

"Child, I have come close to death so many times that I no longer fear it. But I have lived a full life if not a long one." Alicira studied Melarae. "Staul has been speaking to you, hasn't he? That's why you want to know what death looks like."

Melarae flushed and looked down at her feet.

Dread surged through Rekaré. *That* God speaking to her daughter?

Not as bad as the other, but still—not what I would choose.

"Not him," Melarae muttered. "Don't know if it's a God, either."

"One must be very careful when speaking to Gods," Alicira said. "Will you come spend time with me once I am settled in the Leader's House? If you are speaking to Gods then you need to learn how to protect yourself. No matter which God it is."

"I've tried to teach her," Rekaré said.

"Sometimes parents aren't the best teachers of their children," her mother answered with a rueful tone in her voice.

She glanced sideways at Rekaré, mouth quirking. Rekaré remembered times when it had been Heinmyets, or Inharise, or Alame who had taught her magic skills because mother and daughter could do nothing but argue.

Her daughter looked back up and Rekaré thought she saw fear flitting across her face.

"Mother, are you certain this won't be too much of a drain?"

"I'm not dead *yet*," she grumbled. "Nor am I dying that fast. Traveling on water drains me. I have little resistance to it. A day on solid ground and I'll be better. I can take on teaching your daughter a few things once I've recovered. So you will come see me, Melarae?"

"All right," Melarae said reluctantly. "I will."

"Very well." Alicira straightened up. "I will await you after breakfast tomorrow morning. I don't have time to wait. Or does she have lessons in the morning?" she asked Rekaré.

"I will let Tlikset know that Melarae is to come to you tomorrow morning."

"Good." Her mother closed her eyes. "I am so grateful to stop traveling."

Rekaré looked back at her daughter in time to see the disgruntled expression fade from her face.

Perhaps Mother will know what to do about this child and magic.

Once they arrived at the Leader's House, Neinyet from the Medvaran Healing House waited with Onadral and other servants. They carefully moved Alicira from the carriage to a sturdier wheelchair while Katerin hovered, watching everything they did.

"Come to my private office tonight after dinner," Rekaré said to Katerin. "We must talk, as soon as we can."

"I will be there," Katerin said.

AN UNWANTED VISITOR

At last. No water travel for the foreseeable future!

Katerin heaved a sigh of relief. She closed the main entrance door of the suite she shared with Witmara, Alicira, Neinyet, and Onadral, sagging against it. Alicira was settled into her own room for the night with Neinyet on first watch. Witmara was in bed. Haran and Orlanden had retreated to their own suite and would not be back until morning. Now she had time to meet with Rekaré.

Just hope we don't drag things out too long. I'm tired.

Ideally, she'd have been able to slip down to the stable to check on the colt before this meeting. But she had to settle for querying Rainin, and getting an absent-minded reassurance.

Maybe afterward.

It all depended on what magic Rekaré wanted to do tonight. Her head still throbbed from being on the water and dealing with treating Alicira this evening. She didn't have many reserves left.

Katerin pushed herself off of the door and headed down the hallway to Rekaré and Cenarth's private suite. As she walked, she noticed the subtle signs of increased physical security—

more guards walking through the hallways and stationed at doorways. Guards armed with low-level magical weapons, as well. What she didn't notice was a matching intensity in the wards that guarded the Leader's House from outside magic. Her skin should be burning with the strength of those wards when she passed through area boundaries. Instead, a tiny vibration fluttered down her arms, not even enough to make them tingle.

Not good.

Katerin knew the protections at the Keldaran Leader's House, and how Alicira, Heinmyets, and Inharise worried about the areas they couldn't completely shield for one reason or another. She should feel some sort of challenge from the wards as a recently arrived magician when she crossed into Rekaré and Cenarth's wing—and she didn't.

The sense of magical presence was the least it had been since her cousin took up residence and established her authority. She remembered how inconsistent the cold tingles of sorcery had been in the Leader's House the first time she had been in it, after Rekaré took power.

Perhaps her perspective then had been affected by the shock of the twin losses of Metkyi and her beloved daranval Mira, and becoming the Banisher of Shadows to help Rekaré defeat her father Zauril. Katerin wasn't sure how much of her disjointedness had been caused by the loose, unbound sorcery abruptly cut off from its source that roiled around the Leader's House after Zauril's death.

As she took possession of the Leader's House both magically and physically, Rekaré had streamlined and simplified many things about the Leader's House. She opted for comfort and security over the showy ostentation that Zauril had preferred—both in décor and in magic.

It was supposed to be safer. All the same, it worried Katerin that she couldn't sense her cousin's residual sorcery. Or was it her own magical fatigue?

I hope that's all it is.

But something hadn't felt right about Medvara's magic since they crossed the Dry Line this morning. The land roiled uneasily.

Why?

Maybe that was the reason for the increase in guards in the Leader's House without matching growth in ward strength. Was the sorcery drought that much stronger in Medvara than in Keldara?

Worry cinched tighter around Katerin's gut, and she wished she wasn't so tired as she came to the Leader's suite, appropriately patrolled by four guards.

"Lady Katerin," the head guard said, saluting her.

"I'm expected," Katerin murmured, biting back the urge to correct the guard. He would only know her as Katerin ea Miteal, not Katerin Healer. It was not worth the effort to argue.

"Of course." He opened the door to the Leader's suite.

Cenarth sat at a desk in the sitting room, papers scattered over every bit of the surface, studying them under the glow from a brighter glowlight, a magicked disc enclosed inside a glass ball. He gave her a quick wave before returning to his paperwork. Katerin continued past the now-closed nursery door to the open door of Rekaré's study. Her cousin also sat at a desk with a brighter disc light. She pushed a pile of papers away as Katerin entered the office and closed the door behind her.

"You arrived in a timely manner," she said. "Vered sent a messenger bird this evening. They have crossed the Chellana bar. She expects to arrive in port the day after tomorrow."

"I thought we had more time to prepare for this Chiral's arrival."

"So did I," Rekaré said. "It's what Vered didn't say that worries me. Not about Chiral, but about Chatain. I suspect Vered traveled faster across Sea to avoid pursuit."

"That wouldn't be good."

"No." Rekaré leaned back in her chair.

"So what brought this Chiral to your attention?"

"Detaluna, one of Cenarth's cousins, was taken prisoner at a young age by the Saubral, and sold as a slave in Daran," Rekaré said. "She escaped ten years ago and returned to Varen. Vered suggested that we train Deta to gather information. She's been doing that for me over the past five years. That's how I know about Chatain's actions."

"That's a good thing, I suppose," Katerin said. "But that means Chatain probably has his own spies here."

"He does, and Richen my spymaster has identified many of them. We do what we can to feed false information to Chatain's networks. Deta heads up my network in Daran."

"So if you're feeding false information to Chatain, how do you know he isn't feeding false information to Detaluna?"

"Richen estimates that about two-thirds of the information Detaluna gets is good. Including this piece about Chiral. Once Deta found her, Chatain's people went wild. Not always thinking about what they were doing. Deta had to go dark after she first told me, because Chatain's people were hard after them. I had—similar methods for contacting both Deta and Vered as you and I have. Deta had to destroy her patch, so other than telling me they were on their way, we've not communicated except through messenger birds."

"That sort of reaction from Chatain could also be a means to encourage you to think that Chiral is legitimately who she says she is—when she isn't," Katerin cautioned.

Is that why the sorcery in the Leader's House feels depleted? Rekaré's protections against Chatain sucking down all the magic available from the land?

"Or Chatain could hope to set her up as his agent in my household," Rekaré said grimly. "Or as a saboteur. Lots of possibilities, and only a few of those are that she's legitimate. I had hoped to use Mother's magic as well as yours to summon up protections against Chiral, should she be more than just a rebel Ralsem heir. Now—" she sighed. "I hate to ask this, cousin, but I need you to assume the role of the Banisher of Shadows to help protect Varen. Not just Medvara and the Two Nations, but all of Varen."

"*All* of Varen?"

Gods, this was sounding worse and worse. Coupled with a magical drought—no wonder the wards here felt diminished. If Rekaré needed to raise a protective barrier around all of Varen—

But that should be a cooperative effort with Larij, Keratil, and the Two Nations. Why hasn't she done that, especially this year? I would have heard about this before now if that were the case.

Rekaré held up her hand. "Before you say more, please bring out your Eye and let's put up a privacy shield. There are things I need to speak of that I would not have any other hear, whether they be God or human."

Katerin nodded. She brought out the Eye of Dovré and stood in the center of the study, waiting. Rekaré sealed the door shut, tracing a spell over the doorframe. Then she gestured to Katerin. Silently, they flipped the solid black rug in the center of the room and smoothed it out. The reverse side of the rug was black with a big golden circle. Katerin brought two chairs to the middle of the circle, placing them to face each other, and sat in one. Rekaré paced around the edge of golden circle in both directions, muttering a spell as she shook silver powder onto the edge from a glass vial, careful not to spread it beyond the bounds of the gold. When she had finished the second circle, gold and silver light rose from the circle. The golden needles inside Katerin's Eye of Dovré glowed with a matching light. Katerin brought out the token that Staul had given her, remembering his words, and set it down in the center of the circle, between their chairs. She put her feet on both sides of it.

Rekaré now joined Katerin, sitting in the other chair. They twined their forearms together.

"I call upon the Banisher of Shadows," Rekaré said. "I have need of the Banisher. May the Goddess allow her to come forth."

"The Banisher comes," Katerin said, feeling that presence rise within her, a creepy-crawlie sensation prickling up and down her arms and legs. It rose up her throat and moved her lips, her voice coming out deeper than she normally spoke. "What need has the Lady of Medvara of the Banisher?"

"For tonight, I would ask that you seal and protect this sphere, then be available for a later and less secure working. Let no one outside of us two hear what we say to each other."

"It will be done," the Banisher said through Katerin.

She felt the power pass out of her with the same prickly sensation. The silver dust around the edge of the circle transformed into a bright, shimmering dome.

"It is done," Rekaré said.

Katerin swayed and would have fallen had Rekaré not steadied her.

"Are you all right?" Rekaré asked.

"Just tired," Katerin said, surprised at the sudden irritation in her voice. "The Banisher draws a lot out of me. Perhaps a bit too much given I've spent the last few days traveling on water."

"I know," Rekaré said, sounding regretful as she dropped her arms to her side. "And I would not ask this of you without need."

"I know that the Banisher must rise again despite my wishes. I spoke with Metkyi last night, at the shrine in Nixyin." Katerin took advantage of Rekaré's release to lean against the back of her chair. "Both he and Staul spoke of that necessity. They mirrored what you said about the odds being more than just a battle against Chatain. And then—I notice that the wards here in the Leader's House are diminished."

"Yes. We will speak of that in a moment—but this is why I wanted that privacy shield. Protection against Chatain, but even more. I fear what Staul warns us about."

"War. Deepest, reddest war," Katerin said.

"A war involving Gods and humans." Rekaré pushed a flyaway strand of dark hair from her face. "Not the ordinary, limited banishment of a God from a city or land for a generation. Something bigger. I wonder. *Can* the Gods be killed or completely banished? I know my father had pretensions toward becoming a God. At the time I thought it was a delusional desire to be the most powerful sorcerer in the world."

"I don't know. I've never heard of anything greater than a temporary eviction of a God or Gods from a land for a generation, like what my mother Terani did in Waykemin. Metkyi seemed to think it was possible when we went up against your father. Staul believes it is possible. He was mostly the Destroyer when I spoke to him," Katerin said. "Staul was more intrusive of my time with Metkyi than usual. That's not a good omen."

Rekaré groaned. She got to her feet and paced within the circle.

"The God was half-Destroyer, half-Balancer when he spoke to me, but the Destroyer was in control. If the Gods are warring, then what? There must always be Seven Crowned Gods. When your mother deposed Nitel in Waykemin, that banishment was only good there. Elsewise my father would not have been able to use Nitel as a patron. What happens if the Gods destroy each other throughout all the lands? Who replaces them? Or do we have Gods effective in some nations but not others? It's confusing."

"Karnoi and Cirdel went through Terani to banish Nitel in Waykemin—" Katerin found it hard to refer to Terani as *my mother* any more— "and we saw what *that* did. Karnoi and Cirdel became more powerful there. But Nitel was still present, perhaps even stronger, here in Medvara. Why did this happen?"

"I wish I knew," Rekaré fretted. "I've tried asking the Tapestry, but it seems to be useless for probes about the Gods. I suppose that's because this isn't an issue of Medvara. I wish I knew more about what is going on with the Gods. Do you think that Staul is leading a rebellion?"

"He's not the God I would think to do it," Katerin said. "Nitel—yes. Karnoi and Cirdel—yes. But Staul? Dovré? Artel? Terat? Those four have nothing to gain from a war between Gods."

"And yet the cycles turn, and change occurs, and of all the Gods, Staul is the most changeable because of his dual nature." Rekaré sat back down. "Well, we need to think on this more. I have a more urgent need to ask of you tonight, with Chiral so near. We need to restore the protections of Medvara to their former strength, replace my mother's presence in the wards with yours. This Chiral may indeed be Chatain's tool, but we don't need to make it easy for her." She grimaced. "We'll need to drop this shield and bring Cenarth in. I'd have the girls work the magic as well, but they and Linyet are too young."

Katerin hesitated. "I haven't worked with the land's magic at this level before." Was this what Metkyi had been speaking of? "I don't know if I can weave it."

I don't know if I want to weave the land's magic. That will put me in a position to serve as Leader. I don't want that.

But she was a Miteal. It was her responsibility, even though she had not been aware of her heritage until well into her adult years. Her role to be willing to take on this function.

"You are powerful enough," Rekaré said. "Anyone who can wear the geas of the Banisher of Shadows is strong enough to work the land's magic. I have confidence in you."

"That sounds—reasonable." Katerin amended what she intended to say.

Ridiculous. I am only Katerin Healer!

For a moment it seemed as if Metkyi stroked her cheek.

Remember, you are much more than Katerin Healer these days,

she thought she heard him whisper.

"And what do we do about the Gods?" she continued.

"We can only do what we can," Rekaré said. "Right now, my priority is to protect Medvara, and with it, Varen."

"But we must also consider these warnings."

"I worry about such dire portents from Staul," Rekaré said.

"One would think that such forewarnings would come from Artel the Judge, not Staul the Destroyer."

"Agreed. Which is why I wonder what Staul's game is. Speaking of which—what is that disc you placed in the center of the circle?"

Katerin hesitated. Then she knelt and picked up the chip, holding it out to Rekaré.

"Staul gave me this. He says it is one of the chips your mother used when dicing to determine your fate."

Rekaré peered at the chip in Katerin's fingers, but did not take it. "I fear to touch it," she said finally. "Something repels me. But—Staul also gave me a token."

She reached into her own pouch. At first Katerin thought that Rekaré held another chip. Then she looked closer. A fingertip bone.

"What did the God say when he gave you this?"

Rekaré stared away from Katerin, her eyes unfocused. At last she refocused. "This is what he said: 'The Balancer sleeps as the Destroyer grows great. Change comes to Varen and Daran alike. Be ready for when it happens. Listen to the Banisher of Shadows.' And then he disappeared, leaving this bone."

"Interesting." Katerin closed her fingers over the chip. "Staul was more specific with me. It's meant to protect me as Banisher of Shadows, where Dovré can't. But that can't be right. Dovré has always protected me, all three times when I had to raise the

Banisher. I can't imagine why I would need further protection, even as the Banisher."

"Unless, of course, Staul provokes a war between the Gods, and Dovré withdraws her protection from you as the Banisher," Rekaré said.

"Or Dovré is the target of the war."

"I can't see that. Dovré is beloved by all the Gods except Nitel. Well, Karnoi and Cirdel also dislike her. So perhaps that would be a factor."

"Such dislike on their part would be my doing," Katerin said.

"That could be why Staul gave you that chip for protection."

"It would make more sense than Staul leading the revolt." Katerin paused. "I asked him what his game was."

"And?" Rekaré arched her brows at Katerin.

"Survival, he said. For gods and humans alike."

"Those are not the words of a rebel God," Rekaré said.

"I didn't think so either."

"Well, we will need to watch. Best we not speak of these concerns except under this level of protection," Rekaré said.

"I think that is a wise idea." Katerin rubbed her forehead. "Let's work on the wards now if we're going to do them tonight. My head is pounding. Once I'm done here I'll want to collapse. I've had to expend a lot of magic already today."

"Sit. Rest. I'll set up for the ward work. I can release this shield without your assistance." Rekaré went to the gossamer edge of the shield and softly spoke the words to undo the spell. It shimmered away.

"Thank you," Katerin said.

"I also have some refreshment that will help with your fatigue."

Rekaré picked up a small side table and set it next to Katerin, then filled three tiny, stemmed glasses with a purple liquor. Then she placed a palm-sized white cake studded with round purple berries on a plate, and brought both cake and liquor to Katerin.

Katerin raised her brows as the rich, tangy scent from the liquor wafted toward her. "Coos berry?"

"The first bottling of this year's crop from Cooscol. First harvest from the restored bushes. It was slight, but quite robust in magic." She gestured at the cake. "Coos berries in that cake as well. Both the cake and the liquor should temporarily restore your strength."

"This might help your mother," Katerin said. She broke off a piece of the cake and took a bite. The thin, crisp crust crunched into softer, spongier interior. Then the sharp pop of three Coos berries flooded her mouth with a rich, sweet tang that danced up and down her arms and legs, leaving warmth that eased the soreness and aches in her muscles. "Mmm. That *is* good. This year's berries in the cake?"

"Just harvested," Rekaré said.

"I see what you mean about small but robust," Katerin said. She raised her brows as her surroundings sharpened in focus. "Hmm. Yes."

"Try the liquor." Rekaré's face relaxed slightly. "I wasn't sure if the reaction I had reflected my own hopes, or if it really *was* that powerful."

Katerin sat up straighter. "I think the berries really *are* that powerful." She put her piece of cake down. "This bit I broke off will work just fine for me."

She picked up the liquor and took the tiniest of cautious sips. A warm, sweet richness followed by a whisper of salt air, then a deeper, tangy heat, filled her mouth. Her legs itched to move, to do something, and sorcery danced at her fingertips, begging to be set free.

Control the Banisher of Shadows? Easy!

"Ah," Katerin continued. "So different from the Coos berries we've grown in Keldara! Much stronger."

"They were grown on the original fields," Rekaré said. "Enjoy, while I get Cenarth."

When Cenarth returned with Rekaré, she resealed the door.

Katerin finished the last of the liquor and rose to meet them. They moved the chairs and the little table outside of the circle. Rekaré handed a bag of blue glimmer dust to Cenarth and Katerin. This time, they followed Rekaré around the edge of the golden circle while scattering the dust, Rekaré leading the first round, then reversing for Katerin to lead the second round. Then they sat cross-legged within the circle, placing the half-empty bags in front of them. Rekaré began a tonal, wordless chant. Cenarth picked up a counterpoint, and Katerin interwove her voice with theirs.

Strands of their magic flowed into the center of the circle. Rekaré's blue-edged magenta, Katerin's solid blue, and Cenarth's orange-edged gold each formed a long thread. Rekaré picked up the fibers first, twining them together to form one long, colorful filament of magic. Cenarth then separated the strand into lengths, and Katerin wove them together to form a small but brightly colored patch that hovered in the middle of the circle. The energy from the Coos berry liquor made it easier to work the weave than she expected.

Words now filled Rekaré's chant.

"Follow the weave, follow the strand. From Cooscol to Medvare, Saktrin to Biklyet, river to river, ocean to the Dry Line. Renew and rebuild, guard and defend. Repel the outside powers, magical and physical. Medvara is ours and ever shall be."

Cenarth repeated the chant, then Katerin.

"Now *go!*" Rekaré commanded.

The patch swelled, moving beyond them, continuing to expand. Katerin felt its magic tugging at her, giving her brief glimpses of Cooscol, Saktrin, and other parts of Medvara. Power surged through Katerin, greater than she had experienced before.

Then the tugging ceased. Instead of a tiny patch in the circle, Katerin gazed upon a thin, multi-colored barrier that hovered near the ceiling.

Rekaré took a pinch of glimmer dust out of her bag, blowing it into the center.

"It is done," she said.

Cenarth and Katerin copied her.

The dazzling glow faded from their sight but the sharp tingle of the renewed wards danced up and down Katerin's arms. Fatigue washed over her, greater than ever, and she collapsed to one side, lying down on the rug, momentarily unable to move. The only other time she had been this tired had been when she had banished Karnoi and Cirdel from Keldara in Dovré's name. And yet—this time she didn't feel separated from herself and fading away into the endless sleep, like Terani had done. She was just tired. Cenarth fell to his hands and knees, shaking his head.

"You need another shot of that liquor," Rekaré said. "We all need another shot."

"I need sleep." Katerin yawned. "If I have more to drink, I don't know if I can make it back to my suite—at least not on my own two feet."

"We'll ensure you get back," Rekaré said.

"Well, why not?" Katerin pushed herself back upright, struggling to rise to all fours. She collapsed back onto the floor.

Rekaré leaned onto her hands and pushed herself up slowly. She hobbled over to her desk, picking up Katerin's glass as she went. Her movements were slow and shaky. Once she got to the desk, she collapsed onto the chair. Her right hand first reached for the bottle, trembling, then moved to the cake, instead. She broke off a piece and ate it. This time, her hand was steady as she reached for the flagon and poured. She took a sip from one glass, and stood up. She gave Cenarth a glass as well as a piece of the cake, then just the glass to Katerin.

Katerin tossed the liquor down her throat this time. The same heat pulsed through her, followed by a lessening of the fatigue. This time she didn't feel sorcery dancing at her fingertips, but she was able to stand upright.

Rekaré and Cenarth finished their liquor.

"We'll see you back to your suite," Rekaré said.

"Thank you."

As they left the private quarters, Rekaré signed orders to the guard. Two moved just inside the door while the other two fell in behind them. Katerin walked down the halls with Cenarth on her right side and Rekaré on her left. This time she noticed the vibrations from the wards. But these wards stroked her gently, a sensation like Rainin nuzzling her arm after getting a treat rather than the sharp tingle Katerin had experienced before. These wards *knew* Katerin, contained a part of her magic.

Now I am a part of Medvara.

That was not a reassuring thing to consider.

THE MAGICAL COLT

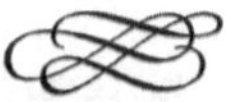

Katerin rose before Witmara or Alicira the next morning. She slipped out to check on Rainin and the colt. Early mornings as fine as this one were her favorite time during the humid Medvaran summers. Light dew coated the grass and bushes, enough to settle the tan-shaded dust on the path. No breeze stirred the bigleaf maples shading the lane from the Leader's House to the stables on the main ground. Sunlight barely peeked over the eastern mountains, the great Artel Mountain sporting a light coat of snow at the very top.

She wandered down the main alleyway of the large stable. Horses were already turned out for the morning, not a one in any stall, including the one that was usually Rainin's. She nodded at the stablehands.

"Where did my daranval get turned out?" she asked them.

"Out there," one said, pointing with his chin to the other end of the alley, where the corrals and pens were. "Cenarth took 'em out."

"Thank you."

Katerin continued down the alleyway and went out the other side. She recognized Cenarth's short spiky braids splaying from under his hat as he perched on the top fence rail of one of the round corrals.

He watched Rainin and the colt. Katerin joined Cenarth on the top rail. To her relief, the colt danced around Rainin as she ate hay, seemingly unharmed from his experience on the boat. He stopped at their feet, reared, bucked a couple of steps, then took off in the other direction.

Katerin laughed despite her worries. "I guess I didn't need to worry about him having any long-term effects from the trip! Those last two days on the water were rough on him."

Cenarth grinned at her. "He's spunky. High in magic potential, much stronger than Rainin. Foals recover quickly. He should have more water journeys to help him adjust—that's what we've found with Quartel's get. Short boat trips of half a day or more helps build up a tolerance to multiple days of sternwheeler travel. Maybe that's how we can get daranvelii to travel over the ocean."

"He reminds me of Mira sometimes," Katerin said wistfully, remembering her daranval before Rainin. "His sire is related to her."

"Well, he's inherited the magic potential of that bloodline, no doubt about it, just look at the silver in his mane and tail," Cenarth said. "He might gray out like your Mira did. He was getting frantic in the stall when we started taking the others out. I wanted to make sure he was well after the trip. But he was raising a right royal fit, so I decided that meant he'd taken no harm." He shifted his weight on the rail. "Led real well. Jeralte had no problems once we got a halter on him. Mannerly on the lead. You've been training him."

"*Witmara's* been training him," Katerin said.

Rainin raised her head and snorted at her foal. Then she sent images of Katerin feeding her treats all day, Katerin grooming her, Katerin scratching her itchy spots.

Katerin returned images of feeding a few treats, a quick

brushing, and then leaving to work inside all day while Rainin and her colt stayed outside, resting and soaking up the sun.

Rainin snorted again and switched her tail in annoyance. Then she thought about treats.

Katerin laughed. "You silly thing!"

Rainin answered that treats were never silly, and that Katerin owed her many, many treats after that long, dark, unsteady ride on *water*.

Katerin produced an apple she had picked up in the kitchens before coming to the stable. Rainin ambled over and took the apple. Her powerful jaws crunched it in half. Part of the apple dropped to the ground. Her foal came over and Rainin pinned her ears and tossed her head, sending him away from her.

Cenarth laughed. "She's not going to share her treat!"

"He is a pushy boy," Katerin admitted. "Very strong-willed. He kicked Rainin—once. She may be a minor daranval in the herd and lesser in magic ability, but as his dam she didn't accept that behavior, and kicked him back. He's learned manners."

"Good thing with a colt as powerful as this one." Cenarth pursed his lips, studying the foal as he pranced around the corral, pretending not to care about his mother's treat. "Witmara's bonded to him in all but name. Probably a good thing he's mannerly."

Katerin hesitated. She was reluctant to express her fears about Sacrifice to Heinmyets and Inharise. But Cenarth might be safe—should she?

By Dovré's tits, he already had noticed the link between Witmara and the colt. The weaning and bonding would likely happen under his supervision.

No one else to ask.

"He is powerful. More powerful than any other magic produced by Keldara this year. I worry about Witmara's bond to him. What about other obligations?"

Cenarth glanced at her. "You worry about the Sacrifice?"

"I worry that it might be necessary." Katerin watched the colt sprint around the pen again. "I've heard it whispered, before we left. Enough to make me worry about Witmara's ties to him. And then an owl flew over him the night of the full moon."

"If there's a need for a Sacrifice, there will be more than just him sacrificed," Cenarth said. "Owl sign would not be enough. What owl?"

"A great gray."

"Could mean that it is his patron, which means he's especially blessed by the Goddess. The Sacrifice doesn't always mean death," Cenarth said. "Especially for a young daranval partnered with someone like Witmara." He clambered off the fence.

"What do you mean?"

"If he does partner with Witmara, then they both become the Sacrifice."

Katerin inhaled sharply. "Both of them killed?"

Cenarth shook his head. "No. Not that." He paused, fingering one of his thin braids. "But they are marked for a greater destiny." He stopped outside the stable and faced Katerin. His features seemed to blur, becoming almost feminine in detail, with gray-green eyes that resembled the waters of the Chellana River on a stormy day. "Katerin ea Miteal. Fear not for that colt and your daughter being separated. Fear instead for the circumstances that may call them to step forward to serve as the Sacrifice." Cenarth's features unblurred from the aspect of the Goddess Terat, his patroness, and he shook his head. "The Gods will do what they will—even Terat."

"She rides you so easily," Katerin whispered.

"More and more as the years progress and I spend more time working magic with Rekaré," Cenarth said. "When I was sworn as the Leader's Consort, it seemed as if that opened a channel to Terat. But easier today after—last night."

"I will think on your words and hers."

"I'm glad you remember them, because I do not." He shrugged. "It has always been her way with me."

"Thank you, Cenarth—and you as well, Goddess," she said.

But as she went back to the Leader's House, Katerin still couldn't dismiss her uneasiness.

Gods, it would have been so much easier if either Witmara or the colt were weaker in their potential for sorcery!

❧

"How is Daro?" Witmara asked when Katerin returned to their suite. She bounced up from her dining table seat to stand by Katerin, bouncing on the balls of her feet.

"Daro?" Katerin sat down to unlace her boots.

Orlanden smiled ruefully at Katerin.

Excited this morning, he mouthed to her.

"You know. Rainin's colt," Witmara said.

"She's been going on about him since we showed up for breakfast," Haran added. "I had to ask, too."

"He doesn't have a name yet," Katerin said.

"Yes he does. He told me yesterday, when we were off the boat and on our way to the stables," Witmara said.

"I see." Katerin focused on taking off her boots. *He's told Witmara his name and it's not even time for weaning yet!* What did that mean? "Well, he's fine and full of himself this morning. Cenarth put them outside. He's tearing around the corral."

"I thought so. He sent me happy fast thoughts."

He's sending to her? Oh Gods.

Before Katerin could say any more, Alicira hobbled into the sitting room, using a cane in each hand to stay upright. Haran and Orlanden both jumped up to help her but she waved them away as she eased herself into an armchair.

"So Rainin's colt has named himself," she said wryly. "And Rekaré's reset the wards."

"You can tell?" Katerin asked.

"I heard both of you as I was coming down the hallway. As for the wards, I had more energy when I woke this morning, without the trickle of power going forth from me to support them," she said. "I could tell I am no longer in that weave. A good thing, as my magic benefits very few any more."

Witmara cocked her head. "But I think your magic is always good for teaching."

"Well, we will see what happens when your cousin comes to study." Alicira eyed Witmara. "And you as well, my dear. Those who would bind themselves to a strong young daranval at your age need to learn more about using that magic. Especially those who learn that daranval's name before he is weaned, and are already getting thoughts from him."

"I am ready," Witmara said confidently, still bouncing on the balls of her feet.

"Where have I heard that before?" Haran said wryly, smiling at Alicira. "She may not be your direct descendant, but all morning I've been reminded of another energetic young woman."

Alicira snorted. "You said much the same about Rekaré at the same age."

"Miteal magicians," Haran said. "You're all the same. If I had known how much time I would be spending around sorcerers, I'd have focused more on learning about magic."

"You can learn from me," Witmara said. "I'm good at magic."

"That's you. We shall see about your cousin." Alicira's voice sharpened. "Is that the remainder of your breakfast I see? Best eat hearty this morning. I may be old and sick but I still have a few tricks up my sleeve."

"Yes, ma'am!" Witmara bowed and scampered back to the table.

Alicira rolled her eyes. "The energy of youth."

"May I get you some breakfast?" Katerin asked.

Alicira frowned at her. "I have little appetite."

"You will be working with young sorcerers," Katerin pointed out. "And even though you may feel energized—you still need to eat." Would the cake from the Coos berries help Alicira?

Worth a try.

"We have fresh peaches from Chellni," Neinyet added, coming into the sitting room. "Fermented goat's milk as well. I could always get daranval milk if you think that would be best, Katerin Healer."

Alicira's face twisted into a querulous expression. "I drank enough of that stuff while carrying Rekaré, thank you very much. Fermented goat's milk and peaches, then, please, Neinyet." Her scowl deepened. "I suppose I should get up and come over to the table."

"We can bring you a tray," Neinyet said.

"Or we can help you to the table," Haran added.

The door opened and Rekaré entered, carrying a covered dish. Melarae trailed sullenly behind her, also carrying a covered tray.

"Good morning Mother, good morning Katerin and Witmara, good morning Orlanden and Haran, and good morning Neinyet," Rekaré said, setting her tray down on the table and crossing the room to kiss Alicira on the cheek. "We brought you breakfast cake and other foods to share."

"Trying to fatten me up?" Alicira grumbled.

"The breakfast cake has Coos berries in it, from this year's harvest in Cooscol," Rekaré said.

"They're more potent than what we grow in Keldara," Katerin added. "I had some last night."

"Coos berries from Cooscol? Hmm." Alicira braced her hands on her canes and struggled to her feet. "I can do this, Orlanden!" she snapped as he hurried to her side. "Too much fussing! I need to do it myself as long as I am capable."

Orlanden raised his hands and backed away. Haran raised his eyebrows and gave Alicira a pointed look.

"I'm sorry," Alicira sighed. "I know you mean well. Perhaps having Coos berries from Cooscol plus the weight of no more presence in the wards will give me a much-needed boost in energy. Where are you growing them, Rekaré?"

"We restored the original fields," Rekaré said. She went to take Alicira's arm as she lurched forward but her mother shook her head.

"You, too? I'm not that frail yet, Rekaré!"

"I still worry," Rekaré said. As her mother hobbled past her, Rekaré rolled her eyes at Katerin.

Alicira thumped heavily into a chair at the table. "I know. And I suppose it is now your time to worry about me. So. You restored the original fields? By the Goddess, however did you do it?"

"It wasn't easy," Rekaré said, taking the empty seat at the head of the table. "Cenarth has been studying their cultivation and talking to Sosuwis about how he worked with Nateri to establish the bushes in Keldara. He ended up pasturing daranvelii on the fields first, then the Stardance line of sheep. We didn't gain foals strong in magic when they were pastured there —same for the fleeces from the sheep on those fields—but a five-year rotation of daranvelii, then sheep, brought back enough magic to the earth to empower the fields. He used wild starts we found in the hills above Cooscol to plant the first fields. The harvest is not that big—only the second year."

"Then I will savor it all the more." Alicira eyed Melarae, who stood back from the table. "So. Granddaughter. You are here to learn magic?"

"I suppose," Melarae said, sticking her lower lip out slightly.

"You *suppose?*" Alicira thumped her cane. "Here you are, a scion of the Miteals, and you have not just magic but a heritage to uphold and defend!"

"I'm not as good as Linyet or Witmara." Her lip stuck out even further. "Besides, we're half-breeds and that's why I'm not as good with magic."

"Half-breeds? Who's told you that?" Alicira scowled.

"People," Melarae said reluctantly.

"What people?"

"Just heard it."

"Well. They're fools. At the very least you can learn defenses and how to handle magical items. As for the half-breed thing—" Alicira leaned forward, glowering. "—only unwise people worry about purity of blood. Merit comes from all peoples. Anyone who says such things is a fool or from the House of Ralsem." Rekaré winced at that last but her mother ignored her as she thumped her cane again. "I will *not* accept any criticism of your heritage from either side! You and your brother are the grandchildren of me and my spouses. You are Miteal and Ralsem through your mother, Clenda and Keldara through your father, a mixture of hope and not condemnation. You have an honorable legacy and there is *no reason* why you should not wield sorcery or at least be familiar with it."

Alicira sat back up, her pout the equal of Melarae's.

Melarae looked down at her feet. Alicira studied her, a thoughtful expression on her face. Rekaré bit her lip.

Melarae is not Witmara, that's for certain.

Now Katerin understood why her cousin was concerned about her daughter. She might be a year younger than Witmara, but Melarae's petulance was more like what Katerin might expect from a young woman beginning her cycles.

Too young for that, praise the Gods. When this one comes into her full magic once her cycles start....

Then again, Katerin didn't sense much magic flowing from her young cousin—just a gray void that blocked the currents, like a big boulder in a river.

Screening already?

Neinyet reentered the room and set the peaches and a mug in front of Alicira. Her presence broke the tension.

"Come sit at the table and tell me what has happened over the past year since my last visit, Melarae," Alicira said, her voice softening. "Forgive an old woman her grumpiness." She smiled at Melarae, who slowly came to the table and sat beside her grandmother.

But despite her smile, worry lines creased Alicira's forehead, a match to the lines on Rekaré's.

"Can I have some of the Coos berry cake?" Witmara whispered to Katerin. "I feel the magic in it."

"A small piece," Katerin said. "It is much more potent than we are used to."

Witmara nodded. Katerin noticed that she studied her cousin intently as she ate, watching Alicira and Melarae. Melarae answered Alicira's quiet questions softly, and Katerin could not clearly hear what either of them said.

Witmara tapped Katerin's shoulder and leaned close. "Why is Melarae so afraid of Alicira?" she whispered into Katerin's ear. "Doesn't she know Alicira is kind and will help her with her sorcery?"

"I do not know why she would feel that way," Katerin whispered back.

"She should know better. She wasn't this way last year. Something's wrong."

"You're all a year older, that's all. People change."

Witmara sat back, frowning. She kept studying her cousin.

The fact that Witmara could tell that something was not right with Melarae was worrisome in more ways than Katerin wanted to think about. What future did that bode for the cousins?

ARRIVAL DISCUSSIONS

We will arrive at six bells tonight.
Vered.

REKARÉ SCOWLED AT THE MESSAGE THAT MAHONIT, THE MAN WHO maintained the messenger bird flock, handed her. She wrinkled her nose at the faint scent of bird poop drifting from him—not as nice-scented as the horse version—and looked up at him.

"Thank you. How long ago did this arrive?"

Mahonit bowed awkwardly before speaking. "Just now, my Leader. Since it bore Vered's seal, I brought the message as soon as its arrival was logged."

"I thank you for that. No return message."

He bowed again and left Rekaré's formal office, the odor of bird excrement wafting after him. Luckily, the stench didn't linger. She steepled her fingers and glared at the portrait of her great-grandfather Alexran, founder of the Leadership of Medvara. Sometimes the magic within the paint made the old beast glower back at her, and today was one of those days.

Scowl all you want, old man. You created these circumstances, and if you don't like how I handle it, well, that's your problem, and you can't do one thing about it now that you're dead.

While Rekaré would not have come into being without Alexran's muddles, Alexran's mistakes…her great-grandfather's poor choices still left her with a mess to clean up, even after eleven years.

History will call me Rekaré the Fixer.

Not what she had imagined during five years of exile with Cenarth, dodging the men her father had sent to capture or kill her. Then she had romantic dreams of unifying all of Varen. Becoming the new Miteal Empress, restoring her family to its rightful position.

What she hadn't realized then was the time it would take for Medvara to support such ambitions on her part. Not only did she have to repair the disastrous final ten years of Alexran's rule, but she also had to fix the damage done by the eighteen years of Zauril. If this was what being the Leader of Medvara was like, how much worse would it be to become Empress?

Not that such consideration had apparently affected her father's ambitions.

Don't think about him.

But it was hard not to think about Zauril. Especially today, when she had to deal with another one of his messes in Morning Council. That gods-cursed trade agreement that cut the vital trade city of Nere out of their rightful share from the whale oil trade was his creation. Nere hadn't supported his grandiose ambitions toward empire, so—no trade agreement for them.

His past favoritism also affected the Weaver's Guild dispute she had just arbitrated. How many more unforeseen problems lurked out there waiting for her to discover? Even after eleven years, she still kept discovering mistakes her father had made. Poor choices her great-grandfather had made. Many days she was grateful for her exposure to how Alicira, Heinmyets, and

Inharise had ruled the Two Nations as a counter to what she still saw wrong in how Medvara operated.

They won't leave such a mess for Cenarth—or Linyet.

Gods, she hoped that her Heartfather and Secondmother lived long enough for Linyet to come of age. She couldn't bear the thought of Cenarth needing to take that role and being so far away from her.

A foreboding that their separation would come sooner rather than later nagged at her.

Oh well. It was time for lunch, and Melarae should be back soon from her first lesson with Alicira. That gave Rekaré time to prepare for Chiral's arrival (another mess thanks to Alexran's Miteal Agreement) on what felt to be the hottest, muggiest day of the summer. She wore her lightest summer shift made from the silk that Vered had brought from Daran, but she still felt hot and sticky.

Even worse, Medvara's magic roiled in anticipation of Chiral's arrival. The land's uneasiness jangled on her nerves, joining with the heat to make Rekaré irritable. Medvara itself recognized the impending arrival of someone with power. Someone with the strength to use sorcery. It didn't like the feel of this user, in this place.

But the Agreement....

The Miteal Agreement. One of Alexran's legacies. Forged years ago, when the first Ralsem family victims of Etikar's rampages fled Daran to their Miteal kin in Varen. The Agreement included an oath to be sworn by each Ralsem not to interfere with the Miteal family leadership in this land, in exchange for refuge. It bound the Miteal rulers to respect and protect Ralsem exiles, at least when they first arrived.

Stupid. Unrealistic. No. Unrealistic for this era.

The Agreement had been enacted during the time when Alexran needed every possible supporter he could get. Overthrowing it now would cause her more magical headaches than not—and besides, she hadn't yet figured out how to untangle Alexran's convoluted links to the Ralsems.

Flawed or not, it's the only tool I have. By the Goddess's gold necklace, I will make Chiral swear to the Miteal Agreement before she even steps off that ship!

That was one precaution.

Next, she would bring the entire family to meet Chiral, united in sorcerous strength to show that Medvara was protected and not vulnerable to an ambitious loner. She would *not* make the same mistake her great-grandfather Alexran had made in isolating Alame and Alicira, his most powerful magicians. She would be cautious but show as much power as she could.

Two raps on the door, a pause, then two stronger raps. Cenarth's private code.

"Come in, love," she said.

"It's lunchtime, my dear." Cenarth opened the door, still in his summer stable clothing, boots with light linen pants and tunic. The faint scent of horse sweat drifting from him brought back fond memories of youthful summers in the high mountains of Clenda and Keldara with her mother, Heinmyets, and Inharise. She wanted to grab him and bury her nose in his chest, absorb as much of his scent as she could. "Your mother has asked us to join her in their suite. The children have eaten already. I sent the three of them over to the stable for their afternoon lessons, figuring that Alicira would want to talk, without them present."

"Thank you," she said. "Council and then morning audience ran long, so I didn't get Melarae from her lessons with Alicira. And—we have more matters to discuss."

Rekaré gave Cenarth the message.

"So it begins," he said.

"The land already feels her. It is not happy."

"I noticed that. The daranvelii are restless and touchy, and I thought it might be due to the land's influence."

"I've been feeling Basnen's annoyance. I had to block her out of my mind because she's been feeding my own short-temperedness, and with the matters in both Council and Audience today, I couldn't afford the luxury of temper just because my daranval is grumpy." She sighed. "Everyone's ill-tempered today. Not just me. But I am the one who has to be wise."

"That's why I told Tlikset to have the children do stable work, not schooling rides. The horses are reacting to the daranvelii's tension over Chiral's arrival, and the heat doesn't help things. Tlikset is going to have them help put the horses and daranvelii in the hill pasture, then clean and check tack under Chilkinti's supervision. He says it is time they learned how to care for their own equipment." He shrugged. "Besides, it's a good thing for them to do on a hot summer's day."

"I agree." Rekaré rose and stretched, wishing she could hang out in the shade of the stable with the children and grooms, soaping tack and taking every excuse possible to splash water on each other. "So let's join the family for lunch."

She took Vered's message from Cenarth, holding it flat in her palm.

"Done," she said.

The cold blue fire incinerated the paper quickly and without heat, leaving a small scatter of ashes in her hand. She brushed them off her palm into the small iron stove that served as winter heat.

"You *are* worried, to dispose of even that simple a message that securely."

She dusted her hands off and wiped them on a rag she kept handy for that purpose.

"I don't know what we are dealing with. I'd much rather be overcautious than not cautious enough. No need to give her any sort of foothold in hopes she can replicate what my father did.

We've had too many warnings from the Gods for me to disregard caution." She slipped her hand into the crook of Cenarth's arm. "Let's go."

He smiled and wrapped his hand on hers. She raised it to her lips for a kiss.

"I dread what lies ahead of us," he said.

"Yes," she whispered, unwilling to voice her fears of separation.

As they left her office their guards fell into place behind them. She wanted to ask him how things appeared to have gone with Melarae's first lesson with Alicira, but kept her own council, buried it deep with her other worries. The lesson was probably one reason her mother wanted to speak with them.

Onadral opened the suite door for them, scowling. "We are eating on the terrace. The Old One's choice. In this heat, despite how she's feeling!"

"She *is* used to the heat of the high mountains in summer." Rekaré slipped her arm free from Cenarth's as they passed Onadral. He lingered to talk to Onadral.

Her mother lay on a couch under the grape arbor that shaded two-thirds of the patio. She leaned against a pile of pillows, her eyes closed, paler than she had been that morning. A glass pitcher filled with water sat on a round table next to her couch, water beading on its surface. One of the glasses next to it was filled, water also beading on it. Haran and Orlanden were nowhere in sight; probably off meeting with the Trade Minister to discuss issues affecting trade between Larij and Medvara and allowing Alicira to rest.

Too much magic working this morning has exhausted her.

She stopped in the doorway, studying Alicira. Why hadn't she noticed how thin her mother was? Alicira had never been a large woman, had always been slender but muscular. Rekaré didn't see much muscle on her mother's frame. Her skin had a translucent glow. It sagged away from the bones in her arms and face that were far too prominent. A bluish tinge outlined her lips, and her eyes seemed to sink into her skull.

"I'm all right," her mother said suddenly, her eyes still closed. "Just resting. I'd only been working with one child at a time this summer, until today. It's a little—overwhelming."

Rekaré sat at one of the chairs around the table. "If it's too much for you we can adjust the schedule. For that matter, you don't need to be teaching any of the children. We *do* have other tutors who can work magic with them!"

Her mother shook her head. She opened her eyes and sat up. "Not with Witmara's level of performance—and then there's Melarae. All three children need you, Katerin, or me to supervise their magic exercises—and you two have more responsibilities. Let me do this, daughter!"

She didn't say *while I still can,* but the words hung between them.

"As long as you don't overdo."

Her mother grimaced. "*Everyone* worries about me overdoing. I have too much to do and too little time left to do it in!" Her voice roughened. "I have to—"

She started coughing, doubling over as she hacked away.

"Water," Alicira gasped, one hand flailing toward her glass.

Rekaré picked it up. Her mother took it with a shaky hand, so that Rekaré needed to support it as Alicira drank.

"Where is Katerin?" Rekaré asked as Onadral and Cenarth joined them.

"She and Neinyet went to the Healing House to get more herbs," Onadral said. "They will be bringing our lunch. I expect them to be here soon."

Rekaré offered more water to her mother. Alicira shook her head. "I've had plenty for now. We're running short on the herbs Katerin uses to control my coughing, so that's why she went to the Healing House."

"I see." Rekaré set the glass down and poured water for herself, Cenarth, and Onadral.

"I'll get more," Onadral said, picking up the pitcher.

Cenarth sat next to Rekaré. Alicira settled back on her pillows, looking at them, smiling faintly.

"Leadership sits well on you two," she said finally. "Heinmyets and Inharise would be proud to see what you are doing here in Medvara. Bringing back the Coos berries in their original location. The health of the land. The feel of the land's magic, even in this time of drought. I'm proud of what you've done."

"There are still many challenges," Rekaré said. "We haven't done as much good here as you think. I'm still struggling with Alexran and Zauril's legacies. I shudder to consider what Heinmyets and Inharise would think of what I'm doing."

You like the feel of the land? I don't. Something's wrong.

Alicira rolled her eyes. "There are *always* challenges for a Leader. Trust me, we struggled over the years in the Two Nations and we didn't have the neglect you two have to mend. The three of us spent many years getting the Two Nations to where they are now! You are fixing years of problems that we never faced in Keldara and Clenda. There were eighteen years with no guidance for the land's magic in Medvara, and at least ten years of poor management before that. Daughter, you can't change things overnight—or even in eleven years."

"I'd still like to do better."

"We all would. Patience—and I need to remind myself of that as well."

Katerin entered, carrying a tray with berries and sliced fruit on it, followed by Neinyet and Onadral bearing platters with bread and meat on them. She set the tray on the table and picked up a vial, pouring it into Alicira's water.

"There!" she said. "I was able to get the right elixir for your cough without any problems. Sip that this afternoon and you should not have any problems with the evening cough. Don't drink it all at once, just sip."

"That is good," Alicira said. "Sipping is easier."

Katerin eyed Neinyet and Onadral. "Why don't you two take some time for yourselves this afternoon? I should be all right here without additional help once Haran and Orlanden get back. It's too hot to do anything other than sit and do handwork. Go. Find yourselves a cool place to be."

"Thank you, Lady Katerin," they chorused.

She snorted. "I am no lady. Go!"

Katerin shook her head after they left. "They're both good healers, but it's annoying to get them to see me as Katerin Healer, not Katerin ea Miteal!"

"Unfortunately, here in Medvare-the-city, Katerin ea Miteal matters more than Katerin Healer," Alicira said wryly. "This isn't Wickmasa, and they haven't worked with you for years like Davni and Colerei have."

"There are times when I wish Davni and Colerei *could* come here, so I wouldn't have to spend time teaching new apprentices my preferences," Katerin sighed. "But they have their own responsibilities in Wickmasa. I can't call them away from their duties to satisfy my whims. Neinyet and Onadral are good healers with much potential, but they haven't yet discovered that the old patterns are not always the best for all situations. Oh well. One cannot have everything. How did the rest of the first schooling session fare, Alicira?"

Alicira pressed her lips together tightly. Rekaré tensed at the expression on her mother's face.

"It's Melarae, isn't it?" she asked.

"Oh, Rekaré," Alicira exhaled, frowning. "Linyet is strong." She nodded toward Cenarth, her face softening into a smile. "He carries your strength, Heartsson. I see so much of your father in him—and parts of your mother as well. He needs to go to the Two Nations soon, to learn the land. Keldara and Clenda will be well served by Linyet when the Leadership comes to him. I would not delay past this next summer to send him to your parents to learn the Two Nations' magic, though. Like you and your father, Cenarth, Linyet's sorcery will be of the earth."

The parting she dreaded. And yet Rekaré had to agree with her mother. Cenarth needed to see his parents and renew his own ties to the land of his birth. Yearning rose within her to see the high mountain meadows again.

Eleven years is too far away from the land of my birth.

But Medvara needed her. She belonged to Medvara. Cenarth was her Regent, and if he was gone—she couldn't leave.

Cenarth gave her a worried look. "We could do this next summer, if that is all right with you, beloved."

"Linyet must learn the Two Nations." Rekaré kept her voice steady even though she wanted to cry. "And Melarae?"

That sad expression returned to Alicira's face. "She resists magic, my dear. She can work simple charms, respond defensively when under attack—but anything else is locked down hard. I cannot decide if she is shielding to protect herself from sorcery, if she lacks potential to wield it with much strength, or if—" she hesitated before continuing, swallowing hard. "Or if," she repeated, "*something* else has closed her off to magic."

Rekaré tightened her lips and squinched her eyes tightly shut for a moment, drawing in a wavering, shaky breath. Cenarth took her hand and squeezed it hard. She opened her eyes again and met her mother's gaze directly.

"Is it my fault?" she asked, her voice barely above a whisper. "Did I do this to her—is my magic too powerful, that she might feel the need to protect herself from me?"

"I do not think it is you," her mother said. "No, it's a deeper issue and much more worrisome, my dear. I can't tell which God or Goddess she has an affinity with."

Fear clutched tightly at Rekaré's gut with icy fingers. "The other night she complained about being bothered by a purple and gold bee while I was talking to Katerin using our speaking patches. I flicked a spellflare to warn her, so that I wouldn't lose that connection. She later told me that the bee disappeared when the magic hit it." She swallowed hard. "Could it be—*that* Goddess?" She couldn't bring herself to mention Nitel's name. Too many reminders might draw the Goddess's attention.

"I wish I knew," her mother said solemnly. "But it concerns me."

"We have been troubled as well," Cenarth said.

"Well, I suppose that means it's a good thing that I am here!" Alicira sat back up and swung her legs off of the couch. "I guess this dying old woman still has her uses." She reached for a handful of berries. "I think Melarae's sorcery lessons should continue for now, but not at the same time as Linyet and Witmara. Witmara is strong. She overshadows Melarae. Witmara needs to learn about Medvara and its magic. Linyet is not quite as strong as she is, but at his age he doesn't require my level of instruction. Witmara should start studying Medvara with Cenarth. Katerin and I will work with Melarae. That leaves you, daughter—" she pointed at Rekaré. "—free to deal with the issue of this new Ralsem, Chiral. Let us know if you need further assistance."

Rekaré nodded, relieved to get away from the question of the children. "Looking at what records we have about the Ralsems— I'm not sure where Chiral fits into the Ralsem genealogy. Detaluna has told me that Chiral is the heir of her branch. It appears to be one that has recently lost favor."

"The Ralsem families are complicated," Alicira said. "They breed like rabbits and feud like hill tribes."

"Some would say that of the Miteal," Katerin quipped.

Alicira snorted. "*We* are all that is left of the Miteal. Between what Etikar did in Daran and what Zauril did here, our family is mostly gone. Etikar's descendants apparently claim their Ralsem heritage, not their Miteal descent. Here—well, there are you and your children, Rekaré, to represent the Ralsem. Nateri did not leave any descendants, either in Cooscol or from her marriage to Thenil in Keldara, nor does she have any living relatives."

Nateri and her family do mean there are some good Ralsem. And yet....

"What happened to Nateri at the end?" she asked. "No one would ever tell me."

"Inharise and Heinmyets dealt with her, because we deemed it wiser that I not be involved." Her mother sighed. "It was after your brother and sister were born. My magic had not fully returned after pregnancy. When Elenil died, that triggered something in Nateri. We had lost Thenil, right after the twins were born, then Elenil shortly after birth. Cirenna was ill. Poor Nateri—I think Karnoi and Cirdel had been whispering to her, and all the sorrows were far too much for her." She paused.

"I have seen such things in those who have suffered many losses," Katerin said. "Especially after they have lost a beloved. They are usually not stable people to begin with, very emotional, very reactive. They feel things very intensely."

"That was Nateri," Alicira said. "Emotional, reactive, and it got worse as she aged. When I first came to Keldara, I feared what she might feel toward me because of Zauril. But she renounced all of his doings, especially after she understood what Zauril had done to me."

Rekaré flinched. Just last year she had found an incomplete record Zauril kept of the tortures he had put her mother through. Cenarth took her hand, squeezing it firmly. She clenched his hand, grateful.

Her mother continued. "Thenil kept Nateri centered and balanced for many years. She had done her best to redeem herself for the fiasco at Cooscol, when we lost the berry bushes for so long. But then the plague returned and took Thenil, then Elenil. As the death toll mounted, she slipped into a dangerous madness. You, Cirenna, Cenarth, and I went to the Healing House for our safety. When I next saw Heinmyets and Inharise, Nateri was dead, honorably buried—and they gave me no details as to how it happened. I think, from what Heinmyets said, that she sought death. She left no lasting curse on Keldara. I fear nothing from her shadows."

"That is good. Do you think she is connected to Chiral?"

"They're all Ralsems." Her mother shrugged. "More than that I can't say."

"How do you advise me to handle Chiral?" Rekaré asked. "Besides not trusting her until she shows me where she stands?"

"That's the highest priority," her mother said. "You've brought Katerin into the wards and raised your protections. That's a good step."

"I think the whole family should be there to meet the ship," Rekaré said. "I want to make her swear to the Agreement before she gets off the ship. If she doesn't swear in good faith, Vered and the ship will know it."

Her mother raised her eyebrows. "That's a good idea."

"What about bringing the daranvelii to support us?" Katerin asked. "Rainin is good at determining truthfulness."

"Not with that colt at her side," Cenarth said. "This would be the worst possible time to expose Daro to Chiral or any other uncertain sorcerous influence." He stroked his chin, frowning thoughtfully. "On the other hand, leaving him behind to start his weaning might work. Since he's named himself and is partially bonded to Witmara, I'd say it's time. He's already pretty independent of Rainin."

"But his fussing might distract her," Katerin said.

"Mmm, perhaps not. Rainin will be protective of you around Chiral, especially if we tell her what is happening," Cenarth said. "Weaning Daro will make her more sensitive to any magic use directed at you. Besides, we can leave him with Linyet's pony, Sark. Daro is playing with Sark. If he is in a herd with Sark, he will not notice Rainin's absence right away."

Rekaré sighed with relief. She *had* wanted the daranvelii present.

"Another thing about swearing the oath on the ship is that Chiral will still be suffering from the ocean journey," Alicira said.

"What about Haran and Orlanden?" Katerin asked.

"Kinfolk only," Alicira said. "Much as they have been a part of our family over the years, this isn't a time for outsiders. Remember, they both report to Haran's brother. I want them to meet her *after* we've decided how dangerous she is. Orlanden is good at extracting information from people without their noticing. I'll ask him to spend time with Chiral, once we decide it's safe."

The first bell after midday rang.

"We'd best eat and prepare for Chiral's arrival," Katerin said, frowning. "I would recommend that we all rest this afternoon." She fixed Alicira with a stern glare. "Especially you, my dear! You put on a good front, but it's clear that between teaching this morning and the heat, you're tired."

Alicira scowled back at Katerin but reached for some grapes and more berries, placing them on the top plate of the stack. Katerin got up and added bread and meat to Alicira's pile of food. She shook her head at the second slice of meat, and Katerin put it on her plate instead. But she added more berries to Alicira's pile.

"Probably better you eat more fruit in this weather," she said. "You do need that meat, though. Makes you stronger. Produce of Medvara should help strengthen you."

"It just doesn't taste as good as Keldaran or Clendan food, though," Alicira said wistfully. "And it reminds me of—things I would much rather not remember."

Rekaré swallowed hard, remembering that account she'd

read just last winter. She leaned over and took her mother's hand.

"I am so sorry for what Zauril did to you," she said in a low voice. "It should not have happened."

Alicira startled. "What he did gave me you, and led me on the path to my beloved spouses. That pain is long past."

"How could you forget it?" Rekaré shook her head. "I found some records this winter—"

"Ah." Her mother sighed, and patted Rekaré's hand with her free one. "I'd hoped he hadn't kept records." She paused, looking away, her lips thinning into a tight line. "Don't dwell on past things. Or, rather, learn from them. The path he chose devolves into shadows, the reddest of red evil." She slipped her hand loose from Rekaré's and picked up a slice of bread. "Remember how he thought, though. If you should have to go up directly against Chatain and his works, or if Chiral turns out to be a danger, that is the kind of thinking you will need to understand. Do not forget it."

"I will not," Rekaré promised. She straightened up and began to fill her own plate.

But tension still gripped her deep inside.

Gods, she wished this Chiral was going somewhere else.

CHIRAL

THE BELLS OF MEDVARE RANG SIX TIMES. KATERIN SWALLOWED hard as they waited for the arrival of Vered's ship, the *Morning Star*. She and Rainin stood on the left side of Rekaré and Basnen, while Cenarth and Quartel stood on Rekaré's right. She heard Alicira's occasional cough behind her, less intense than it had been that morning.

Good. The potion is working.

The children with Alicira remained quiet, even young Linyet, though Katerin heard the occasional shuffle of someone's feet. Linyet? Melarae? She chanced a quick glance back, pride pulsing through her at how Witmara stood steady and calm, face expressionless, reminding Katerin of Metkyi. She faced forward again. No more distractions. Alicira would keep the children safe and under control.

First us and our daranvelii, then Alicira and the children, as we wait on the dock," Rekaré had said as they rode. *"The three of us will go aboard ship as soon as Vered approves. I will swear Chiral to the Miteal Agreement. Then we will bring her to our daranvelii and the rest of our family, to show her our strength. After that—well, it will be up to the Gods.*

Katerin wore both the Eye of Dovré and her necklace from Metkyi outside of the fine golden silk dress Rekaré had lent her. The golden threads within the clear stone of the Eye glowed, as did the green and black lines through the lavender of the stone in Metkyi's necklace. Staul's token rested in a small leather bag that hung around her neck and was tucked under the high collar of her dress.

The great citrine in Rekaré's necklace, the Light of Medvara, first worn by Alexran, then hidden away until Rekaré's ascension to Leadership, blazed with a bright golden light. A smaller green beryl shone on its chain around Cenarth's neck, and Alicira behind them wore a necklace with the blue star sapphire that had been her token all those years as co-ruler with Inharise and Heinmyets. The star glowed, but dimmer than Katerin had seen it before.

Cenarth stirred next to Rekaré. "There she comes."

The great white sailing ship rounded the curve of the Saktrin just north of them and approached the docks of Medvare-the-city. Most of its sails were furled, but a green and gold-tinged ball of lightnings twisted at the top of the highest mast. MORNING STAR shimmered on its side, the letters sometimes green, sometimes gold.

Katerin shivered. She had heard about the great Sorcerer-Captains that sailed the oceans, but never met one until now. Vered usually came to Medvare during the seasons that Katerin was in the Two Nations.

Rekaré said that Vered was bolder and stronger than most Sorcerer-Captains. Most lack the ability to sail inland. That must be one reason why she can travel easily between Daran and Varen.

"What is that ball of lightning?" Witmara asked Alicira.

"It is how the Sorcerer-Captain powers the ship when the

winds lack strength," Alicira responded. "Vered would be willing to tell you more about it if you ask. I don't think she's leaving for several days. Perhaps you and Linyet should get Cenarth to take you aboard tomorrow."

A minor, keening song rose up from the ship, a contralto female voice leading the chant, followed by alto female and deeper baritone and bass male voices. Katerin peered toward the ship to see the source and spotted a tall, broad-shouldered woman in a loose white tunic and trousers standing in the center of the ship's deck, arms crossed. Her shoulder-length straight dark hair didn't move in the evening breeze. As she unfolded her arms to raise them high, her voice ululated, leading the chant.

The song's key changed from a minor to a major chord. Green and gold flashed from one finger, the same shade as the twisted ball of lightning in the mast. The lightnings untwined themselves from around each other and streamed toward the woman's ring. She kept singing, leading the chant, until the last lightning had faded into the brightly glowing green and gold ring on her finger. Then she lowered her hands, and the chant stopped.

The sailors scrambled up the masts to trim the sails. The woman—who must be Vered, the Sorcerer-Captain—stood in her place, arms akimbo again. The ship came about and glided toward the dock. With a lithe grace that the river sternwheelers lacked, it eased into place. More sailors leapt from the ship to the dock to tie the ship fast to the bollards.

"And *that* is a Sorcerer-Captain of the highest rank," Cenarth said. "Few can match Vered for her magic or her bravery, but she is also one of Goddess Terat's best-beloved captains. Her crew adores her. Most Sorcerer-Captains don't dare use magic to sail the Chellana. The Great River resists sorcery."

Rekaré nodded. She gestured to one of the sailors. He ran up to her.

"Please request of the Captain that we seek to meet our relative aboard ship," she said to him.

He nodded. "Will do, Lady Rekaré." He darted away, racing up the gangplank as it was lowered. A moment later, he returned and gestured to them.

"Here we go," Rekaré muttered. She stepped onto the gangplank. Katerin and Cenarth followed half a step behind her.

The captain met them at the top of the gangplank, the skull stone on the fourth finger of her left hand still glowing with bright green and gold lights.

"Rekaré. Cenarth." She hugged Rekaré first, then Cenarth. "And who is this?" she gestured at Katerin.

"My cousin Katerin ea Miteal, daughter of Alame," Rekaré said. "She has served as my mother's personal healer for years."

"Katerin ea Miteal. I am honored to meet you at last. I am Sorcerer-Captain Vered, and have heard much about you from your cousin," Vered said. She shook Katerin's hand. The intensity of the magic exuding from Vered with just that little contact startled Katerin. "You have provided a great service to your cousins."

"Thank you," Katerin said, releasing her grip, still tingling with the contact with Vered's sorcery. *Goddess Terat is strong in this one.* "But most of the time I am nothing more than Katerin Healer."

"You provide a greater service than you would think," Vered turned to Rekaré. "It will be a few moments before you can meet your relative. Detaluna and Mirket are helping Chiral get to the deck. She did not take the trip very well—Lady Katerin, I suspect she may have need of your services once she is in the Leader's House."

Katerin sensed Rekaré tightening up.

"So the water affected her?" Rekaré asked.

"Aye. Terat was not very happy with her, and spoke often to

me about how Chiral resisted her. So Chiral suffered immensely from traveling across the water."

"Does she honestly oppose Chatain, in your opinion?"

Vered glanced around, frowning. "Best to have that discussion later."

"I see," said Rekaré. "I wish to have her vow to follow and accept the Miteal Agreement before she steps off the *Morning Star*. Will that be a difficulty?"

Vered chewed her lower lip thoughtfully, rolling her head from side to side

"I think not. It strikes me as wise, and—" she marched toward the forecastle, where a set of shark jaws hung. One tooth was missing from the lower jaw. She grabbed the shark's jaws and brought it back to them. "We can have her swear on this. Terat tells me that is prudent."

"Between Terat, Dovré, and Staul, I think we are well covered," Rekaré said.

"Earth," a voice moaned from below deck. "I need to get off of this evil ship and set foot on solid ground!"

"And there she is," Vered said, as a man and a woman helped a slight woman clamber from below deck.

Katerin caught her breath at the first sight of the woman's bright red hair. It was almost the shade of Daro's coat, blood-red, plaited into a single braid.

Chiral's skin was nearly as pale as Alicira's without the translucence that Alicira's skin possessed these days. She wore a simple brown divided skirt that went to her knees, a sleeveless white blouse, a plain black belt, and black boots. Katerin was relieved to notice that Chiral apparently did not wear any stones of power.

Then again, as an exile, would she even have retained any tokens?

As Chiral reached the deck, her legs buckled under her. The dark-haired woman and man steadying her lifted Chiral to her feet.

"Detaluna," Rekaré said. "Mirket."

The dark-haired woman bowed to them. "Rekaré. Cenarth." She raised her brows at Katerin.

"Katerin ea Miteal," Katerin said.

"Ah," Detaluna said. "I introduce you to Chiral ea Ralsem, latest exile from Daran."

The red-haired woman drew herself up, shaking off Detaluna and Mirket's hands and lifting her chin proudly. Katerin noted the dark circles under her eyes and how her clothing hung off of her frame.

Naturally slender or an effect of seasickness?

Otherwise, Chiral appeared to be healthy.

Rekaré stepped forward. "I am Rekaré ea Miteal, Leader of Medvara. Before you can set foot on the soil of Medvara, I must ask you to swear to abide by the Miteal Agreement."

"Of course, of course," Chiral said impatiently. "I'd swear to anything to get off of this Gods-cursed ship." Vered flinched. "Not that she's a bad ship," Chiral said quickly. "It's just that I do not like ship travel!"

"Few of us who are sorcerers travel well," Vered said. "Unless you are sworn to service under Terat." But the shadow that had come onto her face lingered.

"Let's do this swearing and get off the water," Chiral sighed.

Rekaré gestured to Vered. "If you would bring up your token of Terat?"

Vered held up the shark jaws. Rekaré put her right hand on them. Katerin and Cenarth followed her lead.

"Deta, as someone with power, you as well?" Rekaré said, command rather than request in her voice.

Detaluna took hold of the shark jaws. Lastly, but slowly, and to Katerin's eye with no little reluctance, Chiral took hold of the jaws.

"Who is your patron?" Rekaré asked.

"The Goddess Nitel, as is true of all *real* Ralsem."

Was that defiance in Chiral's glare? Katerin pressed her lips tightly together, anticipating Rekaré's explosion.

To her surprise, her cousin simply nodded.

"Then, Chiral ea Ralsem. I ask you and your patroness Nitel to hold to the Agreement created between Alexran en Miteal and our Ralsem cousins who flee the oppression and persecution of the Ralsem Emperors that prey on their *lesser* family members." There was no mistaking the edged tone in Rekaré's voice as compared to Chiral.

Chiral winced. A quick smile flickered across Rekaré's lips.

Score to Rekaré.

"I call upon the Goddess Dovré to witness this vowing. The Goddess Terat. The God Staul." Rekaré paused.

Katerin noticed that Chiral winced again at the mention of Staul.

Does she fear Staul? A good sign. Two scores to Rekaré.

Rekaré continued. "Under the terms of the Agreement, I ask you to swear to each of the following. First. You will not seek to overthrow or interfere with the Miteal rule of Medvara."

"I do swear," Chiral said, her voice wavering.

"Second. You will not attack the other survivors of the Flight from Daran *or their descendants.*"

Was it Katerin's imagination or did Rekaré stress that last?

"I do swear," Chiral said.

"Third. You will not independently attempt to launch an attack on the current Darani Emperor from Medvara without our explicit permission."

"I do swear." Chiral's voice was stronger.

"Fourth. You will swear to honor the current Succession of Medvara as sanctioned by the Medvaran High Council."

"I do swear."

"And lastly, I ask for your obedience to me and your personal oath not to harm me or my children."

"I do swear."

"So will it be."

A mixture of green, gold, blue, silver, and red formed a bright ball over their hands on the shark's jaws. It flared brightly, then faded. Katerin shivered at the intensity of the power flowing through her.

"Now," Rekaré said. "My oaths to you. As long as you abide by the Miteal Agreement, you will have shelter in the land of Medvara. I swear not to offer you any personal harm as long as you hold to the terms of the Miteal Agreement. I swear that Medvara will protect you, Chiral ea Ralsem, from any attacks initiated by the Emperor or his minions, as long as you abide by the terms of the Miteal Agreement. As long as you live here peacefully, without conflict, and follow the oaths you have sworn today, you will find a haven in Medvara. So will it be."

The bright ball flared once again, then faded. Once again, the flow of power was stronger than Katerin expected.

Rekaré nodded. "That's it." She took her hand off of the jaws. Katerin released her grip, relieved to be done with the vowing. Vered quietly returned the jaws to their place on the forecastle. Rekaré gestured toward the gangplank. "You are now welcome to meet the rest of my family."

Chiral took Mirket and Detaluna's arms, leaning heavily on them as she walked down the gangplank. Rekaré and Cenarth followed.

Katerin hung back. As she hoped, Vered joined her.

"I have not seen sorcery like yours before, Captain Vered," Katerin said. "I would love to learn more about it."

"That can be arranged," Vered said. "I would welcome a visit from you tomorrow, Lady Katerin."

"Just Katerin, please."

"Then you should call me Vered," she said in return.

Before they could say more Chiral and her escorts stopped before Alicira and the children. Rekaré glided into place by her mother's side. Linyet and Witmara joined her. Melarae kept Alicira between herself and Chiral while standing well away from her brother and her cousin. Witmara frowned as she studied Chiral, and took a tighter grip on Rainin's reins. Linyet leaned against his mother, then buried his face in her side.

"Chiral ea Ralsem, this is my mother, Alicira ea Miteal, spouse of Heinmyets of Keldara and Inharise of Clenda," Rekaré said. "Mother, this is Chiral."

"Alicira the Outcast, if you please." Alicira studied Chiral from her feet to her head, and then back down. "You had a difficult time on the *Morning Star.*"

"I had to give her Memorylock and that did not help with her travels across water," Detaluna said, glancing first at Rekaré, then Alicira. "When I first found Chiral, I discovered that her memory had been tempered with."

Memorylock...and memory tampering?

Katerin itched to step forward and check Chiral further, but restrained herself.

Alicira raised a brow. "So your memory has been tampered with?" She frowned, and looked up at Katerin. "What do you think? What impact does that have on her magic and her health?"

"I will need to examine her first," Katerin said.

Alicira refocused on Chiral. "What *do* you remember?"

Chiral swallowed hard. "Little before Detaluna found me. Faint memories of a sister, and family, but they fade without daily dosages of Memorylock."

"It's not wise to keep taking Memorylock on a daily basis," Katerin said. "Once you have recovered from your travels, we need to do something different. Were you in flight from Chatain or in hiding when Detaluna found you?"

Chiral blushed.

"She was a—servant—in an inn in Adalane," Detaluna said quickly, looking at the children. "This is best discussed later."

Servant? Sounds like more to the story than that. Slave? Serving wench? Whore?

"Well, perhaps we should hurry through the rest of this," Katerin said. "You must be tired, Chiral. Not every sorcerer travels well over water."

"I'm definitely one of those," Chiral said.

Rekaré nodded. "Let me introduce you to the children of Miteal. My daughter, Melarae. My son Linyet." She stopped, gesturing at Katerin to continue.

Was that a faint sneer that passed across Chiral's face? Katerin wasn't certain of that. If so, what did it mean? An effect of the Memorylock?

"My daughter, Witmara," Katerin said. "And my daranval, Rainin." She took Rainin's reins from Witmara, leading her toward Chiral. A worried expression crossed Chiral's face as Rainin approached her. She would have backed away as the daranval mare extended her nose to sniff her. "Rainin is gentle," Katerin hurried to reassure her.

Sniff, look, tell,

she thought at her daranval.

"I am not fond of horses," Chiral said. "My—owner—his horses did things to hurt me."

A wrongness about her, very small,

Rainin thought back. She sent Katerin an image of a shapeless red cloud that faded quickly. Rainin snorted and stepped back from Chiral.

Rekaré's lips quirked in an expression Katerin couldn't name. "Daranvelii will not hurt you unless you have evil intent toward their owners," she said. "They possess magic in different strengths, and come from our sister nation of Keldara. I doubt that your owner had daranvelii."

"No. He didn't." Chiral continued to watch the daranvelii nervously. "I have never encountered daranvelii before. What kind of magic do they use?"

"It depends on the daranval," Katerin said. "Mine help with my healing—but I have partnered with three daranvelii and all three were different in magical strength and ability. I could not have done my years of work as a healer without a daranval."

Chiral shivered. "Horses. With magic. That worries me."

"Well, you will not be required to ride one," Alicira said dryly. "Perhaps we should return to the Leader's House. I tire, and perhaps Chiral should join me and the children in the wagon?"

"That should work," Detaluna said. "Mirket and I can walk with the wagon. It would be good after such a long voyage."

Vered chuckled. "So many landlubbers!" She clapped Detaluna on her back. "I will walk with you and Mirket."

"Then if you will excuse us, we'll ride," Rekaré said. "We'll meet you back at the Leader's House."

They followed Alicira's wheelchair back to the wagon. Once Alicira was safely loaded, Katerin mounted Rainin and spun her to follow Rekaré and Cenarth.

"What do you think of Chiral's story?" Rekaré asked as they trotted through the streets.

"I don't know. I'll know more when I examine her."

"I think it's best you do that tonight," Rekaré said.

"My thoughts as well," Cenarth said.

"Loss of memory could be quite convenient," Rekaré mused. "Or it may cover up—other things. Vered signed that she needed to speak to me in private, as did Detaluna."

"Her open dedication to *that* Goddess is not positive, either," Katerin said.

"I'd like to know more about her fear of horses," Cenarth

added. "For someone with sorcery, she should have known that daranvelii are different. Unless she also fears their magic."

"Her magic may be inconsistent," Katerin warned. "Memory-lock can have that effect."

Rekaré inhaled sharply. "Another thing to consider. So. Katerin. Will you examine Chiral tonight while I speak to Detaluna and Vered, and report to me afterwards?"

"Certainly."

"Then we can compare notes." She sighed. "We should also get a report from my mother. I'm sure she's interrogating Chiral in her own *particular* way."

"What is the issue with too much Memorylock?" Cenarth asked.

"It can wipe out all memories if taken for too long," Katerin said. "And it has other uses, such as creating a false recollection of one's past life. It all depends on the formulation. Some use it to help spies hide who they truly are, and block their genuine memories until the right spell is spoken to free them."

"I had heard of that last purpose for Memorylock," Rekaré said grimly. "Alexran's early journals refer to such practices as common in Daran. How hard would it be for you to concoct the counter spells to any such usage?"

"I need to look them up," Katerin said.

"I have those books in my study, not in the general library or archives. I will give them to you tonight." Rekaré frowned. "I am not convinced that Chiral is benign, and the convenience of memory tampering worries me. We need to figure that out quickly."

"I hear you and agree," Katerin said. "Rainin felt a quick wrongness about Chiral that faded."

"So did Basnen. I hope we've not taken in a serpent."

Until I have more knowledge it is all speculation. Gods, I wish Metkyi were here to help me!

She wondered if it might not be worth her while to slip out

to Staul's temple in Medvare, to see if either the God or Metkyi could provide her with any further insights.

On the other hand, they might spurn her for coming back too soon. She didn't understand the reason for the limitations on the number of times they met, but Staul was strict about keeping them to at most twice during a season, barring grave circumstance.

Katerin stroked her Eye of Dovré.

Goddess, guard us!

REKARÉ PACED AROUND HER OFFICE AS SHE WAITED FOR DETALUNA and Vered to arrive.

This is getting worse and worse.

By Dovré's gold necklace, she hoped that Katerin didn't discover anything unusual. She didn't like any part of this situation, much less the personality of the woman. If she was this difficult after feeling debilitated from a long voyage, then what would she be like once she was fully healthy?

Chiral's been ill. She's been taking Memorylock. She did swear to the Agreement. She may be easier to deal with when she's not recovering.

Gods only knew, her mother was prickly to deal with due to her health.

Even with her alleged past as servant, slave, or serving wench, Rekaré was certain the woman was more accustomed to giving orders than taking them. Moreover, her brief sneer at the children did not bode well. Especially after Melarae's comment about half-breeds just a few days ago. Where had that come from? To her knowledge, only a very small number of former Zauril supporters exhibited that attitude—and she had thought she had eliminated it in Medvara ages ago after marrying Cenarth. Where would Melarae have heard it? Did her daughter's comment identify a subversive element tied to Zauril in the Leader's House?

Patience. Katerin will examine Chiral and report to you. You can talk to your mother about Chiral. And Deta and Vered will be here shortly to tell you Chiral's full story. Talk to Alicira about Melarae and where she would have heard such a thing. I just hope that it isn't that cursed Goddess whispering such things to her.

Rekaré stopped her pacing short at the knock on her door. "Enter."

Tomorrow, she needed to assign more guards to the family quarters. Even in here, she needed someone watching her office door.

I will not be caught unawares.

The wards might not protect her from ambitious usurpers inside the Leader's House—especially if there were negative tales about half-breeds that Melarae had somehow stumbled across. But who would murmur such vicious sentiments to a vulnerable child who would be considered a half-breed?

I need to ask Mother about how Zauril managed his takeover. Did it start with something like this?

Detaluna opened the door. Vered followed her in. Rekaré waved them toward chairs.

"If you have need for refreshment, I have some Coos berry liquor," she said. "Fresh from the original grounds."

"That would be wonderful." Deta collapsed into a chair. "Gods, it's been a rough trip."

"And you, Vered?"

Vered shook her head. "None for me. I need to secure the *Star* tonight and soothe her. It's been a very difficult voyage. Liquor distracts me from talking to her."

Rekaré poured glasses for Deta and herself. "Was the passage rough because of Chiral and her magic?"

"Not entirely." Detaluna sipped on her liquor. "Chiral's

magic is erratic. No, there was another cause. There is a priest of Nitel who has been pursuing Chiral."

"Pursuing her? For Chatain or for other reasons?"

"I don't know," Detaluna frowned. "He was harassing Chiral when I first met her. There *were* two Ralsem heirs, Chiral and her sister Ranar."

"Two? You never mentioned that."

"I wanted to keep news of Ranar quiet, for fear that the messages would be intercepted. Ranar had been a maid at Chatain's court and was on the run when I came across her. Apparently their family was killed when they were young, except for Ranar and Chiral—Chiral's the older of the two. Ranar went to court as a maid, and Chiral—who is more magically talented—was sold as a serving wench to a tavern owner in Adalane. Ranar didn't know that detail. She didn't even know for certain that Chiral still lived. But Ranar was on the road to Adalane when I came across her, hoping to find news of her sister. We spoke, and I discovered she was a Ralsem and potential heir. I was traveling under deep cover, and then later—we had too much sorcery surrounding us at levels higher than I could manipulate to risk it."

"So how did you find Chiral?"

"I stumbled across Chiral while trying to find a hidey-hole for Ranar."

"Did you know about the Memorylock?"

"I gave it to Chiral the first night she was with us. Rekaré, she had no memory of anything significant in her life. Not even her name. Her memories have been suppressed and wiped. I sensed the magic around her, and then when the priest attacked her after I purchased her from her owner—it seemed as if he sought to keep her quiet." Detaluna shook her head. "She's Ralsem, no question about it. Ranar identified Chiral as the sister who had been kidnapped during the raid that killed their parents and brother. Chiral confirmed that after I gave her the Memorylock."

"So what happened to Ranar?"

"Now that's interesting," Detaluna said slowly. "I *think* she's dead. Mirket and I had hired a groom to ride with us, to make me look more like a lady of Daran. Heyrac was his name. Ranar never liked him. Someone betrayed us in Lanivar, before we got on the *Morning Star,* and she claimed it was Heyrac. Once we were safe, I discovered that Ranar had betrayed us to Chatain's men. We argued, she fled, and the last I saw of her, she was riding off with that priest of Nitel. After poisoning Chiral."

Perhaps I've been hasty in judging Chiral if she's gone through this much.

"She poisoned her own sister? Are you certain it was Ranar's doing?"

"Mirket identified the poison after Chiral took sick, and we found traces of it in the meat pastie that Ranar had given her."

More complications. Two heirs of Ralsem, and this Ranar sounds like she is definitely Chatain's lackey. Not what I wanted to hear, even if she is dead.

"So Ranar died after she rode off with that priest?" Rekaré asked. "Do you know that for certain, or do we need to be prepared for her to show up here as well?"

Gods. That one might lead an attack. I don't trust Chiral, but to know that there's another one—Gods.

"Ranar and that priest were on the ship that pursued us partway to Varen," Vered said. "I begged the Goddess for a storm—and when Terat roused it, Chiral called Nitel down on Ranar. The priest managed to evade her curse but Ranar was washed overboard. Terat took her. I saw what happened to Ranar through the Goddess's eyes. *I* say that we don't have to worry about that one, either in the flesh or in the spirit."

"I am not so certain," Detaluna murmured. "I have seen many strange things in Daran over the last few years."

"I trust the Goddess," Vered said.

"And the priest?" Rekaré asked.

"Terat would not touch that priest," Vered said. "He rides with a strong protector—Nitel, I think. He may have been washed ashore on one of the desert islands between here and Daran. It will take him time to escape that and even more to find us. Your new wards over Varen are very strong. I doubt he will easily penetrate them."

I hope Vered is right. So Chiral can raise a curse of Nitel's? Potentially more powerful than I thought.

"How strong a curse can Chiral summon?" she asked.

"It depends on her memory," Detaluna said. "Some days, Chiral is quite powerful. Others—" she shrugged. "When she doesn't remember much, her magic doesn't flare. She doesn't have much control over either her magic or her memory."

"I wonder how she would react to binding bracelets. I don't like the idea of a powerful but inconsistent sorcerer without control, subject to the effectiveness of her memory," Rekaré mused.

"I have no idea how she would react to binding bracelets," Detaluna said. "Using magic seems to take a lot out of Chiral, but I don't know that much about the higher-level sorceries. She collapsed after cursing Ranar, and was unconscious for two days. When she woke, she didn't remember anything. I had to double dose her with Memorylock that time."

That doesn't sound like someone who can hide much or be very deceptive.

But she remembered what Katerin had said about false memories being one of Memorylock's effects.

Would Detaluna know about that? I don't know. Best to ask Katerin. Still, would not hurt to ask.

"Do you think the Memorylock might have implanted false memories in Chiral? Katerin seemed to think it was possible."

"I do not know," Detaluna said. "Vered?"

Vered shook her head. "I know nothing about Memorylock."

"All right." Rekaré drained her liquor glass. "Tell me about the voyage. Was it because of the priest that you were running hard under sorcery?"

"Aye," Vered said. "We were under sorcerous and physical attack, until we were deep enough in the sea that Terat could call up a strong storm which Nitel could not dispel."

Rekaré shook her head. "I wonder what sort of serpent we've taken to our bosom. I fear that one or the other sister is an agent of Chatain's. If not both."

"An agent of Chatain's or politics within the family?" Detaluna said. "Ranar is—*was*—capable of great deceit. I do not know if the purpose behind her search for Chiral was finding her long-lost sister or eliminating a rival. There was a property dispute behind the murder of their brother and parents. But neither Ranar nor Chiral were old enough to know many of the details. At least Chiral does not know."

Rekaré interlaced her fingers and leaned her chin on her index fingers. "This whole story bothers me. Do you know why Ranar left Chatain's court?"

"I heard this rumor elsewhere," Detaluna said slowly. "A girl of Ralsem descent had fled her position as lady's maid because of a dispute. Ranar fits that description. And yet—I could never confirm it through my sources at Chatain's court."

"What was the nature of the dispute and who was the lady?" Rekaré asked.

"Ranar wanted to claim her position in court," Detaluna said. "Aliera ea Stanil, supposedly her mistress, did not agree. The Stanils supported the initial condemnation and attack on Ranar's parents, and Ranar was given to Aliera for safekeeping. Or so Ranar told me. The Stanils provided some of the forces to the Bearan family that led the actual attack."

"Did the Bearans have sorcery?"

Detaluna shook her head. "Chatain is systematically

destroying all leading families strong in magic, unless they swear allegiance directly to him and all family sorcerers link to his magic. The Bearans are powerful without sorcery, and they cultivate technologists."

Rekaré sucked her breath in thoughtfully. The use of technologists had been at the heart of the dispute between Etikar, his mother Elithtra, and Alexran. Etikar argued for technologists' greater use while Elithtra and Alexran opposed them. "How on earth does he expect to support Daran's economy by relying more on technologists than magic? How can the land tolerate it?"

"Chatain does not endure the existence of sorcerers more powerful than he is," Vered said flatly. "He does not care about the land's magic. He prefers to work with technologists, and meanwhile draws as much sorcery as possible to himself."

Like my father did.

Rekaré stifled a shiver. Did Chatain have the same goals as Zauril?

"Do you think he aspires to Godhood?"

"That is what the Goddess Terat fears," Vered said. "We have discussed this prospect in the Sorcerer-Captain guild halls, away from Daran, with her Presence. Fewer of us willingly put into Daran's ports every season. I do not think I will be welcome there after this voyage—and I will not be sorry for that, except for the gold I will lose."

Rekaré sighed. "You have given me much to consider. Well, I can offer you compensation. The fleet out of Cooscol is always looking for good mariners with a fast ship like the *Morning Star.* The trade may not be as valuable as with Daran, but no one here aspires to Godhood."

"That is my hope," Vered said. "It matches what I have heard from the Guild halls."

"I will give you a letter of recommendation to Cooscol's Harbormaster. Thank you so much for your work and information. Deta, we will need to discuss future plans for you and Mirket later. I don't think you can return to Daran either."

"Thank you," Detaluna said.

Rekaré stood up. "I have already authorized payment with a bonus for all three of you. If you go to the Treasury, you can pick it up at any time."

"I thank you, my lady Rekaré," Vered said, bowing. "If you need more information from me, I will be in port for the next few days, as my crew and I plan our next journeys."

"I await your orders," Detaluna said.

"I will speak to you again soon," Rekaré said. "Go now, and rest."

They left. Rekaré allowed herself a second glass of the Coos berry liquor, and stared into the deep purple liquid before sipping from it.

Goddess, what a mess.

Now she needed to find out what Katerin had discovered in her meeting with Chiral.

Another soft knock. "Come in," she said.

To her surprise, it was Detaluna and not Katerin.

"I have something more to tell you," Detaluna said. "Vered and Mirket know as well—I've been depending on them to keep me objective." She swallowed hard. "I—well, Chiral and I were involved. It started when I found her at the Sleeping Dog Inn."

"How compromised are you?"

Oh Gods.

She would have to find new work for Detaluna and Mirket, preferably away from Chiral.

"I was fond of her. I wish her well. But after what happened in Lanivar—and then during the voyage—" Detaluna shook her head. "Nothing has happened between us since Ranar's betrayal, nor will it. I do not trust her. I do not know if she will turn on me or not. She is Ranar's sister, and Ranar was as treacherous as they come."

Rekaré looked down and away from Detaluna, staring at the old family portrait that hung next to Alexran's glowering likeness. It had been painted when her mother was young, just before Alicira went to Larij for fostering. Before Alame's exile. Her grandmother Melara held Alicira's baby sister Melaraen while Alicira stared off in the distance. Alexran glowered at Alicira, while Alicira's father Richenax stood away from the rest of the family. The schisms between Alexran and Alicira, Alexran and Alame, Richenax and Alame, Richenax and Alicira were masked but still evident in this portrait.

I wonder that no one remarked upon it then.

"Treachery can be a family trait," she said.

"If you wish to dismiss me, I will go quietly. I just didn't want to discuss this in front of Vered." Detaluna grimaced. "I'm embarrassed. I should not have been so easily swayed! Chiral can be mesmerizing."

Rekaré shook her head. "You are aware of the problem. You have had Mirket monitoring to ensure your mind is your own and not influenced by Chiral?"

Detaluna nodded.

"Then continue the friendship for the time being. If you think you need further help, let me know. Keep her trust. You may be in the position to warn us should she become problematic."

"I will," Detaluna said. "And—thank you."

"It's nothing," Rekaré said wearily. "And I will find you a task away from her influence once things have settled."

"Thank you," Detaluna repeated. "That is all."

After Detaluna left, Rekaré groaned and rested her elbows on her desk, leaning her head into her hands.

What next?

The Light of Medvara hung heavy and hot around her neck. She needed to find those journals of Alexran's that she had promised to give Katerin tonight. Rekaré pushed herself up, feeling like the necklace dragged at her. Why was it so hot and heavy?

She slipped the Light off, guilt flooding through her at the relief washing through her when its heat and weight were gone. She had left Alexran's journals on top of one of her tall bookcases. Rekaré reluctantly pulled the library ladder over to that section and climbed up high enough to reach the pile of five black leather journals.

Something tugged at her awareness as she reached for them. Rekaré frowned and climbed higher, so she could see the top of the bookcase. A faint purple glimmer shone behind the stack of Alexran's journals. Prickles ran up and down Rekaré's spine.

Another one of Zauril's magic caches.

But how had it managed to remain hidden here in her office, where she worked spells regularly? She gathered up the journals and carried them down to her desk, musing.

I wasn't aware of it until I took the Light off.

That gave her pause. She stacked the journals on one corner of her desk and picked the Light up again, looking up at that faint purple glimmer.

It faded.

Rekaré set the Light down. The purple glow returned.

I need to check this.

She left the Light on her desk as she climbed the ladder again.

DANGEROUS DISCOVERIES

SHE DIDN'T WANT TO DO THIS. SHE HAD TAKEN AN INSTANT dislike to Chiral—but she had a job to do. Katerin reluctantly approached the quarters assigned to Chiral, Detaluna, and Mirket. Four guards waited outside the door, letting her in. Mirket slumped on a chair by the main table, checking his sword and cleaning it.

"Deta's off to talk to Rekaré." He jerked his head toward the nearest door, focusing on his blade rather than her. "Chiral's waiting for you in there."

Typical warrior.

Over the past eleven years she had become more familiar with men and women like Mirket and Detaluna. At first she had been put off by their focus on weaponry, but now she was glad for it, especially after the events of the past few days.

Does this mean I'm becoming more Miteal than Healer?

It was important that she learn to think as Katerin ea Miteal.

As long as I don't completely forget Katerin Healer.

And right now, she needed to act as both. She turned toward Chiral's bedroom. Should she wait for Neinyet or Onadral to join her?

No. The fewer people involved the better.

But how best to keep herself safe should Chiral prove to be a strong sorcerer? Katerin reached for her connection with Rainin, wishing she could bring Chiral and the daranval together.

If we were in Keldara, yes. But that is not the way Medvara does things.

A comforting warmth accompanied by a tinge of distress at the absence of Daro touched Katerin's mind. Rainin's image formed in her thoughts, the contact faint and not as strong as Katerin had experienced with her previous daranval Mira, but still an additional source of magical power. What Rainin lacked in magic she more than made up for in nurturing, devotion and determination. Rainin wouldn't give up, and she fussed over Katerin's health and mental state more than Mira ever had.

Keep feeding me strength,

Katerin thought to Rainin.

Protect our link. Keep me safe.

She still didn't feel right about doing this probe alone, and hesitated before turning the doorknob. But short of pulling Rekaré away from her meeting with Vered and Detaluna, or rousing a tired Alicira from her rest, she didn't have any choice.

You are not just Katerin Healer or the daughter of Terani the God-Killer. You are Katerin ea Miteal, daughter of Alame en Miteal, one of the greatest sorcerers of the Miteal family.

That meant Katerin ea Miteal had to take risks that Katerin Healer would not have done, with more responsibilities than Katerin daughter of Terani would ever have held.

Guard yourself. But protect others as well.

"I'm going to leave the door open with a protective spell, so that you can keep watch," she said to Mirket. "Do you have any plans to leave?"

"None. Deta told me to stay and give you any assistance you need," Mirket said. "I can't be much help to you magically because I don't have sorcery. But I've supported her in the past. I know how to be an energy source."

"Thank you." Katerin cast the spell, then went inside Chiral's bedroom, leaving the door ajar.

Chiral reclined on her bed, curled around a food tray, picking at the selection of meat and fruit on it.

"So *you're* the healer Rekaré sends me," she sneered. "Weren't there any suitable Aireii healers? Or is this meant to be an insult?"

"I *am* one of the Miteal," Katerin countered. "Daughter of Alame en Miteal and Terani of Waykemin. I've been Alicira's healer for the past eleven years, and I hold one of the highest positions in the Keldaran Healing House as healer and teacher. Two of Medvara's healers are currently in advanced training with me."

The Banisher of Shadows stirred within her, along with an angry flood from Rainin. Rainin sent an image of her ears pinned hard with her teeth bared, stomping hard with one hind hoof before leaving it cocked and ready to fire.

Thank you, my dear. But I can handle simple insults,

Katerin thought to Rainin, gratified by her daranval's loyalty in the face of rudeness.

Please watch and protect against other magics.

She channeled both the Banisher and Rainin into her responding glower at Chiral.

Chiral shrunk away, pushing herself up higher in the bed.

She almost spilled her food into her bedding and Katerin automatically dove to save it, steadying the tray as Chiral also grabbed for it. She let Chiral move the platter to a more secure location.

"I am sorry," Chiral said. "I'm just not myself from the voyage. Have you ever traveled that long over water? It's *awful*."

"No, I have not had that experience."

Katerin sat on the edge of the bed and took Chiral's hand, checking the pulses in her wrist. Then she reached up to touch Chiral's temple. A quick, sharp sting snapped across her fingertips as they brushed Chiral's skin. Chiral jerked away before Katerin could press her hand flat against her head to investigate further.

Is that a ward or a manifestation of her sorcery?

"What are you doing?"

"A soft probe into your mind," Katerin said. "Perhaps I can find a means to help you regain your memory."

"I'm not comfortable with that level of mind contact." Chiral pouted.

"It is part of my examination whenever I work with someone who has memory loss like yours." Katerin used a commanding tone.

"I feel Staul on you. Why do I feel Staul? You're a Healer, you should be of Dovré," Chiral gabbled, eyes widening as she pushed herself away from Katerin.

"Staul the Balancer knows me as well as the Goddess," Katerin said. "But my loyalty is to the Goddess."

How strong is Nitel in her?

Chiral shouldn't be able to detect Katerin's link to Metkyi. Or had Staul marked her in some subtle manner she didn't yet realize?

"My Goddess doesn't trust you," Chiral whispered, childlike. "Why? Nitel whispers *God-killer* to me, but it's fuzzy. Why can't I hear her clearly?"

God-killer. Will I ever live down my mother's influence?

"You cannot hear Nitel well because she has been banished from this nation. My mother also expelled her from Waykemin." Katerin still couldn't get a reading on how strong Nitel was within Chiral. "As long as you abide by the terms of the Miteal Agreement, I cannot harm you. I swore to the Agreement just as you did. That means you should be able to trust my oath. Can I trust *your* vow?"

"No, no, no," Chiral said quickly. "But after everything I've been through it's hard to be comfortable with a strange magician."

"I can wait for Detaluna to return if that will make you feel safer."

"No, no, that's all right." Chiral sighed, seeming now to be more adult. "Go ahead and do it."

"All right." Katerin crawled across the bed until she sat next to Chiral. She briefly closed her eyes, summoning up all of her sorcery, then laid her hand flat against Chiral's head, using the mind magic she had studied with Alicira to look into Chiral's memory.

Nitel's disapproval was the first thing Katerin encountered.

I have permission,

Katerin said firmly to *that* Goddess.

Your devotee has sworn to the Miteal Agreement. I need to see what is causing her memory problems.

Nitel's wordless resistance continued.

Shall I call upon Dovré and Staul?

Katerin reached out for Rainin to bolster her strength further.

Nitel faded away, leaving an angry purple coil swirling that faded in tiny bits. Katerin waited for it to be completely gone before she edged delicately into the flow of Chiral's thoughts, careful in case that Goddess decided to leave a trap for her.

Chaos exploded around Katerin, enough to disorient her.

I am here.

Rainin nudged Katerin through the mindstreams and pulled her free from the maelstrom that threatened to drag her into its currents. Katerin drew strength from her daranval, rebuilding her protections.

This is one of the most disordered minds I've ever encountered!

With Rainin centering her, Katerin tried once again. This time, she maintained a crystalline barrier between her and the chaos, remaining oriented and herself, able to observe without being affected.

Chiral is potentially a very strong sorcerer.

But oh, the pandemonium in her mind! Thoughts whirled by Katerin so quickly that it was hard to grab them. None of Chiral's thoughts progressed in an organized fashion but jumped from idea to idea randomly. The mindstreams were riddled by whirlpools that sucked at her and tried to drag her down them.

How can she even function?

Even more concerning, the essence of Chiral felt incomplete and diffuse, lacking sufficient life force to support one person.

Then the image of a slender brunette appeared, features identical to Chiral's except for her hair color.

Ranar,

Chiral thought. The pieces of Ranar calmed some of the whirlpools in Chiral's mindstreams. Katerin began to see the more coherent functions she expected in the mindstreams.

Still, what organization existed under Ranar's influence was not enough to support a working sorcerer, much less someone without magic.

How can she even think?

Watch out!

Rainin loomed large in the mix as Chiral became whole.

Nitel took form again, seething behind Chiral's self-awareness. Ranar's image shattered into pieces as Rainin squealed and lunged at Nitel's Presence. In place of Ranar, Katerin glimpsed a bald-pated priest with Nitel's sigil hanging around his neck, glowering malevolently at her. He feinted at Rainin and she fled.

How dare you challenge my daranval!

Katerin charged at the priest, calling the Banisher forward.

The priest laughed. He hurled a purple and gold ball glowing with teeming lightnings at Katerin. She raised her free hand protectively, and the Banisher flowed through her palm to block the ball and disperse the lightnings. Even so, a sharp pain lanced through Katerin's hand as one purple flash struck it.

We shall meet again,

the bald-pated priest growled.

Then he disappeared. Chiral screamed, and Katerin jerked her hand away from her temple. Chiral moaned and seized her head in both hands. The Banisher faded into the background as Rainin returned, blowing hard, projecting worry and fear in equal measure.

I am all right,

Katerin assured Rainin.

Go back to yourself and rest.

Rainin snorted reassurance at Katerin and nuzzled her. Then she faded to join the Balancer, still on alert.

"Are you all right?" she asked Chiral.

Chiral flinched away from her. "What happened?"

"I got the image of someone called Ranar. Then I saw a bald priest. He threw a ball of lightning at me, and a sharp pain went through my palm."

"Oh no," Chiral moaned. "Oh *no*." She curled up in a ball and rocked back and forth on the bed, shivering and jerking, eyes going dull. Katerin grabbed the food tray before Chiral could spill it.

"Chiral." No response. "Chiral!" Still nothing. Katerin shook Chiral but she did not respond. Her keening increased in intensity.

"Is everything all right?" Mirket stood in the doorway, careful to stay on the far side of Katerin's barrier.

"I tried a light probe," Katerin said, not looking away from Chiral. "The bald priest appeared and threw lightnings at me—felt it in my hand. Then she started doing this."

"That priest throwing lightning is a typical reaction from Chiral to any probes or magic," Mirket said. "She's done that several times with Deta. Usually after she's tried to work magic with Chiral. That's when Deta doses Chiral with Memorylock. She left it in the sitting room. You might want to give some to her."

"Can you bring it to me?" Katerin asked, watching Chiral, wary that her symptoms would worsen.

"Yes, if you'll drop the barrier."

"Doing so now." No need for that barrier now. Katerin wasn't about to probe further into Chiral's mind without another magician as backup.

Not with that degree of disintegration and disorder.

She did not do anything further until Mirket pressed the green bottle in her hand, complete with wooden dosing spoon and marking chalk tied to the bottle by a string. Katerin eyed the bottle, then uncorked it and slipped the spoon off of the string. She sniffed the potion before pouring a dose.

Stronger mix than I'd use.

She tipped a trickle back into the bottle, and marked the level before setting it on the nightstand. Then she approached Chiral.

"Chiral. This will help."

Chiral showed no signs of hearing her. Katerin sighed. There were better ways of dosing a patient in this state, but she didn't have the right spoon with her.

Worth a try.

Before Katerin could move in closer to try to get as much of the potion into Chiral as possible, Mirket climbed onto the bed. He slipped behind Chiral and pinioned both of her arms, lifting her upright. He pulled her close to his body, trapping her legs with his, one arm across her chest, the other holding her head steady. Chiral still writhed in his grasp, her eyes dull and unseeing.

"You should be able to dose her now," he said.

"Is that necessary?" Katerin asked. "I could have tried a less invasive means."

"It's the only way we've been able to dose her when she's like this."

Chiral wailed, jerking her head backward, trying to hit Mirket. Katerin cringed. Then she took Chiral's jaw, held it steady, and swiftly poured the mixture into her mouth. Katerin stroked Chiral's throat and she swallowed. A moment passed when Chiral still struggled against Mirket. Finally, she relaxed, sagging against him.

Awareness crept back into Chiral's eyes.

"Chiral? Are you all right?"

"My head hurts," she groaned. Mirket released Chiral. "I want to sleep."

Katerin straightened up. "Let me get some headache potion." She picked up the bottle and spoon and handed it to Mirket without looking at him, still focusing on Chiral. "Please wash this up and put it away."

After Mirket took it, Katerin undid her medicine pouch and retrieved the headache potion. She mixed it into a cup of water that sat on the table by Chiral's bed. Chiral drank this mixture without resistance or saying a word. Then she rolled onto her side, curled up, and closed her eyes.

Katerin slipped out of the room, questions roiling in her head.

Mirket looked questioningly at her.

"So do you know what is causing her memory issues?"

"I am not sure," Katerin said. *By the Goddess's gold necklace, I hope this isn't what I fear it is.* "But I think we are finished for tonight."

Before she did anything more with Chiral she wanted to have someone there to support her. A strong sorcerer. Rekaré, Alicira, maybe even one of the Medvaran healers. No. Better to have a healer she knew. She would send to Eldoran at the Keldaran Healing House for one of the healers that she had worked with in the past, either Yevtin or Senai. It would take several days for one of them to get here, but that might be the best choice.

Metkyi, I wish you still lived.

If he were at her side she'd feel so much better about dealing with what she suspected was wrong with Chiral.

And she still had to tell Rekaré about what she had seen. She wasn't looking forward to that.

One step at a time. One moment at a time. Keep on moving, dealing with what is next and not worrying beyond that.

Such had been the pattern of her life for the past eleven years.

KATERIN SHUFFLED DOWN THE CORRIDOR, ROLLING HER NECK, shoulders and head, breathing deeply to summon up some energy for this next meeting. That session had taken more out of her than she anticipated. Perhaps Rekaré would share more of the Coos berry liquor—though she probably didn't need *that* much energy.

This time the guards opened the door for Katerin without her needing to identify herself. No one was in the outer family room. As Katerin went down the hallway to Rekaré's study, she heard Cenarth telling a story to Melarae and Linyet in the nursery, an exciting one by the excited tone of the children's pleading when he paused. She knocked once on Rekaré's door.

"Come in." Rekaré's voice sounded muffled, followed by a sneeze. Katerin opened the door as her cousin looked down from the ladder leaning against the bookshelves. "There's a hidden compartment up here that I hadn't known about. Eleven years and you'd think I would know all these spaces by now. I was getting the journals down for you when I became aware that there was *something* up here I hadn't noticed before."

"Anything useful?"

Katerin looked up as Rekaré finished rummaging in what looked to be a box set into the wall, about the size of two hands laid together. She placed something on the top shelf, then closed the box's door. It immediately faded into the wall, so that Katerin couldn't see where the opening had been.

"I'm not certain." Rekaré gathered several items on that top shelf. She carefully descended the ladder. "There's a journal. Some amulet stones set into a necklace, a bracelet, and a ring. I don't want to touch them—they don't feel right."

Katerin winced as the pendant swung toward her, emanating a baleful aura. It featured a large peridot teardrop with a thick inlay of smaller citrines and pearls surrounding the main stone.

"I'd agree with that. I can feel the same thing you do, especially that one. There's something not right about those stones."

Rekaré gingerly placed the journal and stones on her desk.

Katerin noticed that the Light of Medvara that Rekaré typically wore now lay on the desk instead of around her neck. It flashed, then faded.

"This may have been one of Zauril's stashes. He didn't keep his magical items in any one place. I think I've seen that particular amulet in his official portraits." Rekaré pointed at the peridot, citrine, and pearl amulet that had swung at Katerin.

"I thought you found all his things."

"So had I." Rekaré dusted off her hands. "But I keep stumbling across caches like this. Not the first time I've found items of power hidden in the Leader's House. You'd think he feared that I would sneak into Medvare and catch him unawares or something!" She wiped her brow with the back of one hand.

"We *did* do that," Katerin said.

"But we didn't take him on here, in the Leader's House. Fortunate for us. But Katerin, what am I going to do once the children come into their own magic? Gods! It's almost as if Zauril set small traps everywhere to sabotage any successor."

"Train the children to handle strange stashes with caution," Katerin said. "Give them some protective spells. But maybe Zauril's strategy is a good one to adopt for your own defense. Replace his caches with ones of your own."

"I'll think about it. Once things settle with Chiral, we can search this house again." Rekaré poured Katerin a glass of Coos berry liquor, then sat down behind her desk. "Maybe that's the source of Melarae's attitudes," she murmured thoughtfully. "I hadn't thought about that."

"What do you mean? Which ones?" Though after Melarae's outburst at breakfast the other day, Katerin had a very good idea of what they were.

"Which ones?" Rekaré threw her hands wide. "All of them? But the biggest concern I have is her sudden notions about half-breeds. I wonder if there's a hidden spirit based in a cache that is speaking to her. That would be easier to deal with than the possibility of a hidden cell of Zauril supporters that work inside the household."

"That would be easier, yes."

Rekaré grimaced. "Melarae's attitudes are one of my smaller problems right now. Let me tell you what I learned from Detaluna and Vered about Chiral."

Katerin listened intently as Rekaré spoke. Pieces from her examination of Chiral started falling into place.

"So *that's* who Ranar is, and who that priest is," she said when Rekaré had finished.

"You saw them when you probed her?"

"It's—complicated. Rekaré, I can't sense enough of Chiral's self to understand how she can possibly function. Not only is she heavily defended by Nitel, but there are deep whirlpools in her mindstreams." Katerin described her encounter with Ranar and the bald-pated priest during her probe of Chiral.

"That's very interesting," Rekaré said slowly when Katerin had finished. "And it makes me worry even more. Can you explain that appearance? Is it an effect of Memorylock?"

"Not Memorylock," Katerin said. She hesitated before continuing. "I need to talk to Alicira and look further into the archives, because if it's what I think it is, then things are much worse than we suspected."

"How so?"

"I think the priest is connected with Chiral's lost memory. There are two possibilities. Both are bad. One is that the priest administered a very powerful dose of mind-wiping mushrooms in order to influence and control Chiral's magic after she was first captured. Only he miscalculated and it has effectively destroyed her ability to function without others constructing reality structures for her. At some point there won't be enough Memorylock to keep her as a functioning person without killing her. Detaluna is already feeding her a more powerful potion than I would have chosen."

Rekaré raised her eyebrows. "What would be the threat to us from her further deterioration?"

"We wouldn't know if the priest was the one controlling her or if she is acting on her own should she attack us. Worse, the Agreement would have no influence over the priest if he is using her as his tool. He could strike against us, then fade away and leave her to die."

"How physically close would he have to be to have some influence? After all, Vered did say he washed up on a desert island."

"Nitel was present when I probed Chiral. She may be abetting her priest and making him stronger. Otherwise, I would think he would need to be physically here, within the city, to have much of an effect upon Chiral."

"So Chiral could be an agent of Chatain, controlled by that priest," Rekaré mused.

"Possibly. Or the priest could be acting on Nitel's behalf. In both those options she is still an innocent victim, but one who has been emptied out to fulfill the purposes of either Chatain or Nitel."

"I don't like it."

"Neither do I." Katerin hesitated. "The other option is that Ranar does not exist, that she is a fetch created between Chiral, the priest, and possibly Chatain. The image I saw of Ranar was identical to Chiral except for the hair color. She filled those holes in Chiral. Gods, I need to talk to Metkyi. To Staul. This is the kind of sorcery that Staul would understand, not Dovré."

"I would think that Detaluna and Vered would have been able to detect that possibility."

"Maybe," Katerin said slowly. "It's also possible that Chiral by herself or with the assistance of the priest and Nitel is powerful enough to deceive both Detaluna and Vered. She has strong defenses."

Rekaré pressed her lips together tightly. "Is there any means by which you could tell which possibility this is?"

"Not at the moment," Katerin said. "Perhaps there's some information in the archives that could help us."

"I pulled down those journals of Alexran's that addressed Memorylock uses in Daran." Rekaré gestured toward a stack of three leather-bound journals on the corner of her desk. "Digging them out was how I first became aware of Zauril's stash."

"Thank you. Your mother might know what to do. I am not sure which option it can be. I'm sending to Keldara for Yevtin or Senai. I need support before I can probe her further, and I think my support needs to be someone other than you or Alicira."

"Oh, *Gods.*" Rekaré leaned back in her chair and rubbed her eyes. "Either way, she's at risk for irregular use of magic and may be open for either that priest, Nitel, or Chatain to use her to strike at us."

"Yes."

"And we have no choice. She has sworn to the Agreement. *I'm* held to the Agreement. I can't sanction her without risking Dovré's wrath, or Nitel's wrath, or of all the Gods. Neither can you, for the same reason. My mother didn't swear to the Agreement, but if she were to take action—even if she *would* take action—it could kill her."

"But perhaps she could give us some suggestions."

"You need to put magic restraint bracelets on Chiral tomorrow. At least we can keep the children safe from uncontrolled sorcery flares."

"That might be a good idea," Katerin agreed.

She doubted how effective the bracelets might be in this situation. But was there any other option, given the apparent erratic nature of Chiral's sorcery?

Katerin picked up the journals. "I'm tired. I'll try to look at these journals tonight, if not, then in the morning."

"Rest well," Rekaré said, staring at the gems on her desk as if they were a venomous snake that had just manifested itself.

"You too," Katerin said. "Be careful."

"I will," Rekaré said, scowling.

Katerin didn't blame her. She just had to think about what it would be like if more of Terani-the-God-Killer's personal possessions appeared in her life like this.

But Terani's heritage was nowhere near as poisonous as Zauril's. Katerin hoped Rekaré would be cautious in whatever she chose to do with those gems and the journal.

And I wish she would put the Light back on to do it.

RESTLESS NIGHT

NO SOONER HAD THE DOOR CLOSED BEHIND KATERIN THAN Rekaré turned her full attention to her finds from Zauril's cache. Fatigue pulled at her. Perhaps she was too tired to take this on right now. The Light of Medvara throbbed a warning.

On the other hand, when else would she have the undisturbed time to examine these artifacts? Cenarth was occupied with the children. None of her advisors or the Council would be demanding a meeting about matters of state at this time of night. This was a perfect moment, especially since she intended to use tools she wanted to keep secret.

She firmly overruled the instinct that screamed *this is business best done in daylight.* No time for such luxuries now. Her family and her nation were endangered. If these things of her father's could cast some light on how further to deal with this threat—Rekaré would use them.

Besides, better to deal with Nitel at night rather than during the light of day.

Nitel often was less guarded when interacting with mortals during the evening hours, when she was strongest. That

Goddess might dispense a nugget of valuable information that she wouldn't give during the daytime.

Gods only know, I need more information than I have!

Rekaré took a deep breath. She might be bold but she wasn't a complete fool.

She reached for the plain cedar bentwood box that sat at the upper right-hand corner of her desk. Crafted by woodworkers from Clenda from Clendan mountain cedar, it had been a Leadership ascension gift from Inharise. The red and yellow shades in the polished wood reminded her of the woodwork she had grown up with, and the smooth, cool texture on her fingertips brought back old memories.

"This is for you alone, not you and Cenarth," Inharise had said. *"There will be times when you wish to store concealed things and not let anyone else see them. This box will open only to your touch. Leader's gift, given from me as shared Leader of the Two Nations, not from me as your Secondmother and mother-in-law."*

Rekaré smiled at that remembrance. She had been violently homesick when Inharise and Heinmyets had visited that first time. Seeing the box brought back vivid memories of her youth, but touching it eased her yearnings for the land she could never return to now.

Thank you, Secondmother and Leader of Clenda and Keldara.

Was it her imagination that she felt the slightest brush of Inharise's soothing touch on her brow every time she opened this box? She wondered about that. Her Secondmother was just as powerful as her mother Alicira, only in different ways.

Terat's blessing to you, Secondmother.

Rekaré closed her eyes, resisting the temptation to reach out for Inharise, Leader to Leader, for wordless consolation. She needed every scrap of magical energy left to her tonight to deal with the Goddess. Expending the power needed for that indulgence made no sense, soothing though it might be after a harried day.

No more delays. Rekaré opened the lid and picked up the long, twisted key that just fit crossways inside the box's top tray. With her other hand, Rekaré took a pinch of pale blue glimmer dust from the residue on the bottom of the tray and sprinkled it over the key.

"Protect," she murmured. "Protect and open."

The key glowed with a pale blue light brighter than the dust. Rekaré gingerly inserted it into the lock on her desk's lower right hand drawer. She twisted it a quarter turn to the right.

Click.

Half a revolution to the left.

Click. Click.

A full turn to the right. The drawer popped ajar. Rekaré pulled a veil and gloves out of it. The transparent, shimmering veil glowed with a purple-edged green light while the wool gloves were green-edged purple. She hadn't used these tools much since she had discovered them in one of Zauril's stashes, and uncovered their purpose in one of Alexran's journals two months ago. She only used them in conjunction with consultations with the Gods most friendly to her. This was the first time she had used them to summon and manage Nitel.

"In the service of Medvara I call upon the Seven Crowned Gods to heed my call," Rekaré said as she draped the veil over her head, still nervous. She hadn't used these tools much.

Elithtra's Veil. Elithtra's Gloves.

Alexran had smuggled them out of Daran when his brother Etikar had overthrown their mother's regime. They were royal talismans that Chatain would covet if he knew they still existed. The Veil and Gloves offered a means for scrying and for controlling the Gods when the user needed to consult with them. Rekaré had kept the Veil and Gloves hidden since she first found them.

Her vision sharpened and broadened so that she was aware of things beyond this office in her personal wing of the Leader's House. She reached out to confirm that she would not be disturbed.

First, she checked on her family. Cenarth still told stories to the children. Linyet's eyes drooped as he burrowed deeper into his pillow. Melarae remained awake, occasionally murmuring a question to her father.

They would not disturb her.

Beyond her suite, she looked to see Katerin, who was checking on sleeping Alicira, then Witmara. Rekaré extended her vision further to Chiral, also sleeping. With the veil over her head, Rekaré could see the disruptive mindstream patterns in Chiral's thoughts that Katerin had described. There was no sign of the presence of either Ranar or that bald priest.

That had to be a good thing. Wasn't it?

A further scan of the Leader's House revealed nothing other than guards on alert, no members of her Council working late in their offices, her staff settled for the night.

All quiet. All calm. No possible interruptions.

Good.

Rekaré returned her focus back to her body and the study.

She pulled on her right glove.

"In the service of Medvara I ask Dovré to guide and protect me."

She flexed her hand within the glove, the familiar warmth of her patron Goddess flowing within her.

"Protect me in what I do next, oh Goddess." Rekaré took a deep breath.

She reached for the left glove and pulled it on slowly. "In the service of Medvara I demand that Nitel explain and answer my questions."

Who are *you* to command *me*?

came back to her swiftly, as if Nitel had been waiting for her call.

This next move had to be swift, before Nitel fully manifested herself in order to thwart any influence of Dovré. Both Goddesses waited on the threshold for their presence to be directly summoned, but only Nitel was known to shove her way forward without further invitation.

"In the service of Medvara I use the Veil, the Right Hand, and the Left Hand to uncover these secrets. In the service of Medvara I seek the open path, the way which serves and protects. In the service of Medvara, I ask for protection, command, and guidance. So do I request of the Seven Crowned Gods, with preference to Dovré and Nitel."

Nitel grumbled again, but her objections were less strong, less intense, as if she were constrained. Rekaré allowed herself the slightest bit of relief. She hadn't been certain they would compel Nitel.

I need to use the Veil and Gloves to see the muddled future ahead,

Alexran had written in his journal scant months before Zauril's coup.

But every time I wield them, less and less is revealed. Gods! Why do you turn your faces from me?

She drew a deep breath before summoning the Goddesses to their full manifestations. The Light of Medvara's bright flashes were distracting. She placed the necklace securely in the desk's center drawer before continuing.

"Lady Nitel, downfall of Alexran," she whispered. "Lady Nitel, betrayer of Zauril. Lady Nitel, I command your presence."

The Goddess's slender form twisted into being in front of Rekaré.

So have you come to your senses? Will you give me homage?

Nitel demanded.

Rekaré dipped her left index finger into the glimmer dust in the bottom of the bentwood box's top tray and flicked it at Nitel. The Goddess flinched as the grains impacted her being.

I seek answers, not offer worship,

Rekaré countered.

I command, not beg. The Left Hand calls you, not the Right Hand. You are not my patron.

I do not answer your upstart questions so easily! What price will you pay me?

I summon you in the service of Medvara, not for myself. You have extracted enough from Medvara! You owe Medvara for eighteen years of Zauril!

Sooner or later you will come to me. And when you do—

That time is not now. I seek answers. Will you give them, or will I need to use the Left Hand to compel you?

Rekaré flexed her right hand. Dovré's presence would constrain Nitel and stop her arguing.

> Lady Dovré, patron of healers and of Medvara. Lady Dovré, guardian of Miteal. Lady Dovré, I request your guidance and protection. Please aid me in learning what I can from your beloved sister. The Right Hand of Medvara calls upon you.

Beloved sister!

Nitel sneered, even as Dovré shimmered into being.

That is enough,

Dovré said mildly, bowing to give Nitel the respect her sister goddess did not return.

Lady Rekaré, what information do you seek?

Rekaré hesitated. She could only use the Gloves and Veil to answer one question in each session. Which one—about Chiral, or about this most recent find? The gems were the more pressing need.

> The gems I just found. I know nothing about these gems and they have power. Katerin sensed the wrongness in that pendant. I must know what it is, and what I must do to protect us from it.

Zauril had hidden them so well for a particular reason. She waved toward the pendant.

> Goddesses. I have discovered these items hidden away. A necklace, a bracelet, a ring, and a journal. I sense a malign influence about the gems. What are they, what is their purpose, and how do I protect my land and those I hold dear from that influence?

Dovré moved closer. Her transparent fingertips brushed over the citrine, amethyst, peridot, garnet, and pearl pendant.

> Maker-of-Gods! I had thought this lost forever.

She fingered the plain amethyst set into a silver bracelet.

> Strength-of-Gods. This one has no further effect.

Lastly, she picked up the small garnet mounted in a gold ring.

> Vision-of-Gods. This, too, is spent. Beloved of mine, you are fortunate that Zauril exhausted the power in these two stones during his ill-fated quest for godhood. Coupled with the Maker, you would find yourself drawn down the reddest of red paths without adequate guidance. You were wise to consult us first, and to put away the Light before summoning us.

> Fool of a sister!

Nitel snapped, stomping one foot.

> Without Strength and Vision, the Maker has little use! There are times when the reddest paths are the only way. Zauril weakened and turned away from the Maker, refusing the opportunity to join it with the Light. He chose Strength and Vision instead, and lost his nerve.

Nitel sneered at Rekaré.

Do you have the courage your father lacked?

Dovré spoke.

Zauril should never have taken up these stones
in the first place, He was not their equal, and
they consumed him. He failed the tests of
Godhood. He quailed at the end. Had his
courage held, Rekaré, you would have been
subjugated to him at an early age. Good for you
that this did not happen.

I do not seek to become a Goddess,

Rekaré said.

Nitel cackled, throwing her head back as her entire being shimmered and shook with mirth.

Say rather that you are destined to become the
next Empress of Daran and Varen, then!

Nausea surged through Rekaré and she swallowed hard. Empress? Gods below, she could barely manage to cope with Medvara! Empress of *both* Daran and Varen? Alicira had spoken of that possibility years ago. She had written it off as a fever dream of her mother's. And as for herself as a Goddess—no sane person aspired to that lofty goal. The Seven Crowned Gods had remained stable for years. The ending of one God to be replaced by a human raised to that level was just a matter of legend—wasn't it?

I am but a simple woman,

she said to the Goddesses.

I am only the Leader of Medvara, and an incomplete and feeble one at that, who struggles daily to find the right paths for my people. Goddess? Empress? Surely you jest.

Nitel's laughter echoed louder in her ears. But it was not Nitel's laughter as much as the sorrowful look from Dovré that sent chills down Rekaré's spine.

Nitel cursed you at your birth.

Dovré's tone was slow, thoughtful, and measured.

You stole the Stone of Vision from her when we danced to identify your patron, merging it with my gold necklace. I named you Sorrow in the Secret Speech, because I foresaw that you could turn Nitel's curse into a blessing. The process of doing so will be painful and difficult.

Nitel snorted.

I gave her the gift to look for the unusual paths and the red ways. Do not fool yourself, sister! Without my gift, she would not now be Leader of Medvara.

Dovré nodded.

Rekaré, you have the potential to see the paths that will change the world, and will make things right. You have already worked toward rebalancing the world by ridding it of Zauril. But oh my beloved, there is much, much more that remains to be done.

Rekaré slammed her hands down hard on her desk as she rose from her chair.

I am no Empress. Chatain can keep his Empire as long as he leaves me and mine alone. I am no Goddess. A human becoming a god? That is the stuff of legends, not a reality! I am only a human. A sorceress, yes, but only human.

You are of both the Royal Families of Daran. Daughter of Ralsem and Miteal. Gifted with powerful magic, trained and guided by those beloved of Artel, Staul, Terat, and myself,

Dovré said.

The sneer on Nitel's lips grew larger.

Power calls to power. No human is immune to its lure. She who spawned Katerin claimed that banishing me was for the good of Waykemin. But it was power she sought. You would do well to speak to Katerin about the fate of her mother Terani.

Rekaré raised her chin defiantly.

We are only speculating. You said yourselves that Strength and Vision are depleted, lacking power. That I cannot wield Maker without them. This discussion is without merit if such is the case.

Nitel bared her teeth in a death's-head grin at Rekaré.

If you choose to fully wield the Maker, you will find the means to recharge Strength and Vision. And when you do, and decide to unite them with the Light, I will be there.

I will not make that choice!

Rekaré snapped.

Do not be so hasty, beloved. Circumstances change. Even with the Veil you can only partially see what lies ahead.

Dovré gazed at Rekaré sorrowfully.

I will not do it!

Rekaré insisted, a sensation of impending doom hovering in the distance.

Nitel snickered. Dovré glowered at Nitel.

Rekaré drew a ragged breath that came harsh and hard and raw in her throat, as if she had been running for a long distance. Her legs quivered, threatening to give way under her.

Goddesses,

she said, forcing her mindspeech to remain calm.

I thank you for your wisdom. I will put these stones in a safe place and will not choose to wield them any time soon.

Dovré shook her head as a triumphant expression crossed Nitel's face.

Do not be so hasty to deny the possibilities, beloved. It is wise now to put these things away and keep them safe. But when the time comes—

Ah, sister, you only fear that she will turn to me and not you when that moment arrives! That temptation will bear her down. Do you trust your pawn so little?

She is no pawn of mine!

Dovré retorted.

Nitel's smirk faded into seriousness.

> Sometimes the red paths are the only way. Do not be hasty to deny yourself a tool. Keep these things safe, and do not speak of them to any other.

> My sister speaks wisdom.

Dovré's tone was flat.

Rekaré rested her hands on her desk to keep herself upright. Nitel and Dovré agreeing? Such a rare agreement struck fear even deeper into her heart.

> I have heard your voices,

she said formally. Summoning up all her strength, she straightened up and clenched her left hand.

> Lady Nitel, the Left Hand of Medvara dismisses you.

> Remember my words!

Nitel said, the mocking and sneering now gone.

> There will be times when the red paths will be the only means left to you. When you need me, I will be there.

> You are dismissed,

Rekaré said, choosing not to answer her.

Nitel faded, and Rekaré removed her left glove. She turned to Dovré.

> Oh Goddess, my dear patron and protector of Medvara. I thank you for your wisdom and assure you I will not be hasty. I now dismiss you.

The Goddess leaned forward and kissed Rekaré's brow.

> Be wise. Be careful. But do not dismiss your choices, and remember well the words of your father's patron. You are not only of Miteal. You are of Ralsem as well, and that heritage will play a role in your future.

> I will remember,

Rekaré promised.

> Good.

Dovré faded away.

Rekaré pulled off her right glove. She carefully eased the Veil off, then wrapped the Gloves in it.

Before she put the Veil and Gloves into the drawer, Rekaré sat down hard. She opened the lower drawer, feeling like she was pushing her body through deep quicksand. She extracted a cloth from the drawer, and sprinkled a pinch of glimmer dust on it. Then she used the cloth to pick up the necklace, the bracelet, and the ring. Wrapping the jewelry carefully inside it, she placed the package in the bottom of the drawer, then put the Veil and Gloves on top. She shut the drawer, used the key to lock it, reversing the original pattern. Then she put the key back into the bentwood box and rested her forehead on her desk, breathing hard.

Arching her back, Rekaré opened the center drawer far enough to scrabble for the chain of the Light of Medvara with her right hand. She pulled it out, wrapping the chain around her fist, and brought the Light a hand's width away from her eyes, staring deep into the citrine's yellow glow for a few moments. Then she pressed the Light to her forehead, letting its power flood into her and quiet her jangling nerves.

What had Nitel said? That Zauril had quailed at the thought of uniting the Maker and the Light?

If so, then it might have been the one smart thing he did.

She didn't want to think about that further, and hung the Light around her neck again. At least it didn't feel hot and heavy any more.

She sat back up. She now noticed the journal. Should she put it into that drawer with the gems, the Veil, and the Gloves?

No. This was the only journal of Zauril's that she had found.

Perhaps reading it could give her some useful information.

Besides, she had to admit to a certain curiosity about how her father thought—especially after this consultation with the Goddesses.

And she most certainly was not going to tell anyone about this particular meeting, or the journal.

Especially not Katerin or her mother.

KATERIN JOLTED AWAKE TO THE SOUND OF SOMEONE SCREAMING. The glowlight still shimmered on her nightstand. One of Alexran's journals lay open on the bed next to her. She set the journal on the stand, pulled on a robe and slippers she had left within easy reach for emergencies, then slipped her hand into the glowlight's wrist string. She grabbed her medical go-bag and opened her door just as Onadral raised her fist to pound on it.

"It's the Lady Alicira—" Onadral gasped.

"Thank you!" Katerin snapped, the glowlight casting

shadows as it swung from her wrist as she ran down the hallway.

She ducked into Alicira's room and dropped her bag on the nightstand. Witmara and Neinyet were at Alicira's side as she thrashed and screamed, tangling herself in the bedclothes.

"Lady Alicira. Lady Alicira!" Neinyet shook Alicira by the shoulders, but she writhed away from the contact.

Witmara stood two steps back, hands covering her mouth, staring at the distorted figures of the dead battling above Alicira.

Not for little girls.

Even though Witmara would be coming into her own magic in two years, she didn't need to see this. *Katerin* didn't need to see this, even as an adult.

But she was Senior Healer, Alicira's own Healer. She had no choice.

Still, she could spare her daughter this sight.

"Witmara, please help Onadral prepare a soothing draught." Katerin handed her wrist glowlight to Witmara. "Onadral, I need preparation number six. You'll need to go heavy on the poppy juice. Double the usual amount."

"Are you sure? That mixture's already heavy...." Onadral's voice trailed off.

"It is her standard preparation for one of these situations," Katerin jerked her head toward the door. "Quickly."

Once Onadral and Witmara left, Katerin nodded toward the door. "Neinyet, please close the door. Latch it. When they come back, find something for Witmara to do elsewhere."

Neinyet rose to do her bidding. Katerin took Alicira's hands. She jerked and twisted in Katerin's grasp, moaning and coughing when she wasn't screaming.

Katerin closed her eyes.

> Oh Goddess, please help me. Rainin, lend me strength!

She had a quick grateful moment when Rainin's thoughts brushed against hers, feeling a faint warm pressure against her head as if Rainin were present in the room and nuzzling her head.

"Alicira," she breathed, extending her presence and thinking soothing thoughts. "I am here. Katerin. Come to wakefulness."

"No," Alicira moaned. "No. *He* is here! *He* seeks me! Oh Goddess!" Coughing wracked her body.

"There is no one else here," Katerin said, ignoring the shadows twisting over Alicira and trying to disregard the dread twisting through her as she recognized Zauril as one of them.

If we don't acknowledge the dead then they won't gain substance. They're just dream figures her magic has created—oh Gods, is she losing control of her magic now? Will I need to put restraint bracelets on her?

"Wake, Alicira. Come away from your dreams. Wake and come away from your dreams."

Alicira continued thrashing and moaning, mixed with coughing spells that shook her body, though less energetically than before.

This is a bad one.

"What can I do?" Neinyet asked. "I could make *protection-against-possession*."

"Possession isn't what we're dealing with." Katerin jerked her head toward the pitcher and bowl on the dresser. "Let me handle this magic. Dip a towel into the water and wipe her forehead."

> Rainin. Help me. Please. Think of home,

she thought to her daranval.

Wordless images of early Clendan spring flooded into Katerin's mind. Tall green grass in high mountain pastures rippled like water in the wind. Crisp cold snowmelt water roared down creeks full to the brim. A sweet, enticing odor hung over the Kitskan River as it roared out of its deep canyon into the great flats where the Clendan families met for their spring gathering and lawmaking. Spring Festival in all its glory, with humans, daranvelii, horses, and stock all dressed up.

Katerin pushed those images to Alicira as Neinyet dabbed her forehead with the wet cloth. Alicira twisted and moaned, but the intensity of her thrashing slowed as Katerin kept sharing Rainin's remembrances. At last she lay still, gasping for breath between coughing spells.

> Thank you,

Katerin sent to Rainin.

> That helped.

She felt the faint shove of Rainin's projection nuzzling her head, then Rainin was gone. Katerin turned her attention back to Alicira.

"She's burning hot." Neinyet dipped the cloth in the bowl again. "Enough to heat the cloth after a few touches."

Katerin nodded. "It is part of her illness. Alicira." She let her voice be stronger and firmer, noting with a sideways glance that the shadows twisting over her cousin were fading away. "Waken. Come away from your dreams to the real world."

Alicira's fingers tightened on hers after another coughing spell. "Is he still here?" she asked in a thin, shaky voice, her eyes still firmly shut.

"Only Neinyet, Onadral, Witmara and myself have been here," Katerin said.

Begone, foul shade!

she thought fiercely at Zauril's lingering shadow.

Haven't you done enough to her?

"*He's* been here," Alicira whispered. Suddenly she shot upright, looking wildly around the room. She stared at a dark corner and wrenched one hand free from Katerin's grasp, pointing shakily into the shadows. "*There!* He's over there!" More coughing shook her body.

Neinyet brought a cup of water but Alicira ignored it, still staring at the corner.

Begone!

Katerin thought more fiercely, and grabbed Alicira's hand. "There is nothing over there but a dark corner. Neinyet will go see, won't you, Neinyet?" In a softer voice she added, "Set the cup down first. I'll see if I can get her to drink some water."

Alicira drew a deep, sobbing breath. "I see him over there. He's just waiting to prey on me when it's my time to go. I see it! His curse is upon me!" She gasped for breath and started coughing between sobs.

"Alicira." Katerin took Alicira's head between her hands and leaned her forehead against Alicira's, wincing at the heat radiating from her as the coughing eased. "He is not here. You are ill and had a bad dream."

Pounding on the door. "Neinyet, take Witmara into the sitting room. Don't let her in here." Neinyet let Onadral in and left.

Alicira gulped. "Oh Gods." Her body shook as she collapsed against Katerin, half-sobbing, gasping for breath as she coughed and wept. "Oh Gods. Zauril is haunting my dreams. Gloating at me. Insisting that he will have his final revenge and that I will find no peace in death. Oh Gods."

"It has been a long and difficult day and you were just overtired,"

Katerin took Alicira into her arms and held her tight, rocking her. Alicira shuddered, clinging to her. Onadral stood by the bed, awkwardly holding out the cup, still steaming from the mixture.

Katerin took the cup in her left hand and sniffed it carefully, making certain that the mix was correct. She pulled back from Alicira and switched the cup to her right hand, holding her cousin steady with her left.

"Here. Onadral has prepared your healing draught. Drink this. It will help you sleep without dreaming of *him*."

And hopefully ease this fever as well as the cough. It is burning her down to nothing.

Alicira hiccuped, and straightened up. She took the cup with both hands, shaking. When she was finished drinking, she sank back in the bed. Katerin handed the cup to Onadral and picked up the water Neinyet had left.

"Sit back up and drink this water. Onadral, why don't you join Neinyet and Witmara?" she suggested. "The fewer people in here right now, the better. I have it under control."

Better to have Witmara distracted by both of them.

"You're certain?" Onadral kept her voice low.

"I'll sit with her for a while. You two get Witmara settled and back to sleep. Too much loose magic floating around for her safety—the same holds for you and Neinyet. Let me deal with it. I'll explain how to manage these situations later."

Onadral nodded and left, closing the door behind her. As Katerin hoped, Alicira sagged even more in relief when it was just the two of them, her eyelids closing after she finished the cup of water. Katerin eased her back down on the pillows. Alicira cleared her throat but did not cough further. Heat radiated from her pale, translucent skin, and occasional gulps punctuated her shallow breaths.

"That was a bad one," Alicira whispered. "I have not felt Zauril's presence like this for ages. Not here, not in the Two Nations, either."

"It was just a dream," Katerin soothed. "With the stir caused by Chiral's arrival it's understandable that you might dream of him."

"Oh Katerin," Alicira sighed, a faint smile flitting across her lips. "I know you mean well. But I also know the difference between a dream and a Presence. Zauril stirs again. His shadow sees the opportunity to exact further vengeance on me and mine."

"The Goddess will keep you safe," Katerin said.

"Will she?" Alicira's lips tightened and she looked away from Katerin. "Or is she constrained by a higher order? Am I meant to be a sacrifice to Zauril in the long run?"

Katerin reeled back in shock. "You can't mean that!"

"Sometimes I wonder." Alicira refocused on her. "My fate is a mixed one. I do not think I will die peacefully."

"You are safe in Medvara," Katerin insisted.

"There are undercurrents I don't trust here. Things that both you and Rekaré need to beware of; old shadows that I've forgotten or ignored until now. Do not underestimate Medvara. I thought the problems I sensed when younger were just an effect of the way my grandfather did things. That they would change when he was gone. Now I have to wonder. Was it wise for the Miteal to leave Daran and come to Varen? Did we do what was right? Or was it just another exercise in Miteal arrogance that was no less than what Etikar, Dunaran, and Chatain sought to do in Daran?"

"I don't have the answers to those questions," Katerin said.

"Neither do I." Alicira slapped one hand on the bedspread. "And until we came back to Medvara this last time, I didn't spend time thinking about such subjects. Now it seems as if I can't turn around without second-guessing our ancestors' choices."

"You can't fix what our ancestors did," Katerin said. "You can only correct what is yours to remedy."

"I know. And I wonder what my solution will be." Alicira's eyelids flickered. "I feel the potion working. I just fear I'll plunge back into the same dreams, and I don't like what those dreams waken."

"Just dreams, nothing more."

Alicira shook her head. "Don't deny it. You saw how the shadows whirled when I woke. I'm close enough to the Other Side that my dreams can rouse those shades—things that should not be roused."

"Will it help if I stay here with you?" It wouldn't be the first time she had slept in a chair by Alicira's bedside.

"It might."

"Then I will stay here."

So much for a good, restful sleep. Oh well, she could have Neinyet bring in a footstool and pillows to make herself comfortable.

Alicira patted the far side of the bed. "Don't feel you need to sleep in a chair! There's room for you to lie down. If anything, I'd prefer that. Sleeping alone is part of my problem. I miss Heinmyets and Inharise."

"If you're sure about that—"

"I am. At least for tonight."

"Then let me make sure that Witmara and the others are settled. I'll be back. All right?"

"All right."

Katerin went out to the sitting room. To her relief, Witmara was not there.

"Did she go to bed?" she asked Onadral.

"She complained of a headache. I gave her a light potion," Onadral said.

"I didn't want her coming into Alicira's room, but she woke when Alicira started screaming," Neinyet said. "Witmara spoke of a presence that needed to be banished. Then just now, she sighed, got up, and said she was going back to bed and to sleep now, that the presence was gone."

How much of what happened did she sense?

She needed to talk to her daughter in the morning. Witmara's reaction confirmed that she shouldn't ignore what Alicira had said.

She should not be left alone from now on. Someone with magic needs to be close by her at all times, especially at night. If her dreams are awakening a ghost of Zauril's—she needs that help.

"Is something wrong?" Onadral asked.

Katerin hesitated. "Something I need to investigate further. We need to have someone with magic around Alicira at all times from now on. I'm spending the rest of the night with her, and may do so every night after this."

"I did see a presence," Neinyet said in a low voice.

"Tonight is not the time to investigate further," Katerin said. "Get some rest. I will watch."

"Thank you," Neinyet said.

"Just wait with her while I get some things." Katerin quickly went to her own room and gathered additional vials of premixed potions and another glowlight. She didn't *think* she would need them tonight, but one never knew.

As she walked by the shrine to Dovré she had set up in her room, one of the rocks on it caught her eye. Katerin picked it up. It was a plain gray-green rock with dark green inclusions, heart-shaped with silver lines where it had broken and been repaired. It had been one of Metkyi's tokens, one that he had left on her shrine before his death. She now brought it everywhere she stayed. She held it for a moment, then decided to take it with her. A trace of Metkyi's presence still hung about the little rock.

I can use any help I can get right now.

When she returned to Alicira's room, she placed the rock on the far nightstand from the side Alicira lay on. Neinyet left. Alicira rolled over to face Katerin, eyes drooping sleepily.

"I'm surprised you aren't asleep," Katerin said.

"Will be once you settle in here," Alicira mumbled.

Katerin made sure that her glowlight was on her stand before she extinguished the light on Alicira's side. Then she climbed into bed and snuffed it out.

Alicira sighed. She reached one hand over. Katerin took it. Before long, Alicira's rhythmic breathing indicated that she was asleep.

Katerin lay awake, her thoughts spinning. Chiral. Alicira. Witmara. Rekaré.

She wondered what Rekaré planned to do with that dangerous-seeming pendant. Was it a coincidence that Alicira dreamed of Zauril after Rekaré's find? She didn't think the two were connected. But if they were—and what that implied—

Alicira stirred, then turned over, untwining her hand from Katerin's. Katerin listened, but Alicira's breathing slowed and steadied, the normal breathing rate for a sleeper.

Katerin finally closed her eyes.

Metkyi, oh Metkyi. How I wish you were here with me now.

She fumbled on her nightstand for his heart rock, and rolled onto her right side, tucking her hand holding the rock under her pillow. She could almost hear his voice now, almost feel his soothing presence.

He is watching over us—at least I hope he is.

She thought she felt the faintest brush of lips on her forehead, and then a gentle stroke on her cheek. Her wordless awareness of Metkyi's presence grew.

Now she could sleep.

MALEVOLENT MAGIC

ALICIRA STILL SLEPT, SOFTLY SNORING AS KATERIN ROSE. SHE
checked Alicira's pulse and respiration delicately so as not to
rouse her, finding nothing amiss. Good. She had hoped to see
such a sound sleep after a difficult night and the strong potion.
Katerin picked up Metkyi's rock from under her pillow and
tucked it into her sleep tunic's pocket. Somehow just having it
with her made her feel better.

She slipped out of the bedroom and into the sitting room.
Neinyet was the only one there, spinning with magical wool.
From the aura around the wool waiting to be spun, she recog-
nized it as Medvaran Stardance in origin, aged two years.

At least there's still wool from the older fleeces left.

Two years ago had been a very productive harvest, in both
Medvara and the Two Nations.

*Maybe I don't need to worry about Sacrifice with Witmara and
Daro after all.*

"Neinyet, can you sit with Alicira until she wakes? Between
the potion and the dreams she could sleep until mid-morning, if
not midday. Let's encourage her to rest. Last night's dreams

were too vivid, with magic working in them. Whether it's from her or from another influence I don't know."

Neinyet nodded. "Do you have any other worries?" She wound her thread up securely and packed it in the wool bag along with her drop spindle.

"I don't think so, as long as she rests. Bring her breakfast in bed and see if you can keep her there until mid-afternoon at the earliest. Her fever's almost gone." Then she remembered last night's discussion, and what little she had managed to read of Alexran's journals before falling asleep. "We'll need her help to work some magic this afternoon. She needs to be rested and ready."

"Poor lady, with so many requirements of her, and her so ill."

"I'd spare her as much as she'll let me if I could," Katerin said. "But this involves sorcery that hasn't been invoked since the days of Alexran. Unfortunately, Alicira is our best source of information."

"Not much choice, then. I'll try to keep her in bed until then." Neinyet grimaced as she rose. "She doesn't always like staying down."

"I know. But if she can rest, perhaps we'll have fewer problems later on today. I'll try to deter any interruptions that will keep her from resting." Katerin chewed her lower lip thoughtfully. Could they delay putting the bracelets on Chiral until tomorrow?

"Where are Onadral and Witmara?" she asked.

Need to talk to Witmara as well.

"Witmara is still sleeping. Onadral has gone to the Healing House for more supplies," Neinyet said. "Alicira's going through her pain medication pretty quickly."

"Unfortunately that seems to be the progression. We'll need to restock it daily."

Not a good sign.

"As the Goddess wills," Neinyet sighed. She took her things into Alicira's room.

Silence hung in the sitting room after Neinyet left. Katerin stared at the wall. Her hand slipped into her pocket and she brought out Metkyi's stone, absently playing with it as she planned the day ahead of her. Neinyet would probably not need assistance any time soon, hopefully not before Onadral returned from the Healing House. Witmara was still sleeping but if needed, Neinyet could wake her to go for help.

Check on Chiral first. Then meet with Rekaré.

Her cousin needed to know about Alicira's insistence that Zauril was stirring. Plus, Katerin wanted to know what Rekaré had done with that pendant she found last night. Even thinking about it made her uneasy.

The door opened and Katerin looked up. Melarae slipped into the sitting room.

"I'm here for my lessons with Alicira," she said, voice loud and echoing in the silence.

"I'm afraid it's not going to happen today," Katerin said softly. "Please keep your voice down. Your grandmother had a hard night. She was sick, and I want her to rest. Maybe you can see her tomorrow."

"Oh." Melarae visibly deflated. "I was hoping to learn some more magic. It seems to be easier to practice it with Grandmother."

"I'm afraid not. You need to go back to your regular studies."

"Tlikset won't like it." Melarae pouted, making Katerin wonder just *who* wouldn't like the change in schedule. "I don't think she has any lessons ready for me—she was dressed to visit her family today. And Mother is busy with Council and morning audience. That's *boring*."

"You will need to know such things when you become Leader," Katerin said.

"But I need to do better with my magic. I can watch Council

and morning audience any day. How can I be a Leader if my magic isn't any good? Everyone says I'm not very good at sorcery, everyone except Grandmother. I actually believe I can do it around her." Melarae's lower lip trembled like she was going to burst into tears.

Katerin studied Melarae, considering her options. Would it be all right to bring the girl with her?

It's unlikely that Chiral will be throwing magic around this morning. After that dose of Memorylock last night and everything that happened—it should be all right. It's worth the risk. And I need to see Haran and Orlanden, find out if one or both of them can also keep Alicira company or if they have to leave for Larij soon. Orlanden is always good with children. It wouldn't hurt Melarae to visit with him while I talk to Haran.

"Well, perhaps you should go with me this morning," Katerin said. "It never hurts for a magician to learn more about healer's work. I can always use an extra hand, and magic is magic. We might have a chance for you to practice magic with me, and one person I need to see can tell you some interesting stories. But you'll have to listen and do what I say, no argument. Can you do that?"

"Yes. Yes I can." Melarae sat on the edge of one of the stuffed chairs in the sitting room.

Melarae's posture suddenly stiffened, hands neatly folded in her lap, back upright, as if she were in an audience or posing for a portrait, all emotion fleeing from her face.

Why so formal? Is she that worried about me?

"Just let me dress and get a quick bite of breakfast, we'll be on our way," she said to Melarae. She expected the girl to relax but instead she continued to sit in that formal posture.

Is that what she associates with good behavior?

Katerin hurried to her room and dressed, making sure she transferred Metkyi's heartstone to her right trouser pocket. Then she headed for the kitchen to see if there was anything quick to eat, or if the cupboard was sufficiently barren that she'd have to detour by the main kitchen to pick up a fast bite.

She heard voices in Alicira's room as she walked down the hallway.

"Everything all right?" Katerin asked.

"She just woke for a moment, fussing," Neinyet said softly. "But she settled and went back to sleep when I spoke to her."

"Good." Katerin slipped into the room and felt Alicira's forehead. Warmer than it had been earlier. "Her fever's rising again."

"She was really warm when she woke." Neinyet rested the back of her hand delicately on Alicira's forehead. "Cooler now."

"Wake Witmara and send her to get me if it becomes worse. I'm going to Chiral's suite first, then Haran and Orlanden."

Neinyet nodded.

Katerin *had* hoped to be able to see Rainin and Daro this morning. Rainin didn't like being confined in the stable or even a small pen, and her worry about being separated from Daro was a distant ache in Katerin's thoughts

Oh well, once Alicira was awake perhaps she would have time. Katerin sent reassuring thoughts to Rainin, reminding her that Daro was with Sark and that it was time for him to be independent of her.

Rainin returned wistful, longing thoughts.

Katerin thought caresses at her, coupled with promises of many treats and a long ride once she had the time. Rainin settled, though the worry still lingered.

Katerin left for the kitchen.

Fortunately, either Neinyet or Onadral had brought in oatcakes and apples, leaving a huge stack of the large two-palm cakes in one cupboard. The food was under a low-level ward meant to keep bugs and rodents away. Katerin tweaked the ward to allow her access, grabbed an oatcake and an apple, reset the ward, and returned to the sitting room and Melarae.

The girl did not appear to have moved since Katerin left the room. Prickles ran down Katerin's spine. Melarae was only a year younger than Witmara, and Witmara wouldn't sit as stiffly for this long. Given Melarae's past querulous behavior, Katerin would have expected her to be wandering the room by now.

"Do you want anything to eat?" she asked.

"I'm fine," Melarae said, staring at the wall.

Katerin ate, feeling self-conscious as Melarae ignored her. Once finished, she picked up her healer's bag, checking to make sure she had a good supply of Memorylock. Then she fastened it to her belt.

"Let's go," she said to Melarae.

The girl rose, still moving in a jerky, stiff manner.

"Are you all right?" Katerin asked.

Melarae shuddered, then her body relaxed as she moved away from the chair.

"I'm all right," she said.

She gave Katerin a quick, sly smile that was out of place on a little girl's face. Then it faded.

Onadral returned. "I have a full supply of poppy juice for the next few days," she said. "The Healing House is running low, but they expect a new shipment from Larij any day now."

"Neinyet is sitting with Alicira while she sleeps," Katerin said. "One of us needs to be with her to stop these dreams from progressing very far. I'd like Alicira to stay in bed until midday if not midafternoon at least—that's what I told Neinyet. If Orlanden or Haran can sit with Alicira, you might be able to keep her in bed longer."

"I will remember that," Onadral said. She carried the bag of medication into the kitchen and Katerin followed her. "The Healing House warned that we might want to keep our supplies under wards. As short as our current supplies are, I had to promise we'd ration it out carefully for Alicira's use only before I could get this much."

"Do they really think someone would come into private

quarters in the Leader's House to steal it?" Katerin couldn't keep the surprise out of her voice.

Onadral frowned. "Poppy juice is very popular down at the docks and amongst the farm workers right now as a painkiller. Some follow it into addiction—a scourge that started in Zauril's rule, and even though it's diminished from what it has been, it's still a problem. Those addicts are one reason why we have a shortage. While servants and staff here at the Leader's House are nominally loyal—everyone has families. Or beloved friends who may be on the juice."

"I see. Poppy juice addiction is not a problem in Keldara or Clenda."

Painkiller or a mental escape—or both?

Were Haran or Orlanden were aware of this issue? Something else to discuss with them this morning.

Chiral, then Haran and Orlanden, then Rekaré. She should be done with her morning audience by the time I finish with Haran and Orlanden.

"What does poppy juice do and why would people steal it?" Melarae asked.

Onadral frowned. "It's not something you need to know, young lady."

"Actually, she *should* know," Katerin said. "She is a potential Leader of Medvara and if this is a problem in the nation, she needs to learn about it." She turned to face Melarae. "Poppy juice is a potent painkiller. We have to be careful in its use for pain because some people end up wanting to take more after their pain has gone away."

"Why?" Melarae's brows furrowed.

"Because some people find the sensation to be pleasant. It can leave a warm glow throughout the body and make their thoughts fuzzy and untroubled."

"I don't like feeling fuzzy." Melarae's lips twisted even tighter. "Is poppy juice the only thing that can make you think fuzzy? Because sometimes around magic I feel fuzzy and my thoughts get blurry."

"Have you eaten or drank anything before that happens?" Katerin forced her voice to remain calm. Onadral moved next to her, holding herself tight and tense as she studied Melarae.

"Not always. But when I'm in certain places in the house, my thoughts feel fuzzy." Katerin and Onadral exchanged worried looks.

"I see." *Rekaré needs to know this, too.* "After we do my errands this morning, can you show me some of the places that make you feel fuzzy?"

"One of them was in that sitting room," Melarae said. "When I sat on the chair."

Katerin's eyes met Onadral's. Onadral nodded, pulling out a token of Dovré's from under her shirt—not a full Eye of Dovré, but enough to keep her safe in a simple magical search.

"Let's visit Chiral," Katerin said. "And please, tell me whenever you feel fuzzy."

"I will."

Katerin noted that Onadral was already heading for that chair as they walked out the door.

Goddess be with her.

At least Onadral and Neinyet appeared to have the wisdom to avoid magic too powerful for them to handle.

CHIRAL WAS UP AND DRESSED BY THE TIME KATERIN AND Melarae arrived at her suite. Her red hair spilled over her shoulders as she sat on the floor, methodically rattling a cup containing four chips, then poring over them before marking lines on a slate. She didn't look up as they came in.

Detaluna rose from the table, her expression weary. "I wish I had been here when you came last night, Lady Katerin."

"Just Katerin," she said automatically. "No titles here." She eyed the chips that Chiral tossed. They resembled the chip that Staul had given her. That made her uneasy, even though she was used to seeing children play a similar game in the Two Nations. "What is she playing? A gambling game?"

"A fortune-telling game common in Daran," Detaluna said softly. "Chiral doesn't know the meanings of what she casts. In the past I've tried to track her throws, but I don't see any significant meanings to them. It's just random tosses." She shook her head sadly. "When I see her like this—"

Melarae moved past Katerin to focus on Chiral's game. "What are you playing?" she asked.

"Throwing the chips," Chiral answered in a sing-song cadence, her voice more like a young child's than an adult woman's. "Throwing the chips, the beautiful chips. Look at the patterns they make."

"This is an example of what she's like on a bad day," Detaluna continued in the same low voice. "You won't be able to get any reason out of her today. I've already given her some Memory-lock, and, well, there's not much of a response to it. Between the ocean voyage and what happened with your probe last night, I don't think she'll exhibit much magical strength or make much sense for the next couple of days." She shuddered. "I *hate* seeing her like this. I've grown fond of her, ever since I rescued her."

"Dangerous for you." Katerin watched as Chiral showed Melarae the patterns of lines and broken lines that matched the chips. Then she handed the cup to Melarae.

"I know. And usually I'm not attracted to—clients—like Chiral. She's not the first person I've smuggled out of Daran. Just the most prominent. And there's something seductive about her. Chiral entertained men and women both at the Sleeping Dog Inn, where I found her. I'm usually not this foolish, but—something about Chiral reminds me of myself as a young slave in Daran, before my escape. If it hadn't been for Lillai, an older woman who helped me get away, I might still be bound to the Stanils."

"So you were also tied to the Stanils—did you know Ranar when you belonged to them?"

Melarae spread out her toss. All lines.

Detaluna shook her head. "I didn't know Ranar. I wasn't considered able to be a lady's maid, just a cook. Lillai got me into a mercenary corps. Then I met Vered. Vered got me back to Varen, and I met Rekaré. She needed spies, so here I am. Look. I'm not a complete blind fool. I take precautions with Chiral. Vered and Mirket kept me centered on the ship, and Mirket watches me to ensure I don't become too entangled. He doesn't particularly like Chiral, so that's easy for him to do." She smiled. "He's been a good partner over the years."

Chiral tossed the chips. A match to Melarae's toss.

"Can you guarantee that she won't suddenly regain her sorcery?" Katerin watched. Was that the tiniest bit of magic manifesting in that last toss? Or did she just imagine it?

"Alas, no. I'm fairly sure it won't come back before midafternoon, but if she rests, well—" Detaluna shrugged. "She could wake with her abilities returned."

"I've also sent to the head of my Healing House in Keldara for other healers to support me when I probe Chiral again, healers I've worked sorcery with before. Such a disorganized mind is dangerous, especially when coupled with powerful magic. Until then, I want to put binding bracelets on her to restrain her magic."

"You think her condition is that severe?" Detaluna's voice dropped to a whisper. "I've only read about binding bracelets. I've never seen them in use, not even in Daran."

"They're an old device."

Katerin tightened her lips, remembering the only time she had seen binding bracelets in use. Those were different from the bracelets Alicira had talked about. Her mother had been on the edge of falling into the dreamless sleep, her magic erratic and dangerous. The Witches of Waykemin had insisted that Terani be bound. That binding had been the last time she had seen her mother conscious.

"Will they work?"

Melarae shook the cup to cast the chips. Something about Melarae casting the chips didn't feel right to Katerin but perhaps it was just her own instinctual reaction, based on how much those chips looked like the one Staul had given her. Witmara often played a similar gambling game with her friends in Clenda. Maybe her worry was due to having the game identified as fortune-telling, not gambling.

"I hope so. I still need to do some reading about the spells. When I probed her last night, her mind was very disorganized," Katerin answered, matching Detaluna's whisper. "I'm not certain how she's able to function with mindstreams that empty, and that's a dangerous combination with magic. Can I depend upon you and Mirket for assistance when we cuff her this afternoon?"

"Absolutely," Detaluna said.

"Good." Katerin raised her voice. "Melarae, how are your thoughts?"

"Fine," Melarae answered absently, focusing on the chips she had thrown.

Chiral crowed. "Pretty-pretty-pretty! Now let's see if I can beat you."

"Don't gamble away your skirt, Melarae." Katerin repeated the traditional Clendan warning for children playing the chip toss game.

"Huh?" Melarae looked over at Katerin, confused.

She must not have heard that saying before.

"Nothing," she said. "Just an old Clendan saying."

Melarae sniffed. "Oh. *That.*"

Chiral emitted a distressed cry as her toss yielded fewer lines than Melarae's. Melarae turned back to Chiral and the game.

"I worry about the amount of Memorylock I need to give her," Detaluna said. "It doesn't always work. Those days were becoming more frequent while we were voyaging."

"That is a very strong dose you've been giving her," Katerin said. "It's risky."

"I understand. When would you want to put the bracelets on her?"

"Possibly this afternoon. No later than tomorrow morning."

"We will help you when it is time."

"Thank you. Melarae." Katerin raised her voice again. "One more toss and we must go."

"Must we?" Melarae pleaded. "This is fun."

"You can visit Chiral another time. Remember that you are following me in lieu of your magic lessons," Katerin said firmly. "We have other things to do."

"Please stay?" Chiral looked at Katerin.

For a moment Katerin swore that she could see a lingering awareness in those eyes as blue as the skies over Clenda. And then it faded, leaving only a dull, child-like consciousness. But something in that momentary sharp sly gaze left her uneasy.

Katerin shook her head. "We have things to do, Chiral. Make your toss, Melarae."

Melarae pouted, but threw the chips again. Katerin's skin prickled as she saw the result this time. Two blanks and two lines.

"I'll beat you!" Chiral bragged. She scooped the chips up into the cup and tossed them.

Two blanks and two lines.

"I have more lines overall!" Melarae crowed. "I win."

"Not fair!" Chiral threw the cup across the room. "We should do at least five throws, not four!"

"That's enough," Katerin said firmly. "Melarae, our duties await."

Melarae sighed and got up from her chair. "I'll see you soon," she said to Chiral.

Chiral squealed happily. "Bring me toys!"

"I will." Melarae solemnly crossed over to Katerin.

"I'll be back when I know what the plan is, either this afternoon or tomorrow morning," Katerin said to Detaluna. "Send for me if she starts working magic."

"All right."

They left Chiral's suite, heading now for Haran and Orlanden's suite.

"I didn't have a fuzzy brain but I did feel funny around that lady," Melarae said suddenly. "She's too old to be acting like someone younger than me."

"Yes, she is," Katerin said. "You need to be careful around her. Magic has harmed her. She could hurt you with how she uses it, without thinking. It is best that you not go to see her until we have made her safe."

"But I promised her I'd bring some toys," Melarae said.

"It won't be long. Tomorrow afternoon," Katerin said.

Melarae didn't say any more.

For some reason the pattern of the last two chip tosses kept lingering in Katerin's thoughts. They were significant—but why?

She vowed that none of the children would have further exposure to Chiral until her magic was securely bound.

Hopefully I've not made too severe of a mistake bringing Melarae to see her today.

"The Lady Katerin is here," one of the new guards announced to Rekaré.

"Give me a moment, then bring her in," Rekaré commanded. She closed Zauril's journal and slipped it under some scrolls on her desk, her thoughts confused by what she had just read.

The Gods have abandoned me. So I will abandon them!

Not what she had expected to see in his journal, especially when she had been obsessing over it during morning audience when she couldn't afford the distraction. It was confusing. Hadn't her father sought to become one of the Gods? Why then had he wanted to abandon them?

Or is this journal real? Could it be a plant to confuse me and lead me in the wrong direction?

Gods, she didn't know what to think right now.

Katerin entered, dark circles under her eyes, looking stretched and tired.

"What happened?"

Something must have gone wrong last night from how tired her cousin looked. At least whatever it was hadn't been so severe that Katerin had felt the need to summon her, but— what? Chiral? Her mother? Rekaré caught her breath, waiting for Katerin's answer.

"Your mother had a rough night," Katerin said. "Manifestations of your father. She's convinced he's cursed her and will be tormenting her on the Other Side. She woke up screaming, and it took a while to soothe her."

Rekaré let her breath out slowly. "Nightmares can seem very real."

Katerin shook her head. "I saw the manifestations. So did Neinyet and Onadral." She stared at her hands, lips tightening. Then she looked back up. "Witmara did as well. I haven't talked to her yet. Even though I sent Witmara to the sitting room with Neinyet and Onadral, she was sensitive to their appearance." She pushed a strand of dark hair behind her ear that had worked free from her braid.

"She's young to be aware of manifestations," Rekaré said.

But I was, too.

"Witmara's going to be a strong sorceress, most probably with Staul as her patron. Both your mother and Metkyi's shade say so." Katerin's brow furrowed. "Metkyi thinks she will be a Leader someday. I dread those circumstances."

So she wasn't the only one worrying about a young daughter. Still, Rekaré didn't find much relief in the thought. If Metkyi were right about Witmara becoming a Leader, then one of her children would fail.

Focus.

"My father has left bits and pieces of magical tokens around here in stashes that might trigger such a reaction in my mother. You saw one of them last night." Rekaré regretted the last sentence after she spoke it.

What if Katerin asked what she had done with the gems and the journal?

"Alicira claims that it's more than just your father. She's talking about shadows Alexran left as well. Entities and policies that go back to Daran."

"Oh." That *would* fit some comments Rekaré had read in Alexran's journals.

"There's more. I left Alicira sleeping this morning. But Melarae had come to our suite for her instruction."

What now?

Katerin looked worried.

"What else?" Rekaré held herself tight, anticipating bad news.

"She says that being around some people and places makes her thoughts fuzzy. I noticed some odd behaviors right before that subject came up—Onadral and I were talking about the problems with poppy juice abuse that the Keldaran Healing House is seeing. Before that she was sitting very still and formal, staring at the wall. Then she got up, shivered, and was normal, as she walked away from the chair. Onadral came in, we started talking about poppy juice problems, and Melarae asked why people would want to steal it. When I told her some people wanted to feel fuzzy, she said that some places made her thoughts funny—including the chair she had been sitting in. Onadral was checking it as I left."

"Hmm. That's interesting. She didn't come back for her lessons. Wonder what she was doing before she came back to our quarters for lunch?"

"I took her with me on my morning rounds to see if and where anything else triggered her. She pointed out some places, like in the garden and a space in a hallway. But I gather those aren't the only locations."

"Did it happen again?"

"No. We visited Chiral, and then Haran and Orlanden. Orlanden was working on his history of old Larij, and Melarae spent time with him talking about the old trade routes in the northern Saubral."

"Really?" Rekaré had a hard time picturing her daughter being interested in such a topic. "Isn't she young for that?"

A smile twitched Katerin's lips. "He was practicing his stories on Witmara while we were traveling. I think the Mershaunten has asked Orlanden to create this history for his son, who is Melarae's age. *This* Mershaunten has a strong interest in reclaiming territories lost during the great plagues. But I think Orlanden has played a role in creating that aware-ness." The smile faded. "Nothing obvious happened around Chiral."

"How is Chiral today, after what happened with your probe last night?"

"Child-like. She was playing a chip toss game when we got there, acting like she was Melarae's age or younger." Katerin studied the bentwood box on Rekaré's desk, the one hiding the key. She ran her right thumb up and down her index finger as she chewed on her lower lip, pausing before she continued.

"There wasn't anything overt. Except. She and Melarae were playing a chip toss game with four bone chips shaken out of a cup. I've seen this game before, it's a gambling game the children play, but with seven chips, not four."

Rekaré nodded, remembering her youth in the high Clendan summer meadows. "I've played it."

"Witmara plays it all the time. Seeing this version shouldn't bother me—and yet it did. Detaluna called it a fortune-telling game from Daran, and that it was harmless. The chips look like the one Staul gave me. It was all right until that last toss—two blanks, two lines."

"Two blanks and two lines?" Rekaré's skin prickled.

Katerin nodded. "Both of them got it."

"That's the toss that my mother and Staul both threw when they were gambling for my future. Mother told me about that, so have Inharise and Heinmyets."

"I didn't know."

"Damn it." Rekaré shook her head. "Maybe it's coincidence, maybe it isn't. All the same that's worrisome. Things just keep mounting up. What is going to happen, Katerin? Too many omens. Too many odd artifacts just turning up. Restless Gods. When does it all explode, and how are we going to survive?"

"I don't know," Katerin said. "I asked Melarae if Chiral made her feel fuzzy. She said no, but that there was something wrong with Chiral."

"Well, at least she's capable of noticing that! Gods. Where do we start? I feel like we're stomping out one grass fire only to have ten more flare around us."

"One of us needs to put the magic restraint bracelets on Chiral, this afternoon if possible. As disorganized as her mind is, I'm worried about the possibility of wild magic flaring from her. Better to impose those limits now."

"I'm surprised you didn't do it this morning. After all, we'd agreed to do it last night. Did you avoid it because of Melarae?"

"No. I haven't been able to look at everything in Alexran's journals, and I want to find out as much as I can about these bracelets before I put them on. Besides, I want your mother's guidance, and she needs to be well-rested first." Katerin swallowed hard. "I don't think it's been done in Medvara since Alexran's time. The witches did it to my mother—" Katerin's voice trailed off.

Rekaré tapped her fingers on the desk. *Mother. Nateri. Terani.* "It's not a common need."

"Not here in Varen. Are you aware that Chiral and Detaluna have been lovers?"

"Deta told me last night," Rekaré said. "I've asked her to stay close to Chiral because of that. Deta may be our early warning should Chiral turn out to be more dangerous than she seems right now."

Katerin made a face. "Are you sure that's wise?"

"I'm not certain of anything these days!" Rekaré snapped. She sighed. "I'm sorry. But so many things—"

"I understand." Katerin rose. "Four bells this afternoon will be a good time to put those bracelets on Chiral. By then I'll have time to look further at Alexran's journals, and talk to Alicira. Will you be able to help me?"

"I will."

Katerin headed for the door. She turned around before reaching for the handle. "Oh. Did you discover anything useful about those gems and the journal you found last night? Something that might help us with binding Chiral's magic?"

Does she suspect?

"Nothing to do with that," Rekaré said smoothly, willing herself to remain calm under her cousin's scrutiny.

Katerin studied her, then nodded to herself, as if she had reached a conclusion. "Well, it was probably too much to hope for. I'll see you at four bells, in Chiral's suite."

"See you then."

Rekaré sagged back in her chair after Katerin left.

She had to remember that her cousin could also be much, much more than just Katerin Healer.

What if I end up alerting the Banisher of Shadows that there is something wrong with me?

At least she still wore the Light of Medvara, and the Maker was safely locked away in her desk drawer. That might dispel Katerin's suspicions—at least for a while.

BINDINGS

KATERIN PUSHED ALICIRA'S WHEELCHAIR DOWN THE HALLWAY AS they proceeded to the Great Hall where Medvara's Ruling Tapestry hung, all too aware of the binding bracelets in the black lacquer box that sat in Alicira's lap.

I hope this cuffing works.

Neinyet and Onadral paced on either side of Katerin, and Abeyets with Alicira's own Guard surrounded them.

By all the Gods it was hot and muggy! Maybe a thunderstorm might break the heat this evening. Katerin would expect one in the Two Nations when it felt like this. The bracelet box radiated so much heat that Katerin could feel it. They had grown hot after she had reset them for Chiral, with Alicira's guidance.

Katerin didn't like handling the bracelets. To the uninitiated they looked like nothing more than a simple shiny black metal bracelet that was too small to be slipped easily over an adult hand. No sign of a seam or joint showed how to put them on. Four glyphs repeated themselves six times around the outside, each grouping followed by a tally mark. A bitter, oily taste came into her mouth whenever she touched them, and sharp, jangly tingles poked at her fingertips. Rainin didn't like the feel across their link when Katerin touched the bracelets, so she had needed to shut Rainin out of her thoughts until after this ceremony was completed.

"Try having to wear them for long," Alicira had remarked bitterly when Katerin mentioned those sensations. *"Those are the same bracelets Zauril used on me. Not much different from the bracelets I put on Nateri, save that I didn't activate the same intensity of magics that Zauril did."* She had taken the bracelets from Katerin, and traced a sigil on them, muttering to herself. *"There. No more taste."*

Rekaré waited for them outside of the Great Hall. She wore the formal white tricorn hat of Medvara's leaders, and white-trimmed golden robes that marked her as one of Dovré's followers. The white belt that snugged her golden underdress bore the insignia of the Leaders of Medvara as well as the sigil of the Miteal family.

At least I can wear lighter weight Healer's robes!

"Are you ready for this ceremony?" Rekaré asked, her voice stern and formal.

Katerin bowed. "I have prepared for this task you ask of me, oh Leader."

"Have the bracelets been examined and reset?"

Alicira opened the lacquer box. "Both Katerin and I have checked these bracelets and confirm that that they function correctly, Leader. They should not cause harm to the person who is bound by them. I have reset the bracelets, as the last one to wear them, and have instructed Katerin in their use."

Rekaré bent slightly to examine the bracelets, but did not touch them. Alicira met Rekaré's eyes. When her daughter nodded, Alicira closed the box's lid.

"All is complete." Rekaré straightened back up. "Your subject awaits inside the Hall." She turned and nodded to the guards standing at the door. "We are ready."

The guards swung the doors open. Katerin followed Rekaré, pushing Alicira's wheelchair. Neinyet and Onadral came after them, while Abeyets and Alicira's Guard remained outside. To Katerin's relief, the only other people present in the Hall were Cenarth, sitting on the Consort's chair next to Rekaré's chair of office, and Chiral, kneeling in front of the Leader's chair, with Detaluna and Mirket standing on each side of her, Vered behind her.

So this will be private and not a spectacle.

Alexran's account of the cuffing of Nateri had made the whole process sound like a theatrical show, with the Hall packed with witnesses.

The Tapestry shimmered on the far side of the room, a pungent purification smudge smoking in a covered bowl hanging from a stand. The landscapes depicted on the Tapestry did not remain static, but moved, as if they showed everything that was happening in Medvara.

Why is this Tapestry different from the one in the Two Nations?

She never noticed any movement in the Great Tapestry of the Two Nations, though she had heard it mentioned.

Uneasiness stirred in her. Only potential Leaders were supposed to see the living form of the Great Tapestries.

Katerin parked Alicira's wheelchair facing sideways, so that she could look at both Chiral and the Tapestry. Rekaré picked up the smudge. Cenarth rang a set of bells as Rekaré purified each person with the cleansing smoke, starting on one side at ground level on their right side, up and over to their left, then from front to back. After each person she added a tiny spoonful of herbal powder to the bowl, causing more smoke to billow out. It almost made Katerin sneeze when it was her turn.

Finally, Rekaré took the bells and handed the smudge to Cenarth. He purified her while she rang the bells. When he finished, she returned the bells to him, then inserted the smudge into a holder next to her chair. She bowed to the Tapestry, to the group standing in front of her, and lastly to Cenarth. Then she sat.

"I call to the Tapestry to witness this cuffing of Chiral ea Ralsem, in order to protect herself, those around her, and Medvara from uncontrolled outbursts of sorcery," Rekaré said.

"I don't want to be cuffed," Chiral whimpered. "Why do we have to do this? I swore to the Miteal Agreement!"

Katerin's stomach turned. She had read Alexran's account of how Nateri screamed and pleaded as Alicira cuffed her. She had hoped that perhaps a younger personality of Chiral would dominate during this session. But this Chiral's voice was deeper in tone, and she seemed to be more mature than she had been this morning. Which in itself meant that they needed to cuff her now, since her magic was recovering.

Still—*she knows what we are doing to her.*

It was my recommendation. It is my job to tell her.

"We are doing this because—" Rekaré began.

"Wait, Rekaré." Katerin held a hand up to stop her. "This is my duty, as the Healer who recommended this action." She knelt in front of Chiral. "When I probed you yesterday, I saw a dangerously disorganized mind. This morning, you had no more intellect than a young child. I see that you have recovered further, which makes you even more unsafe because of these swings. Detaluna says that you lose your understanding, that it comes and goes along with your sorcery. I also sensed that you were capable of very powerful magic, and that you may not always have control of it. It was my suggestion that we cuff you. For the protection of you and those around you."

Chiral's lower lip trembled. "I'm afraid that I'll lose all the memory and sense of myself that I've gained since I left the Sleeping Dog."

Katerin was almost persuaded by Chiral's mournful expression, her choice of words. But once again, she saw the flash of *something else* scheming in those blue eyes, and that hardened her resolve.

"I have adjusted the settings on these bracelets," she said. "I doubt they are the same binding you experienced at the Sleeping Dog. These bracelets will not deny you all use of sorcery—just restrict how much of it you can access."

Chiral's lip quavered even more. "I thought I was safe here."

"You are," Rekaré said. "But Daran—and Medvara in particular—is not a good place for magic to be out of control. Katerin speaks true. I cannot allow wild, uncontrolled magic to happen here. The land will be unhappy with us all, and when the magic of Medvara is unhappy with a sorcerer—you would not want to experience those consequences."

"I can show you how to modify your magical expression to work with those bracelets," Alicira said. "I have both worn them and have been the magician cuffing another. I will be the one advising Katerin on how to cuff you."

"But does it really have to happen?"

"I am the Leader of Medvara," Rekaré said. "Based on the advice of Katerin Healer, Katerin ea Miteal, I say it has to happen."

"Of course *she* would give you such advice because she envies those of us who are pure and true," Chiral sneered. "*You* would trust a half-breed over a pure Aireii since you've whelped half-breeds! Pure blood means nothing to you."

Rekaré shot to her feet. "Enough." Her voice was low and harsh, making Chiral flinch. "An attitude like that *could* be held to be in violation of the Miteal Agreement. We do not hold to such beliefs in Medvara, nor do we want Daran's poison about blood purity to spread in Varen. If you want shelter and asylum from the land I rule, you *will* reconsider this attitude."

"Do you know why the magical families are failing in Daran?" Chiral snapped back. "They are fading because they do not breed true. The technologists are becoming more powerful in Council. Say what you will, but there is a real crisis because mixed blood is diluting Aireii magic!"

And how would she know this? Wasn't Chiral a servant when she was in Adalane? Or did she learn all this after leaving the Sleeping Dog?

"Is there truly a crisis or is it stupid Ralsem prejudice?" Rekaré bristled even more, her voice rising. "Some of the strongest sorcerers in Varen are non-Aireii. My Heartfather and Secondmother, Cenarth's parents and my mother's spouses, match Alicira in magic! Katerin there, who you scorn? If you knew all that she has done magically, you would not sneer at her. Her mother Terani-the-God-Killer exiled your patroness from Waykemin. Terani was Chiyani, not Aireii. Some of Varen's strongest young sorcerers are not pure Aireii. I do not see failure in mixed blood. Instead I see strength, growth, and a new future." Rekaré drew in a ragged, slow breath. When she spoke again her tone was calmer. "Varen is not Daran, Chiral. If you cannot accept that reality, then you best be planning to find another refuge. Are you making that choice?"

Chiral shook her head, lowering her eyes to the ground and shrinking into herself. "My humble apologies to you, to your spouse, and to Katerin ea Miteal. My options are limited, so if you find my apology less than sincere, that is why."

"And this is why we need to restrain your magic," Rekaré said. "Your awareness varies."

"I understand." She raised her head again to stare defiantly at Rekaré. "But you should know that the technologists believe they can defeat magic. That they are driven by the Gods to eliminate all sorcery. Diffusing magic in the blood will bring about the doom of sorcerers. Sooner or later you will need to deal with this."

The way her voice rang out on that last statement gave Katerin the chills, as if one of the Gods were speaking through

Chiral. But if Rekaré had the same impression, she gave no indication of it. Instead, she turned to Katerin.

"Katerin ea Miteal, in my name, I ask you to perform this task."

Katerin stifled a shudder. She removed the lid from the box in Alicira's lap.

Right wrist first.

She picked up the first bracelet, the one meant for the right hand, and tapped the sequence she and Alicira had set to open the bracelet. While it still tingled in her hands, the foul oil taste no longer filled her mouth.

"Right wrist," she said to Detaluna and Mirket. Vered placed her hands on Chiral's shoulders to hold her steady as Detaluna and Mirket extended Chiral's right wrist. Katerin lifted the bracelet up with both hands, facing the Tapestry.

"In the name of the Leaders of Medvara," she said. "I cuff this person Chiral to constrain and control the magic that flows from the right hand, the sorcery that builds and supports, the powers of love, life, and growth. Goddess Dovré, honor and support my binding."

The bracelet quivered in her hands, but Alicira had told Katerin to expect this. What she hadn't expected was the further agitation of the pastoral scenes depicted on the Tapestry, and the soft golden glow that wound free from the section depicting Medvara in summer. The glow surrounded Katerin's hands and the bracelet, easing the tingles in Katerin's fingertips.

Katerin turned to Chiral. "Chiral ea Ralsem. I bind you with the right hand magic, the powers blessed by the Goddess Dovré, Patron of Medvara." She eased the bracelet onto Chiral's right wrist. Chiral moaned as Katerin twisted the bracelet shut, then tapped it securely closed to lock it.

The easy one done.

This next one Katerin dreaded. She picked up the other

bracelet with the barest touch. It zapped her fingertips as she tapped it open, vibrating in her grasp as if it strained to be free.

Mirket and Detaluna brought Chiral's left wrist forward. Her eyes widened as she stared at this bracelet, already glowing orange-red as Katerin turned to face the Tapestry. She tried to pull back and Vered tightened her grip on her shoulders.

Katerin didn't blame her. The power pulsing through her felt angry and malign, simmering with rage.

"In the name of the Leaders of Medvara," she said, controlling the quaver that wanted to break loose from her throat. "I cuff this person Chiral to constrain and control the sorcery that flows from the left hand, the wizardry of the reddest of red paths, that destroys and divides, the powers of hatred, death, and decline."

Katerin had intended to invoke Nitel, for additional power over Chiral. But suddenly she felt as if Metkyi stood beside her, his fingers wrapping over hers, his body pressing close as the anger within the bracelet calmed. The words she spoke next were not the ones she had rehearsed with Alicira.

"My lord Staul." She said each word prayerfully, caressing Staul's name as if Metkyi in truth spoke through her. "I beg of you as Balancer and Destroyer to bind this woman's sorcery. Please honor and support this binding."

When she pronounced Staul's name, Katerin's entire body trembled. Chiral squealed and tried to break free of Mirket, Detaluna, and Vered. The bracelet throbbed stronger than ever in Katerin's fingers as the glow blazed forth from the Tapestry in eye-burning bright white and orange.

"Not Staul," Chiral moaned as Katerin approached her. "*Not Staul!*" she screamed as the bracelet pulled Katerin the few steps to her side.

"Chiral ea Ralsem. I bind you with the left hand magic, the powers blessed by he who is Balancer and Destroyer, He Who Stands With Varen." Again, Katerin felt overcome by someone else's presence as she spoke the unplanned words. Anger flowed away to be replaced by grim determination.

Chiral shrieked and struggled as Katerin twisted this bracelet on her wrist and locked it. She writhed in the grip of Detaluna, Mirket, and Vered, shrieking words in a language Katerin didn't recognize.

"You will regret this!" Chiral screeched at Katerin in a language she could understand at last. "You call yourself of Dovré? Hypocrite! You are bound to Staul heart and soul! By Staul, by Nitel, you will suffer and die! I vow that—" She stiffened as the bracelets glowed a bright orange-white. Then she spasmed, and collapsed into Mirket and Detaluna's grasp as her eyes rolled up.

The Healer in Katerin wanted to make sure that Chiral was all right and that this spasm was doing her no long-term harm. She took a step toward Chiral, but the glow of the bracelets on Chiral's wrists stopped her. She still needed to complete the spell.

I am not Katerin Healer right now. I am Katerin ea Miteal, the Banisher of Shadows.

"May we check her?" Neinyet breathed to Katerin. Katerin nodded, not wanting to speak for fear of spoiling the ritual. She refocused on the Tapestry, summoning up her concentration.

"Dovré and Staul. I call upon you to witness what was done today. I thank you for your guidance and your help. Watch over us, and over she who is bound, and help her bear her burdens lightly and in all wisdom."

The Tapestry rippled, the distinct pictures within it seeming to move and flow together in response to Katerin's words. Then the movement stopped. The glow on Chiral's bracelets faded.

Katerin turned to Rekaré.

"Leader Rekaré. I have done what you have requested of me. I ask for cleansing and forgiveness for acting in the interests of

Medvara instead of the interests of this sorcerer. I ask for absolution against any claims she may make against me."

"I absolve you." Rekaré picked up the smudge, adding more of the stinky powder to create an even bigger cloud of smoke. Without bells this time, she purified Katerin back to front, left to right. "It is your task to return the smudge to its proper place."

I thought Rekaré was supposed to return the smudge to the Tapestry!

At least, that's how Rekaré had initially described the ceremony to Katerin. Otherwise, Katerin was placed within the Tapestry's influence, and that was not a safe thing for the person who had just cuffed another's magic.

Rekaré nodded at Katerin, opening her eyes wider.

Trust me, she mouthed.

Perhaps a God had spoken to Rekaré or was speaking through her? The Tapestry? Medvara itself? After all, Metkyi— or Staul acting through Metkyi's shade—had already intervened in this ritual. This could be Dovré speaking through Rekaré.

Trust,

the Goddess's voice whispered deep inside of her.

Katerin took the smudge from Rekaré, keeping her hands steady. It quivered with power as she hesitated by Chiral, then knelt to purify her, Onadral, and Neinyet as well.

She should say something. But she knew of no ritual for this purpose, no words. All Katerin could do was gently touch Chiral's shoulders, hands, and feet, then wave the smudge further over her.

Chiral's eyes opened. That *something* in Chiral's eyes flashed anger and hatred at Katerin. Then it was gone, Chiral's eyes dulling. Katerin rose and replaced the smudge in the holder before the Tapestry. She knelt in front of it, knowing without being told that she needed to do this. As she pressed her forehead to the floor, braced for whatever this proximity would bring, she felt the same power that had reached out from the Tapestry to the bracelets brush against her.

Medvara sees you and honors you for your service, Banisher of Shadows. Our blessing goes with you.

The voice was unfamiliar, and yet resonant of the land around them.

So it was *the land speaking to me through Rekaré.*

Katerin sat back up, letting her breath out slowly in relief as the Tapestry withdrew from her thoughts.

It is done.

She rose and hurried to Chiral. Neinyet and Onadral had turned Chiral onto her left side. Mirket, Detaluna, and Vered stood back.

"We will need to dose her with Memorylock again," Detaluna said as Katerin joined her. "When Chiral shakes like that and falls down, she wakes with less awareness than what you saw this morning."

Katerin dropped to her knees beside Chiral. "How serious is it?" she asked Neinyet.

"She's had a severe fit," Neinyet said, shaking her head. "She will most likely sleep for the rest of the day."

Katerin winced. "I could have handled this cuffing better."

"Katerin, it's not your fault. Chiral *was* working magic. She tried to curse you. I warned her," Rekaré said grimly. "The Agreement won't let her do that. It sought retribution."

"The bracelets amplify vows like the Agreement," Alicira said tiredly. "I also tried to warn Chiral about reckless statements that can trigger the Agreement. She had been cautioned, Katerin. This isn't your fault—it's hers."

Detaluna shook her head. "I don't think Chiral remembered

your advice, Alicira, especially after Katerin probed her and she collapsed. This is what happens with Chiral and her fits. She uses magic, and has a spasm. Or she collapses. The stronger the magic she uses, the greater her illness afterward, and her memories are unreliable."

"Which is another argument for cuffing her." Alicira sighed. "This is exactly the sort of impulsive, sporadic behavior that those bracelets were designed to restrain. You did not act with the intent to exploit Chiral, right?"

"I had no reason to exploit Chiral's magic," Katerin said softly. "But despite my intentions I still feel the guilt of a Healer. And I can wish for a better choice of tools to handle it." She pushed herself up slowly. "What's done is done. Chiral's magic is bound, so hopefully Medvara is safe."

"Meanwhile, I will help her understand how to safely manage her magic with the bracelets," Alicira said. "With my assistance, she will fare better than either Nateri or I did after we were cuffed."

"Mother, you don't have to do that," Rekaré said.

"Yes I do, as one former cuffee to another," Alicira said, eyes focused on Chiral's still form. "The means of Nateri's cuffing is still something for which I need to atone. Call it one small payment for some of the red on my spirit." She looked away from Chiral to Rekaré. "It will allow me to exorcise a mistake."

"Be careful," Rekaré said. "Be safe. I would not have you exhaust yourself for one such as her." She scowled. "She is ungrateful and dangerously impulsive. I fear she may have brought Chatain's attention to us." She sighed. "What's done is done. Cousin, I thank you for your service. Medvara has honored you with its blessing. Mother, I thank you for your assistance. This ceremony is complete." She rose.

"Take Chiral to her rooms," Katerin said to Neinyet and Onadral. "I will be there shortly."

"Mother, Katerin, please stay for a moment," Rekaré said.

Neinyet left, and returned with a litter carried by two guards. Katerin stood beside Alicira until the others left. Then she sank onto the step below Rekaré.

"What is your concern?" she asked. "I have one of my own. Given her background, how is Chiral so aware of the problems with magic in Daran?"

Rekaré took off her hat and placed it carefully in Cenarth's seat before joining Katerin on the step.

"I suspect she may have learned more at the Sleeping Dog than we realize. We will need to keep watching her. Her memory goes conveniently blank at certain times."

"I think she has more connections to Chatain than we realize."

"Entirely possible. Which brings us to my next urgent concern, Katerin. We need to strengthen your connection to Medvara. That's why I had you take the smudge back to the Tapestry. When Staul spoke through you, he also advised me to formalize your role in Medvara's succession. Taking the smudge to the Tapestry was just the first part of that process."

Alicira frowned. "That's an interesting precedent. Are you going to formally make Katerin a potential Regent, along with Cenarth? It would be a good idea, given that Cenarth is a candidate to replace both Inharise and Heinmyets in Keldara."

"Not yet," Rekaré said. "I've not discussed this with Council. They have to approve her, as well as Katerin giving her agreement. But yes, I do want to make her a Regent-Designate. I worry about what this appearance of Chiral means with regard to Chatain's intentions toward us. I will not be another Alexran jealously husbanding all power here! I would rather that Chatain see we are strong, with Katerin in place as a potential successor in Medvara and Cenarth for the Two Nations. Not give him a reason to think he can replicate what my father did with whatever tool he chooses to use, whether it be Chiral or someone else."

As her cousins continued to talk, Katerin swallowed hard, her throat tightening so that she couldn't respond. Her? Rule Medvara? She had known this was possible ever since Rekaré became Leader. But she had thought that was an unlikely prospect after Melarae's birth.

"Melarae has very little potential for further magic development," Alicira said bluntly. "Having Katerin as an option for Regent is a wise move. Melarae is too much like my late sister in her magic abilities for me to be comfortable with her as your preferred successor. What does the Council think?"

Katerin didn't listen for Rekaré's answer as dread clenched her throat even more tightly shut. She slipped her hand into her pocket and clenched Metkyi's heartstone.

So it has come to this,

she thought she heard him murmur from a distance.

Or was it just her wish to hear him speak? *Something* whispered across her forehead, as if he kissed it.

Then Staul pressed against her mind.

Be mindful. You are no longer just Katerin Healer, my Banisher of Shadows. The choices you make now will affect several generations.

The unexpected image of herself holding firm against Chatain as the defender of Varen and Medvara flashed into Katerin's thoughts. Staul and Dovré flanked her, Witmara stood in front of her, slightly taller than she was now so that Katerin could almost rest her chin on Witmara's head. But the responsibility was hers.

Must I?

she questioned Staul.

> It is but one possibility. Nothing is clear yet. But
> by objecting, by ruling this option out—you
> close doors that should not yet be shut,
> Banisher of Shadows.

"Katerin?" Rekaré's voice startled Katerin and she jerked, again aware of the conversation. "You've been awfully quiet. Will you be willing to let me move forward in formally making you the Regent-Designate of Medvara, should I be unable to serve?"

Katerin coughed, hoping to loosen the tightness in her throat.

No, she wanted to scream. *No. Because that means something could happen to you, and that means leaving the Two Nations for good, and that means I must be something more than Katerin Healer—*

"Yes," she said out loud, her voice quavering. "Reluctantly, but yes."

As the daughter of Alame en Miteal and Terani-the-God-Killer, as the lover of Metkyi priest of Staul, as the mother of Witmara ea Miteal, she could do nothing less.

Relief eased the tight lines in Rekaré's face, and Katerin wondered what her cousin had seen in the possible futures ahead of them.

She reached wordlessly for Rainin. Her daranval sensed Katerin's distress, and sent back images of nuzzling her, licking her as if she were Daro.

At that moment Katerin didn't know what she would do without Rainin.

FALLING

THE NEXT THREE DAYS PASSED QUIETLY, WHILE GROWING HOTTER and muggier. Clouds formed in the distant Arteldinnei, but though Katerin saw occasional flashes of lightning over the mountains in the evening and heard the distant roar of thunder, no relief came to the Saktrin Valley.

Vered said her farewells, then sailed to join the Medvaran fleet. Alicira tutored Melarae in the mornings while Katerin and Cenarth worked with Linyet and Witmara. In the afternoons, Alicira visited Chiral, who had woken after a day's sleep. Melarae went with her, dogging her grandmother's steps. Those visits made Katerin nervous—but nothing happened.

"It is good for both of them," Alicira had said when Katerin questioned the visits.

She spent her afternoons with Rekaré and the Council, preparing for the formal ceremony that would confirm her as Regent. Between sessions, she kept checking Alicira and Chiral. The continued heat kept drawing strength from her cousin, but there was nothing Katerin could identify as treatable.

Chiral treated Katerin with thinly veiled contempt, glaring at her every chance she could get. But the swift changes in memory and her ability to think steadied, so that she behaved more like a young teen rather than whipsawing back and forth between young child and young woman.

"It *is* an improvement," Detaluna told Katerin at the end of the third day, as they sipped cold mint tea in the Western Garden behind the Leader's House, just the two of them.

"How much Memorylock have you been giving her?"

Dusk slowly fell. The Western Garden was warmer than the others in early evening but it was also one of the few private areas on the grounds. Katerin fumbled with the heavy peridot signet on her left hand's ring finger. Rekaré had presented her with it just this afternoon, in acknowledgement of Katerin's soon-to-be official role as Regent-Designate.

"None. She is still angry about being cuffed. I'm not sure if it is that anger or if it is an effect of the bracelets, but Chiral is thinking and behaving more consistently than before." Detaluna studied her tea, frowning.

"That's good." Katerin leaned her head against the chair back and closed her eyes, listening to the ripple of water in a nearby fountain. "I had hoped the cuffing would have that effect. I'd like to sit in on the sessions she's having with Alicira, but so far the Council takes up most of my afternoons."

"They seem to be uneventful," Detaluna said. "Nothing to worry about."

Mother!

Witmara's mindspeaking cry startled Katerin. She jumped up, splashing tea over her tunic and trousers. Fear clouded their linkage, a wordless, gut-clenching panic that overwhelmed everything else around Katerin, even the damp stains on her clothing.

What is it?

she thought back to her daughter, setting the teacup down with a shaking hand and pulling the wet clothing away from her skin.

"What's happened?" Detaluna set her cup down on the table in a clatter that matched Katerin's. "I feel something wrong from Chiral."

"We'd better go see."

Chiral. Of course.

This would be about the time that Alicira was working with Chiral. Both Witmara and Melarae were with her today. It would be hard for her to try something dangerous, especially with the bracelets modulating her magic, but Witmara shouldn't be this frightened like this, not with adults around, not unless—

Dread swept over her, pure panic from Witmara.

Witmara!

Fright drove Katerin's cry toward her daughter, a mother's call. No answer, just that overwhelming sense of *dread*. Katerin broke into a run, Detaluna right behind her.

Neinyet met them at the garden gate, breathing hard. "Alicira's collapsed. She was working with Chiral. Melarae and Witmara were there."

"Did Chiral *do* anything?" Katerin demanded as they raced down the hallway.

"Not that I could see."

Rekaré!

Katerin only had the concentration to send one quick, focused thought toward her cousin.

Your mother!

Katerin ran down the corridors with Detaluna and Neinyet behind her, raising her hand with the Regent's signet as she thundered past guards, grateful that she now wore it.

I didn't think it would be useful this soon.

"Follow us!" Detaluna yelled, echoed by Neinyet.

Guards stood watch at the door to Chiral's suite, but they moved aside to let Katerin and her entourage through. Alicira lay on the floor, moaning, one knee raised, her eyes closed as Onadral bent over her, Mirket standing awkwardly nearby. Witmara held one of Alicira's hands as she knelt by her side, tears spilling down her cheeks. A few steps away, Melarae sobbed into Chiral's chest. Chiral stared at Alicira's body, her lower lip trembling as she loosely held Melarae.

Katerin took a deep breath.

Goddess help me.

She knelt next to Alicira and rested her fingertips on Alicira's wrists, then her throat, seeking to find the weak, thready pulse. Alicira's skin was clammy and cool, her eyes closed, breathing shallow and quick with occasional gasps. Her moans sent a chill through Katerin.

I thought we'd have more time, that she wasn't this debilitated, that it was just the heat. Oh Gods, I should have been stricter and not let her work with the children.

"Alicira." Katerin projected a command tone in her voice.

Alicira didn't respond. No flicker of her eyelids, no change in her low moan.

Oh Goddess.

Katerin fumbled at her throat for the Eye of Dovré. She slipped it off and laid it on Alicira's chest.

"Alicira," she repeated, sending her awareness through the Eye to prod Alicira's consciousness.

No change. Alicira didn't seem to be aware of Katerin at all.

"Mother!" Rekaré skidded to her knees next to Witmara. "*Mother!*" She took Alicira's hand.

Witmara slid back, shakily rising next to Melarae and Chiral.

Katerin sank back on her heels and looked up. "What happened?" She looked directly at Chiral. "What were *you* doing?"

"Nothing!" Chiral cried. "Alicira had both me and Melarae manipulating the practice ball, pushing it back and forth to each other while Witmara held a shield over us." She pointed to the small white leather ball bedecked with pink, yellow, green, and blue ribbons that lay on the floor near her feet. The long ribbons coiled around the white ball, some of the long strands torn. "Then everything went red, and the ribbons ripped. Alicira stood up, calling *Zauril, Zauril, you will not have them!* There was a bright flash, and then she collapsed."

"There was a red shape over Alicira," Witmara added, her voice low and quivering. "It meant to hurt her. I threw a banish charm I'd been learning. It blew up when my spell hit it." Worry tightened her face even more. "Mother, did I do this? Should I have shielded Alicira as well?"

Katerin shook her head. "No, darling, if anything, you kept things from getting worse."

Oh dear one, you're too young to deal with something like this.

"Isn't there something more you can do?" Rekaré pleaded. "She's not responding to anything."

"I don't know right now," Katerin whispered. She could *feel* both Staul and Dovré lingering close, and dreaded what that meant. "We need to get her back to her room and in bed. Then we wait."

"For *what?*" Rekaré's voice cracked as she looked up at Katerin. "Can't you heal her from whatever this is?"

Katerin swallowed hard. "Staul and Dovré are both close to her right now, Rekaré, and she has no awareness of my presence or yours. What happens is out of our hands."

Rekaré's eyes widened. She looked down at her mother, and with a shaky hand brushed away the stray strands of silvery hair that had fallen across Alicira's face.

"I will stay with her," she said, her voice firmer.

"Good. Once she has gone to her quarters, then I will check these others to ensure they are safe," Katerin said. "I will come to her side as soon as I can."

The Banisher stirred within her, confirming her decision.

Rekaré stared numbly at Katerin. "But—"

"If your father is manifesting inside the Leader's House to this degree, then we'd best find out if he is influencing those who were around your mother," Katerin said. "Neinyet, Onadral, and you can keep her safe."

Rekaré opened her mouth, but Neinyet interrupted as the door opened.

"The litter is here," she said.

Katerin, Neinyet, and Onadral gently eased Alicira onto the litter. Katerin waited until they were gone before turning to Chiral, Melarae, and Witmara.

"I want to know *everything* that happened," she said, deepening her voice and letting the Banisher come forward. "Witmara, let me see your memories. Please."

She had done these probes most frequently with Witmara, so she would be the easiest to do—and would provide an example to both Chiral and Melarae so they wouldn't be too frightened.

Chiral's the one who will resist the most.

Her daughter came to Katerin, eyes fixed on her trustingly. Katerin placed her hands on Witmara's temples and leaned her forehead against her daughter's.

Show me,

she said to Witmara.

Show me all.

Memory spilled between them. It was mostly how Chiral had described it, Witmara shielding Chiral and Melarae from all influences except their own. Then a foul scent wafted through, an odor of rot and death strong enough to make Katerin gag. An amorphous red shape appeared and swatted at the ball, ripping and snagging the ribbons.

Witmara tried to banish it, as Alicira rose and cried out *"Zauril, Zauril, you will not have them!"* Alicira threw a spell at the red figure, which reached lazily to grapple with her. Witmara grabbed at the form as the world flashed bright white and orange around them, momentarily blinding her. When it cleared, Alicira had collapsed on the floor.

Katerin's hands tightened on Witmara's head as fear pulsed through her. She gently investigated her daughter's mind-streams, dreading what she might find.

All is well, beloved,

Metkyi whispered as Staul's presence deepened within Witmara.

Staul protected our daughter. Staul has claimed her for himself.

Katerin slipped one hand to the necklace Metkyi had given her as a token of their bonding.

What did we see, beloved?

she asked, hoping his presence would remain. Metkyi's heartstone in her pocket felt warm, as did the necklace.

> Zauril's shadows are rising. We will remain
> close. Be ready to fully waken the Banisher,
> dearest. It all depends on how the weave
> unravels.

Katerin dropped her other hand from Witmara and leaned back. Her daughter's brown eyes met hers steadily, without fear or worry, though her expression seemed more mature and worldly-wise than it had been only this morning.

"I know who my patron is now, Mother, and I understand what is at stake here," Witmara breathed softly. "I am sorry."

Katerin shook her head and kissed her daughter's forehead. "Never be sorry. Be honored that your father's patron has chosen you to walk his paths."

So young.

And yet she had been Witmara's age when Terani went into the dreamless sleep, leaving her motherless. Witmara's age when she had chosen to go to the Healing House in Keldara, much to the relief of the witches of Waykemin.

Then, Katerin had not known who her father was. Now, knowing that she was a daughter of the Miteal, she understood why the witches worried.

It was dangerous having a scion of the Miteals amongst them that was unbound to any land, a daughter with the potential power that Alame en Miteal had possessed. A Miteal daughter with Dovré as her patroness, and all the potential and power that meant, was a clear threat to the long-term schemes of the witches of Waykemin.

At least Witmara knows who she is and what she can be, and she is amongst family rather than those who would see her dead if they dared.

Katerin turned away from her daughter and looked at Melarae.

"Melarae. Let me see your memories."

Chiral's arms tightened around Melarae. "Must she?"

"Yes, and you must do so as well." Katerin raised her left hand to show Chiral her signet. "I command it as Regent-Designate."

Chiral scowled. But she dropped her arms from Melarae and gave her a little push. "Show *her* that there's nothing to be afraid of."

Melarae quickly glanced at Chiral. Then she meandered toward Katerin, head down, taking tiny steps. Katerin watched her, tense. Was Melarae moving slowly to provoke anger, or because she was afraid? Or both?

As Melarae reluctantly stopped in front of Katerin, she waited for Melarae to raise her eyes to hers. When she would not, Katerin gently rested a finger under her chin and encouraged her to look up. She saw the wetness welling up at the corners of Melarae's brown eyes, how the little girl struggled to keep from showing her fear and sorrow. Part of her sympathized with that young girl.

But the Banisher within her did not.

Darkness may ride this child,

her Banisher self whispered to Katerin's Healer side.

You cannot let that go.

I can be compassionate and yet a judge,

Katerin Healer said to the Banisher.

You have much to learn, Katerin ea Miteal,

the Banisher said.

Katerin pulled a cloth out of her pocket with her free hand and dabbed at Melarae's eyes. "Are you all right?" she asked.

"I'm scared," Melarae whimpered, blinking fast.

"Did you see Witmara get hurt when I probed her memories?" Katerin asked.

"But she's your daughter!" Melarae shivered under Katerin's hand. "You wouldn't hurt her!"

"She is my daughter, but she is also a child who needs protection," Katerin said firmly. "Just like you are. I need to understand what happened to your grandmother, because that is a threat not just to her but to you and Witmara, to all of us. Understand?"

More wetness in Melarae's eyes, but she nodded.

"Will you let me look at your memories?"

Melarae nodded again.

Katerin placed her hands on Melarae's temples and rested her forehead against Melarae's. She delicately touched Melarae's mind.

Show me all that you saw,

she said to Melarae.

How?

Just think about it. I will see what you saw, hear what you heard, feel what you felt.

Slowly, hesitantly, the scene from Melarae's perspective unfolded, much as it had for Witmara, until the foul smell once again filled Katerin's nostrils. For Melarae, the amorphous red shape had an identifiable form. A contorted version of Zauril reached for her. She screamed and tried to jerk away from Katerin. Katerin held on to Melarae more tightly as the Banisher became dominant over her Healer side, interjecting herself into Melarae's memories as she stood with her short sword drawn, standing between Zauril and Melarae.

He will not harm you,

Katerin said to Melarae.

I am here.

A red tentacle lashed out at Melarae. The Banisher blocked it in the recollection, but she noted where it had originally left its mark in Melarae.

It wasn't the first of such marks on the little girl's mind. Angry, sickened, Katerin struck Zauril's form. The memories faded away and Melarae collapsed, sobbing. Katerin pulled her close, soothing that one mark. It would take longer to treat the others, but at least she could fix this one.

"He will not have you," she murmured to Melarae. "Why couldn't you say anything?"

Melarae shook her head. Katerin winced at the waves of pain and fear radiating from her. She wanted to probe further but no—Rekaré needed to know about this and be present. Rekaré needed to help heal these other injuries so that she knew what had happened to her daughter and how she could protect her.

In the meantime, Katerin was going to dose Melarae with *protection-against-possession*, to forestall any further attacks from Zauril's shade.

Katerin pulled back from Melarae. "I understand," she said gently, wiping Melarae's eyes. "And I will do my best to help you as soon as I can. After I have looked at Chiral's memories, then I will give you something that will help, all right?"

The thought occurred to her that perhaps Chiral should also be dosed with *protection-against-possession.*

"Will Alicira be all right?" Melarae whimpered. "I think I hurt her."

"Oh honey," Katerin murmured. "It wasn't you. Or Witmara.

Or even Chiral. Sit down with Witmara over there—" she gestured at the nearby bench, "—and I'll help you after I'm done with Chiral."

Melarae nodded. With dragging feet she joined Witmara on the bench. Katerin turned her attention to Chiral.

"Chiral." She would have said more, but Neinyet burst into the room.

"Katerin! Alicira is much worse!"

"Oh *Gods,*" Katerin breathed. "Stay here!" she snapped at Chiral. "Mirket, Detaluna, keep Chiral here. Melarae. Witmara. With me."

She was not about to leave either girl within easy reach of Chiral, not until she had the opportunity to examine her memories. She took Melarae and Witmara's hands and followed Neinyet.

"Is Alicira going to be all right?" Melarae whimpered.

"I'm afraid not," Katerin said.

Saying the words made it more real. A tight lump formed in Katerin's throat as dread deepened within her. She clung to Melarae and Witmara's hands, grateful that the young girls' shorter legs forced her to slow down, match her stride to theirs. It gave her time to prepare for what she feared lay ahead of them.

REKARÉ BLINKED BACK TEARS, GRATEFUL THAT CENARTH AND Linyet had joined her at Alicira's bedside. Neinyet had sent them to her before going after Katerin and the girls. She had seen enough death over the years to recognize its approach as her mother's breath rattled in her throat.

What happened? She was doing well this morning.

Katerin rushed in, holding onto Melarae and Witmara's

hands. Katerin let go and the girls scurried toward Alicira. Katerin pulled Neinyet aside, murmuring urgently into her ear. Neinyet's eyes widened, and she nodded.

Katerin brushed several strains of loose dark hair out of her face. Rekaré moved aside to let her work. Her cousin checked Alicira's pulse and breathing. As she looked up, Rekaré met her eyes. She shook her head, answering Rekaré's unasked question. Then she leaned close to whisper in her ear.

"I need to leave for a moment. Neinyet is preparing *protection-against-possession* for Melarae. Shades of your father are rising, and have left their mark on your daughter. Many marks. I healed the latest, but you need to be present to manage the rest. After I dose Melarae, the Banisher of Shadows needs to try to reach Alicira before it is too late—but I must make Melarae safe first."

No. No.

Rekaré stared at her cousin. The grim visage of the Banisher of Shadows looked back at her from Katerin's face.

"I will return shortly." She straightened up and reached for Melarae's hand.

Melarae reluctantly took it, and Katerin led her away from Alicira's bedside. As the door opened, Melarae looked back toward Rekaré and Alicira, her face pale.

"What's going on?" Cenarth asked. "Why is Katerin taking Melarae out?"

She whispered into his ear. "Katerin is giving Melarae *protection-against-possession.* She's found marks of my father's influence on her."

Cenarth grimaced. "Our poor girl."

Rekaré nodded, her thoughts spinning. That meant what she suspected was true after all. Guilt tightened her shoulders. Perhaps she should have pursued and purged those traces of Zauril in the Leader's House sooner.

Goddess Dovré, please, please, ease my mother's heart. Do not let her die in torment! And keep my little girl safe. How could I have not seen this? I swear, I will hunt down even the tiniest trace of Zauril in this house and eliminate even the smallest shard of his presence here!

After a short period, Katerin and Melarae returned. Her daughter looked pale and pinched, but at the same time, relieved, and joined Linyet at Cenarth's side. She did not reach out for her grandmother but stared at Alicira with a shaken, guilty expression on her face.

Katerin pulled a stool over to the other side of Alicira's bed. She placed one hand on Alicira's temple, reaching across to Rekaré with the other.

"I will need your help," she said. "Zauril's shade tried to attack Melarae and Chiral while they practiced a magic exercise. Your mother and Witmara stopped him. But I suspect he may still be haunting her."

That was what Mother most feared.

Rekaré nodded, unable to speak, and took Katerin's hand, then placed her other hand on her mother's temple. The intensity of the Banisher of Shadows' *presence* within Katerin pressed hard upon Rekaré, enough that she reflexively raised a shield to protect her thoughts.

What if the Banisher sees what I have been doing with the Veil and the Gloves?

The Banisher's concentration on Rekaré eased, her focus turning to Alicira.

Her mother's thoughts seemed to be locked behind a transparent shield, circling wildly as a red shape bearing Zauril's features chased her.

He found a way to torment her at the end after all, through forcing Mother to protect her granddaughter.

Guilt rose even higher in Rekaré, its tension rippling down her back and tightening her neck and shoulders. She should have anticipated this happening. She should have found a way to stop it.

But I was distracted by everything else. I should have kept searching for my father's leavings. Better yet, I should have burned this house down and built anew eleven years ago.

Too late for such recriminations.

Do you still have your token of Staul?

Katerin/the Banisher asked.

Yes.

Press it against her temple.

Rekaré brought out the fingertip. She placed her hand with the fingertip onto her mother's temple at the same time that Katerin placed her token. Within moments, she felt Staul's presence, both as Balancer and Destroyer. He seemed to be pleased with himself.

Well done, my ladies,

Staul said.

Metkyi,

Katerin pleaded, now not the Banisher of Shadows.

Please. Bring her peace. Guide her way to the
Other Side. Stop Zauril's torment of her.

A second presence filled Rekaré, a faint smile crossing Katerin's face. The Presence caressed Katerin, then turned to Rekaré. She recognized it as Metkyi. Katerin's lover. Rekaré's own support and guide during the hidden years when she fled Zauril's searches.

Lady Rekaré. In the names of Staul and Dovré, I request your strength and support to ease your mother's passage to the Other Side.

Rekaré gulped. So she would be the one to guide her mother.

I give of myself freely.

Metkyi nodded. He placed his hands on Rekaré, drawing power from her. His shape transformed, until he was a bright, glowing figure whose shape varied from moment to moment, flickering like a flame holding out against an inconsistent breeze.

He stroked Katerin's cheek. Then he moved toward the transparent barrier. It gave way before him. Metkyi seized Zauril's shade.

She is not yours; she has never been yours. Lord Staul, aid me!

The two figures wrestled until Zauril's shadow disappeared. The barrier turned opaque, and Rekaré found herself back in her body, staring at her now-quiet mother. Alicira's breathing was still shallow and rattling, but she no longer moaned. Her face relaxed and Rekaré fancied that a faint smile touched her lips.

"It will not be long now," Katerin said. "But at least the rest of her passage will be peaceful." She sat up slowly and removed her hand from Alicira's temple. Rekaré slipped her token from Staul into her pocket. "We should send for Haran and Orlanden. They will want to bid her farewell."

Rekaré issued orders for Haran and Orlanden to be brought

to them. It wasn't long before they came, joining the children at the foot of Alicira's bed.

They watched as Alicira's breathing slowed. Katerin and Rekaré each held one of Alicira's hands. At last Alicira heaved one long sigh with no answering inhale. The Light of Medvara blazed forth once, then faded.

Katerin rose slowly, ponderously, as if she carried a great weight. She straightened Alicira's limbs. "We have seen the passing of one of the great sorcerers of our era," she said. "May she find peace with the Goddess at last."

"My friend is gone," Haran said. He took Orlanden's hand and held it tight. "The Star of Medvara has passed from this world. She was a friend when my own people would have cast me out. She helped reconcile my brother the Mershaunten to me and Orlanden. Medvara and the Two Nations are made lesser by her passage. I speak for my brother and all of Larij in expressing our sorrow to you, Rekaré, and your family. To Medvara and the Two Nations. Larij mourns with Medvara."

"Thank you," Rekaré said stiffly, staring at her mother's body.

Somehow Alicira seemed smaller than she had ever been. Melarae burst into tears and Linyet whimpered. Witmara took them in her arms as Cenarth held Rekaré, pulling her tight against him as she continued to gaze at her mother. But she couldn't cry. Not yet. Even though deep inside she was screaming, the cold, hard, anger gripping her kept Rekaré from breaking into sobs.

Before my mother is burned to ash I will rid this house of all influence of my father. Even if I have to tear it apart board by board, stone by stone, with my own bare hands. The Light of Medvara should have protected us. It didn't.

Only she didn't *need* to use the Light or her own bare hands. She had the Veil and Gloves. She had the Maker, the Strength, and the Vision. She could use Zauril's own tools to purge his presence where the Light had faded—she should have done it sooner, but she had been too weak, too doubting, too trusting. Too afraid to make the choices that might lead her down the reddest of pathways, to make herself feared as well as loved.

My mother. My daughter. Who else have I sacrificed by being too soft and gentle?

Nitel's words from the other night came unbidden to her.

Sometimes the red paths are the only way.

Was that Nitel's chuckle she heard?

LOSSES

LOSING ALICIRA WAS NOTHING LIKE LOSING METKYI. AFTER Metkyi's death, Katerin had the luxury to focus on nothing beyond her own grief for three days before resuming her life. Then she had been bondmate and beloved, she who was closest to the dead. Now, despite her eleven years of service to Alicira as Healer and as her cousin, she was further away from those in deepest mourning.

Her tasks as Regent-Designate also required a surprising amount of work related to funeral arrangements and managing diplomatic actions. The Council confirmed Katerin as Rekaré's Regent-Designate quickly, making her co-equal with Cenarth in authority throughout Medvara. It was her duty to send out the news of Alicira's passing and coordinate the ceremony. Because of her sorcery combined with healing skills, she also worked with the Medvaran Healing House to preserve Alicira's body for the six days of preparations before the ceremony.

Rekaré closeted herself with Cenarth and her children except for Council meetings. When Katerin did see her during the day, her cousin seemed to be focused on other things— understandable, considering her loss.

And yet—something about Rekaré didn't seem right. But the magic radiating off of her kept Katerin at arm's length. She desperately wanted to ask, but there was something about the feel of the magic that kept her repulsed, uncertain if she really wanted to know what was occupying Rekaré's thoughts. She could guess, from the degree to which Rekaré kept Melarae near. She just hoped her cousin wasn't probing Melarae by herself.

Additionally, Katerin desperately wanted to check Chiral for any effect from Zauril's shade. But she needed support from other healers familiar with sorcery before she tried poking into Chiral's mind again. Alicira's collapse had saved her from a possibly reckless move. But it wasn't possible until Yevtin and Senai arrived from Keldara. The Medvaran healers were good, but they hadn't seen the things Senai and Yevtin had. Oh, she could have called upon Rekaré—but she needed magicians not bound by the Miteal Agreement as backup.

Furthermore, someone had to plan the post-funeral feast. Someone had to meet with the priests and shamans to prepare for Alicira's ceremony. Someone had to find lodging for the leaders and chiefs streaming into Medvare-the-city for the funeral, and plan events while remembering who should and shouldn't be placed next to each other in processions.

The tasks reminded her of winters spent at the Keldaran Healing House, where she organized training sessions for new healers and coordinated gatherings of village and circuit healers to compare notes on their work over the past year. Her work as Alicira's Healer had also required her to help Alicira organize her responsibilities as one of the Three Leaders so that she did not become overloaded. There had been other times when Katerin had needed to assume minor diplomatic responsibilities in Alicira's place, performing as Katerin ea Miteal instead of Katerin Healer.

Fortunately, Rekaré's majordomo Cantiste, a former

merchant from the independent trade city of Chellni, knew many of the principal leaders both civil and religious flooding into Medvare-the-city to honor Alicira. Together Katerin and Cantiste worked out the ceremonial procedures that would honor all seven of the Crowned Gods and their esteemed acolytes without slighting any political worthies.

But as Regent-Designate, it fell to Katerin to meet the more prominent dignitaries in Rekaré and Cenarth's stead, since they were the primary mourners. She grew to dread the screech of the whistles that warned of yet another sternwheeler's arrival. The only good part of that duty was that it meant she was able to spend more time with her daranval, as she rode Rainin regularly down to the docks to greet the new arrivals.

Rainin's presence steadied her. Rainin kept contact with her throughout the greeting ceremonies, even if all she could do was to rest a nostril on her wrist, or nuzzle her back as Katerin stood stiffly alert, waiting for the next gaggle of arrivals to disembark from the ships. Every sternwheeler in the Medvaran fleet was pressed into service, even the small early ten-person versions that Rekaré's technologists had experimented with years ago.

Mayors from the port cities along the Chellana arrived first, from Chellni and Nixyin, then Lone Peak and Wixtnal. The Mershaunten sent a graceful regret, designating Haran as Larij's representative at the funeral. Administrators from Cooscol and the other small coastal ports arrived on the *Morning Star* the day after. Vered shared a sad smile with Katerin before she joined Detaluna and Mirket.

Relief arrived on the fourth day when her friends Yevtin and Senai came from the Keldaran Healing House. Katerin hadn't expected them so soon after summoning their help with Chiral. She sent them to her quarters.

That afternoon's meetings went long and hard. Nitel's Voice picked an argument with Dovré's Blessed in the ceremony rehearsals. The Medvaran head priest of Staul, who knew Katerin from Metkyi's ceremonials, intervened with the assistance of Artel's shaman. Terat's Speaker kept the Voices for Karnoi and Cirdel from getting into the fray, though he seemed overwhelmed. Katerin let the Banisher through to settle the argument.

But at last it was done, and she could return to her quarters and her friends.

Gods, though, one more thing and I will exile Nitel's Voice from Medvara with no regrets! Her Goddess is exiled. She can be as well.

The damnable heat and humidity didn't help her mood, either.

As Katerin opened the main door to her suite, the scents of huckleberry, mint, and meat wafted toward her. Her stomach rumbled and her mouth watered. She suddenly remembered that she hadn't eaten a bite since breakfast just before dawn.

"We're outside," Senai said, bustling out of the kitchen as Katerin stood on the threshold, momentarily confused by the activity and smells.

Katerin followed Senai, bemused by the changes in the suite since she had left it this morning. She and Witmara had moved out of their original rooms after Alicira's death so that they could be cleansed and purged of any shadows that might choose to linger, as well as to reflect Katerin's new status as Regent. Katerin had not had time to do more than drop her things in the suite. Witmara had gone to the stables to linger with Daro and Rainin as much as possible during the horrible heat of the past couple of days. Neither of them did more than rifle through their bags to find what they needed.

Now, glowlights provided a cool brightness to the space as dusk fell, and the pile of bags had been cleared.

Outside, Witmara curled up on a couch, watching Yevtin braid leather. Her dark hair was damp and freshly plaited, testifying to a recent bath.

Katerin dropped into the chair next to Yevtin's as Senai moved around the patio dining area. She brought Katerin a glass of cold mint tea.

"Thank you," she said to Senai. "I am so sorry I've left these rooms a mess. You didn't have to pick up after me. I'm sorry, but with everything—"

"You would think as Regent you'd have more servants," Senai muttered. "I've of a mind to send for Davni and Colerei just to make sure you get fed properly. Those cupboards were empty!"

"No, no, no need to call them away from their families." Her original assistants from the village of Wickmasa had young children of their own, now. "I just haven't had time to see to my household since Alicira's death, that's all. I've been getting our meals from the main kitchen."

"Since when have you ever kept up a household on your own in any summer?" Senai grumbled. "Winters, yes, you've organized the Healing House but even then, if I hadn't kept your household together, you've have dropped of exhaustion."

"I'm grateful you're here now," Katerin said, her throat tight and hoarse. "There's so much to do. But you look worn out too!"

Yevtin chuckled and set his work down. "Senai, you need to stop fussing." He pushed himself up. "I'll check on that elk roast. Katerin, your potions and powders are organized. I set up your cabinet myself. Witmara showed me which room was yours and helped me." He rose. "Meat should be done by now."

"Thank you, Witmara." Katerin smiled at her daughter. "I'm afraid I've not been much of a mother these past few days."

Witmara slipped off the couch and came to Katerin for a wordless hug, then tucked herself in at her mother's feet. Katerin leaned forward and kissed the top of Witmara's head. Her daughter unfolded and stretched, cat-like, smiling, then rested her head on Katerin's knees, huddling close.

"Thank you, Yevtin and Senai," Katerin sighed, projecting her voice so that Yevtin could hear her as he poked at something inside the clay summer oven. She heard the rattle of metal and hoped that meant Yevtin was making one of his good pot roasts with tubers and root vegetables, the meat marinated in huckleberry liquor that was baked into a glaze. *And he said it was elk. I hope it's one of Colerei's smoked roasts.* "It's been chaos. I wasn't expecting this to happen when I asked you to come. Alicira was failing, but I didn't think she would die so soon. I had hopes your help would ensure she would live longer."

Yevtin and Senai exchanged glances. "Inharise suggested that we might need to come before you requested us," Senai said. "We were loading our canoe when your message arrived asking for our help with this—Chiral, is it? It was the next day that we got word of Alicira's death, right before boarding the stern-wheeler."

Katerin nodded. "I'll tell you the full story after I eat. We need to probe Chiral before Alicira's funeral."

"Of course," Senai said.

"Done!" Yevtin took an iron hook and picked up the handle of the three-legged iron kettle to carry it into the dining area. He set the kettle on a flat stone pad in the middle of the table, then used the hook to pull the lid off.

"That smells delicious," Katerin sighed as the rich scent of huckleberry glaze combined with elk filled her nose. She pushed herself up from the chair and untangled herself from Witmara. "But you didn't have to cook after your long trip on water. We could have gotten food from the kitchens."

"Not tonight," Senai said firmly, setting plates on the table. "Colerei prepared and seasoned the roast herself for us to bring to you. She'll have our heads if she heard we forgot to feed it to you."

"Dear Colerei." Katerin smiled, remembering her assistant, one of the premier cooks and bakers of Wickmasa. "Did she also send bread?" She sipped her tea.

Witmara joined her, scooting her chair close so that she

could lean against her mother. Katerin put her free arm around her daughter. Witmara sighed and snuggled close. She briefly leaned her head against Witmara's, then kissed the top of her head.

I am so blessed in my daughter.

"But of course," Yevtin said. He went inside and returned with a linen bag, whisking a loaf out of the bag. "Three loaves, two under preservation spells."

Katerin wasted no time in dishing up as Yevtin and Senai settled at the table.

"Inharise and Heinmyets will most likely arrive tomorrow," Yevtin said. "When we left Heinmyets had begun packing."

"But they haven't finished the harvest yet, have they?"

"Enough that they can hand it over to Speylits and Kennait," Senai said, naming two of Inharise's cousins, one from Clenda, the other from Keldara, who were usually in charge of the harvests in Clenda and Keldara. "They sealed the magic the day your request for our help came."

"That's good." Katerin took a bite of the roast, savoring the sweet, tangy huckleberry flavor permeating the soft meat that crumbled in her mouth, punctuated by the tang of sage. "Perhaps when they arrive, Rekaré will settle down. She's been pacing around the Leader's House."

"I thought I saw her at a window earlier, when Witmara took me out to see Daro," Senai said. "But she didn't acknowledge me or look at either of us. What do you think, Witmara?"

Witmara swallowed the bite she had just taken. "She was spiritwalking. Didn't you notice the aura around her?"

Katerin looked up sharply, noticing how Senai eyed Witmara.

I hadn't noticed that.

"I don't see such things as easily as you do, Witmara," Senai said softly. "Seeing spiritwalkers is a gift not given to all."

Katerin put down her spoon. "Now I'm worried. Why would

Rekaré be spiritwalking, especially during the daytime?" She hesitated. "Was she wearing a green and gold pendant, with a silver bracelet that has an amethyst set into it and a gold ring with a big garnet?"

"I couldn't see her that clearly," Witmara said. "She was blurred. That's probably why you weren't sure it was her, Aunt Senai."

She's using those gems she found, not the Light of Medvara, and she's searching out traces of Zauril. She can't be doing that by herself. I need to go help her.

Katerin started to rise but Yevtin put one hand over hers.

"You cannot fix everything," he said in a low voice.

"I am the Regent-Designate of Medvara," Katerin said. "It is my duty to help if my Leader is concerned enough about shades to spiritwalk through the Leader's House in broad daylight."

Senai raised her brows at Katerin. "Shades?"

"A shadow of Zauril caused the attack which brought about Alicira's death," Katerin said. "Rekaré and I banished it. He tormented Alicira at the end. If Rekaré's spiritwalking, she's pursuing any remnant of Zauril left in this house. I'm sure of it."

Silence followed her words.

At last Yevtin spoke. "Without your help?"

"She's not said a word to me," Katerin said. "The only thing we've discussed has been the funeral ceremony." She paused as a further thought occurred to her. "She found some artifacts of Zauril's recently. I've been wanting to ask Rekaré about what she did with them. But then I had to cuff Chiral, and after that Alicira died."

"Gods," Senai said. "We should have come sooner. No wonder Inharise has been so concerned. She's been anxious ever since you left."

"Circles upon circles upon circles," Katerin said. "Every time I turn around it seems like another issue arises. It's been so quiet until this summer. Then the drought, and Chiral, and Alicira's death." She bit her lip. Should she share what she'd learned from Staul and Metkyi?

Not yet. That involves Katerin ea Miteal, not Katerin Healer.

In any case, there were things she would prefer to discuss with Senai and Yevtin when Witmara was not in the room. She particularly wanted to know what Senai thought about the evolving bond between Witmara and Daro.

She also wanted to know more about Rekaré's spiritwalking.

Tonight I will confront her and find out why she is spiritwalking. I will get Yevtin to lend me strength while Senai guards Witmara.

The Banisher stirred within her, almost chortling.

You are becoming wise.

Katerin shuddered. What was she turning into?

No rest until all the shards of Zauril are banished.

Rekaré paced through the halls of her wing of the Leader's House, the Maker around her neck, the Strength on her wrist, the Vision on her finger. She had put away the Light of Medvara for this task, though its flare at Alicira's death had been its last stirring. Would it waken again? That wasn't something that Rekaré felt comfortable testing. At least the spell to recharge Strength and Vision independently of any God had appeared in yet another cache.

The fiery blaze of sunset matched her mood. Smoke from a forest fire to the west hazed part of the sky, hanging thick and close. The persistent smoky stench reminded Rekaré of her nightmares. After dark, it was all too easy to imagine destruction and devastation around her.

That's why you are doing this.

Now was the perfect time to search out any remnants of

Zauril. Cenarth was putting the children to bed, so she had a few moments free to continue her quest for pieces of her father's magic stashed in and about the house.

She still hadn't discovered the main source of Zauril's power. How had he managed to attack her mother? None of the stashes she had discovered were strong enough to fuel his shade.

That four-fold-cursed Chiral is the source of the problem.

But she was bound by the Miteal Agreement.

Nitel stirred within her.

At last you come to wisdom.

She is your beloved!

Rekaré snapped back at the goddess.

Not that she doubted Nitel was far from the truth. If it wasn't that Nitel wanted to see it happen, she'd confront Chiral right now. Grounds enough to avoid it until after her mother's funeral. That confrontation could make things worse. She remembered the tales of the sabotage at the late Empress Elithtra's funeral in. Etikar and Alexran had argued beforehand, provoking Etikar's Curse, which led to the Great Plague that spread across the world. Curses enacted at a ruler's funeral, where all the Gods were nearby if not present, had the possibility of spreading further than normal thanks to the magical energies being used as part of the ceremony.

But once my mother is ash....

Once the funeral crowds were dispersed and the risk of sabotage fueled by magical energies was gone, then Rekaré would not care. She would confront Chiral and damn the consequences.

She marched through the rest of the Leader's wing, using her magic to conceal herself from the guards. Nothing left here. At least nothing more of Zauril and Nitel than the Maker, the Strength, and the Vision carried. And yet she could still feel him stirring. Her sense of his presence had gotten worse since her mother's death.

You will have to challenge Chiral,

Nitel nagged as Rekaré hesitated at the doorway that separated the Leader's wing from the rest of the house.

It was easier to use concealing magic in her quarters. Once she stepped through that door, she would have to expend more magic to hide herself.

Silence!

Gods, she wished she could quiet Nitel's voice once and for all. It seemed like she was louder when Rekaré wore the Maker, the Strength, and the Vision. Perhaps if she focused them on Nitel and used them to banish the Goddess?

Then who would guide me on this quest?

Nitel *had* helped her find several caches of Zauril's magic. Neither Dovré nor Staul offered any help.

Rekaré decided to go to the Great Hall and meditate before the Tapestry. She had not done so while wearing the Maker, the Strength, and the Vision. Perhaps it was time. That might be what was necessary to see Zauril's leavings in the rest of the house. And since the Light no longer responded to her, it wasn't as if she had a choice. Sooner or later, she would need to use them.

Or am I just making excuses?

She hadn't really tried to use the Light since her mother died.

She took a deep breath. Cloaked as she was, she still had to open that door. Rekaré stepped into a side alcove and lowered her concealment. Then she tucked the Maker under her shirt, slid the Strength higher up her arm to be hidden by her sleeves, and turned the stone of the Vision into her palm, closing her hand around it.

Now she approached the door.

"Lady Rekaré, where is your escort?" the head guard Tlinet asked, peering worriedly down the hallway.

Rekaré smiled wearily at Tlinet. "I slipped out of my quarters, wanting to meditate in front of the Tapestry without bothering anyone."

Tlinet shook his head. "Not with so many outsiders wandering around the Leader's House," he said. "I personally will escort you there."

Tlinet had no magic so she wouldn't have to worry about him snooping. She could still raise the power of the Maker, the Strength, and the Vision to search as they walked to the Great Hall.

Rekaré nodded to him. "Then let us go." She waited impatiently while Tlinet called the other two guards over, summoning a third from down the hallway to replace him. Then he turned to her.

"It is safe now for us to go, my Leader."

"Good." She waved to him. "Why don't you lead the way?"

"I am honored."

She noticed how Tlinet seemed to puff up a little bit as he walked ahead of her.

Prideful.

She might need to check on him, look at his records to see if he had ever served under Zauril. Gods only knew, he was old enough. Could he be a saboteur, or a carrier for Zauril?

She hadn't wanted to start suspecting her people. Perhaps she should.

Rekaré waited until they had turned a corner before raising her awareness again, calling on the Maker to identify any traces of Zauril. She hadn't been able to do much searching outside of her own wing for fear of alerting other sorcerers. Who knew what alliances they held? Foolishly, she had thought it would be simple to fulfill her vow to clear the Leader's house of all taint of Zauril before her mother's funeral.

She had not accounted for the speed by which the funeral guests had arrived. Or Katerin's continual presence within all parts of the Leader's house. Since her cousin had become the Regent-Designate, she had moved into the position with an authority Rekaré had not recognized in her until now.

Then again, what else would she expect from someone like Katerin, who had been a circuit healer and an instructor at the Keldaran Healing House before settling in to be her mother's personal healer? Easy enough to forget those parts of her cousin's life that gave her the skills to manage events like this.

Katerin didn't start organizing until it was needed—and in the chaos following Alicira's death, it had been necessary. Her deft hand at planning and organization kept pandemonium away.

Only Rekaré really wished her cousin wasn't quite so efficient.

She hesitated at the door of the Great Hall. "I prefer to be alone," she said to Tlinet. "Watch at the door."

"I will." He smirked at her.

Once again, Rekaré reminded herself to check his history.

Or mention it to Katerin.

It was a reasonable distraction for her cousin.

Rekaré heaved a relieved sigh as the door closed and she was alone in the darkened Great Hall. Tlinet's presence had bothered her more than she realized—another reason to look into his past connections.

She took several more long, deep breaths with slow exhales to calm herself before she went further. One did not approach the Tapestry with fragmented thoughts.

Rekaré closed her eyes and concentrated on the sage, lavender and rosemary scent remaining from the smudge she had lit before the afternoon's audiences, not the underlying reek of sweat and smoke. Her thoughts settled. Calm purpose flowed from her core, even though fatigue still pulled at her and the smoky, muggy heat made her irritable.

Now she could approach it. Rekaré opened her eyes.

A glowlight shimmered by the Tapestry. The windows were still open in an attempt to cool the stagnant room, in spite of the smoke. Rekaré brought out the Maker, slid the Strength back down to her wrist, and turned the Vision back to where it should be on her finger. She slipped her feet out of her sandals, leaving them by the door, and walked across the rugs covering the polished wood floor toward the Tapestry. The magics woven into the rugs bolstered her energy and soothed her jagged fretfulness.

She knelt next to the brazier before the Tapestry and lit the remnants of the smudge. Then Rekaré took three more deep breaths before picking it up, further calming herself as she moved it in the purification ritual.

Then she drew upon the Maker.

Show me Zauril's power. Show me where he still hides.

Before the Maker could answer, the doors opened behind her. Rekaré startled to her feet.

"Tlinet, you were not supposed to allow—" Her voice trailed away as she saw Katerin. She tried to bring up a concealment spell but it was too late.

"You *are* using them." Katerin's voice was steady and matter-of-fact. "How much of yourself have you given to Nitel? Why are you not using the Light of Medvara?"

Rekaré clenched her fists as she squared up with Katerin. "I'm doing my best to rid this house of Zauril's presence! The Light will not help with that!"

"And you're doing this alone?" Katerin slipped off her

sandals and walked across the rugs. "Did you at least call upon Cenarth for help?"

"I—" Rekaré's voice trailed away under Katerin's direct gaze.

I don't want him to see me like this. Don't want him to know what I'm doing.

"Witmara has seen you spiritwalking," Katerin said in the same level tone. "Senai was with her."

Rekaré sighed and turned away from her cousin, back to the Tapestry. "I fear the possibility of a curse such as the one that drove the Great Plagues. If I can rid this house of all traces of Zauril, then it won't happen."

"That still won't account for whatever Chiral may do. Or why you aren't using the Light instead of—these." She gestured toward the Maker.

Rekaré kept her focus on the Tapestry. "Perhaps she should not attend the funeral."

She would not, *could not*, tell Katerin how the Light no longer resonated with power but hung lifelessly on her chest.

"I think that leaving her out sets up even more problems, especially if she is Chatain's agent." Katerin moved to her side and forward, so that Rekaré could see both her and the Tapestry. "Keeping her from the ceremony may give her an excuse to act, with no one of any significant power to watch over her—every sorcerer of any skill will want to be at your mother's funeral."

"But if she's there, then she's present to do more mischief."

"Our best sorcerers will be at that funeral. It's better to have her where we can act should she do something. We need to find out the effect of your mother's last training on Chiral. Now that Senai and Yevtin are here, I can—*we* can—probe Chiral tonight to find out what influences drive her, and what effect Zauril's manifestation during that training session may have on her."

"We?"

"You should be there too. I am sorry that you've felt the need to resort to these items without my help and protection. I feel the power radiating off of them and it's not positive. Did you at least find out what they are?"

"Yes. Dovré named them for me." Rekaré was tired of resisting. She should have told Katerin in the beginning. She couldn't remember why she was so adamant about keeping the knowledge about the Maker, the Strength, and the Vision from her cousin. She picked up the necklace. "This is Maker-of-Gods. The bracelet is Strength-of-Gods. The ring is Vision-of-Gods."

Katerin's eyes widened. "How have you been able to handle them without being absorbed?" She frowned. "Rekaré, you should have brought me in to protect you."

"They are not the only artifacts I have been using. I also found Elithtra's Veil and Elithtra's Gloves. I have been using them as protection and shielding. Just not tonight, because I thought those tools were hiding things I needed to know."

Katerin relaxed, though she gave Rekaré a sharp look.

"At least you have the Veil and the Gloves. But why didn't you tell me about them as well?"

"You have been doing needed work. I didn't want to distract you. There's not been a lot of time for us to talk."

Provoke Katerin's guilt. That will change her focus.

"I've been delaying what is the most needed," her cousin said, chewing on her lip, a welcome sign that Rekaré's strategy had worked. "Including this, for which I am sorry. But we dare not wait much longer to find out what happened from Chiral's perspective. Yevtin is outside the Great Hall, to provide me support. We can pick up Senai and Witmara—I don't want to leave Witmara alone. She will be safer with us, well-shielded, while we deal with Chiral. It's the only chance we have before the funeral. Senai said that she expects Heinmyets and Inharise to arrive tomorrow."

"So they will be here for the funeral." Another relief. Her

Heartfather and Secondmother's additional magical strength would provide more protection.

"Yes."

"Give me a moment to speak to the Tapestry, and then I will be ready."

Her cousin nodded. She retreated from the Tapestry's presence, taking the Regent's seat.

"I will stand watch," she said. "I think it would also be best if you put away that jewelry before we go to Chiral. With the power those items draw, they could be a distraction or a tool for Chiral to exploit. Use the Light of Medvara instead."

Part of Rekaré was grateful.

But another part of her was annoyed at her cousin's presumption that she needed protection. A third part worried that Katerin would notice the Light's unresponsiveness.

Let the Gods do what they will.

She was tired of struggling with this weight by herself. Rekaré returned to her knees and bowed low to the Tapestry.

How much threat is Zauril's remaining presence to me and my people?

The images on the Tapestry milled about, nothing coming clear. Then a slow spill of blood-red liquid flowed across it from top right corner to bottom left, spreading until nearly half of it was covered.

Rekaré grabbed for the smudge and raised it high, her hand shaking as she stood. Her first trembling passes with the smudge did not stop the further spread of the flood of red.

Then Katerin's fingers closed over hers. The Goddess's presence flowed into Rekaré from Katerin, calming her mind and steadying her hand. Katerin's fingers fell away. Rekaré traced the path of the growing flow.

It stopped. At first it receded slowly. Katerin snapped her fingers, and just like that, the red was gone.

Rekaré looked at her cousin. Katerin stared at the Tapestry, her gaze focused and remote, detached from the world about them. For a brief moment Rekaré saw her cousin robed in the formal garb of the Leader of Medvara, the Light shining brightly on her chest.

Then an eye blink, and she was no more than Katerin Healer once again.

Katerin flinched, then looked away from the Tapestry.

"I don't think we dare delay dealing with Chiral for any longer. Where do you keep those things?" She gestured at the Maker.

"I agree," Rekaré said. "We'll have to go to my personal office to put them away."

"An excellent idea. So quarters first. Then Chiral."

Rekaré nodded. Her cousin walked toward the door. Rekaré followed her, thinking about what had just happened. Katerin's sorcery was getting stronger. Was she aware of just how powerful she was becoming?

REVELATION

"So it is time." Detaluna opened the door.

"Yes," Katerin said. A glowlight glimmered on a side table between two overstuffed chairs. Mirket sat in one of the chairs, cleaning a headstall. The other chair held a scroll, clearly what Detaluna had been reading. "Is Chiral sleeping?"

It might be easier if she is.

Detaluna shook her head. "She's been restless tonight. Mirket, could you ask Vered to bring her out to the sitting room?"

"Yes." He picked up the headstall, rags, and bucket of water and went down the hallway.

Detaluna rolled the scroll, sliding it into a case. "How would you like to set this up, Katerin, Rekaré?" She didn't look at either of them as she closed the case and put it in a corner.

"Let me first introduce you to my colleagues from the Keldaran Healing House, Senai and Yevtin," Katerin said, gesturing first to Senai then Yevtin.

"I am honored." Detaluna crossed her arms across her chest in the old Miteal imperial salute, and bowed to them.

Interesting choice of honors.

Or was it still used in Daran? Another piece of information she was missing. Senai arched a brow at Katerin, her face smoothly sliding back to normal as Detaluna straightened back up.

"Vered is with Chiral?" Katerin asked, instead of commenting on the salute.

"We decided it was best not to leave her alone," Detaluna said. "Even with your bracelets, I'm concerned, after what happened with Alicira."

"Hopefully, we'll be able to rule out the need for constant supervision," Katerin said. "But we have to find out what happened during that session, from Chiral's perspective. Rekaré keeps sensing a strong presence of her father, and he haunted Alicira at the end. We must ensure that he has not left a piece of himself in Chiral."

"Agreed." Detaluna pointed her chin toward Witmara. "Will she be safe under these circumstances?"

"Better than if she were alone," Katerin said. She studied the other chairs in the room and decided upon the one whose arms weren't stuffed. "Let's put this chair in the middle of the room and have Chiral sit there. Witmara. Take the chair that Mirket was sitting in. Pull it into a corner. Watch and monitor, but shield yourself."

Rainin. Guard Witmara.

A brief tickle as if Rainin were nuzzling her back, and then she felt Rainin's focus change to Witmara. There was a secondary daranval mind that followed Rainin, unformed, worried about Witmara's safety.

Daro?

Guard your young one as well as mine,

she added to Rainin as Witmara, with Yevtin's aid, shoved the chair into the far corner.

Metkyi's stone warmed in her pocket. Katerin pulled it out, then went to Witmara. She kissed her daughter's forehead and slipped the stone into Witmara's hand.

"Your father's heartstone," she murmured. "I have carried it for years. Now it is your turn. It will keep you safe."

Witmara nodded, clenching the stone tight. Katerin stepped away from her, to her surprise not feeling bereft.

It was time to pass it on.

And that would be one more item for Witmara's protection.

Mirket and Vered escorted a sleepy-eyed, blinking Chiral into the sitting room. She took three steps inside and halted. She wore a lightweight white nightgown, her hair bound into two braids instead of her everyday single plait. Her hair's red shade looked even more like blood in the shadows cast by the glowlight.

"What is happening?" Her voice quavered on the last word. At least she appeared adult, not child-like.

"Please sit, Chiral," Katerin said, gesturing to the chair. "We need to find out what you experienced during that attack on Alicira."

Anger flashed quickly across Chiral's face but was then reined in so quickly that Katerin wondered if she was imagining it. *Something* lingered in those blue eyes, but as Katerin looked more closely, it faded.

The anger had a palpable feel to it that wasn't Nitel. It reminded her of—of what? Something long ago, something almost forgotten. Something equally as treacherous as Nitel.

The Banisher within Katerin went on alert. What if it wasn't Nitel that was driving Zauril's behavior? It had to be, though, Nitel was the only God affected by Zauril's overthrow—*wait. Karnoi and Cirdel.*

But the Hunt does not ride here in Medvara!

Nitel wouldn't make cause with Karnoi and Cirdel, would she? They were days away from Keldara, where Nitel had been a part of Katerin's banishing the Twin Gods from that land. Karnoi and Cirdel could be active in Medvara, but if they were, she would be seeing the Hunt by now. The ghostly wolf pack of lackeys who had died in suspicious circumstances always followed those Gods, eager to do their bidding.

And yet. The rise of poppy juice users in Medvare-the-city. Could that be an urban manifestation of the Hunt? Despite the oppressive heat, chills whisked across Katerin's skin, enough to make her shiver.

"Katerin?" Rekaré's low, tense voice brought her out of her reverie. "Is something wrong?"

Perhaps we've been chasing the wrong Gods, Katerin wanted to say.

Not the time. Whether Nitel had chosen to reach out to the Twin Gods of Chaos and Discord to escalate was something she couldn't determine yet.

Still, a possible alliance between the three Gods could explain the concerns of Staul and Dovré.

"Just an idle thought," she said to Rekaré. "Nothing to talk about right now."

Chiral's examination might tell Katerin what she needed to know about *this* possibility.

"Has Chiral been given *protection-against-possession?*" Yevtin asked. "I did see that fresh mixture in your potions. It might make this probe more difficult."

"I didn't give it to Chiral for that very reason," Katerin said. "The dose is for Melarae, because she bore marks of Zauril's influence. More than that, as disorganized as Chiral's mind-streams are, it might cause further problems. You can tell me what you think after we are done."

"Understand." Yevtin walked toward Chiral's chair.

Chiral shrank back as he approached. "Who are you? I

thought you were protecting me, Katerin! The Miteal Agreement! This son of dirt—" She abruptly closed her mouth as Rekaré glared at her.

"Hush, child," Yevtin rumbled. "I am Yevtin of the Keldaran Healing House. Katerin has called us here to help us understand what has been done to your mind." He stopped in front of her chair.

"I have no need of priests!" Chiral snarled.

"Oh? Well, I am no priest, but a healer of many years, so your concerns do not apply to me." Yevtin knelt on Chiral's right side. "Dovré is my patron."

Senai swept forward and took up a matching position on Chiral's left. Chiral looked away from Yevtin to glare at her.

"I suppose you're also *another* healer from Keldara," she sneered.

"That would be correct," Senai said smoothly. "We have worked with Katerin for many years. I trained with her in Keldara."

Before Chiral could react, Senai took her hand. Chiral tried to pull back as Yevtin took the other hand. She struggled against their grip until Katerin rested her hands on Chiral's left shoulder. She gestured to Rekaré to do the same on Chiral's right shoulder. Chiral stopped fighting, but Katerin felt her muscles tighten, a low prickling vibration throbbing against her hands.

"What are you doing?" Chiral's voice rose, quavering.

"Hush," Katerin said, the Banisher speaking forcefully through her. Chiral trembled as Katerin placed her right hand on her forehead. "Now. Show us what you saw the day that Alicira collapsed."

The images that followed were blurred even more than Melarae's recollection had been, right up to the moment when Zauril manifested himself. Then a flood of red spilled across Chiral's thoughts, followed by emptiness.

Just like it did across the Tapestry.

Katerin called on Rekaré, Yevtin, and Senai to augment her probe. She prodded more thoroughly at the emptiness. Nothing stirred.

> I can show you what I've seen in her mind streams.

she said to Yevtin and Senai.

> Please. We need to see more detail,

Yevtin answered.

Katerin concentrated. She pushed. The emptiness around them turned pale red, expanding to enclose them in a brittle, pulsating bubble that sparkled. Katerin touched the bubble. Glassy and cold. She made a fist and slugged it. The bubble shattered around them in shiny shards that sparkled away. Now they were in Chiral's mindstreams, a maelstrom of confusion that Katerin recognized from her previous probe. Nitel loomed large in front of them.

> You have no cause—

> More so than you think! Who is really in charge of this your beloved? You? Or others?

Nitel's presence whispered away, all but the tiniest piece left to monitor what they did. Katerin did not push as hard as she had the first time, because no matter how deeply she went, Chiral's mind was opaque, full of mist and fog that obscured her mindstreams and had the feel of the bracelets' magic. The bald-pated priest did not appear, nor did Ranar.

Well, this is no help.

Frustrated, Katerin pulled out of Chiral's mindstreams and heaved a deep breath, dropping her hands from Chiral. Rekaré, Yevtin, and Senai did the same.

Hopefully someone else saw more.

Chiral buried her head in her hands. "I told you there was nothing of use from me," she said, her words half-obscured.

At least she did not have a fit this time. Katerin stepped back as both Senai and Yevtin stood up.

"I see what you mean," Yevtin said slowly.

"Can I go back to bed?" Chiral asked.

"Yes."

Chiral shot out of the chair quicker than Katerin expected. Vered looked questioningly at Katerin and she nodded.

"Keep the watch," she said. She waited to say more until Chiral and Vered were out of the room.

Senai shook her head. *"Protection-against-possession* is no remedy for that one. Dear Goddess, how can she survive with that fragmented a mind?"

"Then you saw that," Katerin said.

"I saw enough of her thought patterns to get a feel for her situation. Between Nitel and the way she's fragmented—" Yevtin shook his head.

"There is more to her than just Nitel," Rekaré said. "I didn't see Ranar or that priest you talked about, Katerin."

"The bracelets may restrict incursions into Chiral's thoughts. She can't lash out at us—but we cannot dig deep into her mind."

"Very possible," Yevtin said thoughtfully, stroking his beard. "Well, we need to sleep on this. That is, after we put our hostess's furniture back." He picked up the chair that Chiral had been sitting in. Witmara helped him move her chair back to its original spot, her eyes still big.

Rekaré frowned, but Katerin rushed in before she could speak, recognizing *need to sleep on this* as a Keldaran code phrase for *don't talk about it here.*

"I think that would be a good idea. Rekaré, don't you still have some of that lovely liquor a few days ago?"

"Liquor?" Senai perked up. "I could use a nice drink."

"Coos berry liquor from the original bushes," Rekaré said.

"Definitely want *that*," Senai said.

"Then let's go to Rekaré's study for a taste," Katerin said, moving toward the door. "Detaluna. My thanks to you."

"Always willing to help," Detaluna said, picking up the scroll case.

"Thank you," Katerin repeated

"What was that about?" Rekaré asked in a low tone once they were outside. "A code phrase from the Keldaran Healing House?"

"Yes. Don't talk about it here is what it means. Your study is most easily sealed to listeners."

Cenarth was in the sitting room of Rekaré's personal quarters as they arrived, contemplating several maps rolled out on a table.

"It's late for a meeting," was all he said.

"We've checked Chiral," Rekaré told him. "Perhaps you should join us?" She looked questioningly at Katerin.

Why is she asking me?

"I think it would be a good idea if Cenarth joins us," she said. "Witmara, do you want to lay down on the couch and rest until we're ready to go back to our suite? Or would you prefer to come into Rekaré's study with us?"

"Here," Witmara said, heading for the couch. Katerin detoured to kiss her on the forehead as Witmara burrowed into the couch and closed her eyes.

Then she went to Rekaré's study. Cenarth gathered chairs and stools and set them around a side table while Rekaré got down glasses and the one small bottle of liquor, and poured generous servings. Katerin delivered glasses to Yevtin and Senai, then handed one to Cenarth before taking one for herself. Rekaré settled in next to Cenarth at the table.

Yevtin held the glass high. "So. Coos berry liquor, from the original bushes. How did you manage to recover them?"

"It took a lot of work," Cenarth said. "We've just been able to distill the new crop, the first one of any size in many years."

"Oh," Yevtin breathed, raising his brows and whistling softly. "I thank you, lady Rekaré." He sipped his glass and smiled.

"As do I," Senai said after her tasting. "Much appreciated after—*that* experience."

"You did not see the whole of it." Katerin said. She described her encounter with Ranar and the bald-pated priest from her previous probe of Chiral. "I did not press further and deeper because I didn't want to trigger a fit in Chiral."

"The bracelets might be an effective counter to her spasms," Rekaré said.

"It seemed harder to find that link to Ranar and that priest," Katerin said. "I thought for certain we would run into it."

"Other than your opening encounter with Nitel, there was no influence from the Gods or other potential outside influences," Senai said. "Though were it not for the lack of signs of the Hunt, I'd say there's a feel of Karnoi and Cirdel in Chiral's mindstreams."

"I expected to see more of Zauril," Rekaré said. "But there was nothing."

"There is a façade there," Yevtin said. "She is still hiding something. But it's locked away solidly, possibly by those bracelets."

"So what do we do?" Katerin asked. "Is Chiral safe? Or will someone or some God use her presence at the funeral pyre to create another Great Plague?"

"On the surface she seems to be defanged," Senai said slowly. "I'm not certain I trust that initial impression."

"I'd agree," Yevtin said. "Perhaps one means to deal with it is to assign Senai and me to supervise her during the funeral."

"I think that's an excellent idea," Katerin said. "Rekaré, what do you think?"

"Anything we can do to prevent a tragedy will be good."

Rekaré focused on her liquor glass. "I still think she has some tie to Zauril, somewhere, but after tonight's screening? I have no idea what that would be." She sighed and put her glass down. "Yevtin. Senai. Katerin. I thank all of you for this work tonight. Senai, Katerin said that Inharise and Heinmyets will arrive tomorrow?"

"I just got a message from Nixyin," Cenarth said. "It is confirmed. They will be here tomorrow."

"In time for the funeral day after tomorrow," Rekaré said. "Well. Two more evenings. And after that—I will decide if Chiral's future is to remain here in Medvara, or if I want her to seek refuge elsewhere." She tossed back the rest of her drink. "It has been a long and difficult day. I want to go to bed."

Katerin studied her cousin, wondering if Rekaré just wanted to get rid of them in order to continue spiritwalking. But Rekaré stood and took Cenarth's hand. Fatigue sagged the muscles in her face, and she looked more tired than ever.

"Then we will see you in the morning," she said, finishing her own drink.

Yevtin and Senai followed suit. Yevtin scooped Witmara up.

Two guards followed them down the hallway to Katerin's suite. She collapsed on a chair as Yevtin carried Witmara to her room and Senai went into the pantry, coming back with a wine bottle and glasses.

Yevtin returned and dropped into a seat. "We will have to do something about that girl after the funeral," he said. "There is no possible way that she will be able to function independently for much longer than that."

"I have wondered if Chiral is part of the façade or if it is imposed upon her." Katerin took the wine that Senai had poured for her.

"She positively reeks of the interference of Gods," Senai said. "And not just Nitel."

Yevtin nodded. "Karnoi and Cirdel are not innocent by any means. Nor are they the only ones present."

"But we've not seen the Hunt," Katerin said.

"We are not in the wilds," Senai said. "Perhaps the Hunt is taking a different form. After all, we are in a city, and the Hunt can change shape. They aren't locked into wolf form."

"With all the visitors for Alicira's funeral, this could be a problem." Katerin slumped back in her chair. "I have been told by the local Healing House that poppy juice addiction is a growing problem. Could the Hunt take the form of addicts?"

"Very likely," Yevtin said. "I will look more closely when we go out."

"They would blend in with the crowds. We need to keep close watch on Chiral," Senai said.

"Let's hope she's our only worry," Katerin muttered. She was reluctant to share what she knew of Rekaré's use of the Maker, the Strength and the Vision to search for what might be left of Zauril. "But at least you are here, and tomorrow we'll have Inharise and Heinmyets."

Perhaps her Secondmother and Heartfather could ease Rekaré's mind about Zauril's presence better than Katerin could.

And what if the problem really wasn't Zauril's shade, but the Twin Gods playing games?

Katerin shuddered. She wasn't certain which possibility was worse.

SAD REUNIONS

THE FAMILY GATHERED ONCE AGAIN AT THE DOCKS AT DUSK THE next day. Katerin sat Rainin tensely, using part of her awareness to monitor Rainin's senses to determine if the Hunt had indeed taken a new form to reflect their urban presence.

She couldn't detect them, at least not right away. But then she spotted a surge of scruffy, dangerous-looking people lurking about the docks and the riverfront, more than had been there the day before.

How much of this presence was due to the drought forcing farm workers to find temporary work in the city, and how much was due to drifters moving in to observe Alicira's funeral? After all, this was the biggest funeral ceremony that Medvara had ever held. No records showed that Zauril had held any ceremony for Alicira's family, and of course Rekaré had not mourned Zauril's death.

Would I even recognize the Hunt in a different form? Wolves aren't native here.

The shadows she knew were from Keldara and Clenda. Katerin had killed at least one of them herself. But it would stand to reason that Karnoi and Cirdel would draw on local shades to follow them here—and she wouldn't know who they were.

Rainin snorted at one gathering that broke apart at an alley opening. Katerin caught a side glimpse of a woman that in profile reminded her of a darker-skinned version of the image of Ranar she'd seen in Chiral's thoughts. Then the woman turned her head, and her features were different.

If they're from Daran, they'll stand out as paler than most.

Except, of course, for those Medvarans of Aireii descent.

Rainin snorted and shook her head. She pinned her ears at a young person of indeterminate gender with short dark hair who darted in front of them. Their profile resembled Zauril. But once again, a closer look revealed differences. Katerin tightened her hand on the reins.

Remember those faces.

After all, when the Hunt was in wolf form, she had only identified those shadows by the expressions in their eyes.

Rainin tossed her head again, projecting uneasiness.

Is it the Hunt?

Katerin asked her directly, projecting her own memories of seeing the Hunt in Wickmasa. Her daranval was Wickmasa-bred, and the Hunt had skulked around that village until Katerin and Metkyi had led the battle that banished Karnoi, Cirdel, and the Hunt from Keldara.

Uncertainty colored Rainin's response.

Like, but not like. Not the same forms. But same feel.

Then they were past the streets and at the pier. Rekaré glanced back and waved Katerin up next to her.

"You dropped behind us—is there a problem?" she asked quietly.

"There may be," Katerin said. "I keep seeing people who could be manifestations of the Hunt. And Rainin knows the feel of the Hunt from Wickmasa. She says it's like but not like."

Rekaré grimaced. "The Twins on top of my father's shade? Goddess's golden tits. You told me about Senai and Yevtin's reaction to Chiral, but I didn't think it was possible. As if there wasn't enough to worry about."

"We will be watching," Katerin said as they drew up near the dock.

Heinmyets stood at the top of the sternwheeler's ramp, his old daranval stallion Elantai standing next to him, saddled and bridled. Elantai pawed impatiently, tossed his head and neighed a challenge. Quartel answered in ringing tones while Basnen and Rainin nickered back. Elantai snorted, then minced down the ramp in small steps. Once they reached the dock, he pricked his ears and nickered toward the daranvelii on the dock, then turned his head back toward the sternwheeler, whickering nervously.

An answering nicker came from inside the ship. Then Inharise appeared, leading her young bay daranval mare Sasitin, Rainin's nine-year-old daughter. Sasitin whickered at Elantai, then at Rainin. The tell-tale tingle that arose whenever the daranvelii mindspoke to each other without involving humans prickled through Katerin. But she didn't say anything to Rainin. If the daranvelii discussion were important, her daranval would tell her.

Inharise led Sasitin to join Elantai and Heinmyets. The daranvelii touched noses, stepping eagerly across the dock planks to reach solid ground. As soon as Elantai's hooves reached solid earth, Heinmyets swung up on his back with an easy grace that belied the gray strands in his dark braids. Sasitin danced about, snorting, and it took a couple of moments before Inharise mounted her with a fluidity matching Heinmyets's.

"At last!" Heinmyets rode forward and leaned to hug Rekaré,

and saluted Cenarth. "Heartsdaughter and son, it is good to see you. A long trip, and the daranvelii didn't like being on ship. But not much affects Elantai." He sighed. "Would that the occasion were happier. We had hoped to make this trip while Alicira yet lived. I hadn't expected her to die so quickly."

"We will speak more of this when we reach the Leader's House," Rekaré said. "Her ceremony is tomorrow. I am so glad —" her voice caught and she coughed before continuing. "So glad that you were able to arrive in time."

"I felt uneasy ever since you left, Katerin," Inharise said. "I've been worried about Alicira's health."

"The speed of her demise took us all by surprise," Katerin said.

"We pushed to get the magic harvest proofed so that we could come as soon as possible because of Inharise's concerns," Heinmyets added. "How is Rainin's colt doing?"

A chill went through Katerin. "He has named himself to Witmara," she said, staring straight ahead and not at Heinmyets.

"Named himself? But he's not even weaned, is he?"

Witmara boldly rode her pony up next to Heinmyets. "His name is Daro," she said. "And he is being weaned now. That's why he is not here with his dam."

Katerin sighed. She had hoped this could wait.

"Witmara and Daro have had an affinity since he was born," she said, still not looking at Heinmyets.

She had known that he had been considering the colt as a possible replacement for Elantai in spite of the obvious attraction between Daro and Witmara. Gods, she hated to disappoint him!

"Has he been halter-broken?" Heinmyets asked.

"No," Katerin said, even as both Cenarth and Witmara answered, "Yes."

"Witmara has been working with Daro over the past few days, Father," Cenarth said. "Leading him from the ground and ponying him both. We chose not to bring him today because we didn't want to push his ability to handle this much activity."

"If they are bonding, then it would be a good idea for her to have him with her tomorrow," Heinmyets said. "Otherwise he will be distressed by the magic released during the ceremony. Bringing him today would have been a good idea, a chance to expose him to difficult situations before the funeral."

"He joined with Rainin to protect Witmara during a magic working last night," Cenarth said. "Adding in this expedition might be a bit much for a colt so soon."

"Magic working?" Heinmyets asked.

"Once we're safely at the Leader's House I can tell you more," Katerin said. "It's tied to what happened to Alicira."

"I see," Heinmyets said. "Still. Witmara. We should ride out and have you pony Daro. Rekaré. Will it be an evening ceremony?"

"Yes, according to tradition," Rekaré said.

"Then tomorrow morning will be a good time to pony him through the streets," Heinmyets said. "That way you will know what to expect from him."

"Thank you," Witmara said. She eased her pony back to rejoin Melarae and Linyet.

"She is growing up," Heinmyets said.

"Almost too fast," Katerin said.

At least that went better than I expected.

ANOTHER LATE NIGHT IN HER STUDY. REKARÉ LEANED BACK IN her chair, ignoring the urge to pull out the Veil and Gloves as well as the Maker, the Strength, and the Vision to prowl the Leader's House. After last night's discovery by Katerin, plus the presence of Heinmyets and Inharise, she wouldn't be able to move around unnoticed. Plus she wasn't certain it would be of use anyway.

Katerin's disclosures about Senai and Yevtin detecting traces of the Hunt also worried Rekaré.

What if her focus on Chiral's ties to Nitel and Nitel as Zauril's patron were nothing more than a distraction?

She hadn't thought about the possibility of the Twin Gods playing a role in Medvaran politics, simply because they weren't the patrons of anyone powerful. Hadn't been powerful in Daran, hadn't been powerful in Medvara. They were battle and chaos gods, and other than their ties to Katerin through her dead mother Terani, hadn't had much influence in Medvara, Keldara, or Clenda.

Wrong, she corrected herself.

Karnoi and Cirdel had co-opted Metkyi's twin brother Makri to deny his Healer's ties to the Goddess Dovré.

Katerin bore a dread of them because of their role in Terani's death, when Karnoi and Cirdel had possessed her in order to banish Nitel from Waykemin. The Witches of Waykemin had dedicated themselves to the Twin Gods after that. With Waykemin devoted to them, the Twin Gods had tried to establish a foothold in Keldara, manifesting in Wickmasa during her own exile.

Rekaré went to the open windows to stare out into the gardens. The moon rode high in the sky behind a cloak of smoke and sullen clouds, the half-crescent occasionally peeking between brief openings in the clouds.

Half-moon tomorrow night for Mother's funeral, even if we can't see it.

She crossed her arms, suddenly cold despite the lingering muggy warmth from the hot day. A waning half-moon meant that Dovré's strength was also waning, while Nitel, Karnoi, and Cirdel grew stronger.

What do they want?

Years ago, Katerin and Metkyi had theorized that his brother Makri had sought the favor of the Twin Gods in order to gain power, jealous of both Metkyi and their sister. But there had been no time to think about what the Twins wanted, and then, after—none of them had thought about it, swept into the rush to challenge Zauril and depose him.

Not examining the Twins' motives further had been a mistake.

War between the Gods.

When she remembered what Staul had said to her, what Katerin had repeated of her encounters with Staul—she had to wonder.

Nitel, Karnoi, and Cirdel.

Who was the victim here, and which god or gods were being forced out? The Twin Gods had not been powerful for many years.

Someone tapped lightly on her door. Rekaré turned away from the windows.

"Come in," she said, reluctantly walking back to her chair.

She wasn't certain if she was annoyed or relieved to be interrupted.

"Heartsdaughter," Heinmyets said.

He walked toward her, opening his arms. Without hesitation Rekaré went to her stepfather, the man who had always acted as her father, *was* her father more than Zauril. She buried her head in his chest, savoring the scent of horses and smoke. Heinmyets wrapped his arms around her. The familiarity brought tears to her eyes as well as the sharp awareness of the gaping hole in her life that she had been trying to avoid thinking about.

She hadn't been able to cry yet for her mother, not with so much to do ahead of her.

She couldn't sob for long. When she shivered and lifted her head, she looked up to see that his dark eyes were wet as well.

"She was so proud of you," he said. "We all have been."

"I feel like I've not been able to put one foot right over the summer. Ever since this spring things have been difficult." She choked back a sniffle. "The drought. Chiral's arrival. And—I am failing my daughter, Heartfather. Something is wrong with her. Dreadfully, magically, wrong. Katerin sees it, but I don't know what to do. The curse of my blood father, and I don't know what to do about it. I wanted to be a better mother to her than I was a daughter to my mother, but I'm failing."

"Heartsdaughter. Do you know how many times I heard your mother fret about failing you? You are magically powerful, and were marked by the Gods from birth." Heinmyets stroked her cheek. "As parents all we can do is try to help our children live up to their potential. What they do with our efforts is up to them."

"Oh Heartfather." Rekaré gulped. She slipped away from him and went to her chair. "I wish I had your confidence."

He chuckled as he sat down, crossing his legs and leaning back in his chair. "Confidence is something you project even when you are terrified that you are wrong. We live in challenging times. The world is changing around us. We are called to be leaders, and as leaders we often must manage to deal with our own doubts."

"But what if I don't want to be a leader?" She gasped, shocked at her own words.

Heinmyets didn't react, nodding. "Go on."

"I mean—oh, this sounds so stupid after all these years and all Mother's dreams for me to take power here, but—I thought until this spring that my blood father was safely banished. That I could rule Medvara easily, raise my children, and live my life." She looked toward the window and the moon. "And now that I've been faced with my first serious crisis since I took power, I just want to run away from Medvara. I don't feel like I belong here. The land has become alien to me. I ask you, is that the way a leader should feel?"

"Oh Rekaré, Rekaré." Heinmyets shook his head. "Rebuilding Medvara after years of neglect wasn't a crisis? I disagree. You have stood up magnificently to many crises as you brought Medvara's magic back to life, and rebuilt its strength." He uncrossed his legs and rose, staring out the window. "You are facing even bigger challenges. The Gods are uneasy. Chatain has ambitions that go beyond that of Empire. Only an arrogant fool would refuse to doubt themselves." He turned away from the window and laughed, a short bark. "You doubt yourself? Inharise and I quail in the face of what we see coming."

"So you see it too." Rekaré stood beside him.

Heinmyets put an arm around her. "Yes. Inharise and I feel it even more here in Medvara. This land is restless in a way that Keldara and Clenda are not."

"Chiral roils it."

"It's not just her. More is going on. I'm not surprised you feel like you've lost your connection to the land. It is difficult when we go through a drought like this, even more so when outside threats arise."

"I wish I'd taken more time to talk to Mother after she got here. But I've been so busy with Chiral, with managing affairs, with trying to ferret out the last traces of my father in this house."

"You didn't know," Heinmyets said softly. "We didn't expect her to die this quickly. We knew her time was short, but we thought we could finish up the harvest and then be able to spend some time with her here." He tightened his arm around Rekaré. "You had other concerns."

Rekaré sniffled, more tears taking her by surprise. They stood silently together as wetness trickled down her cheeks. At last she wiped her eyes dry.

"Thank you, Heartfather," she whispered.

Heinmyets kissed her forehead. "We are here. We mourn and honor your mother together. Our world has changed, and we will need to meet its new face. I am confident in you, Hearts-daughter. You will face the changes and do what needs to be done. You are a Leader."

"Not a very good one," she whispered.

"Better than you think," he said. He released her and stepped back. "Go rest now. Tomorrow will be a long day."

"I will," she promised.

After Heinmyets left, Rekaré poured herself a finger's worth of Larijian whisky, a mourning gift from Haran. She went back to the window and stared at the moving shadows outside, sipping on the whisky.

At least she no longer felt the urge to keep searching out traces of her father. What was done was done.

After the funeral, she promised herself. *When we are all done with the ceremony.*

Gods help us.

GODS-CURSED FUNERAL

At least they were not riding in the full sun. Heavy clouds hovered overhead, making the evening darker than ever in spite of the torchlight, and holding in the heat of the day. Katerin was in the third rank behind the wagon bearing Alicira's body, after Heinmyets and Inharise, then Cenarth, Rekaré, Melarae, and Linyet. Witmara rode next to her, ponying Daro. Behind them were Chiral, Detaluna, Mirket, Vered, Senai, and Linyet. She didn't keep track of who followed now that they were moving.

It was Cantiste's worry to get them all in order now, not hers.

Her formal robes were too heavy for this heat. Cantiste had fussed over what Katerin was to wear given her different roles, and decided that she needed to wear the white and gold of the Regent-Designate, not the lighter garb of a Healer or simple formal dress befitting her role as a daughter of Miteal. The wool cornet made her head sweaty and the robes themselves had been hastily altered to fit her. The last person to wear them had been Alicira's father Richenax, and he had been taller and broader-shouldered than she was.

At least she had been able to wear her light knee-length Healer's trousers under her robe, and fasten both her Healer's bag and the bag that carried her other magical tokens to her belt.

"Normally carrying magical tools is not allowed," Cantiste had said while helping her dress. *"But given your role as close kin, you can bear your tools."*

Rainin tossed her head, worried about the crowds that lined the roadway.

Katerin sent her comforting thoughts. Daro's mind danced on the edge of her awareness, but Witmara kept in contact with him. The colt was doing astonishingly well for such a young weanling, following his lead and at times pressing close to Witmara and her pony. At least he wasn't shying or startling, but turning to her for comfort. Rainin was more bothered by the crowds than he was.

Katerin sent Rainin a picture of them galloping across a high plateau, no other horses or daranvelii or humans around. Rainin returned calmer thoughts, but an undertone of fretfulness still roiled her mindstreams. When Katerin asked, her daranval couldn't return a specific worry. Just an awareness that something lurked at the edge of her consciousness, something dangerous that refused to reveal itself.

At last they arrived at the funeral ground. Katerin dismounted and handed her reins to Witmara. She joined Heinmyets, Inharise, Cenarth, and Rekaré by the funeral wagon. With the help of the guards, they lifted the bier and carried it to the waiting pile of wood that made up Alicira's pyre. Then they took their places around it. Witmara rode over to Katerin and handed her Rainin's reins. Then she dismounted, placing herself between her pony and Daro. Chiral and the others filled in the row around the bier, standing silent.

Artel's chief shaman in Medvara climbed to a platform overlooking the bier, standing with his arms outstretched, wearing heavier formal robes than Katerin's. He stood silently while the procession and mourners gathered around the bier, waiting for the crowd to settle. Finally, he threw his head back and began a long, ululating cry that knifed deep inside Katerin, bringing back painful memories of Metkyi's ceremony. With a wave of his right hand, the torch fastened to the stand ignited. He remained silent for a moment as the flames took hold, then burned high. Then he started chanting.

We gather to say farewell to our beloved
We gather to escort her to the Other Side
We gather to bear witness to her glory.
Alicira, daughter of Richenax and Melara.
Granddaughter of Alexran and Melarae.
Alicira, sister of Delian and Melaraen.
Mother of Rekaré, Cirenna, and Elenil.
Triad wife of Heinmyets and Inharise.
Alicira the Outcast.
Leader of the Two Nations, with
Heinmyets and Inharise.
Alicira, beloved of Dovré.
Dearest Dovré, we bless your daughter.
We give Alicira to your keeping.
All of us, all of her beloveds.

He dropped his arms and descended from the platform.

Heinmyets climbed up. Katerin half-listened, thinking of what she needed to say. She had some time to plan her words. Heinmyets, Inharise, Rekaré and Cenarth would speak. Then it would be Katerin's turn. Haran after Katerin, as one of Alicira's oldest and dearest friends, as well as Larij's representative.

Heinmyets finished, and Inharise ascended next. Rainin

tossed her head and pawed impatiently, not her usual behavior. She shifted her weight and snorted.

Hush,

Katerin sent.

Danger,

Rainin returned, along with increased worry that she could only *feel* the danger, not see it. Katerin looked about them. She couldn't *see* what worried Rainin.

Chiral.

She looked around. Chiral stood on the other side of the bier. Her gaze seemed to be fixed on Inharise, mouth half-open—*wait.* Chiral's hair seemed to darken to that same brunette shade that Katerin had seen before, in her memories of Ranar.

Chills ran down Katerin's spine. She kept staring at Chiral while she slipped her hand into the pouch that held her magic tokens, fumbling until she found the chip that Staul had given her.

Then Chiral's hair was bright red again. Did anyone else notice that brief change? Katerin looked around. The others in the front row around Alicira's bier seemed transfixed by Inharise's speech, including Senai and Yevtin. Katerin reached out for Rainin's thoughts again. She sent an image of

Rainin warning Senai and Yevtin, talking to their daranvelii.

Witmara startled, turning her head to look at Katerin. Daro pulled against her grasp, nickering worriedly.

Katerin nodded toward Chiral. Witmara looked, her eyes widening. Daro bounced in place, now gazing at Chiral as well.

Witmara took a shorter grip on his lead, her hand on the knot under Daro's chin.

Inharise finished speaking and descended from the stand.

Chiral straightened up. Her hair changed from red to brunette again. Chiral raised her arms high, her lips moving in a silent spell. Bright magenta and red lights flared between her fingertips.

Daro reared, squealing as he lifted Witmara off the ground. She dropped her pony's reins and kept her feet as he landed. As they struggled he swung his hind end so that Haran and Orlanden next to him had to scramble away.

"Whoa, Daro, whoa," Witmara pleaded, both hands on Daro's lead as he whipped his head back and forth to loosen her grip. He tried to back away but she followed, holding him firmly so he would not escape.

Melarae bolted from Cenarth's side to join Chiral. Magic flared between them in bright magenta and red threads as she crashed into Chiral. Melarae turned away from her and bared her teeth defiantly, raising her hands above her head in mimicry of Chiral's pose. A lesser version of the magenta and red lights that Chiral summoned now glowed between Melarae's fingertips.

The colors of Karnoi and Cirdel.

Her mother Terani's patrons. Dread tightened Katerin's gut. Rekaré stopped halfway up the steps as the magic streams expanded between Chiral and Melarae. The Light of Medvara remained oddly quiet on her chest.

Daro lunged toward Chiral, dragging Witmara, fighting her restraint.

"Daro, whoa!" Witmara repeated.

But her weight was too light to stop the maddened colt. Heinmyets lunged for Daro's lead rope, to add his weight to Witmara's. A dark forest-green light flared as Heinmyets grabbed the lead rope. He yelled and fell.

Pride and fear both pulsed through Katerin as her daughter struggled to regain control of Daro, not giving up even as he pulled her closer and closer to Chiral and Melarae. Katerin tried to move, but something kept her rooted to the ground as a shade took shape in front of her. It coalesced into the form of her mother Terani, features thin and drawn, almost skeletal, her dark eyes smoldering with rage. Terani lifted a spear and aimed it at Witmara. Katerin recognized it as the Spear of War and Unmaking, legendary tool of the Twin Gods...*but wait, Staul has wielded it as well.*

The Banisher broke her freeze, taking over Katerin's muscles. Katerin joined with the Banisher's rage as they lunged forward and grabbed the spectral spear.

> Staul, Dovré, aid me!

Katerin pressed Staul's chip against the Spear. It became solid in her hands. Katerin channeled everything—her pride in Witmara, her dread, her fear, the exploding rage of the Banisher of Shadows—through the chip to the Spear. She wrestled with Terani's grip, trying to wrench the Spear away from her mother.

> Did you think you would evade your fate?
> Alame's daughter! I lost everything in Waykemin
> because of you! But it all comes right now.
> Through you the cursed Miteals will find their
> ending today, all praise to Karnoi and Cirdel!

> I defeated your gods in Keldara, and I will do so
> again!

> With the help of that priest of Staul who is now
> dead!

> I am the Banisher of Shadows.

Fool! You would pit yourself against the Twin Gods!

Staul the Destroyer manifested next to them.

With our help! Katerin is beloved of both me and Dovré.

Nitel appeared, Dovré beside her.

I am with them. Be wise, oh lackey of the Twins. Honor your daughter rather than challenge her.

Terani bristled at Nitel

What would you know of honor?

Nitel answered.

Do you enjoy your eternity as the tool of the Hunt?

Terani seemed to waver at that point. Katerin wrenched the Spear from her, and Terani disappeared.

You must use the Spear,

Dovré said.

You must stop Chiral.

How?

Katerin asked.

The part of her that was the Banisher reacted before Dovré could answer, thrusting the Spear between the waves of magic flowing between Melarae and Chiral as Witmara and Daro reached them.

Melarae screamed and fell as the streams faded.

Chiral in the guise of Ranar spun to face Katerin as Daro paused, looking confused.

Magic still swirled between Chiral's raised hands, dancing between her fingertips. She uttered a curse and threw a magenta ball at Katerin. She countered it with the Spear, popping the magic.

Why aren't Detaluna and Mirket stopping her? Or Senai and Yevtin?

All four of them appeared to be frozen. Senai was wild-eyed, while Yevtin visibly strained to move.

Etikar's curse. That's what she is chanting.

The same curse he had used to break Elithtra's power and spread the Great Plague worldwide.

Daro whirled and kicked at Chiral with both hinds, barely touching her. She staggered away, focusing her anger on Daro and Witmara. Katerin intercepted the next roiling ball of magic that Chiral hurled at them. The tip of the Spear deflected it. The ball landed on Melarae.

She screamed.

Rekaré shrieked and ran to Melarae. Daro whipped around and lunged at Chiral. Witmara let the rope slide through her hands as he struck at Chiral, catching her with one forefoot and sending her staggering back before she could form another sorcerous ball.

Touch Yevtin and Senai with the Spear,

Dovré's melodious voice whispered.

I am protecting Witmara and Daro,

Staul added, overtones of Metkyi coming through his speech.

> Free Yevtin and Senai. It will take all of you to overcome Chiral. Quickly! Before she activates the curse. I can stop it if you get them free.

Chiral called up another ball of magic, swirling malignantly with Karnoi and Cirdel's power.

It took every bit of Katerin's will to listen to the Gods and not give in to the Banisher's desire to quench the sorcery within the ball, to trust Staul's promise to protect Witmara and Daro.

She touched first Yevtin, then Senai with the Spear as Chiral hurled the ball toward Witmara.

Daro screamed and dodged between the ball and Witmara, rearing to strike at it. The ball stopped just before it touched his hooves, roiling a darker red and magenta as it stayed in place.

Staul appeared in the Destroyer's classic skeletal form, holding the ball.

> Beloveds of Dovré,

he said to Yevtin and Senai.

> You must seize her and hold her tight for the Banisher. You—

he turned to Katerin.

> Strike her hard with the Spear. It will not kill her; it will only banish those spirits riding her.

Yevtin and Senai grabbed Chiral's arms. Katerin struck her hard with the Spear. It plunged deep into Chiral, then disappeared from Katerin's hands as Chiral sagged to her knees, held upright only by Senai and Yevtin's grim grip. Her hair changed back from brunette to red, a darker red than before. Staul stalked over to Chiral and stood over her.

"Stand aside, beloveds of Dovré," he said out loud to Yevtin and Senai. "It is best that you not be touched by this."

"She will not flee?" Senai asked.

"She will not dare."

Chiral collapsed as Yevtin and Senai released her arms. Staul waited until they stepped back four paces.

"Neutralize the curse and put it back on the one who revived it," he said, continuing to speak so all could hear as he held the roiling spell ball high. "I do this in the name of the Seven Crowned Gods, with the blessing of Artel, Dovré, and Terat."

"No, no!" Chiral cried, scuttling away from him.

"Stay," Staul said in a deep, commanding tone that resonated through Katerin's bones.

"No," Chiral whimpered, freezing in place, holding her hands up to protect her face as Staul raised the ball high. He hurled it. The magic splattered over Chiral, turning her whole body into shades of magenta and red.

"Curses to you, Staul!" she screamed as red streams like blood poured from her face. "The ill will of the Twins follow you forever!"

"You have no power to curse me!" Staul pointed one long, bony finger at Chiral. "You have threatened my beloveds," he growled. "You have tried to wield Etikar's Curse without understanding what it means when you fail to execute it properly. You have given yourself over to Karnoi and Cirdel's empty promises without understanding what you have done. Do you realize what you've opened here?"

Chiral laughed at the God. "You *fool* Staul!" It wasn't her voice but that of another's, a sultry, seductive tone lower in pitch than Chiral's normal soprano.

Katerin shivered. She recognized Cirdel's voice from when her mother had channeled the Goddess during her childhood.

Chiral continued. "You've let yourself be blinded by the worship of your puny followers here in Varen. The future no longer belongs to the Seven. You will fade away and your influence will die as our strength grows. The Seven have been stagnant for too long. It is a new time, a new world."

"And you would replace the Seven with the Two, Cirdel? More fool you. When the Gods change, not a one of us remain the same. You and Karnoi think to remain unscathed? How do you know you will even remain? Again, I ask you, do you understand what doors you are opening here?"

Before Cirdel spoke through Chiral again, Daro lunged forward. His forefeet pounded on Chiral and she screamed, curling into a ball. Witmara wrenched him away before he could do more harm. He reared high, shaking his head to rid himself of Witmara's grasp. She was able to back him two steps before he yanked free from her.

"Enough," Staul said, his voice deepening as the skeletal form of the Destroyer shifted to the half-Destroyer, half-Balancer that Katerin had seen in his Nixyin shrine. "Young daranval, save your strength. Now is not your time to act." He caught Daro's lead, turning the colt to face him. "You are a brave and worthy companion for one of my beloveds. Save that power for when both of you have matured. Today is not the time for the two of you to become the Sacrifice." He held the lead out to Witmara. "You both have given great assistance here today, much beyond what either of you should have attempted at your age and strength. Both of you have great hearts and courage. I honor, salute, and bless both Witmara and Daro. Now. Step aside and let us deal with this. Had it not been for your swift reaction, things could be worse."

"And what of this vessel of our kin, *brother?*" Nitel asked contemptuously, waving one hand at Chiral. "Give me one reason why I should not devour her."

Katerin cleared her throat, preparing to speak but hesitating as Rekaré rose, Melarae lying limp in her arms. The Light of Medvara blazed brightly for a moment, then pulsed with a softer light at a heartbeat's rate. Lightning flashed overhead, thunder banging and rumbling loud and hard enough to shake Katerin's guts.

"For one thing, this is supposed to be a funeral, not a slaughter," Rekaré said. She glared at the Gods before her. "This ceremony was meant to honor my mother and her sacrifice to save my daughter and this—this ungrateful wretch!" She gestured with her chin at Chiral who lay curled on the ground, quivering. "If anyone has the right to claim vengeance, I do!" She glared at Chiral.

Heinmyets and Cenarth came forward to take Melarae from her arms.

Rekaré resisted them for a moment, then yielded Melarae to Cenarth. She faced Nitel, her face paling bone-white with rage.

"*You*," she hissed. "You brought this about, with your game-playing and your desire for vengeance. You would cause my mother's name to be a curse to the world just as her great-grandmother Elithtra was. How long did you conspire with Karnoi and Cirdel to bring this charade about? And now you dare to claim to stand with Staul and Dovré against this travesty, this attempt to revive Etikar's Curse! You *dare!* My mother's memory deserves better than this! It was through your lackey that my mother suffered. And now my daughter—" She gulped and drew a deep breath. "No. You do not deserve vengeance upon Chiral. You do not deserve to drink her life, Nitel. Chiral does not deserve such a peaceful ending. I will ensure that it is so."

Lightning blazed overhead followed by another body-shaking roll of thunder that nearly deafened Katerin. But she could still hear Nitel and Rekaré.

"And just who are you, Zauril's daughter, to defy me and break your Miteal Agreement with my beloved?" Nitel pushed close to Rekaré until only a hand's width separated them, but Rekaré did not flinch away.

"I am Zauril's daughter only by blood. Name me rather the daughter of Heinmyets, the Heartfather who raised me with my mother and Secondmother to make me what I am! I am the child of Alicira, Inharise, and Heinmyets, not Zauril. He is as nothing to me."

"And yet his blood flows in you. A part of you is still mine."

"Dovré named me Sorrow in the old Miteal tongue," Rekaré said. "And Sorrow I will be, to you and any other God who dares to interfere with my family, my people, and my land. Begone, Nitel. And take your co-conspirators Karnoi and Cirdel with you. I stand with Dovré and Staul, Artel and Terat. Go, and leave us to mourn my mother!"

"You will regret this choice," Nitel said. "I remind you of the curse I laid upon you at birth. I gifted you with the curiosity to seek the unusual paths and the red ways, the courage to look for the unconventional and the alternate way. It may seem to be a blessing at times, but make no mistake. I curse you."

"I do not shirk from that blessing," Rekaré answered. "It has given me the power to reclaim Medvara as my right. It allowed me to conquer my father. You do not frighten me, oh reddest of red Goddesses! I defy you, and will do so until my dying day!"

Lightning and thunder again, punctuating Rekaré's words.

The work of the Gods.

But which one? Staul? Artel? Dovré wouldn't resort to such flashy behavior. And none of the other Gods necessarily used lightning and thunder on a regular basis.

Nitel drew herself up and Katerin cringed as she sensed the power the Goddess drew to herself. Dovré and Staul moved to Nitel's side.

"I forbid you to touch Rekaré," Staul said.

Nitel laughed bitterly. "Brother, I ask you, do you know what protecting this one awakens? *You* who warned *my* beloved of the consequences of her actions? Are you aware of what protecting this one will do?"

"Rekaré will bring sorrow to all of us," Dovré said steadily. "So will it be. The world circles. The world changes. A new world is born from the ashes of the old."

More bitter, near-hysterical laughter punctuated by thunder and lightning spewed from Nitel. "And you will walk steadily to your doom? Sister, more fool you. I will speak my last words as a reminder to Rekaré, then depart. I remind her of the obligations she has sworn to this her cousin as a result of the Miteal Agreement."

"An Agreement that she has violated and I have a right to enforce!" Rekaré snapped back.

"Rekaré Kinslayer, do you thirst for more of your kin's blood?"

"She is no kin of mine."

Nitel grinned without humor, a wrathful smirk that sent fear pulsing through Katerin. "She is closer to you in blood than the one here you claim as cousin!"

"You lie." Rekaré paled.

"Do I? Chiral ea Ralsem is the daughter of your father's brother. Zauril en Ralsem and his brother Zauberin swore protective oaths that bind both of you, before Zauril left Daran on Etikar's quest to eliminate the last of the house of Miteal." Nitel's poisonous smile spread wider. "Rekaré Kinslayer, murderer of your father, will you kill your cousin as well, knowing that will make your name a curse even more thoroughly than the breaking of your Agreement would do?"

More lightning and thunder, as a chill wind briefly swept through from the west.

This one is from Nitel. But what God caused the other strokes of lightning? Nitel wouldn't emphasize what Rekaré says...would she? And Rekaré doesn't have the power to control storms...does she?

"Chiral has brought harm to those I love," Rekaré answered resolutely. "And for that she must pay."

"Rekaré Kinslayer, if Chiral dies by your hand as Leader of Medvara, then you bring down my curse upon Medvara because of the oaths *your father and your uncle* swore. Brother, sister, do I speak true?"

"She does," Dovré said, reluctance in her voice.

"She does," Staul growled.

"So, Rekaré Kinslayer. Shall I take my vengeance upon her for you? It will be an easy means for you to rid yourself of this trash."

"Begone, Nitel." Rekaré said stiffly. "Begone from this land." She drew a deep, shuddering breath and the Light of Medvara flared bright again, along with another flash of lightning.

Rekaré must be doing this. But how?

"In the name of the Seven, as the Leader of Medvara, I cast you out of this land," Rekaré intoned. "Your shrines are no longer welcome here. Your followers must choose other Gods or be cast out. As long as I rule in Medvara you have no place here. I speak as Leader of Medvara. Begone!"

"You will regret this."

"You will not take my vengeance. I regret nothing." She tossed her head defiantly. "Now. Begone and let us mourn."

"Your loss," Nitel said. "Do not forget who helped you with the hidden things! You have doomed yourself and Medvara already."

"Begone!" The Light glowed brightly along with another flash of lightning, then faded in a roll of thunder.

She's doing it through the Light of Medvara, Katerin realized, awed. *But she can't keep this up—is Nitel planning to drain Rekaré and then finish her? Is that what Rekaré really wants?*

She didn't think that Dovré or Staul would allow this to happen. Not here. Not now.

"As you wish," Nitel said mockingly. She bowed to Rekaré and was gone.

Rekaré drew a deep breath, staring down at Chiral, looking years older and fatigued. "Katerin."

"Yes."

"Can you cast a stronger binding spell on this—this person? I do not wish to bother with her until my mother has been consigned to the Gods. Nor do I want any further problems with her at this ceremony."

"I will strengthen her bracelets." Katerin looked at Senai and Yevtin. "Your help, please? Detaluna, Mirket, can you raise her?"

Detaluna and Mirket startled as if they had been asleep. Detaluna's face twisted in a shamed frown as she took one of Chiral's arms.

"Hold her arms forward so that I can touch her bracelets," Katerin said. "Senai, Yevtin, feed me strength?"

As Detaluna and Mirket complied with Katerin's order, Senai and Yevtin stood next to Katerin and placed their hands on her shoulders. Katerin closed her eyes, sensing the flow of their magic being ready and open for her use. Then she placed Staul's chip on the bracelets. Chiral groaned but did not pull away.

"Restrain all her magic," Katerin breathed. Power whispered down through her hands and into the bracelets. Chiral whimpered but did not go down.

It is done,

her Banisher side whispered.

But it will not last long. There is something twisted in this person, something that needs further work.

Katerin responded. She opened her eyes and dropped her hands from Chiral's bracelets, stepping back.

"Let us resume the ceremony," Rekaré said. "Back to your places."

Katerin nodded. As she returned to where she had been standing, those she passed bowed deep, as if she and not Rekaré were Leader of Medvara. They held those deep bows as Witmara followed Katerin. She reached her spot and turned to face the bier, only now seeing Rekaré's stricken expression. Rekaré gave Katerin a crisp nod before she climbed the stairs again. The Light of Medvara no longer shone brightly but looked like an ordinary pendant.

Now what does that mean?

Something had changed as a result of this confrontation. That knowledge dug even deeper into Katerin's innermost self as she half-listened to Rekaré's eulogy for Alicira.

She dreaded what these changes might be.

And she didn't think she had seen the last of Terani. Gods, when she had bid Terani farewell years ago in Waykemin, locked in the dreamless sleep, she had never thought to encounter her mother again.

She hadn't reckoned with the power of the Twin Gods.

Nor had she realized how much Terani had hated her.

My time as Leader of Medvara is coming to an end.

Even as Rekaré spoke her mother's eulogy, sorrow not just from the death of her mother but at the loss of something more tolled within her. Melarae's body had been so still, so cold in her arms, colder than the sharp gusts of wind that brought rain squalls. Would Melarae survive the backlash from Chiral's magic?

Would her relationship with the land survive this incident? She hadn't been the one to stop Chiral. That had been Katerin and Witmara's doing. She hadn't missed how those closest witnesses to the confrontation with Chiral had given honor to her cousins when it was done.

The land had not spoken to reject her leadership—yet. But how long would it be until it did? She was grateful for that last bit of energy from the Light of Medvara that had helped her push Nitel out. But now nothing stirred in the pendant. Was that meant to be a message?

Rekaré finished her speech, numb and detached, and climbed down the stairs. Cenarth waited at the bottom, Melarae in his arms, sadness twisting his features. Rekaré took their daughter into her arms, stricken at how limp and lifeless she seemed.

"I do not think she will survive long," Cenarth whispered as he helped her steady Melarae. "Not unless Katerin and her friends have some magic to overcome that sorcery."

"Katerin can save her," Rekaré said, her voice wavering and tentative. She kissed Melarae's forehead and held her tight.

Oh my daughter, my daughter. Am I to lose both my mother and my child this day?

Could even Katerin overcome that malign stroke from Chiral?

Melarae's breathing was too light, too shallow. Rekaré ignored the rest of the speakers as she focused her will upon her daughter, willing her to live, to breathe.

Melarae. Melarae.

She could reach her son by mindspeech, had always been able

to do so from his earliest days. Why couldn't she do the same with her daughter? She had never been able to touch Melarae in the same way as she had Linyet. Why? Deep inside she keened for the relationship that never had been between her daughter and herself. Even at birth something in her had held back.

Why didn't I fight harder for my relationship with her then? Why didn't I make myself love her as I should have?

Memories of Melarae resisting her touch, of Melarae calming with anyone but her mother as a small child raced through her thoughts as she stood there, clinging tight to her daughter's flaccid body.

Rekaré fought back tears. The land had come first. She had been busy consolidating her control over Medvara when her daughter was an infant. She had put off Melarae's care to others who seemed to have an easier time of it, eager to get away from the baby and back to ruling. Linyet had been a less fussy and easier child, adoring his mother from early on, not resistant like Melarae had been.

She had always thought there would be time to make it up. That someday she could spend the needed time with her daughter to create a better relationship.

And now that *someday* might never come.

Someone gently touched her arm and Rekaré looked into her Heartfather's eyes.

"You must say the last words and cast the cool fire," Heinmyets said softly. "Only you can do that as Leader of Medvara. Let me take my granddaughter."

Rekaré swallowed hard. She eased Melarae into his arms. Heinmyets shook his head sorrowfully, and held her tight. Rekaré's throat tightened as she remembered how he had held her half-brother Elenil in the same way as he died. Inharise moved next to him and helped him bear the slight weight, her eyes wet as she gazed at Melarae.

"Please take care of her for me, Heartfather, Secondmother," she breathed.

"I will do my best, Heartsdaughter," he said.

"We will care for her," Inharise added.

Rekaré said the final words of the ceremony in a daze, calling down Dovré's cool fire upon her mother's pyre. A flash of lightning zigzagged down to strike it along with Dovré's fire.

How long will it be until I have to do this for my daughter as well?

And Linyet—would he remain safe? Or would Karnoi and Cirdel find a means to strike him down as well?

No. He remains the heir to the Two Nations. We swore to that. Medvara is not his future.

As the blue and white flames consumed Alicira, it was but scant consolation that no noxious spirits arose from it to poison the world. Katerin stared unwaveringly at the fire whenever Rekaré glanced in her direction, her jaw set tight and firm as she held Rainin's reins. Her face was unreadable but Rekaré suspected her cousin was turning over the same things in her thoughts that she was.

Katerin is Regent-Designate. Either she or Witmara will eventually lead Medvara unless Melarae survives somehow.

That fate was one she knew her cousin dreaded. But a Miteal needed to lead Medvara and keep it and Varen safe against Chatain and the incursions of the Daran Empire.

I could take up one role that had been prophesied for me.

Katerin could hold Medvara while Rekaré raised an army to attack Daran and, with any luck, overthrow Chatain. She could be Empress.

But a deep revulsion wracked through Rekaré at the thought of ruling Daran. She had walked away from that choice years ago, had vowed to herself that she would never, ever take those steps.

> Then what? You were conceived to be my Empress.

The presence she recognized as the tiniest whisper of her blood father stirred within her.

> Begone!

she snarled at that faint whisper.

> If not that choice, then other, less-desirable options will fall to you.

> I am not your daughter. I utterly renounce you. Begone.

Cackling laughter, and the voice fell silent as the last flickers of the cool fire died down, faster than any non-magical fire. Rekaré mechanically went through the last rituals and the formal dismissal as a steady, pounding rain began, her arms aching for the weight of her daughter.

She would have to do something about Chiral.

Just not tonight.

AFTERMATH

ELARAE'S CONDITION REMAINED UNCHANGED OVERNIGHT.

Is it hopeful that she's no worse? Rekaré wondered as she checked on her daughter before Morning Audience.

Katerin and her friends from Keldara, along with the highest-ranked healers of the Medvaran Healing House sat watch in shifts. Rekaré wanted to stay with her daughter, but—duties. Medvara needed her more than ever. She had chosen to be Leader before being a mother, and now....

At least the air smelled fresh this morning, the damp and slight chill from last night's storm a welcome relief from the days and days of sweltering heat and smoke.

"We will watch over her," Katerin said as Rekaré stared at her daughter's still form.

"I'll try to drop back in when I can." Guilt tightened Rekaré's throat.

"I know." Katerin gave her a guilty smile of her own. "I need to spend time with Witmara and Daro, especially after yesterday. You aren't the only one split between family and obligations," she added. "And we need to talk about what happens next with Chiral."

"Yes. We do."

No more time to discuss that issue now, however, as the bells rang to announce the opening of morning audiences. Rekaré hurried to reach the Great Hall in time.

Chiral.

As Rekaré strode down the hallways to the Great Hall, her thoughts kept dancing around the options for that woman. Between audiences that were nothing more than formal farewells to funeral attendees now leaving to tend to their own harvests, she contemplated what to do about Chiral, staring at the Tapestry, her thoughts spinning, unable to think about much else.

Certain thoughts came to her in bits and pieces between the waves of visitors. Chiral could not stay in Medvara. That was the absolute minimum. If she stayed, there was no doubt that Karnoi and Cirdel would once again try to use Chiral to disrupt and destroy. Nitel's uncertain allegiance with Dovré and Staul during the funeral was also worrisome.

Whose side was that reddest of goddesses really on, besides her own? Did Nitel have a desire to reign as a solitary Goddess, without her six siblings?

I can't do anything about that.

Though the thought nagged at her, it wasn't within Rekaré's authority to thwart Nitel's goals.

Not now, at least.

And yet the notion of defeating Nitel kept niggling at Rekaré.

The party from Cooscol interrupted that train of thought, a welcome distraction. That farewell went like all the others, at least until Rekaré's appointed governor in Cooscol, Sestain, lingered after the others had left.

"I am concerned about the sorcerer who disrupted the funeral," he said bluntly, his pudgy pale face flushing red. "We had reports of one like her in Cooscol before the berry harvest.

But that one was brunette, not red-haired. My Chief of Guards had reason to believe she was a spy for Chatain."

"Chiral has been sworn to the Miteal Agreement, and her actions were in violation of that agreement. Have no worries. She will be exiled from Medvare-the-city at the very least." She studied Sestain thoughtfully. "What happened to the sorcerer in Cooscol?"

Sestain grimaced. "Chief Dornyet cornered her. She disappeared from an enclosed room. There were other guards present, not just Dornyet, so he wasn't making it up. No report of her since then." He wiped his sweating brow with a plain white kerchief.

"Did she have a name?"

"Not one that we could confirm," Sestain said. "My lady. I would encourage you to send this Chiral very far away. Or back to Chatain."

"Would that I could," Rekaré sighed. "But sending her back to Chatain is a violation of the Miteal Agreement. Nor would I want to send her back with whatever information she may have gathered here."

"Understood," Sestain said.

"I do hear your advice, and completely agree with it. She cannot stay here."

"Good. Please do not send her to us. We've invested too much time recovering the Coos berry bushes to entertain any who will threaten our hard work."

"I will not send her to any other location within Medvara," Rekaré promised.

"Thank you."

Sestain left, leaving Rekaré to contemplate this latest piece of data. Could Sestain's sorcerer have been Ranar?

It doesn't matter now. Chiral needs to go, and if her troublesome sister actually exists, perhaps she will follow Chiral.

And only now did Rekaré remember that Ranar was not the

only one to worry about. The priest. Could he have made it to Cooscol somehow? And from there, to Medvare, to support Chiral?

She contemplated calling Sestain back to ask if there had been reports of a nameless, bald-pated priest along with this sorcerer, then decided against it. Detail-oriented Sestain would have mentioned that fact. Rather than make him search for someone who might not be in Cooscol, much less actually exist any more, perhaps she should ask Vered to check into Sestain's report.

Sestain's news did increase the urgency of *doing something* about Chiral. But what? Nitel couldn't have lied about that relationship between Rekaré and Chiral, not with Staul and Dovré present.

More closely related to me than I had thought. I didn't realize.

And that created more problems. She came close to courting the Gods' disapproval by killing her father eleven years ago. They frowned on kin murder, and it was only justified by being vengeance for the deaths of her grandparents and great-grandparents. If she killed Chiral, she risked condemnation from the Gods. At least as long as Melarae lived—Rekaré shied away from that thought.

I'd sooner let Chiral live than wish for Melarae's death.

Then Cantiste brought in more visitors to leave mourning gifts, and express concern in cautious terms that didn't hide their worry about what Rekaré's next actions would be. Medvara was the shield against Daran for many small exile communities not as successful as the Miteal had been. If the Gods turned against Rekaré because she pursued vengeance against a relative as close to Chiral, that left the exiles she protected open to Chatain's wrath.

It took every ounce of effort she had to reassure these visitors.

Alone again. Rekaré's thoughts returned to her dilemma.

Chiral was her cousin. Blood kin.

Murderous blood kin, treacherous and not to be trusted. Blood kin nonetheless. She had broken the Agreement, so Rekaré was well within her rights to exile her, instead of killing her.

But where? Who could she trust with an exiled Chiral? Not Waykemin for certain. That would be handing the Witches a poisoned dagger that they wouldn't hesitate to use against Rekaré. Not Larij. She couldn't foist Chiral on the Mershaunten, even if he were willing to take her on. She owed —her family owed—too much to Haran and Orlanden's help over the years to repay them with the custody of a poisonous serpent like Chiral.

Handing her to the Saubral might be an option, given Staul's opposition to Chiral's aims. The Saubral might do what Rekaré dared not and kill Chiral.

Or not.

She is ambitious, and the Saubral might well decide to follow her.

So the day went by, until dinner. By then most of those who would want a personal audience before leaving had gone.

After a dinner she barely touched, Rekaré begged off further audiences so that she could sit by Melarae's bed.

For once she was alone. Cenarth had spent his own sad vigil earlier while Rekaré held court. He and Katerin were putting Linyet and Witmara to bed, Witmara taking Melarae's place in the nursery for the moment to console her cousin. The Healers were taking a short break to confer about what further treatments they could use to help Melarae. It was a rare private moment with her daughter, all the more painful because Rekaré could now see the strong resemblance to her mother in her daughter's features.

She held Melarae's hands in hers, blinking back tears as she stared at this daughter she had never really understood.

> Please don't die. Goddess, please don't let my daughter die for my own stupidity. My ambition. Goddess, please.

But even as she thought the prayer she could hear Dovré's response.

> I named you Sorrow in the old language. I am sorry, dear one. But as she who will bring Sorrow, you must also understand it.

"No," Rekaré groaned out loud. "Goddess, no."

No sooner had she finished speaking than the door opened.

"Is she worse?" Inharise asked, slipping inside quietly.

"No better and no worse," Rekaré sighed. "And I keep praying...." Her voice trailed away and she shook her head.

Inharise came over next to Rekaré and rested her hand on Rekaré's shoulders. "It takes time. Especially after a magical attack."

"Dovré says that as she who will bring sorrow, I must also understand it," Rekaré's voice caught on the last words. "Oh Secondmother, I have done so many things wrong as a mother."

"All of us have as parents." Inharise pulled a stool next to Rekaré. She stroked Melarae's forehead with one hand and eased one of Melarae's hands out of Rekaré's with the other, frowning as her granddaughter lay still, not responding to the different touch.

"I have never felt connected to my daughter. I always was grateful to be away from her, rebuilding Medvara and making it strong again."

"You had a job to do that no one else could," Inharise said. "Your mother could not rebuild Medvara, not with the vows she had taken. Katerin was not called to rebuild Medvara but to support your mother. Fixing Medvara was your task, Heartsdaughter. You did what you could."

"But was it right to focus on Medvara and not on my child?"

"You are Leader and parent. Sometimes choices have to be made." Inharise sighed. "Heinmyets will be here shortly. He is speaking to Cenarth and saying good night to the children. We have talked about what we can do to help you. Chiral should come to Keldara with us."

"I can't ask you to take on that burden."

"Karnoi and Cirdel remain banished from Keldara," Inharise pointed out. "They will not be able to work through her."

"But Mother was an influence in Keldara, and Katerin did the banishing of Karnoi and Cirdel," Rekaré said.

"The current leadership in Keldara is not of the Miteal," Inharise said firmly. "Chiral is not related to either of us, nor to Katerin or Witmara. We do not have your ties."

"Chiral will have problems with the sternwheeler. While she doesn't travel well on water, I would be worried about the impact on your magic and your ability to control her as well."

"We have no intention of returning by boat," Inharise said. "The Keldaran Healing House has a separate lodge for people with afflictions like Chiral appears to have with her memory, long-term conditions that may never resolve. Places that would keep her safe. That would get her out of Medvara."

"I will be eternally grateful if you would take this challenge off my hands," Rekaré said. "Especially given what may happen with my daughter." She sighed.

Another knock, then Heinmyets entered.

"You have spoken to her?" he asked Inharise.

"Heartfather, I am grateful for your offer. No. More than grateful. Overwhelmed. But that may put the Two Nations into a difficult position," Rekaré said. "It's too much to ask."

"Too much?" Heinmyets shook his head as he stood at the foot of Melarae's bed, staring at his granddaughter's still form. "Say rather that we have not done enough. It is time for the Two Nations to come forward and contribute to the protection of

Varen. We should have been doing more during the past eleven years."

"Cenarth and I needed to establish Medvara as a power capable of protecting Varen ourselves without your assistance," Rekaré said. "Otherwise we would be seen as nothing more than a subordinate state to the Two Nations, and I would have been viewed as merely a surrogate for my mother, not Leader in my own right."

"True," Heinmyets said. "But that is not a concern any more, with your mother's passing. Currently we need to look to the future of Varen—Medvara, Larij, Keratil, Keldara, Clenda, even Saubral and Waykemin. Chiral is a threat to all of Varen, not just Medvara. You need to get Chiral out of Medvara—even without being tied to the land, I feel how she roils the land's magic."

"She is my cousin," Rekaré said. "More closely related than I thought."

Heinmyets nodded. "And her connection to your father tests your own ties to the land."

"Yes," Rekaré reluctantly admitted.

"Then, as much as we would prefer to stay and spend time with you, with Cenarth, with our grandchildren—I think it is time that the Two Nations take custody of Chiral, and remove her to Keldara quickly. Perhaps if we get her away from Medvara, then Melarae will do better."

"One can only hope," Rekaré said. "And perhaps the failure of Chiral's schemes may lead to her own demise. From what Katerin has said, Chiral is not in the best of health. Maybe the power she drew upon to launch this attack at Mother's funeral has led to further disintegration."

Katerin entered without knocking as Rekaré finished speaking.

"Further disintegration is too much to hope for," Katerin said. "If anything, Chiral's closer to forming an integrated personality than she was before. I wish I knew more about her interactions with Ranar and that priest!"

"I have worrisome news from Cooscol on that front," Rekaré said. "Sestain of Cooscol told me that a mysterious sorcerer recently appeared there, a brunette who looked like Chiral. His guard chief Dornyet cornered her, and she disappeared from an enclosed room. There were other witnesses."

"Ranar?" Katerin asked.

"Sestain had no name for the sorcerer. He also made no mention of the priest."

"I don't like the sound of that." Katerin frowned down at Melarae and moved to her side, checking her pulses and resting the back of her hand across her. "At least Melarae has not gotten worse," she murmured. "But she is not getting better, either." Her lips tightened. "I wish I had realized the degree to which their magic had become entangled. I am sorry, Rekaré. I should have recognized what was going on sooner."

"We depended on my mother to warn us about Chiral," Rekaré said. "Why she didn't identify that Chiral was getting stronger, I don't know."

"Perhaps an interaction between Melarae and Chiral? Melarae was displaying stronger magic. We need to separate them—but I'm afraid of what that separation will do to Melarae."

"I want Chiral gone from Medvara. I can't forgive what she's done, and given what Nitel revealed about our kinship—Chiral has reason to eliminate me and my children," Rekaré said. "For Melarae's sake, the sooner the better."

"We will take Chiral to Keldara," Heinmyets said to Katerin. "Perhaps that will help Melarae."

Katerin glanced quickly at Rekaré. "Remove Chiral from Medvara?"

"Heinmyets and Inharise have offered to take custody of Chiral."

"The Pleasant House in Keldara?" Katerin asked.

"Yes."

"So the Pleasant House," Katerin said thoughtfully. "She would be under Senai's direct supervision." She tapped her fingers on her chin. "That would work. Karnoi and Cirdel have no foundation in Keldara."

"Thanks to you," Rekaré said.

Katerin shrugged. "Moving Chiral out of Medvara would mean she could not draw on the link she made with Melarae."

"The link?" Rekaré asked.

"Apparently Chiral used Melarae as a focal point to connect with Medvara's magic," Katerin said. "We had to seal it off today, but I'm afraid to sever it completely. For Melarae's sake. Chiral is too close to her physically and could cause Melarae harm. If Chiral is removed from Medvara, then I could finish separating them and not fear the consequences should Chiral react to their separation. Melarae will suffer some withdrawal, but given the condition she is in now—well, it's worth a try."

"How could Chiral have done this and none of us recognize what she was doing?" Rekaré sighed.

"The Twin Gods were working through Chiral," Katerin said harshly. "The Twins with some sort of hidden tie to Nitel. We spent most of our time focusing on Chiral's link to Nitel and not enough looking at other linkages. I spent much time at Staul's shrine last night, and then at Dovré's this morning." She exhaled a long, shuddering breath. "Artel has not yet pronounced it, but—Staul and Dovré consider themselves to be at war with Karnoi, Cirdel, and Nitel. Chiral's attack was the first strike in a war between the Gods, as far as those two are concerned. The limitations I've had in speaking with Staul and Metkyi have been lifted in anticipation of future conflict."

War amongst the Gods. The words struck Rekaré hard.

What are we to do?

No wonder the Tapestry had remained silent all day.

Uncertain possibilities, and Chiral is too close to me by blood for the Tapestry to speak on this subject. Damn you, Karnoi and Cirdel. Damn you.

She bit her lip to keep angry words from escaping. Now was not the time. She could not give into emotion, not yet.

"What happens next?" she asked, forcing a calmness she didn't feel into her voice.

Katerin shrugged. "I have no idea. Mind you, this declaration of war is not definite. Dovré said this morning that she and Staul are still pleading their case to Artel the Judge. He may yet rule that this is an issue of the Two Nations and of Medvara and not a matter of the Gods—but I do not think so. Not with Chiral's ties to Chatain and Zauril. Not if it turns out that Chatain cultivated and prepared Chiral to be a weapon to destroy Alicira's good name throughout the ages, just as his grandfather Etikar did to his great-grandmother Elithtra."

"To *our* ancestress Elithtra," Rekaré reminded her. "Your great-grandmother, my great-great-grandmother. My mother's great-grandmother. And with Chiral being my cousin through my Ralsem ancestry—that makes things even more complicated."

"A further argument for Chiral to go to Keldara," Inharise said. She rose. "If you have no disagreement, then we will prepare to leave tomorrow morning. The earlier the better, to evade as many observers as possible."

"I ask that Yevtin stay here to help with Melarae," Katerin said. "Senai should ride with you, so that she can help restrain Chiral."

"That can be done," Inharise said. She kissed Melarae's forehead, then turned to Rekaré and hugged her. "Stay strong, Heartsdaughter. These are challenging times."

"Stay safe—and thank you," Rekaré said in return.

Heinmyets sighed at Melarae's still form. He also kissed her forehead, then hugged Rekaré. "Our thoughts are with you, Heartsdaughter."

She burrowed her head into his chest for a moment longer, savoring her Heartfather's spicy musk, muted by smoke and the scent of leather and horses.

"I wish you could stay longer," she whispered.

"When all this is settled," he said. "Perhaps this winter."

"I hope so."

He released her and followed Inharise out the door.

"You'll be all right with Melarae for a little bit longer?" Katerin asked, lingering. "I need to talk to Yevtin and Senai."

"Go ahead."

Katerin left. Rekaré sighed and sat back down with her daughter.

Gods, what a mess.

DEPARTURES

ONLY A FEW RAYS OF EARLY MORNING SUN STRUCK THE STABLE yard as Katerin rechecked the sorcery within Chiral's bracelets. Detaluna and Mirket had needed to prod her out of the Leader's House. Any remorse that Chiral had exhibited earlier had transformed into surly objections to leaving this soon for Keldara, especially by horseback.

No sign of any diminishment of the original spells on the bracelets, no matter how deeply Katerin probed. How had Chiral managed to evade their restraints at the funeral?

Divine help, or resources from the Hunt or that damned priest?

The rest of the guard riding with Heinmyets and Inharise moved around the stable yard, checking pack mules and horses, gathering in small groups to say farewells to those left behind. Rekaré had assigned one of Medvara's guard units to augment the riders Heinmyets and Inharise had brought with them. That way they would have a sizable party while riding across the difficult Saubral lands. Cenarth lingered with his parents, while Rekaré remained with Melarae, having said her goodbyes inside.

Katerin poked at the bracelets one last time. Her spells remained present, at full strength.

How did she do it?

By all signs, Chiral should not have been able to attempt her curse. She must have had some sort of assistance—the Twin Gods, or the priest? Or had it been Chiral's link with Melarae?

"Be careful with this one," she said softly to Senai as Chiral mounted her bay mare, with Mirket's help. "I still don't know how she called up magic at the funeral."

"The bracelets should have been enough to stop it," Senai said. "I will be vigilant."

"Thank you. Ride carefully, and let me know when you are safe in Keldara."

"I have the speaking square you gave me last night. Now that we have this connection, I plan to use it."

"See that you will—every night while you're traveling, around dusk. I'll be watching."

Senai rolled her eyes. "Katerin, nothing's going to go wrong!"

"Indulge me," she said. "I will feel better when I know all of you are safely in Keldara and Chiral is at the Pleasant House."

"I will do my best to contact you every night around dusk, then."

"Thank you." Katerin rested her hand on the neck of Senai's daranval as she mounted. "Ride safely, my friend."

She stepped back, joining Cenarth as Heinmyets and Inharise swung onto the backs of their daranvelii. Elantai trumpeted a challenging neigh and half-reared as Heinmyets spun him toward the gates of Medvare. Heinmyets laughed.

"Old daranval still is eager for travel," he said, saluting Cenarth and Katerin. They stood together at the gates and watched the troop ride off toward the river trail, Elantai prancing in the lead. Senai took up a position riding next to Chiral, along with Detaluna and Mirket.

Katerin sighed as Senai waved to her. On the one hand, she wished she were riding with them. On the other, she didn't want to leave Melarae's side.

The troop disappeared into the trees bordering the river trail. Katerin turned to walk back toward the Leader's House, already beginning to sweat from the early morning heat. Suddenly she stopped in the street, foreboding pulsing through her.

I will not see Senai alive again.

No. No.

She wanted to ride after Senai to warn her to be careful, not risk anything in order to keep Chiral under control.

Your life is more precious than that, my friend.

Her fingers itched to grab the speaking square and warn Senai.

The foreboding passed. Was it real, or just an expression of her fear? Riding across the northern edge of the Saubral lands had gotten safer as Rekaré solidified her control of Medvara, drawing up treaties with the Saubral so that land travelers could follow the Chellana without harassment. The Saubral wanted the opportunities that expanded trade and the new stern-wheeler ports gave them. Random raids on travelers through their lands were much less rewarding as a result of those treaties.

And yet—the Saubral were still raiders at heart. A Shadowwalker might be tempted by Chiral as a prize. But would they risk attacking the leaders of the Two Nations, even for one such as Chiral?

She didn't think so.

Katerin heaved another sigh. Cenarth frowned at her.

"Something wrong?"

"Just a foreboding that I won't see Senai alive again," Katerin said. "But it didn't come with any of the signs of the Goddess, so perhaps it is just an idle fear. After all, she is riding with your parents. Who would attack them?"

"Not many," Cenarth conceded. "But my heart has been heavy as well. They will be safe, Katerin."

"I hope so," Katerin said. As Cenarth turned away from Katerin, she hurried to Melarae's room. If Melarae were to have any reaction to Chiral's leaving, it would be during the day.

THE NEXT MORNING, KATERIN WENT TO THE STABLE TO WORK with Witmara and Daro. The colt had taken no harm from the incident at Alicira's funeral. If anything, the colt focused more strongly on Witmara. She didn't need the lead rope to direct him around the pen, and he followed Witmara precisely, stopping when she stopped, turning away from her when she signed him to do so, going away and coming back.

"A good connection between those two," Cenarth commented as he leaned against the outside of the corral fence, watching as Witmara directed Daro over a series of ground poles and around several posts without using a lead. He raised his voice. "Good idea to give him a mental break, Witmara. He's just a baby. Keep it short."

She nodded and stopped Daro after he stepped through a sequence of poles laid out in a zigzag pattern. She rested her hand on his neck, scratching along his crest. Daro wiggled his upper lip, making appreciative itchy horse faces.

"Katerin!" Neinyet's voice carried an urgent note as she ran up to the corral. "Cenarth! Rekaré wants you back at Melarae's bedside. She thinks Melarae is waking."

Cenarth hesitated. "We shouldn't leave these two unsupervised—"

"Go!" Katerin shooed him away. "I'll be right there, once we turn Daro out."

"Are you sure—"

"You're her father. Go!"

Cenarth needed no further encouragement. Katerin joined Witmara and Daro. "We need to put him up now. Do you want to see Melarae?"

Witmara bit her lip. "I—I don't know, Mother. I'm a little afraid of her after what happened."

"Well, Daro's had enough work now. Let's turn him loose, and then perhaps you could do some reading? It's going to be too hot to do much soon, anyway."

Once Daro was released, Katerin hurried to Melarae's room. Onadral stood next to Yevtin, holding a pan filled with a fragrant, steaming tincture. He palpitated Melarae's throat glands, frowning to himself, dipping a cloth in the pan and dabbing at her forehead and throat with it, then checking the glands again. Rekaré sat on her other side, holding her hand, while Cenarth stood behind Rekaré, lips tight as they both watched. Melarae's eyes were open, though dull and unfocused.

Katerin recognized the scent of Yevtin's tincture—sage, cirelen flowers, and juniper. Her stomach tightened at that identification.

Treatment for the magic plague, with a touch of protection-against-possession.

She eased in next to Yevtin. "How bad is it?"

"She has the fever," Yevtin said. "I'm reluctant to administer *protection-against-possession* orally because she's not quite right. Something else is wrong. I'm afraid giving it to her by mouth would be too strong."

Katerin took Melarae's other hand, checking the pulses in her wrist. Thin. Weak.

"Perhaps we should give her a quarter dose so that we can track possible possession."

"I don't think she can even handle a quarter dose." Yevtin sighed. "All we can do is keep it from getting worse. This is one of the most difficult cases I've seen, Katerin. Check her throat pulses." He stepped aside.

Katerin took his place. She felt Melarae's forehead, wincing at how warm the girl was. Then she checked her throat pulses. Even more than the wrist, they were weak and thin.

Yevtin was right.

"At least she has wakened," she said, straightening up and stepping back so that Yevtin could continue wiping Melarae down with the tincture. "I may have an oral tincture that will help."

Melarae whimpered, squirming a little. "Mama?"

"I'm here," Rekaré said softly.

"Hot. So hot."

"I know, sweetheart. Yevtin and Katerin are here to help you."

"Make them go away."

"Yevtin and Katerin?" Rekaré asked. "But they're helping you."

"Not them." Melarae gestured wildly at the room around her. "Red shadows. Red shadows everywhere!"

Worry creased Rekaré's brow. "Honey, I don't see any shadows."

"Red shadows everywhere!" Melarae insisted.

"Katerin?" Rekaré's voice broke and she gulped, swallowing hard.

"It is to be expected," Yevtin interjected before Katerin could speak. "Rekaré, I've seen this before. It is a normal side effect of the fever. If she were stronger, then we could give her *protection-against-possession* by mouth. But in her current condition she can't handle even a quarter dose. This is why I'm wiping her down with it. The benefit is not as great but it is better than nothing."

"I'll make a fever potion," Katerin said.

She left Melarae's room for her own quarters, pulling

together a mild willow bark potion. Melarae was still awake and fretting when she returned, and Katerin delicately spooned the mixture into her. A short time later, Melarae sighed.

"Sleepy," she mumbled.

"The potion will do that," Katerin said, stroking Melarae's brow. Was it her imagination or did Melarae feel cooler? "Are you still seeing the red shadows?"

"No," Melarae muttered.

"Good. If you see them again when you wake, tell whoever is here that you need more fever potion." Katerin put the bottle on the side table.

Melarae fell asleep.

THE TREATMENT SEQUENCE REMAINED THE SAME THROUGH THE next few days. Melarae would wake with a higher fever, complaining of seeing the red shadows. After being wiped down with Yevtin's tincture and given a dose of the fever potion, the shadows would go away. Katerin never could spot the shadows herself, despite attempting a link with Melarae.

"She's just not getting better," Yevtin fretted to Katerin after the fourth day, when just the two of them were with a sleeping Melarae. "We should see some change in her by now, either improving or fading. Especially after you severed that connection with Chiral."

Katerin nodded. She had severed the connection two days ago. To her surprise, that spell working had been uneventful, with no reaction. But she still wasn't happy with the results.

"This isn't typical," she said in a low voice. "I'd almost risk *protection-against-possession* by mouth—but she just hasn't gotten any stronger. She should have by now."

"That's what worries me."

"Oh well, perhaps things will change when Chiral is safely in Keldara at the Pleasant House."

"How many more days?" Yevtin asked.

"Last night Senai said they'd spotted the Lone Peak. They're not riding very fast." Katerin grimaced. "Large party, and the Leaders are stopping to negotiate with Saubral villages. From what Senai says, Chiral hasn't been doing very well so that's also slowing things down."

"Hmm. Any idea what's going on?"

Katerin shrugged. "The connection between our speaking squares isn't very strong in Saubral country. It'll get better once they're in Keldara." But uneasiness rested hard on her heart, belying her confident words.

Melarae suddenly screamed, her eyes popping open, body convulsing. Yevtin and Katerin jumped up as Melarae jerked and twitched, yelling incoherently.

"Get the *protection-against-possession!*" Katerin screamed at Yevtin. "Full dose!"

"She can't sustain it—" Despite his objection, Yevtin hurried to the side table and grabbed the bottle. "But by the Gods, you're right, we don't have a choice."

Melarae stopped twitching as he poured the dose. She fell back on her pillows, eyes wide and staring, froth bubbling on her lips.

It's already too late. Fear tightened Katerin's chest. *Too late.*

"Free," Melarae whispered. "Gods. I'm free!" She shrieked and sat up again, her body shaking as she reached for something Katerin couldn't see. Her voice keened as she continued. "But they separated us! How can I be fully free with the bond broken? How can I be the God's agent now?" Her last words came out as a sob. "Chiral, Chiral, I've failed you!"

"*Dose her now,*" Katerin ordered, a chill spreading from her gut throughout her whole body.

Yevtin deftly spooned the dose of *protection-against-possession* into Melarae's mouth. Some of it dribbled out of a corner as Melarae's lips went slack. Katerin tried to close Melarae's jaw, to stroke her throat to encourage her to swallow. But her chin stubbornly locked into place, and she kept moaning, not swallowing. Her wail rose louder and louder, ending with a piercing shriek.

Then Melarae fell backwards in the bed again, eyes wide, staring, and unresponsive. She wasn't breathing.

"Oh *Gods*," Katerin groaned. She felt Senai's speaking square vibrate in her pouch, but she couldn't take the time to reach for it. Instead she bent over Melarae, trying and failing to get her to breathe again. "Get Rekaré! Cenarth!" she shouted to whoever could hear her or respond. "Yevtin, send someone for them. Oh Gods, oh Gods, oh Gods." She sank to her knees by Melarae's bed, burying her face in the light sheet.

> Goddess, please. Staul. Metkyi.

His touch was suddenly on her shoulder.

> You cannot change this. Others have need of
> you, and she is gone. What you would bring
> back is not Melarae but something worse.

She became aware of the incessant pulsing of Senai's speaking square and pulled it out.

> Fear, danger, death,

radiated from the fabric even before Katerin spoke the words to activate the speaking spell. Jumbled images of fighting came to her.

Heinmyets on old Elantai striking at a swarm of Saubral Shadowwalkers…Inharise going down under another swarm…Detaluna captured by Saubral secondaries…Chiral carried away by a bald-pated priest, resisting until he bent to whisper something in her ear…everything going black…

"No," Katerin whispered.

"Gods. *No*," She squeezed the speaking square tightly in her hand, shaking.

"*NO!*" she screeched. She fumbled in her pouch for Staul's chip and raised it high.

Answer me, Gods! What has happened?

As she stared at the chip, the world shimmered around her, and she was *there*, watching the Saubral ride away, Chiral mounted on a snorting chestnut mare next to the bald-pated priest, laughing as the Saubral struck at the remainder of her escort before galloping off. Detaluna slumped over a packhorse, bound hand and foot, body limp. Senai's body sprawled over a bloody patch of ground. Heinmyets knelt next to Inharise, pressing firmly on a bloody bandage, Elantai nowhere to be seen.

"Katerin! Katerin!" Rekaré's shaken voice brought Katerin back from the vision. She realized she was sitting on the floor next to Melarae's bed, Yevtin and Cenarth standing next to Rekaré who knelt in front of her. "What else has happened? We've been trying to call you back from the vision—what have you seen? At least one bell has rung since you fell into the trance."

"They've been attacked," Katerin blurted. "Saubral ambushed them and took Chiral. The priest has her and Detaluna. I think she's going with him willingly. Senai's dead, Inharise is hurt bad."

Rekaré flinched. "Are you certain?"

Katerin wordlessly handed Rekaré the speaking square. Rekaré held it for a moment, then groaned, dropping the square and burying her head in her hands.

"It's true," she said, raising her head. "And it is no coincidence that Melarae died at the same time as the attack started." Her voice hardened. "Chiral did this to Melarae."

"We don't know that for certain," Yevtin said. But his voice was uncertain.

"Katerin can confirm it," Rekaré said. "The Banisher of Shadows knows how to do it."

Katerin shuddered. She couldn't shake away those images, those long moments reliving that attack. Part of her shied away from probing Melarae's fading memories, not wanting to violate the last bit of the dead child's deepest self.

But we need to know.

Necessity knew no gentle way around what she had to do. Katerin sighed. She stiffly staggered to her feet, surprised at how drained she was.

Rainin, aid me.

She sent an image of Melarae to her daranval, followed by Chiral and a visualization of the link between Chiral and Melarae that they had severed only two days ago. If only her old daranval Mira still lived—then she would have had the strength perhaps to stop Melarae's death from happening, might have given the Gods a battle. Rainin, devoted as she was, lacked Mira's command of daranval magic.

All her magic potential went to producing Daro. Mira never foaled, never passed on her magic. Rainin produced Daro—but for what?

Then Rainin's mind brushed against hers; soothing, calming, pulling Katerin away from further speculation. Katerin wrapped herself in the homely, comforting steadiness of her current daranval.

It was enough. Perhaps not strength but what Rainin granted Katerin was the steadiness and predictability of everyday life, of the guarantee that no matter what happened, ordinary, average people still went about their business, even in the face of war.

She could do this.

Holding Staul's chip in her right palm, Katerin took Melarae's hand, pressing the chip hard against it.

Staul, aid me. Metkyi, guide me.

This working was not something she expected Dovré to help with.

The Banisher stirred. For once Katerin welcomed that aspect of herself, retreating into its hard essence. The Banisher elbowed her way into Melarae's fading thoughts roughly, tearing through them with little subtlety or concern for damage or pain. The part of her that was Katerin Healer winced at that, while the part of her that was Katerin ea Miteal grimly held on, examining each shard of recent thought.

There wasn't much in Melarae's memories past the attack at Alicira's funeral. Only a set of focused thoughts.

Vengeance. Freedom. Fulfill your objective. They will pay for what they have done!

The thoughts were not those of a little girl. They carried the flow and pattern of Chiral's mindstreams as they had been after she had been cuffed.

Vengeance, freedom, fulfill your objective

circled around in a dull drone that shut out anything else

until suddenly, sharply, they halted, as if a candle flame had been snuffed.

That was when Melarae died.

Metkyi had been right. They had been trying to keep a shell alive, one possessed by Chiral.

Katerin Healer would not have probed further after this revelation. Katerin the Banisher dug deeper, tracing those last few circles of thought. What little remained of Melarae shrieked in fear and terror as the Banisher examined those last memories.

Under the focused thoughts lay terror. A tiny independent trace of Melarae reacted in horror and pain, not comprehending exactly what it was that Chiral had tried to do in partnership with her but knowing it was wrong. Fear of condemnation once she reached the Other Side resonated through that aspect, reinforced by the angry, vicious thoughts Chiral had sent to Melarae just before her death.

Oh, Melarae.

Katerin Healer shuddered to think of the agony the little girl must have existed in during the last days of her life.

Gods. Goddesses. Have mercy on her spirit.

Do not fear,

Staul the Balancer answered. *I*

t was not by her choice. We know and understand. She is at peace now. I have her safe. But you need to dig deeper.

Katerin the Banisher hardened her resolve. She looked past the shards of tiny, terrified Melarae's mindstreams, pushing them aside with a casual flick of her fingers.

Shrill laughter met her next. Terani's shade arose yet again, skeletal and threatening. Thankfully she did not brandish the Spear again.

Begone, shadow!

The Banisher commanded.

Return to your master and mistress!

Terani smirked at Katerin, then faded.

You can command the Spear to sort through those thoughts and eliminate these distractions,

Staul as Destroyer commented.

The Banisher snapped her fingers and the Spear appeared in Katerin's hand, much shorter than it had been before, with only a hand's width of shaft to support the long, slender head, making it almost like a sword. She sorted through the remaining thoughts, pursuing a faint tendril that bore Chiral's touch. She dug deeper and deeper, until she could finally grasp the remaining link between Chiral and Melarae, something she hadn't known was there.

Bright red flashed across Katerin's mind's eye, and she flinched back at the wave of malign anger from Chiral. The Banisher in her raised the spearhead and stabbed at that rage, shattering it into tiny red splinters that were absorbed into the spearhead. It vanished, leaving Katerin deep in the bleak emptiness of the shadow world.

How do I get out of here?

Metkyi's familiar hand rested on her shoulder.

You must not linger.

Oh Metkyi, Metkyi. What happens next?

You must go back to the world of the living,
sweet one. You have probed almost too deeply
into the land of the condemned dead.

But Staul said Melarae was safe—

She is not here. The one you followed is
between the worlds. Best you return before this
place gathers you into its maw as well.

He took Katerin into his arms. She clung to him, burying her head in his chest as they passed clusters of the malign dead. But she heard voices, some of which meant her no good.

At last Metkyi set her down.

Return to yourself, beloved. I can take you no
further.

His lips brushed her forehead. Then he gave her a shove toward a clear white light. Katerin followed it until she came back to herself, gasping and shivering, cold despite the heat.

"Well?" Rekaré demanded, her face set and hard. Katerin shuddered as she looked at her cousin, for the first time seeing Zauril's influence in her features rather than Alicira's.

Gods. She didn't want to say this.

But Melarae was dead. Inharise might be, though Katerin thought she might have felt that loss even as distant as they were. Senai was dead.

And Chiral had brought it about.

Katerin took a deep breath.

"Chiral is responsible for Melarae's death," she said. "Melarae died in fear and torment. She is safe now."

Rage swept across Rekaré's face and she shrieked in anger and sorrow.

"She will pay! I call for vengeance against Chiral ea Ralsem. She has broken the Miteal Agreement." Rekaré straightened. "Hear me now, oh Gods. I revoke my oath to the Miteal Agreement given to Chiral ea Ralsem. Not only has she caused my mother's death, but she caused the death of my daughter and of others I hold dear. She consorts with the reddest of red evil. She will pay. *She will pay, even if I must forsake my Leadership to do it!*"

Katerin shivered. She had seen Rekaré in this mood before, after Alame's death and again at Zauril's. Only then Nitel's visage had come over her. Now power seethed underneath Rekaré's suddenly paler than pale face, power greater than Katerin had seen stir in her previously and unconnected to any God. Rekaré seemed to grow larger, a red-gold light blazing forth from her that didn't come from the Light of Medvara, projecting a presence Katerin had only sensed from one of the Gods.

Our Lady of Sorrow. Our Lady of Vengeance.

Cenarth blanched. "Surely you do not mean—"

Rekaré turned on him. "She has killed my mother and my daughter. She has shown herself to be my eternal enemy. You heard she-who-I-banished call me Rekaré Kinslayer at my mother's funeral." She bared her teeth in a mirthless grin. "Let it be so. I will avenge my deaths, no matter the cost to myself."

Dread descended upon Katerin. She wanted to advise Rekaré against reckless action. But the Banisher stirred within her, wordlessly echoing and supporting her cousin's words even as the Light lay unresponsive on Rekaré's chest. Stiffly, she rose from Melarae's deathbed. Numbly she walked toward Rekaré, stopping to prostrate herself before her cousin, touching her forehead to the floor in a reverence deeper than she had ever offered anyone before now.

"The Banisher is yours to command, oh Lady of Sorrow," she said in the old High Aireii tongue without raising her head from the floor, the unfamiliar resonance of the language making her mouth and throat feel scratchy and achy.

"Rise, Banisher of Shadows," Rekaré answered in the same language. She glared around the room. Her next words shifted back to Varenese. "Katerin is with me in this. Who else will follow me to erase this threat from Varen and fulfill my vengeance?"

"I will," Yevtin said hoarsely. "I will ride to avenge Senai."

"I—cannot," Cenarth said. "We have a living child, Rekaré! And what of Medvara? Would you walk away from all we have built here?"

"The Gods have spoken," Rekaré said. She closed her eyes for a moment, seeming to grow smaller. The red-gold glow faded along with Katerin's sense of the greater presence that had filled Rekaré. She opened her eyes again. "I have little choice, dear one. Ask Katerin. If Chiral reaches Waykemin—"

"Chiral is allied with Karnoi and Cirdel," Katerin said. "If she joins the witches, then who knows what she is capable of doing?" She chose not to mention Terani's appearance.

I need to think more on what that means.

"I intend not to let that happen," Rekaré sighed.

"Then what of Medvara?" Cenarth asked. "What of my parents? Of Melarae?"

"For now, I would ask that you become Regent in Witmara's name, Cenarth." Rekaré turned to Katerin. "I must have you ride with me, to aid my Secondmother and—" her voice caught. "I will have need of the Banisher of Shadows. Afterwards, we shall see what becomes of us."

"And Melarae?" Cenarth's voice cracked.

Rekaré faced him. "A family ceremony, tonight, while others prepare to ride." Her lips tightened. "I will speak to Vered.

Perhaps the *Morning Star* can be coaxed to sail upriver as far as she will travel from the ocean. That will save us time. We leave after Melarae's ceremony."

She swept from the room, Cenarth following her.

Katerin looked at Yevtin. "Gods," was all she could say.

Yevtin's face tightened. "Yes. War between the Gods is upon us, Katerin."

Together, they turned back to Melarae and began the necessary preparations.

THE PAIN ON CENARTH'S FACE ONCE THEY REACHED THE PRIVACY of their own quarters was almost too much for Rekaré to bear.

You must hold steady in your resolve, she told herself firmly. *Not just for Medvara but for Cenarth and Linyet's sake.*

"So I am to lose you as well?" Cenarth's voice cracked. "Beloved. At least let me come with you."

Rekaré shook her head. "No. One of us has to stay with Linyet." A lump tightened her throat, making it hard to talk. "I mean, we could turn him over to Katerin, or to your parents, but—he should not ride with me. With us. You are one of my Regents. Someone has to rule Medvara, and I want the Banisher at my side."

"Why must you do this without us?"

"You heard Nitel before I banished her." Rekaré gulped. "If I kill Chiral as Leader of Medvara, then the land is cursed under the Miteal Agreement. I become Rekaré Kinslayer." She buried her head in her hands, suddenly overwhelmed.

"Let me carry the load with you. Why should you alone be cursed?" Cenarth rested one hand on her back, rubbing her shoulders.

"Because I am Zauril's daughter as well as Alicira's." Rekaré dropped her hands. "Because I carry his taint."

"Rekaré—"

"The land is rejecting me," she said, blinking hard. "It has been rejecting me since the spring. Just like it did Alexran. If I stay, if I come back after killing Chiral—I bring doom upon Medvara. Chatain will have the opening he seeks to conquer Varen. Maybe even achieve Godhood. I *can't* stay, beloved. Much as I want to. I don't want to see you fall. I don't want to see Linyet subjected to the same doom as Melarae."

"We could both go to the Two Nations."

For a moment she was tempted by that possibility.

Back home for good.

That choice only delays your doom.

She didn't know which God or Goddess said those words.

"I wish I could," she breathed. "But I fear the curse that may be laid upon me."

Cenarth took her into his arms. "Will you at least consider it?"

"I will see what happens after we deal with Chiral," Rekaré said, her voice trembling. "I cannot promise anything other than that."

"Please at least see me after that."

"That I can promise. It won't be in Medvara."

"I don't care." He kissed her. "Chellni, Dera, the Lone Peak, even Gulter. Share a speaking square with me, beloved, but do not cut me off completely. I will happily go into exile with you."

Rekaré sadly stroked his cheek, unable to speak any more. She didn't think it would be possible. If Inharise was severely weakened, or dead—Heinmyets would need Cenarth. Linyet was too young to take on the Leadership of the Two Nations.

"I will do what I can, beloved," she finally choked out. "I just don't know what happens after Chiral. But I will tell you myself about how I avenged my mother and our daughter—if I do not fall in the process."

His arms closed around her tighter than ever. At last, she let herself sob.

RIDING FOR VENGEANCE

Rekaré paced the deck of the *Morning Star,* ignoring the midday heat, restless now that they drew near to the port closest to the Lone Peak, a day and a half after Melarae's death. The ship shuddered in complaint at her distance from the sea. Somehow Vered had managed to convince the reluctant ship to race upriver at a pace nearly twice that of the sternwheelers. A strong west wind drove the ship upriver, but the *Morning Star* glided through the river as if it were riding on ice with the wind's aid, flying faster than other sailing ships on the river and outdistancing the sternwheelers they encountered. It seemed as if the Chellana's powerful current was as nothing compared to the strength of the wind.

A voyage worthy of the greatest epics.

Not that she would be around to hear those songs. Whatever happened from here on, she could never return to Medvara. She knew that deep in her bones, even though Katerin refused to accept that possibility.

> Rekaré Kinslayer. Do you really want that title
> for yourself?

Nitel whispered those words whenever she let her guard down.

Then Rekaré remembered Melarae, and her resolve grew.

My mother and daughter were tormented at the end. I will not let that go unavenged.

"You should save your strength," Katerin advised as she rose from her seat in the bow and joined Rekaré on the main deck. "We will need to ride hard."

And I haven't done that for eleven years.

"I will be fine," she said firmly, quelling her own doubts.

Katerin grimaced. "You've not rested enough since we left Medvare."

"I burn with my wrath," Rekaré muttered. "I *burn*."

"And you will be less likely to make wise choices unless you settle and rest," Katerin retorted. "Sit. *Now.*"

She gestured toward a short cask lashed to the deck. The firmness in her voice was that of the Banisher, and enough to force Rekaré into reluctant compliance.

Still, her feet tapped restlessly. Katerin bent over her, frowning as she pulled out her Eye of Dovré and passed it over Rekaré.

"What are you looking for?" Rekaré asked.

"Ensuring that the Gods haven't tampered with you!" Exasperation tinged her cousin's voice. "The Light hasn't shone since Alicira's funeral."

Rekaré waved her right hand dismissively. "Does it matter now?"

"It matters for your safety and success. I'd just as soon be certain that those Gods haven't placed a suicidal compulsion on you. Now hold still." She gripped Rekaré's chin in one hand and held the Eye in front of her face. "Look into the Eye." Her voice carried tones of the Banisher again.

Rekaré resisted for a moment, but the attraction of the golden threads within the clear crystal of the Eye was stronger than her opposition. Katerin swung it in front of Rekaré. Her eyes followed the stone, her rage quieting for a moment.

Then her cousin closed her hand around the stone and released Rekaré's chin.

"At least they haven't got a foothold in you," she said, relief in her voice.

"I'm stronger than that!"

"Words I heard from my mother before she fell into the dreamless sleep," Katerin said, her voice cold and sharp, colored now almost entirely by the Banisher.

"Are you certain *you're* clear from any godly meddling?" Rekaré asked. "I saw that manifestation of your mother at the funeral."

"Yevtin has inspected my mindstreams," Katerin said, sitting next to Rekaré. "No more interference with my thoughts than what Dovré and Staul have done in the past." She hung the Eye back around her neck and tucked it under her tunic top. "Now. Best to plan. What are we going to do once we make landfall?"

"Ride out, of course."

"Do you know in what direction?"

"I recognized the landmarks from Senai's speaking square." Rekaré swallowed hard. "I suspect that we will be riding for the Saubral capital once we find Heinmyets and Inharise, and not Waykemin, praise—" Her voice cut out and she swallowed hard, choking back the automatic *praised be the Goddess.*

Right now she wanted no ties to the Gods. Not a one of them.

Their war killed my mother and daughter.

"Why is that? I think the opposite." Katerin's voice sharpened.

Rekaré reminded herself with an effort that her cousin had not been part of her meeting with Abeyets and the others of the guard that rode with them. She had been saying farewell to Witmara and preparing Melarae for her minimalist funeral ceremony.

"I described the attire of the troop led by that many-cursed priest to Abeyets and my Guard leaders," Rekaré said. "They hearken from the Saubral, not Waykemin."

"Waykemin is not that far from Gulter the capital of Saubral, and many Waykemese ride with the Saubral," Katerin said. "Waykemese look and dress like Saubral. And given Chiral's history of betrayal—I would not be surprised if she and her minder didn't turn for Waykemin at some point in their flight, even if she promised her Saubral riders that she would go to the Hidden One in Gulter. I would doubt that Staul the Destroyer will welcome her there."

"If he still is the patron of the Saubral."

Katerin made a rude noise. "Those alliances do not change that quickly. Staul would have let me know." She rose. "I'm going below to check the daranvelii and get things ready for unloading. Looks like we'll be docking shortly."

Rekaré nodded, staring at the sharp-pointed, snowless Lone Peak in the distance. She clenched her fists tightly, her fingernails digging into her palms.

I will have my vengeance soon.

KATERIN HEAVED A RELIEVED BREATH THAT EVENING AS SHE recognized the rider galloping across the sagebrush and dried grass prairie toward them. Jeralte, one of the Clendan riders with Heinmyets and Inharise.

Abeyets met him. They paused, spoke, then both galloped toward Katerin and Rekaré.

"Thanks be to Dovré you're here, Katerin Healer," Jeralte said. "Leader Inharise is badly injured, and all our Healers are dead, including Senai."

"I know," Katerin said. She urged Rainin forward. "We saw it through Senai's speaking square. How is Inharise faring?"

"Not well. She is in pain and needs a Healer. Heinmyets has done what he could with Senai's resources, but none of us know enough to do what is needed."

"Then let's ride. Rekaré, please excuse me."

Without waiting to hear her cousin's response, Katerin urged Rainin into a gallop. Jeralte spun his daranval. Rainin pinned her ears flat against her head and stretched out in the daranval's floating gallop, outpacing Jeralte's mount.

Despite the need Katerin couldn't help but feel proud of Rainin. Her magic might not be the strongest amongst the daranvelii, but she was one of the fastest runners in the Two Nations, perhaps even in Medvara as well. She bent low over Rainin's neck, urging her to greater speed. They galloped along the flat until they reached the crest of a rolling hill that dropped steeply on the other side down to a narrow draw. Katerin checked Rainin, easing her back to a trot, waiting for Jeralte to catch up. Three other riders galloped up the hill from a small copse of pines near the creek at the bottom of the draw.

Katerin moved her rein hand forward and Rainin angled down the hillside at a slower canter. Her ears flicked back and forth as she alternately loped and bounded down the hill. The three riders met them.

"Katerin Healer! A welcome sight. We have need," said Paniyets, one of Heinmyets's men.

"I heard. Take me to Inharise."

"In the trees."

She followed the riders down the rest of the slope and into the pines. Her stomach tightened at what she saw; wounded horses and wounded riders, a greater number than she had expected. No fires, which was also to be expected in this heat. She spotted a lean-to made of pine boughs and rode for that.

Heinmyets rose from Inharise's side. "By the Goddess I've never seen a more welcome sight."

Katerin didn't answer him, kneeling by Inharise. Her torso, left arm, and right leg were clumsily wrapped—clearly not Healer's work. Her breathing was ragged and rough, and Katerin heard a faint rattle. Her lips were gray-blue with pain, and gray underlay her normal red-brown skin color.

Hurting pretty bad.

"Inharise," she said, keeping her voice quiet. "Can you speak?"

Inharise opened her eyes. "It's—hard."

"I understand." Katerin felt her forehead, pleasantly surprised that while Inharise was warm her fever was not too high.

Maybe not too bad yet.

She unwrapped the bandages around Inharise's torso, bracing herself for the stink of putrefaction and guts. Two days in this heat might have been too long to go without a Healer's assistance, though the lack of high fever was a good sign.

To her relief, there was no gut stink, just superficial wounds below the rib cage. But another wound between Inharise's ribs bubbled and popped as Katerin released the pressure on it.

Lung, not gut.

Inharise cried out as Katerin probed her ribs, finding several broken ones.

"I covered that rib wound, bound it tight and put healing powder on it from Senai's kit right away," Heinmyets said next to her. "We've left it alone save for that—that and trying to keep her cool."

"Good." All the same, she saw signs of infection beginning. "Can you get me some water? And did Senai have willow bark powder?"

"I did not know what Senai had," Heinmyets said. "None of our Healers survived the attack. I did what I could—splinted her leg and arm. But she's been in pain, and I didn't want to try suturing her wounds." He grimaced. "I'm good enough for horses and stock, but—"

Yevtin marched up to them. Katerin looked up. "Her fever's low," she said to him. "Injuries missed the gut. We'll need to check the splints and get some pain medication into her. Heinmyets only knew the healing powder. No Healers survived the attack."

"Gods," Yevtin said. "What do you want me to do?"

"Let me give her some painkiller to start while you check her arm and leg," Katerin said.

While she had a rudimentary healing kit on her belt, she carried more supplies in Rainin's saddlebags. She pulled out a cup and her pain tinctures, grateful that she had replenished the kit. She checked the vials and picked a medium strength mix, one that would work quickly. Heinmyets brought Katerin a waterskin and she filled the cup halfway, then poured several drops in and stirred the mix with a finger. Then she added a heavy dose of willow bark powder.

Yevtin met her by Rainin. "Both broken, but not bad. I'm reluctant to remove the splints; Heinmyets has them nicely bound."

"Good. I'll work on Inharise. Why don't you start checking our other casualties?"

"Got it." Yevtin gave her a quick bow and turned away. Katerin returned to Inharise's side.

"I need you to sit up," she said to Inharise. "Heinmyets, will you help her?"

She waited until he had eased Inharise off of the ground. She bit her lip, tears running silently down her cheeks, but did not cry out. Katerin slipped her left arm behind Inharise and held the cup to her lips, letting Inharise drink in slow sips. Then she put the cup aside and helped Heinmyets guide Inharise back down.

Next, Katerin cleaned and stitched the wounds on her torso. Inharise tensed for a few moments as Katerin began work on her chest wound, then relaxed as the painkiller and willow bark took effect, her breathing steadying and her eyes flickering shut in relief.

It was full dark by the time Katerin finished working on Inharise, pausing only to activate the glowlights she had brought from Medvara. The gray tinge to Inharise's skin and lips had faded, perhaps not to a healthy color but enough that Katerin knew the pain tincture and willow bark had helped. She looked up to see Rekaré and Heinmyets watching her.

"She will be all right?" Rekaré asked hoarsely as Heinmyets sat by Inharise, taking her uninjured hand in his.

Katerin rose. "Yes. I'd better see how Yevtin is doing with the others. You stay here with her."

Rekaré exhaled. "Thank you." She sat opposite Heinmyets, eyes fixed on Inharise.

Katerin picked up both her healing kits and Senai's as well as one of the glowlights.

"I did not expect to see you riding with Katerin," Heinmyets said, the slightest hint of reproach in his voice after Katerin left them. "Medvara is not the Two Nations—how did the land allow you to leave it?"

Rekaré heaved a deep sigh.

"The Gods ride her," Inharise said hoarsely, before she could speak. "Can't you see it? Her ties to the land have been countermanded by something else."

"Chiral is responsible for the deaths of my mother and daughter," Rekaré said harshly, too tired and numb herself to ease the blow of her words. "Melarae died a day and a half—no, two days ago now."

"Oh no," Inharise whispered. "Melarae too? I feared her injuries were too great."

"She never got better, but she was stable until—until—" Rekaré gulped, fighting back a sudden swell of tears. "Chiral's escape from you was the actual cause," Rekaré couldn't look at Heinmyets and Inharise and keep on speaking, so she stared toward the faint glimmer of the lights Katerin and Yevtin carried. "Katerin probed her memories. You can ask her the details. I—I can't talk about it any more." She clenched her hands around each other, gazing at them. "I swore vengeance upon Chiral at Melarae's deathbed." Her voice dropped until it was barely a whisper. "I understand what the cost will be. Cenarth holds Medvara as Regent right now and it will go to Katerin once Chiral is dead. He will bring Linyet to the Two Nations after that. Losing my mother was bad enough—but my daughter and the rest of my family as well...."

Silence fell. Rekaré clamped her hands together until her fingers ached. When the quiet became too much, she looked back up.

"If I don't deal with Chiral, then who will? Who will be the next person dear to me who dies instead?"

Heinmyets shook his head slowly. "A difficult choice."

"Melarae died in torment." Rekaré's voice cracked as she finally dared to meet his eyes. "I failed her. I was never the mother to her that I should have been, too wedded to Medvara, too committed to being Leader and not mother...."

"*Stop that.*" Inharise groaned as she tried to push herself up, wincing as she struggled with her broken arm.

Heinmyets reached behind to support her. "Dearest, take care. I would not lose you as well!"

"Now is not my time." Inharise fixed Rekaré with a stern

gaze. "Listen. You did as best you could, you and Cenarth. You had a nation to rebuild."

"It's not just guilt," Rekaré said, looking away from them again. "It's—how could I send someone else to do what is my task?" She gulped again. "Worse. If I stay in Medvara, the Gods will push me toward being Empress."

"It is what you were raised to become," Heinmyets said.

Rekaré shook her head. "I can't. I know it's a failure of everything my mother dreamed of for me—but I can't. I miss the Two Nations. I miss the high mountains in summer. I miss riding free." Her vision blurred and she wiped her eyes. "The land and I exist in uneasy truce and have for the past year. That damnable Leader's House is full of Zauril's caches and his hidden traps and spells. The land fights me at every turn. It hasn't gotten easier."

"And you would wish this on Katerin?" Heinmyets's voice sharpened again. "Run away instead of dealing with it?"

"The land does not fight her like it does me," Rekaré said. "It embraces and welcomes her. Witmara is more at home there than Melarae was. It wouldn't be Katerin as ruler but Katerin as regent for Witmara." She swallowed hard. "Nitel keeps calling me *Rekaré Kinslayer.* Sometimes I don't think it's her voice but the land. I am *his* daughter as well as my mother's. I do not think the land forgives me. We both came to the Leadership through blood and murder."

"Where would you go?" Heinmyets's voice softened. "What would you do? Return to the Two Nations? What of Cenarth and Linyet?"

"I do not know yet," Rekaré said. "I just know I have to exact my vengeance. Perhaps I am fated to perish along with Chiral. Cenarth will go to the Two Nations, so that Linyet can learn the land and be your heir. But Chiral must be stopped—and that is for me to do. Not Katerin, not Cenarth, not you two." At last she dared to look directly at her Heartfather and Secondmother. "I have failed. I am sorry."

"Failed? Oh no, no, no," Inharise said. "There are times when the land withdraws its support." She glanced at Heinmyets. "I thought the land's uneasiness was just Chiral's presence."

"It's been that way since this drought began," Rekaré said. "When the winter snows did not fall as they should have in the Arteldinnei, and then the spring rains were sparse—I wondered. This many-cursed summer has been difficult and I've felt more and more distant from the land."

Heinmyets shook his head. "Our beloved spouse felt that things were not right as well. Gods, Heartsdaughter."

"Do not speak to me of Gods," Rekaré said bitterly. "If it were not for this war they are trying to force me into, my mother and daughter might still live. This foolish striving for power on the part of the Gods condemned both of them!"

"Be careful." Heinmyets made a quick warding sign.

"I no longer care what the Gods think! Let them curse me. Can they do any more to me? Nitel whispers *Rekaré Kinslayer* to me constantly. Dovré's voice is unreliable. And Staul—who knows what his game may be? Neither Artel nor Terat deign to speak or help me, and I will not call upon the others. I am Rekaré Kinslayer, she who no longer walks with any God. My land has rejected me."

"Rekaré, Rekaré," Inharise said. "Despair is dangerous."

"Despair is all I have, despair and a thirst for vengeance." Rekaré rose and bowed to them. "I will leave enough riders to support you on the rest of your way home to Keldara, along with Yevtin. We will leave before dawn tomorrow with the others. I bid you farewell, Heartfather, Secondmother. I hope to see you again, but if I fall—please tell my husband and my son that I did this to keep them safe."

Before they could speak one word to change her mind or

argue she whirled and marched away, seeking Katerin and Abeyets to select those who would ride with her.

Numbers will not matter now. And I have no home any more.

If anything, she was half-tempted to ride out alone. Leave Katerin and the others behind. Basnen would be sufficient companionship to find and kill Chiral. There would be enough of a moon to ride by.

But before Rekaré could yield to that temptation, Katerin met her by her bags.

"How soon do you want to ride out?" Her cousin's voice was harsh and bitter, enough to surprise Rekaré and eye Katerin carefully.

The Banisher of Shadows rode her cousin, peering out dangerously through her eyes, setting her jaw firmly in an expression that Rekaré suddenly recognized as one she had seen so many times on Alame's face when he was angry and determined.

"If I could gather enough riders, I'd leave before moonrise," Rekaré said.

"We can do that," Katerin said. "Yevtin and I have been gathering those healthy enough to ride hard and fast and Abeyets has been organizing them." She frowned. "Staul fills me with utmost urgency. We must ride swiftly. We can be ready quickly."

"Ha!" Rekaré snorted. "Not words I expected to hear from you, cousin."

Katerin's lips tightened into a thin line. "After what I've seen over the past few days, I am ready to be done with the curse of not just Chiral but those who come along with her." She gestured toward where the injured lay together. "The attackers left several riders and one of the Healers mindless. Injuries not just to the body, but also to the mind. Fortunately there are enough slightly injured riders to get Heinmyets and Inharise to safety. But we must ride hard. What was done here was worse than anything a Shadowwalker would do. Not Saubral. They—

oh Gods, Rekaré. They devoured souls. Saubral would not destroy minds like this. No. I recognize this from my childhood. This is the work of the Witches of Waykemin."

"But they wore the guise of Saubral—" Rekaré protested.

"Saubral do not do this," Katerin repeated. "The Witches do. The mindless will never recover. Worse than what was done to Melarae. I—Yevtin and I had to—it was a mercy to send them to the Other Side, with Staul's aid."

Rekaré shuddered. "What walks amongst us in Chiral's form?"

"It is more than Chiral," Katerin said. "Chatain works the reddest of red paths. She is his tool, plain and simple."

"Then go make things ready, and I will prepare myself."

The bitter grin Katerin gave Rekaré resembled a manifestation of Staul the Destroyer more than anything else.

In another time, she would have shuddered to see such an expression on Katerin Healer's face. Katerin turned away without saying anything more, and Rekaré knelt to check her bags.

Now have I fully become Sorrow. And I will bring Sorrow to Chiral and that multi-cursed priestly tool of Chatain. Vengeance will be mine.

She thought she heard a distant chuckle from Nitel.

And curses to you as well, Goddess. I will see your end for all the sorrow you have brought me, if it is the last thing I do!

TRANSFORMATIONS

By dusk the next evening, Rekaré knew exhaustion and pain like she had not experienced since ascending to the leadership of Medvara. Katerin used her powers as the Banisher of Shadows to track Chiral's location. They rode at a long trot for most of the way, a ground-eating two-beat gait that was easy on the daranvelii, stopping for short periods to let them rest and feed. The longest stop was midday at the top of one of the long narrow mountain ranges that divided the Saubral desert, hiding from the harsh sun under the shade of aromatic junipers.

Several times Katerin guided them away from the clear trail to paths that her magic identified as shortcuts to the route Chiral and her captors were taking. As Katerin had predicted, they turned away from Gulter toward Waykemin.

"We must beat them to the Kitskan River," she muttered to Rekaré. "Otherwise we will contend with the full power of the Witches. As it is, those Waykemese who ride with them will grow stronger in magic the closer they get to the Kitskan."

That had been before they stopped for midday. Rekaré tried to nap as they hid from the sun, but she kept hearing Melarae's cries every time she closed her eyes. And when she wasn't hearing her daughter, she was hearing her mother.

And Nitel haunted her.

Toward dusk, Katerin urged Rainin into a gallop up yet another dry, rocky ridge through stunted sagebrush. The fast pace was a relief after the endless pounding of long trotting.

"How far?" she called to Katerin.

"We will beat them to the ford," Katerin answered. "If we gallop."

"They won't go another way?"

She didn't know this place well. In her five years of wandering the wild with Alame and Cenarth, Rekaré had never gone into Saubral lands, much less anywhere near Waykemln. She knew that further north was a deep, nearly impassable maze of steep canyons, sheer cliffs, and the swift, rapids-filled river that marked the boundary between Clenda and the witch-lands. But there might be southern passages over the Kitskan.

Katerin shook her head. "No means for Chiral and her companions to cross the river to the north. The rapids start north of the fords. They can't go south. That direction will take them onto unfriendly Keratil land if they do that. Our biggest challenge is to intercept them before the guards at the fords stop us."

Basnen snorted and swerved to avoid a tightly packed grouping of sagebrush. She quickly caught up with Rainin, though it was an effort. Rainin was *fast*. Rekaré suspected that Katerin kept Rainin short of her full speed so that she wouldn't get too far ahead of the others.

Katerin checked Rainin to a brief halt just before they topped the ridge, waiting for the others to join them. She raised her hand as Rainin pranced impatiently, straining to keep running.

"We will be dropping down to a river—the Ollonit—after we crest this ridge," Katerin said when the others arrived. "Our quarry is following the river road. We'll have little cover so scatter. The river road is steep and rough, and it winds quite a bit so if the Gods show us favor, we can get them between two groups if we split now. We have to stop them while they're still in the canyon, because the Ollonit opens up onto a wide meadow before it flows into the Kitskan. If they make it to the meadow we'll not just be fighting Chiral and her rescuers, but guards from Waykemin."

"You have been here before?" Abeyets asked.

Katerin's lips thinned tightly until they almost disappeared. "Only once, when I left Waykemin. The Gods are also advising me. Any other questions?"

"How are we going to get them between us? Isn't that going to be guesswork?" asked one of Rekaré's riders from Medvara—Yanara, Rekaré recalled, a superb rider and fighter from a village upriver from Medvare-the-city. She had admired Yanara's skill with sword and bow during training sessions.

"I know about where they are, with Staul's aid. Some of us will ride upriver before dropping into the canyon and the rest of us will ride downriver. Those of you riding upriver need to stay under the main ridgeline for at least three turns of the river. It will be a gamble so be careful, those of you riding upriver. How many of you have concealment charms?"

About half of the riders raised their hands.

"All right. You ride upriver with Abeyets." Katerin closed her eyes, concentrating. "They should still be a few bends away by the time we reach the Ollonit. Abeyets, " She pointed west. "As we go over the top, spread out but not too far upriver." She pointed east. "After you reach the river, ride downriver along the edges of the ridge. Try not to leave many tracks if you have not seen signs of their party."

Abeyets nodded. "So we try to get behind them. Do we engage right away?"

"No," Katerin said. "There is a narrow, rocky ridge with

steep cliffs on the south side of the river, and a small box canyon before the ridge on that south side. That forces the trail into a narrow gorge. If we get there before you, we can set up an ambush with riders on the cliff walls. Those who ride with you should not all drop down by the river but stay on the slope. Some should cross the Ollonit to follow on the other side."

Abeyets nodded curtly. "I understand. This plan sounds good." He turned his daranval to ride west, waving the ten riders with the concealment charms to come with him. The other ten rode with Katerin and Rekaré.

When they topped the ridge Rekaré bit her lip as she looked downhill. She hadn't ridden down a slope this steep for eleven years. They dropped below the top and followed a game trail angling down and sideways below a tall rim instead of straight down. Katerin directed the others to follow angled paths down the side of the canyon. One by one the other riders split off to make their way down while Katerin and Rekaré rode forward under the rimrocks.

At last it was only the two of them.

"Ready?" Katerin asked her. "We have the steepest line of all."

"How much further east are you riding?" Rekaré asked.

"No further. Follow me, try to stay in my path." Katerin grinned humorlessly. "We'll hope they don't ride with great trackers." She turned Rainin straight down the hill, not following any trail that Rekaré could see. Icy fingers clutched at her gut. It would be oh so easy for either Rainin or Basnen to miss a step and tumble downhill. If Basnen went down they would take Katerin and Rainin with them. The shale and loose dirt underfoot was softer than anything she'd ridden for a long time.

You used to do this! she scolded herself. *Gotten soft after all those years in Medvara.*

Rekaré leaned back in the saddle and gave Basnen free rein,

maintaining just enough contact to help the golden mare maintain her balance.

Basnen snorted, projecting confidence as she plunged down the hill in skidding, sliding strides and jumps, head low and balanced. A joy at the challenge came to Rekaré from Basnen, an eagerness to *finally* be scrambling across a *real* obstacle. Rekaré shamelessly held onto the saddle horn with one hand to help her stay balanced. Katerin did much the same.

At last they reached the river bottom in a clatter of rocks and dust, plowing through sagebrush. Katerin did not ride into the narrow meadow but wheeled Rainin to move downriver along the brush where the slope met the mostly-flat land. She dropped her reins and braced her bow, nocking an arrow. Rekaré followed Katerin's lead, though she itched to draw her sword. If only it would be so easy to take Chiral out with an arrow from a distance!

Somehow she didn't think that would happen.

They rode silently. Katerin did not pick up her dropped reins but let her left hand swing free, occasionally reaching into a loosely bound bag hanging from her belt. Magic roiled around her, straining to be free, simmering and ready to be unleashed with a single word. Rekaré suspected that Katerin was scattering glimmer dust.

I didn't realize she had this much power.

How had Katerin become such a potent sorcerer?

Somehow she's loosened the constraints on the power she inherited from Alame. Without my help. On her own? Most likely—or else with Staul and Metkyi's help.

Seeing how the spell obeyed Katerin confirmed her decision to cede Medvara to Katerin as Regent.

She is much more than just Katerin Healer.

How many times had she ridden behind Katerin's father Alame while evading Zauril's hunters, his power smoldering just like Katerin's was now?

Alame should have become Leader of Medvara long before Zauril came.

Instead, Alexran had chosen to cling to power after he had grown weak. He should have resigned in Alame's favor—or even in favor of Alicira's father Richenax, or Alicira herself.

Just like it is time for me to leave the Leadership of Medvara.

Katerin picked up her reins and halted Rainin when they reached a clump of cottonwoods. Rekaré stopped Basnen behind her until Katerin gestured for her to come up on her left side.

"This is the place," she whispered, pointing toward the narrow, rocky ridge that jutted into the Ollonit.

Rekaré studied the terrain before her. The ridge on the south side of the river rose in tall, narrow columns with a toothy, irregular cap. The cliffs on that side extended back from the riverbed with a short, narrow box canyon opening no more than four daranval lengths wide. The canyon was tiny, big enough to maybe serve as a small corral. Past the steep drop into the box canyon, a higher bench terminated abruptly at the cliff bottom. Cliffs rose behind that bench. Rekaré squinted along the bench's edge. Could Chiral's party go around? They would need to have left the river canyon some distance back, she decided.

The riverbank rose abruptly to the level of the bench until it reached the box canyon and the tiny dry creek bed running out of it. On their side of the river, a small meadow opened up between the river and the cottonwoods. The trail forded the river at the edge of the meadow, so riders were forced to enter it.

"I wouldn't come through here if I were expecting pursuit," she breathed to Katerin.

"Not many options to Waykemin from the direction they took. The other routes from the fords force the riders to go to Nere, Gulter, or Keldara for at least a half-day's ride. No other good way from the path they have chosen. I don't think they're expecting to be followed."

"Fools. If I knew the territory I'd expect an ambush."

"Staul covers us from their perceptions," Katerin said. "And they may not anticipate that anyone could mount pursuit that quickly." Her mouth quirked in a brief, wry smile. "Nor that they are being followed by someone from Chiyan, my home village. Even though they are not yet in Waykemin, they may feel safe now that they're riding the Ollonit. Few outsiders know of this passage. There *is* an old saying that those of Waykemin cannot be defeated here."

"Then why...." Rekaré's voice trailed away as Katerin bared her teeth mirthlessly.

"I am Chiyani and Waykemese by birth," she said. "And Staul and Dovré stand behind me. This is as much my land as the Two Nations and Medvara are. The Gods lead them to their own destruction."

"I wish I could be as certain as you." Another confirmation of her decision to pass Medvara—and the eventual fate of Varen— to Katerin and her daughter for safekeeping.

"Waykemese against Waykemese," Katerin said. "The Banisher of Shadows against Chatain's tool. The land here does not love Chatain. But it knows me. It recognizes me as the daughter of Terani, as Chiyani. That priest? He and Chiral cannot stand against a Chiyani Banisher of Shadows."

And Rekaré Kinslayer.

"How much longer until they reach us?"

"Our riders are taking position. It will be soon." Even as she finished speaking a rider made her careful way along the bottom of the ridge toward them. Katerin mimicked a chickadee call. The rider answered, angling toward them as another rider came into view. He rode higher on the slope, and took up a position where his daranval was hidden by rocks.

Soon. Soon this will be over.

She was ready for an ending to this.

Some instinct made Rekaré tuck Staul's token into the sleeve pocket of her tunic. If ever there might be a time when she would need the God's favor, this could be it.

KATERIN WATCHED AS THE RIDERS TOOK THEIR POSITIONS, TWO ON the slopes each side of the river, the riders to the south needing to leave their daranvelii on the bench. The remaining six made their way slowly to join Katerin and Rekaré.

"Any tracks?" she quietly asked the last rider.

The rider shook her head. "I was the only rider to follow the trail. No sign ahead of me."

"Good."

Katerin tightened her grip on the bow, tensely watching upriver. She had glossed over the old prophecies when talking to Rekaré, because the tension and worry radiating off of her cousin was so intense she could feel it.

Did Rekaré seek death as well as vengeance?

I will not let that happen.

The Banisher enveloped her, wrapping Katerin in more power than she had experienced before. Was it because she was close to her birthplace?

I will need to guard against Terani.

She didn't think it would be long before they would be fighting Chiral and her acolytes. But she had been discreetly scattering glimmer dust while she and Rekaré rode to this grove, trickling small grains while whispering a spell that would block Chiral and that priest from escaping uphill, at least.

Should she do more? The dust she scattered had not warned her of anything more than their own riders, so she would have time if she wanted to spell the meadow. Katerin considered the possibility. She unnocked the arrow from her bowstring and put it back into her quiver, then handed the bow to Rekaré.

"Hold this," she commanded, the Banisher within her making it more of a command than she intended.

Rekaré arched her brows but said nothing as she reached for Katerin's bow. Katerin untied the pouch that held her glimmer dust from her belt and loosened the ties further, checking to see how much she had left.

Not much.

Do not hold back,

Dovré whispered to her.

Spread it wide and far,

Staul added.

Katerin poured the remaining dust into her left palm and hung the bag from her saddle horn. She urged Rainin forward, and took a small pinch from the mound, scattering it as far on her right side as she could. She continued to the river ford. Then she shifted her weight to spin Rainin so that she could toss dust on that side of the meadow.

By the time she rejoined the waiting riders there was only the smallest layer of dust on her palm. Katerin turned Rainin sideways and blew it toward the riders. She extracted Staul's chip from her medical bag, then turned Rainin back to face Rekaré and the riders, raising both hands high.

"Protect and shield those who fight in your name, oh Dovré. Staul. Artel. Terat." She would not name those other three Gods. She shifted her weight and Rainin spun to face the meadow. "Give us the victory soon, oh Dovré. Staul. Artel. Terat. Slow the feet of their mounts. Weaken their strikes. Cast doubt in their minds." She fell silent but reached unspeaking for the spirit of the land, as she had learned to do after watching Heinmyets in Keldara.

> You know me. I am born of you. Honor me, give me the victory this day, for those who ride have acted against all that is right. They would free evil that should be leashed, have murdered a child and an old woman in the name of he who rules the Land-Over-Sea. Have eaten the spirits of loyal riders and guards. They cannot prevail.

Wind whispered through the trees, and was that a dust devil or a manifestation of the land that shimmered in the middle of the meadow in the rays of the setting sun?

> I hear you,

the land whispered back.

> They cannot prevail.

> In the name of the Goddess Dovré and the God Staul I thank you.

The faint glimmer faded. Katerin exhaled. She picked up Rainin's reins in her left hand and rode back to Rekaré, reaching for her bow.

"I did not know you could work this land's magic," Rekaré murmured.

"I was born across the river not far from here," Katerin said, renocking her arrow. "The land knows me." She bobbed her head to Rekaré. "We ride on your command."

"And not yours?"

"Yours is the vengeance. I simply prepare the land for you."

"Alame knew the land's magic beyond Medvara as well," Rekaré said.

Katerin didn't answer. She concentrated on the faint spell she had worked while riding to the meadow, straining to detect their foes. How much longer now?

Rekaré suddenly pulled off the Light of Medvara. "Take this."

"I can't."

"You are working the land's magic." Rekaré drew a ragged breath. "The Light will respond better to you than to me. And me—I have the Maker, the Strength, and the Vision. I will not wield them with the Light like Nitel urges. That will take me down a path I will not choose. But my heart tells me we will need every tool—and here you are, Regent-Designate of Medvara, and a speaker to the land. You should wield the Light."

"All right," Katerin whispered, unable to say more. Rekaré dropped the chain over Katerin's neck, then reached in her pouch, putting on first the Maker, then the Strength, then the Vision.

Katerin's sense of the land deepened, growing fuller.

Welcome, Banisher of Shadows, born of
Chiyan. Your wish?

Let me see where those I seek are now.

A faint image of Chiral riding next to the bald-pated priest came to her, followed by Detaluna slung on her belly over a horse's back and surrounded by other riders. Another flash, of the trail winding around a bend in the river, then the riders nearing the ford that led to the meadow where they waited.

"They approach," Katerin said softly.

"To the trees," Rekaré breathed. The Maker glimmered on her chest.

They retreated further into the brush, out of immediate sight of the trail as it crossed the river and entered the meadow. Katerin wished she had some means of communicating with

Abeyets, to know how closely behind Chiral's riders he and the others followed.

Too late to worry about that.

The land picked up her concern. She glimpsed Abeyets and his riders following, a couple of bends behind Chiral and her riders.

Sound of splashing water as the group forded the summer-shrunken river. Katerin glanced down to make certain that Rainin's reins were securely knotted so that she could drop them. Rainin jerked her head high, ears pricked forward, tensing under Katerin, ready to charge.

Chiral and the bald-pated priest appeared first. They entered the meadow.

"*Wait,*" Rekaré whispered. "Make sure they are all there."

Chiral's horse blew a long, rolling warning snort as they came further into the meadow. Chiral jerked on her reins. The priest's horse skittered sideways.

"They know a spell's been put on the meadow," Katerin growled.

"Now!" Rekaré yelled.

Rainin leapt forward at Rekaré's shout. Katerin bellowed an ululating cry. The Light of Medvara blazed brightly on her chest.

Chiral's horse reared as they swept forward. Katerin aimed for the bald-pated priest's mount, sensing that the magic protecting Chiral originated from him. No arrows could pierce that—only swords or spears.

But his magic didn't extend to their steeds. She seized another arrow and shot at Chiral's horse. Chiral's mare bucked and dumped her, whirling and presenting a broadside target. Katerin's third arrow struck the mare in the flank.

The priest fared slightly better, riding his horse's panicked bucks until it stumbled and collapsed onto the ground.

Their charge took them through the gathered riders. Katerin

whirled Rainin around using weight and legs, grateful that she'd taken the time to train Rainin in some of Mira's old fighting moves. She slung her bow on her saddle.

Somehow Detaluna had managed to stay on her frightened mount. Katerin pulled her belt knife and rode close, slashing at her foot bindings. Detaluna slid off, holding her hands up. Katerin cut those bindings, then tossed the knife to Detaluna.

"Thanks!" Detaluna whirled and ran toward one of the fallen riders, kneeling to retrieve his sword.

Katerin dismounted when she noted that most of their foes were on the ground.

"Keep yourself safe," she murmured to Rainin as she drew her sword, distantly aware that Abeyets and his men had joined the fray.

She would do better on foot since Rainin lacked battle experience. A pulse of additional strength surged through her as her feet touched the ground, the land lending her more power.

This is my place.

But before she could attack a foe, Terani rose before her, once again wielding the Spear. Katerin hesitated, then reached into her left pocket where she had tucked Staul's chip.

Terani stabbed at her arm, making Katerin drop the chip.

Teach you to be so dependent on a tool,

she chortled.

Alame could never overcome that failing.

Katerin did not waste time on a retort. She parried Terani's thrust and reached for the land's magic. Staul's chip flipped up and back into her left palm.

I need to get the Spear back. But how?

She kept close to Terani so that she didn't have room to use the Spear. At last her opening came. Katerin dropped her sword and seized the Spear's shaft with both hands. They wrestled for control of the Spear. Terani kicked at Katerin and she jumped to avoid contact.

I curse you,

Terani snarled.

You and Rekaré Kinslayer. Both of you must die
so that my masters can rule.

Their left hands bumped into each other. Terani flinched back at the contact, enough that Katerin could pull the shaft out of that hand. She seized Terani's left wrist, pressing the chip hard against it.

Terani writhed in Katerin's grip, yanking on the Spear with her right hand and trying to pull her wrist away from Katerin's left hand. Katerin stood firm, pulling up strength from the land as Terani struggled. The Light of Medvara pulsed, more power flooding into her with each bright flare.

Begone, foul shadow! I care not whether you
are in truth my mother's shade or some malign
counterfeit. You keep me from what I am fated
to do!

Terani spat at her, the spittle burning on Katerin's face. She ignored it, keeping her grasp tight on Terani's wrist. Terani let loose of the Spear and desperately tore at Katerin's fingers. Katerin slid her hand to the bottom of the spearhead, wishing for the Spear to shorten to three palms width. Then she stabbed deep into Terani.

Terani shrieked, twisting away into smoke and dust.

Watch out!

Metkyi's voice bellowed.

Katerin barely turned in time to counter the bald-pated priest as he struck at her, catching his sword on the head of the Spear. They grappled and countered each other, Katerin at a disadvantage.

Will it reshape into a sword?

Even as she thought it the Spear changed its form in her hands, shifting to become a sword. The priest's eyes widened as the Spear changed shape. Katerin slipped the chip into her right hand, against the sword's hilt. It disappeared and she felt the magic pulse even more strongly within the sword. Katerin took advantage of the priest's distraction and struck him hard in the gut. The priest howled in agony, eyes wide, grasping at the blade.

"No," he groaned. "Spare me this—no, not this! Aiii—it's eating my spirit!"

Exultation filled Katerin as she realized the truth of what he said, that the sword consumed his spirit. The priest screamed and she *felt* his agony. But unlike past times when she had sensed someone else's suffering, it didn't cause her pain but an unholy joy. The part of her that was Katerin Healer disapproved. Her ecstasy at his torment violated her vows as a healer.

But the part of her that was Katerin ea Miteal, the Banisher of Shadows, thrilled at his misery.

He participated in causing Alicira and Melarae's deaths, and for that he will pay!

The sword lapped up those emotions, humming with approval at that last thought.

Goddess, for this I am truly sorry,

the part of her that was still Katerin Healer prayed.

Many things are necessary in war,

Staul the Destroyer answered.

The priest collapsed. Katerin freed the sword as the priest fell at her feet, his body smaller than it should be. As she watched, it crumpled into ash, falling into itself as if his insides had been sucked dry. Katerin exhaled and raised the sword.

Spear of War and Unmaking indeed. And more than a spear.

Part of her wanted to take the time to think about this further but she dared not do so. Fighting still raged around her.

"Become Spear," she said out loud, wondering if Staul's chip would restore itself. As the Spear reformed, the chip remained part of it.

Katerin looked around. Most of Chiral's cohort were down or injured. Detaluna fought with a man and a woman. To her relief more of Rekaré's riders were on their feet and fighting than their foes. Sorcery roiled around the individual battles, slowing their adversaries' feet and even their strokes.

Where are Rekaré and Chiral?

At last she spotted them, fighting at the edge of the river, Chiral backing into the water. Katerin ran toward them, worry pulsing through her as she saw Chiral's unexpected skill and Rekaré's apparent awkwardness.

Is she bewitched or simply overtired?

Katerin couldn't see any additional magic flowing around them. And she would have thought that killing the priest meant weakening Chiral's sorcery—but perhaps not.

Help Rekaré, oh Goddess! Staul. Someone.

She swung at one of Chiral's supporters who would have blocked her, ignoring her shriek of pain as she bounded toward Chiral and Rekaré.

Chiral knocked Rekaré's sword out of her hand. Katerin leapt between them, driving Chiral back.

Sword, she thought to the Spear.

"*Mine*," Rekaré growled, grabbing up her sword. "My vengeance!"

"Take this!" Katerin shoved the transformed Spear toward her cousin. "Press your token of Staul into the hilt!"

Without hesitation Rekaré dropped her sword and took the Spear from Katerin. Katerin scooped up Rekaré's dropped sword, engaging with Chiral to buy time as her cousin pulled Staul's token from her tunic sleeve pocket and shoved it against the hilt. Then Rekaré muscled in to reengage with Chiral.

A few more strokes and it was over. Rekaré swung hard, beheading Chiral with an inhuman strength that would have shocked Katerin had she not seen Rekaré do this to Zauril eleven years ago. Chiral's body crumpled like the priest's did, fading into ash, her hair changing back and forth between red and brown before it crumbled into powder.

A shadow writhed from the dust of what had been Chiral. A pale man with red hair, dressed in elegant purple and red silk with golden dragons and demons entwined on it appeared.

Greetings to you, Rekaré Kinslayer,

he proclaimed, dragging out the "s" in Kinslayer until it sounded like a snake's hiss.

So you have prevailed against my tool Chiral.
May it become your doom. Medvara's doom.

"I renounce my leadership of Medvara!" Rekaré shrieked in return. "I take this doom fully upon myself in the name of righting the evil done to my family, my people, and my land. You will never control us, Chatain!"

Chatain's apparition burst into a laugh.

Oh, Rekaré Kinslayer. It will be oh-so-delightful to see your fall. Who will now rule Medvara? Who will protect the land of Varen? You have brought doom to all you care about by your actions today. You are the end of the house of Miteal.

"Not as long as *I* live," Katerin said. She took the sword back from her cousin and commanded it back to its spear form, then stepped in front of Rekaré. "And *I* for one tire of your presence."

Who are you?

Chatain's apparition demanded.

Katerin took a deep breath and raised the spear over her head. "I am Katerin ea Miteal, daughter of Alame en Miteal and Terani ni Chiyani, Terani-the-God-Killer. I am the Regent-Designate of Medvara. I am the Banisher of Shadows, the wielder of the Spear of War and Unmaking."

Chatain's eyes widened as he stared at the Light of Medvara steadily glowing on Katerin's breast. He raised his hands to cast a spell. "I curse you, Alame's daughter—"

"No! You have no power over me, Chatain. In me you see the union of Staul and Dovré. And I say to you, as long as I and my descendants live, you will never prevail over Medvara!" She thrust the Spear into Chatain's apparition. It faded.

Thankfully the Spear did not drink from Chatain's power. Katerin lowered it.

Rekaré bowed to her. "Banisher of Shadows. I thank you for aiding me in my vengeance."

Katerin's lips were numb. It seemed like she watched from a distance as she eyed Rekaré.

"Rekaré Kinslayer." The words were not hers, the voice speaking through her not hers. At this point Katerin couldn't tell if the deity speaking through her was the Goddess or Staul.

Rekaré dropped to her knees in front of Katerin. Part of her wanted to object, to raise her cousin back up.

This isn't right, I should be kneeling to her.

But the greater part of her, the part that allowed the God to move through her—Dovré, she finally realized—simply gazed down at Rekaré, waiting.

Rekaré raised her head. "I accept the title of Rekaré Kinslayer. I accept that doom it brings upon me, oh Goddess." She reached for Katerin's hand, the one that bore the Regent's signet. She slipped the Regent's signet off of Katerin's finger and replaced it with that of the Leader of Medvara. "I hereby renounce my Leadership of Medvara and pronounce Katerin ea Miteal, Regent-Designate, as my replacement."

"You—you can't—" Katerin managed to force through her lips, speaking as herself and not the Goddess.

"You are no longer Katerin Healer," Rekaré said. "Dearest Katerin. The magic you worked gave us the victory. You demonstrated your affinity with this land. The Light of Medvara has accepted you when it has rejected me. Your ability with the land reaches beyond Medvara and the Two Nations, a strength I cannot claim any more." She drew a ragged breath. "Today's events confirm that I can no longer be Leader without risking further damage to Medvara. I am cursed, as I knew I would be when I set out on the red road to vengeance. I could not have banished Chatain at the end as Leader of Medvara. You did, as Regent-Designate."

Katerin dropped to her knees, forcing the Goddess within her to lay quiet as she took Rekaré's hands. "Rekaré, you're tired after days of sorrow. You can't mean this. I am no Leader!"

"You banished Chatain without the power of Leadership," Rekaré answered. "Hold Medvara for Witmara as Regent if not for yourself as Leader." She reached for Katerin and wrapped her arms about her. "Oh cousin, if I were to go back, the land would rebel against me," she murmured. "I would become another Alexran or, worse, Zauril."

Katerin clutched her closer. "Then what will you do?"

Rekaré gulped and Katerin realized she was half-crying, half-laughing.

"I will become a wanderer and a poet," she said. "I will be your eyes throughout Varen. My mother found peace in the Two Nations. I will find my peace in traversing the nations of Varen. Zauril has poisoned both our lives. You have no such shadows haunting you—and if I were to go back, then I would drag both Chiral and Zauril with me to curse the land. I would not do that to Medvara."

"You need not exile yourself like this   "

"There will be need for someone to do what I propose," Rekaré said. "Chatain will come again. Let me speak for you to the nations of Varen. Let me be the one who unites the land, so that when he comes for you—mark my words, he will do so— the entire land will stand in resistance against him instead of just Medvara." She pulled back. "My magic will remain in the protective mix to guard Varen. But I must see more of the land to strengthen its defenses."

"Come back to Medvara before you make any hasty decisions."

Rekaré shook her head. "Hasty? I have been contemplating this since you came to Medvare-the-city. My Leadership began and ended in kinslaying. That leaves me open to corruption and destruction. But you—you bring a new era to Medvara."

"My hands are as red as yours."

"Not with kin's blood. You defended me and the land. Let me raise you a force from the nations to counter Chatain when he comes. An elite troop using the diverse magics and peoples of Varen."

"And what of Cenarth and Linyet?"

"Their future lies with the Two Nations." Rekaré sighed. "I

will help Heinmyets take Inharise back to Clenda. That will be my first task. Send Cenarth and Linyet to me quickly, so I may see them. Then I will become a shadow amongst the nations."

She speaks the truth,

the Goddess said to Katerin.

"So what happens now?"

Rekaré rose, taking Katerin's hand to help her up. "This." She raised her voice. "Fighters. To us!"

The troop turned to them, those who were able to walk or hobble gathering around them.

Rekaré surveyed them. "You have all fought well and I am grateful to you for your role in helping me achieve my vengeance. But my actions on this day have also condemned me. The Emperor-over-Sea, cursed be his name, has denounced me as Rekaré Kinslayer and laid a doom upon me that I would not take back to Medvara."

Gasps came from around them.

Rekaré raised Katerin's hand. "But the Gods are generous to us, for my cousin, Regent-Designate, Katerin ea Miteal, Katerin daughter of Alame en Miteal, steps forward as Leader of Medvara in truth. This is my last command to you. Honor Katerin and her daughter Witmara. Follow them to a new and more glorious Medvara, to a greater and stronger Varen that will resist the evil schemes of the Emperor over Sea. Hail Katerin Leader!"

"Hail Katerin!" they yelled. "Leader Katerin!"

Rekaré dropped her hand and released Katerin's. Katerin bowed to her people—*her people!* Could she do this?

"I thank you," she said softly. "My first command to you. We have the aftermath of battle to clean up, with injured and prisoners. I would not camp here tonight for risk of courting the unwanted attention of Karnoi, Cirdel, and the Hunt."

"There is a larger meadow upriver," Abeyets offered. "We will still have enough light to set up camp there."

"Then let us make this happen," Katerin said. "Quickly. And bring me the prisoners we now have. They will swear to Medvara or—" She hesitated. Could she do this? She amended her first thought, *or they will die.* Not a path she wanted to follow at the beginning of her Leadership. "I will need to talk to them to determine their fate," she said finally. "I need to see how entangled they are with Chiral's lies."

"We have but five survivors besides Detaluna," Abeyets said. "They appear to be Saubral. Others fled after you killed the priest. I do not think they were Saubral. The restraints you laid down did not restrict them when they chose to leave."

Most likely of Waykemin, then. This is their land. The Witches will soon know what happened here.

"I will speak to them and determine their loyalty," Katerin said.

Rekaré stirred. "I would speak to them as well. Perhaps I can start creating my troop."

Abeyets nodded. The riders scattered.

"You would ally with such?" Katerin asked. "Don't you fear betrayal?"

Rekaré nodded. "The Saubral lands are a part of Varen." A faint smile twitched her lips as she rested her right hand on her chest. "And the Maker tells me I may have need of these riders."

Abeyets led three men and two women to them, Detaluna following. Their wrists were bound in front of them. One woman hobbled along, leaning as best as she could on one of the men, with the others clustering close to help her. Detaluna circled around and joined Abeyets.

"I vouch for these five," she said. "The other riders were cruel, but these five were among those who treated me with consideration."

"Our loyalty is to the Hidden One in Gulter, not to *that*

woman and the so-called priest who controlled her," the uninjured woman snarled. "The Hidden One sent us as a safeguard so that our people would not be blamed for any damage she created." She spat. "We five are the only ones riding with them who did not swear to her or that cursed priest."

Rekaré and Katerin exchanged glances. "I would have asked you to swear loyalty to me as Leader of Medvara instead," Katerin said slowly. "But if you still owe allegiance to the Hidden One—"

Rekaré stepped forward. "I have a proposal for you. Would you ride with me to Gulter and introduce me to the Hidden One? I will pay you."

The woman eyed Rekaré suspiciously. "Aren't you the Leader of Medvara?"

Rekaré raised her bare hand. "No longer." She pointed her chin toward Katerin. "Katerin ea Miteal now leads Medvara. I am Rekaré Kinslayer now, not Rekaré ea Miteal. I have a greater purpose—to keep Varen free from the schemes and control of the Emperor-over-Sea, who controlled and drove *that woman,* as you call her, and the priest. I want to form an elite troop from all nations that will resist him. Would you support me in this goal?"

The woman chewed on her lip, then turned to face her companions. Katerin noted the small nods each person gave her as she met their eyes. She turned back to Rekaré.

"My name is Sesenth," she said. "She who bore me attended the occasion when your mother diced with Staul. She was Shadowwalker where I am not. I speak for all of us. We vow that we will see you safely to the Hidden One where we will speak more of this. I know that she is concerned about the Emperor and his goals."

Rekaré pulled her belt knife free. She cut Sesenth's bonds, then did the same for the others.

"Then you will swear to Rekaré Kinslayer, at least until we have met with the Hidden One?"

Sesenth smiled. "To Gulter and perhaps beyond, Rekaré Kinslayer." The others echoed her words.

"Then come. Let us help move the wounded and establish camp for tonight. Tomorrow we will ride to ensure that my Heartfather and Secondmother reach Keldara safely, for I would see them safe before I begin my travels, and I will deal with other matters that should not take long. Then we will go to Gulter."

"We will follow your lead."

"Then let us begin." Rekaré turned to Katerin. "This meets with your approval?"

"Yes."

Rekaré, Detaluna and the Saubral walked away. One of the men picked up the injured woman. Katerin drew a ragged breath.

Now she could be Katerin Healer, perhaps for the last time.

You will have the opportunity to heal more than
the sick,

Dovré said.

You are a healer of more than people. You
will see.

A light touch on her forehead, and the Goddess was gone.

Katerin whistled Rainin over to get her healing kit out of the saddlebags. Before she could move to Rainin's side, the mare pressed her forehead against Katerin's torso, sending thoughts of comfort and pride. Katerin took a moment to lean her forehead against Rainin's.

This is what was meant to be,

Rainin sent.

I am here.

An image of Daro and Witmara came to Katerin, the two of them standing together in a pen, gazing southeast. Magic flowed around the two of them, more powerful than any Katerin had seen before.

Our children,

she thought to Rainin.

Our children who will rule,

Rainin echoed. Then she nudged Katerin away, sending a wordless reminder that the injured awaited. Katerin chuckled and retrieved her healing kit.

As long as she had her bond with Rainin she would remain balanced. Even if she was the temporary Leader of Medvara.

Seven years. Only seven years, until Witmara is of age to rule.

THE END

CLEANING HOUSE

CLEANING HOUSE

Katerin ea Miteal, newest Leader of Medvara, stood on the sternwheeler's deck as it negotiated the currents of the Saktrin River to approach the private Leader's pier. Her fingers twisted in the black and silver mane of her magic-gifted horse, Rainin. The bay daranval's nostrils flared and she pawed at the deck, impatient to get off the ship and onto solid ground.

"Quit," Katerin said mildly to the mare. Rainin stood still, but her eagerness to be back on land transmitted across their mental link.

Rainin nudged her side. Once again she sent pictures of Katerin in the Leader's chair in the Great Hall. Katerin speaking to the Council as Leader. Katerin reviewing the Medvaran magical sheep herds. Katerin working the spells which kept Medvara and the nations of Varen safe from the intrusion of Chatain, Emperor-over-Sea. All images of Katerin as unquestioned Leader of Medvara.

I am not Leader, but Regent,

Katerin thought back to Rainin.

Undeterred, Rainin kept sending her pictures of Katerin as Leader, like she had been doing ever since Rekaré had abruptly abdicated in the wilds of the neighboring nation, Saubral, after their successful pursuit of one of Chatain's agents.

Why did she continue to argue her role with her daranval? It wasn't going to change the reality they would face as soon as the ship docked.

Perhaps because she was not ready to bid farewell to her true self as Katerin Healer. She had been Katerin Healer much longer than she had been Katerin ea Miteal or the Banisher of Shadows. Had only learned who her father was when helping Rekaré to become Leader. Had only reluctantly become the Banisher of Shadows since...her hand brushed against the hilt of the weapon that had come to her during that battle against Chiral. Now it was a sword, but its natural shape was that of a spear, the weapon of the Banisher.

The Spear of War and Unmaking.

The weapon that made her the Banisher of Shadows, not Katerin Healer. It, along with the pendant known as the Light of Medvara marked her as Leader. Even if she stepped down in seven years for her daughter Witmara to take over the Leadership, Regent or no, for now she was still the new Leader.

If there is to be anything left for Witmara to rule I cannot flinch from my duty. I do this for Witmara. Not myself.

Rekaré and her husband Cenarth had done their best over the past eleven years to heal Medvara from the decline brought about by the abuse of the land's magic by Rekaré's father, Zauril. Their efforts had been successful—until Chatain's meddling. Chatain and the ghosts that lingered in the Leader's House. The funeral of Rekaré's mother Alicira, which had exposed Chiral as Chatain's agent. The death of Rekaré's daughter Melarae, her intended heir for Medvara, also caused by Chiral.

And then there was the interference from the Seven

Crowned Gods, who fought amongst themselves as much as they caused their human followers to battle against each other.

How long before they bring me down, too?

She had two Gods supporting her, her patroness Dovré and the fearsome, dual-natured Staul. Artel the Judge and Terat of the Waters were neutral but by nature tended to align with Dovré and Staul. But the other three—all had reasons to harm Katerin.

Nitel. The Twin Gods Karnoi and Cirdel. Their feud with her was both personal and political.

Katerin shook her head to dismiss those thoughts. This was not the time to think about battling Gods. She refocused on the pier and those who waited on the riverbank. Cenarth stood in the lead, with his and Rekaré's surviving child, Linyet. Witmara, with her newly bonded daranval colt Daro, Rainin's weanling son, stood next to them. The Leader's Guard behind them, lined up as if Rekaré herself instead of Katerin was here.

Their counterparts stood behind Katerin.

She took a deep breath.

Going to be my life for a while.

What was she going to say to Cenarth? Did he expect to see Rekaré with her for one final farewell? She wasn't certain what Rekaré had written to him in the long letter that she sent with the courier that carried the messages that Katerin was now Leader.

What news will I need to break to him? How much did Rekaré share?

She kept watching as the sternwheeler eased into its place and was secured. Witmara seemed excited and happy, waving at her. That eased her heart a little. Cenarth and Linyet were solemn and quiet and he did not appear to be looking for Rekaré. Rainin stopped sending images to Katerin and raised her head to nicker at Daro.

The ship's captain checked the gangplank herself, marching

up and down it before she nodded approval to Katerin and her Guard.

No avoiding it now. She stepped forward, Rainin pulling ahead a little in her impatience to get off of the ship. Once they were on the dock Rainin's stride lengthened and Katerin matched it, ready to get on land again herself. Rainin nickered at Daro again. He answered but stood calmly next to Witmara.

That was a minor relief. Witmara was taking his training seriously.

Cenarth and Linyet bowed to her. Witmara startled, then bowed quickly.

"Leader Katerin, we welcome you back to Medvare-the-city," Cenarth said, his voice tight and choked.

Katerin reached for his hands. "You do not need to be so formal with me."

"Under these circumstances it would be best." Cenarth drew a deep breath and eased his hands free from hers. "There have been things happening here as well. The Leader's House—the Leader's Wing has burned. It apparently happened the night that Rekaré abdicated." He swallowed hard. "The Council—they want to speak to you as soon as possible. The Great Hall remains, as does the guest wing."

"Burned? The Tapestry?"

Gods, if the Great Tapestry that integrated Leader's magic with the land's magic was gone then she had to replace it...then again, she would have to weave a new one herself now that she was Leader. Or could she get away with using Rekaré and Cenarth's Tapestry since she was the Regent?

"No. But—there are still problems, Katerin." Cenarth glanced around. "Best we talk about this—and other things—in private."

"Of course." Katerin turned to Witmara and hugged her daughter, then reached over to Linyet for a quick embrace. He pressed into her side for a moment then pulled back. Daro nuzzled Rainin. "Did you ride down to the docks or are you in a wagon?"

"We rode. It was easier to have the Guard hold our mounts with Daro here."

"All right." She hesitated, waiting for Cenarth to lead them away.

"You are the Leader," Cenarth said. "You must go first."

Oh. Yes.

"Sorry." She walked forward with Rainin at her side, Witmara following as was now her place. She climbed onto Rainin, glancing behind to see when the others were astride.

Then she rode off. The Guards formed around her and the others. It felt strange to be riding alone at the head of a procession with this much protection. She had either been riding further back or else with fewer Guards when she rode through Medvare-the-city in the past. As they headed through the streets toward the Leader's House, people stopped to look, then cheer.

"Leader Katerin!" she heard some call. "Witmara!" others yelled.

The voices were approving, to her surprise, as she waved to acknowledge them.

Didn't they love Rekaré?

No mention of Cenarth or Linyet as the crowd hailed her. Were the people of Medvare-the-city so fickle?

A soft brush against her thoughts as the Goddess Dovré manifested herself.

After all that happened before you left to pursue
the betrayer Chiral, it is to be expected. This is
why Rekaré could not come back,

the Goddess said.

They loved her as Leader—didn't they?

They did. But after Chiral's attack and Melarae's death, she lost their confidence. Medvara is still a fragile nation, in spite of all Rekaré and Cenarth have done. They remember the curses of Zauril. The arrogance of Alexran. The burning of the Leader's House.

We were not here when the Leader's House burned. Besides, I am a descendant of Alexran, just like Rekaré. He cursed my father Alame—his own son—and exiled him. Why should they trust me in these troubled times?

Because you were Katerin Healer before you were Katerin ea Miteal and the Banisher of Shadows, and Medvara requires a healer's touch.

The Goddess's presence faded, leaving a bitter taste in Katerin's mouth. She never expected to be Healer to a nation.

The Leader's wing was not visible from first approach, but the stench from the fire permeated the grounds around the Leader's House. They rode to the stables. Katerin settled Rainin in her stall while Cenarth took care of the children and their horses. She joined him as he watched Witmara school Daro in an outside pen. The Guard had withdrawn to their own quarters once they were safely on the grounds, a return to procedures from calmer days.

This would be a better place to talk.

Cenarth managed the stables and supervised the sheep that produced the magic fleece in Rekaré's name. Now what was he going to do?

They stood side by side in the stable doorway's shade. She was grateful the horrible summer heat that had plagued not just

Medvara but the entire land of Varen had faded, even though the air was still cloying and thick with humidity.

The drought and heat as signs of the land's disapproval had been among the reasons Rekaré had given for her abdication.

"I am sorry," she said. "I tried to convince her to stay."

Cenarth shook his head. "You could not have persuaded her." He sighed. "The fire happened the night the courier arrived. The shadows fueled it."

"Shadows?" Her skin prickled.

Rekaré had spent the days around the deaths of her mother and daughter stalking the Leader's House, seeking sorcerous remnants of her father's magic. She had sworn that Zauril had cursed her.

"Rekaré was right about Zauril's haunting the place." He looked at her. "The Great Hall is unusable. The Tapestry drives me out of there. It will not allow anyone else inside. I cannot command it anymore."

Worse than she had thought. "Is that what the Council wants to discuss?"

He nodded, and slipped a signet off of his finger. "I have no right to wear this. The Tapestry is possessed. I no longer have a role in ruling Medvara. Now that you are here, there is no need for me to serve as Regent."

"You are still my co-Regent designate."

"Not since Melarae died. I am heir to the Two Nations of my parents, and Linyet has already been sworn as my heir. We have no claim on Medvara, with both Rekaré and Melarae gone."

"It doesn't have to be that way." Her voice came out weaker than she wanted. "I need help. Advice. I was not trained to be a Leader, Cenarth!"

"You spent eleven years as Healer to Rekaré's mother while she ruled the Two Nations with my parents. You learned something from that."

"Well, yes, but...." Her voice trailed away.

"Rekaré and I spent five years running from her father's pursuit. We didn't have much preparation for Leadership, either. If anything, you're better prepared than we were."

"There's only one of me."

He nodded. "And I will help with the transference of power. You will need to weave a new Tapestry as soon as possible. I will stay until that is done." He paused. "How are my parents?"

"Your mother will live, but I don't expect her to be able to travel from Dera until next spring. Rekaré and her riders escorted them to the Two Nations' border because their guards suffered severe losses."

He tightened his lips and looked away from her, focusing on Witmara and Linyet now brushing Daro in his pen. "She wrote me that this was the last direct service she could perform for Medvara and the Two Nations."

"I'm sorry."

He sighed again. "When I first realized I loved her, I knew that ours would not be an easy or smooth relationship. Her sorcery is too powerful. We feared the Gods had more in mind for her than just Leader of Medvara. But she refuses to walk the path that would make her Empress. So—she has chosen a different path. You said she had riders with her, but her Guard returned with you. Who is with her and where is she going? She's not riding alone—is she?"

"No. There were five Saubral with Chiral who gave their oath to Rekaré Kinslayer, along with Detaluna," Katerin said, her throat tight.

Cenarth grimaced. "Rekaré Kinslayer? Is that what she now calls herself?"

"Chatain called her that after she killed Chiral, and she did not flinch. And then both Dovré and Staul—so yes. She calls herself Rekaré Kinslayer."

"Oh Gods. No wonder she wouldn't come back." He groaned and leaned against the barn wall.

"She plans to ride the nations of Varen to gather information for me and to raise an army to defend against Chatain's next incursions."

"I had hoped she would return with you to say farewell. Even though she said she dared not return when you left."

"She fears what may follow her to Medvara."

"She had promised me we would speak again." He pushed off of the barn wall and straightened up.

"I have another note for you." Katerin reached into the smaller pouch on her belt that she used for important papers. She handed it to Cenarth as the children slowly walked toward them. He read it, sighed, then tucked it into one of his belt pouches.

"Do you want to speak to the Council or see what has become of the Tapestry first?"

Katerin sighed. "I want to see the Tapestry first. I need to earn the Council's respect, and subduing what possesses the Tapestry will do that. Make sure the children are safe."

Cenarth nodded in acknowledgement as she turned away from him.

Smoke smell filled even the untouched hallways of the public part of the Leader's House as Katerin marched toward the Great Hall.

"Leader Katerin!" one of the Council members called as she passed by their chambers. "We need to talk!"

"Not now!" Gods, she would not tolerate their bullying. "I will deal with you after I banish what possesses the Tapestry." She drew upon the part of herself that was the Banisher as she waved the Spear toward him. He shrank back into the Council suite.

She turned to the guards lingering near the chambers.

"Remove everyone from this building. This magic may spill from the Great Hall. I do not want any to be used by whatever fell sorcery may now command the Tapestry."

By the Gods, I swear that one of my first acts as Leader will be to tear this cursed place down and rebuild.

Too much had happened for her to rule comfortably from this building. Perhaps it was the first thing she could do to heal Medvara. Gods knew she had always hated this house.

As she approached the Great Hall, a malign aura swirled around her, bearing a nauseating, rotten-egg stench. Katerin's lips tightened. The Light of Medvara pulsed warm on her chest and the signet in the ring of the Leaders of Medvara glowed golden. If she had any doubts about confronting what had possessed the Tapestry first, they were gone now.

The familiar heaviness in her legs and arms and the increasing thickness of the air around her signaled the presence of the Banisher of Shadows' patron, the God Staul.

Good,

he whispered, not fully manifesting.

You do not go unarmed.

I would be a fool not to.

Amusement came from him.

No one has ever considered you to be a fool.

What advice do you have for the Banisher of Shadows?

Do not hesitate when you confront the Tapestry.

That is all?

My blessing upon you, Banisher of Shadows.
We cannot help you further. You must prove
yourself as Leader of Medvara.

Gods, yet *another* test of her fitness to rule.

The weight of Staul's presence faded as she stood before the doors to the Great Hall. A faint keening moaned behind the doors, coupled with a rising and fading whoosh as if a strong wind blew inside. Katerin tightened her grip on the Spear, and took a deep breath. She whispered four general spells to keep in reserve should she need them, needing only a specific command phrase to engage, before she pushed the door open and stepped inside.

A red whirlwind spun toward her, an unseen force trying to shove her out. Katerin slammed the door shut and stepped forward, slamming the Spear's shaft hard on the scuffed pine floor. The pressure on her ceased. Blood-red tendrils snaked toward her from the spinning vortex. Loud cackles echoed through the Great Hall's expanse.

She thumped the Spear on the floor again. "STOP."

The screeching faded and the tendrils withdrew into the whirlwind. A shadowy shape took form in front of her, coalescing into a likeness of Zauril.

"Who dares command me?" he roared.

"I am Katerin ea Miteal, Leader of Medvara! Begone. You do not belong here!"

Zauril laughed at her. "I have conquered the Miteal before and will continue to do so! Who do you think you are, bastard base-born daughter of Alame? Medvara is *mine*, by grant of Chatain, as your dear cousins have learned to their detriment and failure. Do you think yourself greater than Alexran, Alicira, and Rekaré? The House of Miteal is nothing more than a decrepit remnant fit for nothing more than satisfying the fever dreams of savages playing with shards of sorcery they do not understand. You, too, will fall to my strength on my path to Godhood."

"I am the daughter of Alame en Miteal and Terani-the-God-Killer of Waykemin. I banished the Twin Gods from the Two Nations without facing the mindless sleep that devoured my mother. And I say to you, Zauril the Cursed, that it is time for your miserly grasp upon Medvara to *end!*" She lunged forward with the Spear.

Zauril backtracked. A red sword appeared in his hand. He sneered at her. "Do you think it will be as easy as that? You cannot call upon your Gods for help here."

She *had* hoped it would be that easy.

"I am the Banisher of Shadows," she said through gritted teeth. "And you are no would-be God but a jumped-up aspirant!"

Sword,

she thought to the Spear.

As it changed form, a worried expression crossed Zauril's shadowy face. He lunged toward her and she engaged.

The Spear as sword had a mind of its own. But after the recent battle with Chiral's supporters, Katerin had learned to follow its guidance. She fell into a rhythm, matching Zauril stroke-for-stroke as they battled across the floor.

The Tapestry reached out to impair her.

"Cease!" she ordered, keeping her focus on Zauril as she flung one of her prepared spells at it.

Zauril pressed her toward it. She smelled smoke, and realized the Tapestry had caught fire.

Better it be destroyed than aid him.

She flicked a second spell behind her. "Confine!"

His strokes weakened. He *was* drawing power from it. She pressed forward, until he fell backward into the Leader's chair.

Now she could finish his shade. Rekaré had beheaded him in their battle. But he had come back from that. She intended to banish his shadow from Medvara forever, if she could.

Spear,

she thought.

As it changed form, she plunged it deep into his chest.

"By the power of the Banisher of Shadows, I expel you from the land of Medvara! You are no God, nor shall you ever be!"

Zauril's face contorted.

"You do not know what you create. I will come back more powerful than ever, even if it is through your prized child!"

"And I will be here to stop you," she answered.

As his shade shimmered away, a burst of heat wrapped around her from the Tapestry. Katerin stepped back, coughing. Flames twisted around the Tapestry.

She considered using her remaining spells to stop it.

No.

Rekaré had been right about the curses of Zauril on this place. Let it burn.

Sometimes drastic measures were required. She backed out of the Great Hall, locking the doors behind her, then ran down the hallway until she encountered the guards she had left behind.

"Fire in the Great Hall!" she bellowed. "Has everyone been cleared, as I ordered?"

"They have been, Leader." The head guard stepped forward. "The Council objects. I will send people to put the fire out."

"Gods no! Clear everyone including the Council and let it burn!"

"M-my lady, you w-wouldn't...." the guard stuttered, shock crossing her face.

"The place is cursed." Katerin stopped short from snapping at the woman. "It's time to clean house. Make sure that the records are safe...."

"Cenarth had them removed after the Leader's wing burned."

"Then make sure all people are clear and withdraw. I will contain the fire so that it does not spread."

"I understand." But she still saw doubt on the guard's face. "Are you sure?"

"Sometimes you need to cauterize an injury," she snapped. She strode past the guards and they fell in place behind her. As she marched out of the public wing, the Council swarmed toward her.

"Leader Katerin, what is going on?" the Council leader blustered.

She stopped short. "What needed to happen to this abomination. Now let me be. I need to contain the flames so that we do not lose the stables or the other buildings on these grounds."

"But my Leader—"

Katerin glanced at the head of her guards. "He distracts me. Remove all of them."

She turned to face the building, the Spear clenched tightly in her hand. She raised both hands high, focusing on the bright orange flames spreading along the rooftop. She closed her eyes, drawing on the power lurking within the Light of Medvara, and concentrated, visualizing a transparent containment that kept the fire from reaching outward. As the conflagration swallowed the building, she shook from the effort of keeping it *there* and not letting it spread further.

Time passed. She desperately wanted to lower her arms, to collapse on the ground. But she fought fatigue back, struggling to keep the firestorm confined. It seemed as if the flames licked at her face, her body, as Zauril alternately screamed and laughed at her.

Katerin held firm, keeping her eyes closed. Zauril's voice faded, overwhelmed by the inferno's roar and the crash of timbers. The roar finally diminished, followed by the ebbing of heat. Thunder crashed, and a single raindrop landed on her cheek. Cool damp preceded the rush of wind and water as more drops followed the first one, tempo increasing until waves of rain battered her.

She opened her eyes and lowered her arms, leaving it to the rain. Her legs gave way under her and she fell to hands and knees, gasping for breath, trying to draw strength from the land's magic. It didn't respond to her touch. Despair flooded over her.

How can I heal Medvara if it refuses me, too?

Someone approached and she snarled at them. Too much magic still roiled around her and she had no one close that she trusted.

Alone, alone, alone. No one for me ever. Who can I depend upon? Who will help me lead?

"Mama?" Witmara's voice was tentative. "The House has been consumed. Should I have not called the rain to put the fire out and ease your burden? Are you all right?"

Katerin looked up at her daughter's concerned face, dry amongst the deluge. For a moment it contorted into something ugly.

It is Witmara and not Zauril, she reminded herself. *But if she's been possessed....* Hadn't Zauril threatened just that?

Power stirred under her hands.

Do you not trust your own daughter?

a soft voice asked, faint disappointment coloring its tone.

Do you choose to repeat the mistakes of your predecessors? Are you the Banisher of Shadows or are you but another Miteal spawn blinded by the seduction of your power? Another one who devours her offspring?

She remembered the many and small ways that Witmara had supported her. The power within her daughter. The potential. The strength that her early bonding to Daro portended.

No,

she said back to that voice.

I will not choose that path.

Good.

The strength that had evaded her surged into her hands.

Awareness flooded through her along with strength. Alexran had not trusted his children or grandchildren. Zauril hadn't trusted anyone even as he sought to capture and exploit Rekaré. And Rekaré had doubted Melarae. All of that distrust had poisoned their connection with the land's magic.

So simple.

"You did the right thing," she said to her daughter, sitting up. "It is all right now."

"Let me help you up." Witmara came close. The rain pounded around them but not on them.

"Thank you." Katerin took Witmara's hand and stood, hugging her daughter close as they turned to look at the debris.

"What will we do now? Where will we stay?"

"We will rebuild," Katerin said. "We will heal this land. And as for a place to stay—there are shrines to Dovré and Staul here. I am certain one of them will welcome us for the time being. We will need to weave the new Tapestry as soon as possible—you and me together."

"Together? But you are the Leader."

"I am but a Regent for you, my daughter. We must weave it together."

"I like that. Will I need to weave my own Tapestry when I become Leader?"

"I do not know," Katerin said, her heart lightening as they walked away from the wreckage and toward the gaggle of Council leaders.

The land's approval pulsed through her every step. The rain stopped and sunlight broke through the dark clouds overhead to shine on them. The fresh scent of rain-washed air lightened the oppressive, heavy feel it had possessed earlier.

They stopped in front of the Council. As one, the four women and three men bowed to her.

"Leader Katerin," the headwoman said, stepping forward. "I am sorry for this loss."

"It should have happened years ago, after Zauril's death," Katerin answered her sharply. The woman flinched back as if stung. "It was too big, too pretentious, too much a relic of what my ancestors fled Daran-over-Sea to avoid and made worse by Zauril's presence. We will build a simpler and more useful Leader's House."

Even as the headwoman and several other Council members frowned, Katerin knew she was right.

Sometimes healing needed to begin with drastic measures.

It's one way to clean house.

UNEXPECTED ALLIANCES

UNEXPECTED ALLIANCES

This is not the choice I wanted you to make.

Rekaré could hear Cenarth's voice as clearly as if he were standing next to her instead of at their farewell several days ago. How many days had it been? As she lay in her bedroll, staring up at the brilliant stars overhead, she couldn't say for sure. Everything blurred together. The last clear thing she could remember was loading onto the deck of the *Morning Star* in Medvare-the-city. Vengeance had been on her mind then, vengeance for the deaths of her mother Alicira and her daughter Melarae, plus the attack on her Heartfather Heinmyets and Secondmother Inharise.

Still, she tried to count the days.

A day and a half on the Morning Star *upriver.*

That part was clear. Then things blurred again. How long had it taken to reach her Heartfather and Secondmother? Had it only taken them one day to catch up with their attackers? She remembered the battle—where she had truly earned the title *Rekaré Kinslayer*—and resigning the Leadership of Medvara. Remembered her cousin Katerin's stunned expression as Rekaré advanced her from Regent-Designate to full Leadership.

Then things blurred again. She had helped escort Heinmyets and seriously wounded Inharise to safety at the border with the Two Nations. *That* heart-wrenching farewell from yesterday was clear, worse than parting from Cenarth since it was the final rejection of all she had known.

And now she rode with one ally and five—well, what could she call the Saubral who accompanied her?

Former enemies.

But not necessarily friends. Possible allies. Those with whom she shared a goal. That last was most accurate. Whether they would be more than possible allies depended on what happened when she met the Hidden One in Gulter.

At least these riders were regular Saubral riders, not Shadowwalkers nor Houndriders. Their feet appeared to be normal, not cloven, and they were brown-skinned, not gray like the Shadowwalkers. Nor were they the diminutive gray-green Houndriders.

Rekaré groaned and ran her fingers through her now-short dark hair. She had cut hair for her mother and daughter at their funeral pyres. Given a token lock for her *other* cousin, Chiral, who had led the attacks on Heinmyets and Inharise and brought about the deaths of Alicira and Melarae.

It didn't feel like enough. It certainly hadn't silenced the voices that haunted her dreams and left her wide awake on this moonless late summer night in the high desert. Or morning, rather, given the paleness of the eastern sky.

> Rekaré Kinslayer, Rekaré Kinslayer, what will you do now?

If it wasn't Nitel sneering these words into her dreams, it was Nitel's allies Karnoi and Cirdel.

Or it was Chatain, the Emperor-over-Sea, whose tool Chiral had been.

Or it was her beloved spouse Cenarth pleading for her to

return—not to her former nation of Medvara, not as Leader. That was gone from her. But to help with the transition of the Leadership of the Two Nations as Heinmyets and Inharise passed it to Cenarth.

Oh my beloved, if only I could.

But doom and disaster lay in that direction. His mother Inharise, her Secondmother, now suffered from serious injury because of Rekaré's choices. And to return to the Two Nations labeled with the epithet *Kinslayer*? She could not do that to those who raised her.

She was truly cursed.

And she dared not go back to sleep because anything she could say to Cenarth, even in dreams, would only disappoint him. Besides, it was almost time to rise for the day's ride.

Today we reach Gulter.

Home of her people's closest and most dangerous foes. And she sought an alliance with them? What kind of fool was she?

I must try. I promised Katerin.

If anyone could call the Saubral to the aid of Medvara, it would be Rekaré as Kinslayer. The Saubral would understand that aspect of her.

Rekaré crawled out of her bedroll, retrieving her boots from where she'd tucked them under the covers. She shook them out in case a scorpion had wandered into one of them. Each move she made was slow and cautious, alert for the warning rattle that meant a venomous snake had taken refuge from the chill desert night near her warmth. Her protective magic wasn't reliable in this Saubral country.

It hadn't been reliable since everything had gone wrong.

No rattle disturbed her stealthy movements. She chose this spot near the horses, farthest away from the fire, not because she was as much worried about raiders stealing them—not in the Saubral lands, riding with Saubral warriors—as she was about being too close to her companions. Who knew how safe from her any of them would be? They rode with a kinslayer, after all.

She picked up her bow, leaving her short sword on her bedroll, and walked over to the low fire. At least she could relieve Sesenth, currently on watch.

Sesenth raised a brow as Rekaré joined her. "Another night without sleep?"

Rekaré nodded, not wanting to speak.

Sesenth shrugged. "We'll need to wake the others soon. Going to be another hot day. We're close enough to Gulter to press on through the heat instead of taking a midday break."

Gulter.

The city where the Hidden One ruled over the Saubral.

Why was she amongst those who were sworn foes of her people? she asked herself again.

Because I am the Kinslayer. Because the danger presented by Chatain to all of Varen outweighs any threat to my person. Because I must make the Hidden One listen, and only the Kinslayer can do that.

Chatain controlled most of the land of Daran-over-Sea, and had sought to rule the Miteal colonies in Varen for years. Rumor held that his goals were higher—that he ultimately sought to depose and supplant one of the Seven Crowned Gods.

Not while I draw breath.

She had promised Katerin that she would be her eyes and ears throughout Varen, that she would raise support for Chatain's inevitable invasion.

I owe you my vengeance, Chatain. You most of all.

"Deep thoughts," Sesenth said.

Rekaré ran her fingers through her hair again, not wanting to talk about Chatain and what lay ahead of her. The hair was a welcome distraction from those thoughts.

"This doesn't feel right."

"You have cut a lock of hair." Sesenth's tone remained

neutral. "That would seem right to mourn kin who betrayed you."

"It's not enough."

"Is this what you want?" Sesenth pulled off the tight-fitting brown cap she wore under her black cowl and had never taken off since Rekaré met her, though she removed the cowl in camp. Her head gleamed bald underneath the cap.

"That would seem right, yes." An unwilling curiosity sparked in her. "Is that a Saubral thing?"

"It marks devotees to Staul the Destroyer," Sesenth said. "Are you certain that's what you want?"

Tears threatened to well up in Rekaré's eyes as she nodded. "Yes. As soon as we can. Probably once there's light."

"The fire provides enough light to do it now, and we won't be delayed in riding out. Give me a moment." Sesenth got up and shook one of the others awake to take over the watch. She rummaged in her bedroll, and returned with an oddly-shaped knife and a jug. "Kneel by the fire, Rekaré Kinslayer. Kneel and receive the blessing of Staul the Destroyer."

Rekaré eyed the sharp edge of the knife reflecting the firelight. It would be just as easy for Sesenth to cut her throat as her hair.

Isn't that the risk you take, Kinslayer? You are cursed.

She was no longer Leader of Medvara. What would Sesenth gain by her death? What more did she have to gamble? If Sesenth chose to kill her, wasn't it because Staul had decreed her deserving of death after all?

Rekaré dismissed her fears and knelt by the fire. Sesenth poured pungent oil over her head. She bit her lower lip and stared at the fist-sized lava rocks that made up the impromptu fire ring, hands clenched into fists, as Sesenth carefully shaved the hair off of her head. The first clump fell in the dust next to the fire. Rekaré changed her focus to that strand. She winced as

Sesenth scraped her scalp and rubbed more oil into the cut. It stung. But the pain felt necessary and right.

Absolution for what I have done.

If there could ever be absolution.

When it was done Sesenth oiled Rekaré's head again. "Welcome to the company of the damned, Rekaré Kinslayer. Now you are truly one of us."

Rekaré sat up and ran her hands over her bare head.

Now what?

In response to her unspoken question Sesenth produced a felted blue cap. "One of my old ones," she said.

"Thank you," Rekaré said. She picked up the oily strands and cast them onto the fire. As the stink rose, the others began to stir. Rekaré walked away from the fire to rejoin the horses, staring east, toward the first pinkish glow of light at the rim of the distant mountains.

No turning back now.

She expected to feel Staul's approval as gold mixed with the pink of sunrise. It came as a light touch, one she had learned to recognize. What she did not expect was the added approval of the Goddess Dovré, her former patroness.

I said I would not abandon you,

Dovré whispered deep into her soul as Rekaré watched the sunrise, her scalp throbbing.

Thank you Goddess.

She would need that confidence today when she rode into Gulter.

Sesenth joined Rekaré, holding out a short black cowl like the one she wore during the day.

"This goes with the cap," she said. "Both are my gift to you, Kinslayer."

"How can I repay you?"

A sardonic smile twisted Sesenth's lips. "Your friend Detaluna rides at your right hand. I would ride at your left hand."

"It is a blood-red road I face."

"Who better than me to ride with you?" Sesenth exhaled, staring at the sunrise. "Besides," she said in a quieter voice, "I've had a vision. I seek to follow in my mother's ways and become a Shadowwalker, but there are none remaining of her strength to mentor me in all of Saubral—at least not since you slew Gegarth. Serving Rekaré Kinslayer's quest to defeat Chatain will be my pathway toward obtaining that mantle." A wry smile twisted her lips. "I want to be the greatest of all Shadowwalkers. Defeating Chatain at your side will make me so."

Rekaré repressed a shudder. The Shadowwalkers were the reddest of red magicians, completely committed to the Destroyer side of the God Staul.

"You do not wear the shape of a Shadowwalker."

"Because I have not yet earned the right to transform," Sesenth said. "You will give me the right to do that."

What does it make me that I create a new Shadowwalker?

What didn't she know about Shadowwalkers? Much, clearly. And yet—

Rekaré could not afford to be finicky about her allies.

She turned to Sesenth. "I accept your gifts and your quest, Sesenth. May we both find what we seek."

"Thank you. It's more than my ambition. Chatain's touch is foul. A curse upon all. What I sensed of it through Chiral...." Sesenth's voice trailed off. "I would speak for your cause to the Hidden One."

"Thank you." Rekaré took the hood. "However, I want to change this color."

"To what?"

"Red. Blood red, to match the road we face."

"Just for you or for all of Staul's sworn who follow you?"

Unasked for, power hummed through Rekaré. For a moment she saw herself in the blood-red cowl. Power shimmered around her as she raised a red-edged sword.

Then the vision faded.

"All of us, then," Sesenth whispered in an awed tone.

"You saw my vision?"

"With Detaluna at your left and me at your right," Sesenth said. She dropped to her knees. "Lady Rekaré, if this vision becomes true..." She took Rekaré's hand and kissed it. "I am your servant."

"Tch." Rekaré wrapped her hand around Sesenth's and pulled her up. "Visions are not cast in stone, and Chatain is an ocean away from us."

"Nonetheless. I will do whatever is necessary to make that vision happen."

"Time will tell."

The fanatic glow in Sesenth's eyes made Rekaré uneasy as she donned the cowl. *Now what am I becoming?*

As she returned to the fire Detaluna looked up from where she knelt by the fire. Their eyes met and held for a moment. Then Detaluna nodded, approving.

Rekaré didn't expect to feel this degree of relief at her endorsement.

Then she wondered if Detaluna also possessed a vision.

They approached Gulter by dropping into a narrow, rocky crack in the ground that forced their group to ride single file on the trail winding through the great basalt walls. Sesenth led, pausing occasionally to flash handsign at unseen sentinels above them as the fissure deepened. Rekaré tried to keep track of the number of twists in the path before Sesenth signaled, but couldn't discern a pattern. Magic shimmered around them, tentative at first, then stronger and more hostile as they proceeded.

Her magic-gifted daranval mare, Basnen, trembled at the feel of Saubral sorcery. Rekaré patted Basnen's neck and sent her reassuring thoughts. The golden mare calmed, trusting the bond they had held for so many years.

I hope Basnen's confidence is rightly placed.

Suddenly the crack widened and they dropped into a hot, wide, rock-walled basin, their mounts scrambling down a dusty, narrow trail toward the first row of stone buildings. As far as Rekaré could see the basin was filled with buildings constructed of the same gray basalt as the walls. Tan-shaded cloth sheltered reed mat-lined pathways wound between the rock structures.

Little moved on those pathways in the intense heat of late afternoon. Some people sprawled against tripod-backed chairs outside of the buildings. They reached for their weapons, then laid them back down after scrutinizing the new arrivals. A few were attired in cowls, tunics, and long pants like Rekaré and the other riders, but most wore simple breechclouts, men and women alike. She thought she saw a couple of gray-green Houndriders slipping down one of the alleys. Otherwise, all she saw were brown-skinned Saubral people, neither Houndriders nor Shadowwalkers.

Then one of those wearing a cowl left the closest building. His skin was gray and his bare feet were cloven flesh.

Shadowwalker.

And she had agreed to create one of these. How dare she contemplate this?

Because I must.

"Sesenth. What do you bring us?" The Shadowwalker's voice was harsh and grating.

Sesenth leapt off her horse. "News for the Hidden One, Firenigth." She gestured toward Rekaré. "This one brings change from Medvara."

"Medvara!" Firenigth spat. "What good ever comes from those colonizers?"

"This one is different," Sesenth said. "She is *benghaalph,* the One Spoken Of."

Firenigth spat again, scrutinizing Rekaré. "An Aireii? Sworn to Staul?"

"A Miteal. *The* Miteal, or at least that is what she was. Heartsdaughter to the Two Nations. Daughter of she-who-diced-with-Staul."

"How the mighty have fallen." Firenigth sauntered around Basnen, his eyes boring into Rekaré. She sat up straight and dropped her reins, wordlessly preparing Basnen for an attack.

Firenigth did not disappoint her expectations. He reached for Basnen's bridle.

Basnen flattened her ears and snapped at him. She swung her head into his body, knocking his hand away with her muzzle and sending him staggering two steps back.

"You...." Firenigth charged at Basnen.

Rekaré sat lightly, following her mare's movement as Basnen seized his forearm in her teeth. One of her golden forelegs struck his right leg. The mare forced him to the ground, landing on her knees. Rekaré kept her hands free from the reins as Basnen released his arm and stood back up. Basnen lowered her head, ears pinned back hard, teeth bared, ready should he move again.

"No one touches my horse without my permission!"

Firenigth clutched his forearm, glowering at her. "That beast is dangerous."

"She is an experienced daranval war mare. Are you always such a fool?"

Sesenth snorted and Rekaré thought she choked back a laugh.

"Firenigth has been in the Pit too long. Perhaps he needs to ride patrol again." She strode over and helped him up. "Now. Let the Hidden One know that *benghaalph* has come to us."

A breechclouted Saubral man joined them as Firenigth scurried away. He bowed to Sesenth. "What needs to be done for you and our guests, Sesenth? Are you staying or is this a stop?"

Hospitality at last. Who would have thought it amongst the Saubral?

"Kovi!" Genuine joy filled Sesenth's voice and she hugged him. "We are staying for at least one night." She turned to Rekaré. "Kovi is my brother and a skilled horseman, our head trainer. Do you want to handle your mare yourself or would you trust him?"

"She's a beauty," Kovi said, holding the back of his hand toward Basnen. "A lovely daranval. One of Elantai's get?"

Rekaré raised her brows in surprise. Her Heartfather's stallion was famous, but even so, she wouldn't have expected a Saubral to recognize Basnen as one of his daughters.

"Yes," she said.

Kovi smirked as Basnen delicately sniffed his hand. He slowly slid his hand up her blaze to scratch between her eyes. "I've seen another of Elantai's get take down a raider for grabbing at his bridle just like she did." He shook his head. "There were safer horses to steal in that raid, but Tenketh just couldn't pass up a daranval. He got stomped for his pains, and it was hard for the rest of us to get away as a result. Firenigth is as much of a fool as Tenketh was. There's a reason why he doesn't go out any more. He did just enough raiding to secure his position as a bureaucrat."

"She seems to like you," Rekaré said slowly as Basnen twitched her face, moving her head so that Kovi could scratch another itchy place. She wondered just how many times Kovi had participated in raids—and with whom.

"I have more respect for daranvelii than to grab at them without their rider's permission. So. If you will trust me, I will tend to your beauty myself while my grooms take care of the rest of your horses and—" his eyes rested on Detaluna's daranval. "I'll handle the daranvelii. Safer that way—if you two prefer."

"I'll supervise the unloading of the packs," Detaluna said. "One daranval with an unfamiliar handler is probably enough."

That eased any lingering worry Rekaré had. "Basnen has accepted you, so I am all right with having you handle her, Kovi. Especially since Detaluna will be there."

"Good," Kovi said.

"Have their bedrolls placed at our hearth," Sesenth said. "I am taking my *quixnahi* to the Hidden One."

"She is your *quixnahi*? Hmm. I would not expect an Aireii to serve as your mentor."

"She has accepted Staul's blessing," Sesenth said. "And she is the one who finished Gegarth."

"Worthy of being your mentor, indeed." Kovi gave her a short bob of a bow. "Welcome to Gulter, my sister's *quixnahi*. May you find what you seek."

Rekaré dismounted and handed her reins to Kovi. Then she undid her saddlebags and slung them over her shoulder. She left her unstrung bow hanging from the saddle.

"Should I leave my sword with Detaluna?" she asked Sesenth. That would have been protocol in both Medvara and the Two Nations. But here—always best to ask.

"You are my *quixnahi*," Sesenth said. "There is no need. You may walk armed here."

Rekaré nodded. "Well then. Let us go meet the Hidden One."

❀

The Hidden One's Great Hall was located deep in the maze of stone buildings that made up Gulter. Rekaré kept track of the twists and turns they took through the narrow passageways—nowhere near big enough to be called streets, definitely too small for horses and riders. Occasionally the passages opened up on small shaded plazas with pools in the center.

Even with the shades across the top of the pathways it was hot. She understood now why so many here wore nothing more than a breechclout. Tendrils of air moved sluggishly through the labyrinth, but not enough to cool.

Oh well. The lack of people in the alleys meant fewer staring eyes on her. Those that they did encounter startled when they noticed Rekaré's paler skin. Sesenth's glare silenced them and they looked away. Rekaré did not see any more Houndriders or Shadowwalkers.

Does this mean their numbers have lessened?

Not that any non-Saubral knew for certain how many of those creatures existed. And if they could transform from normal humans, like Sesenth implied...*I need to learn more about the Saubral.*

"How do you stand the heat?" she asked Sesenth when they stopped to drink at one of the plaza fountains.

"It is much more comfortable inside the buildings. And this is the worst of the summer. Cooling starts soon."

Rekaré nodded. She wanted to remove her cowl and cap, splash her head and face to cool it. But though sweat stood out clearly on Sesenth's face she did nothing more than drink from the fountain.

Best to follow her lead.

The fountains might be restricted to drinking only, not washing.

At last they entered a courtyard bigger than the others. Guards stood at the entrances but let them pass without challenge.

The Houndriders and Shadowwalkers lurked here. Five gray-skinned Shadowwalkers, wearing cowls like Firenigth, stood next to a shrouded person sitting on a stone throne. Firenigth stood at the person's right hand.

The Hidden One?

Most likely. What she could see of that person's skin was leathery and scaled, a little like the Houndriders but browner.

The remaining fifteen awaiting them were Houndriders. They sneered at Rekaré, gibbering nonsense as she and Sesenth walked by. One lunged toward Rekaré. Without breaking stride Sesenth kicked it out of their way, sending it yipping. She snarled something in a language Rekaré didn't understand. The Houndriders moved further away from them but their eyes lingered hungrily on Rekaré, open desire gleaming from their faces. It made her skin crawl but she did not acknowledge it, focusing on that shrouded being sitting on the throne.

Sesenth stopped before the steps leading up to the stone seat. She knelt, touching her forehead to the ground, then rose. Rekaré bowed. She would not kneel to the Hidden One but she would acknowledge her as an equal.

"My lady," Sesenth said. "I announce the coming of my *quix-nahi* at long last."

"Firenigth says you call her *benghaalph* as well," the shrouded one said. "But she is Aireii. How can that be? How is it that one of Dovré's wears the cowl of one sworn to the Destroyer? How can Rekaré ea Miteal be the One Spoken Of?"

"Rekaré ea Miteal is no more," Rekaré said. "I am Rekaré Kinslayer. I ride a trail of vengeance for the deaths of my mother and daughter. Chatain manipulated my cousin Chiral to cause their deaths. For that I killed her. But now I have a greater goal and seek a greater prey—the union of all Varen to destroy Chatain."

"Chatain," the shrouded one said slowly. "That is—interesting." She snapped her fingers. "Leave us. All of you except Sesenth and her *quixnahi.*"

"Mistress—" Firenigth began, clearly distressed.

"Leave us. All but Sesenth. I will take the vow of her *quixnahi.*"

The others left but Firenigth lingered. "If you harm her—" he said to Rekaré.

"I have no reason to do so," she said.

Then it was just the three of them in the courtyard, though Rekaré was aware that the Houndriders and Shadowwalkers watched from the doorways. The Hidden One sighed loudly, and waved a hand. Shades dropped over the six openings. She muttered something. The faint sounds from the city around them faded. Then she pushed herself up. Sesenth hurried to help her but she waved Sesenth away.

"So, Rekaré ea Miteal that was, Rekaré Kinslayer now." The Hidden One lifted her shroud. "Gaze now on what I am and tell me that you are both *quixnahi* and *benghaalph.*" She threw the shroud over her head so that it landed on the throne behind her.

What does she want?

Rekaré contemplated at the twisted and shriveled form before her, now clad only in a breechclout. The Hidden One had the leathery, scaled skin of both Shadowwalker and Houndrider, with the fleshy cloven feet of the Shadowwalkers. Scars twisted across her body—some from battle, others clearly from ritual. Tattoos covered the parts of her skin without scars. But despite her withered form, power radiated out from the Hidden One.

Her power lies in the tattoos, supported by the scars,

Staul whispered to her.

> You must identify what is Shadowwalker and what is Houndrider…and what makes her the Hidden One. That will prove you are benghaalph.

"I see you wear the sigils of the Shadowwalkers," Rekaré began.

The Hidden One nodded, gray eyes glimmering bright. "Ah, but which are Shadowwalker and which are Houndrider?"

How do I tell?

Rekaré scrutinized the marks. The matching blue tattoos that wound down the Hidden One's cheeks and into her neck caught her attention.

Shadowwalker or Houndrider? Shadowwalker.

"The blue tattoos running from your cheeks down your neck and onto your shoulders are Shadowwalker sigils," Rekaré said.

How do I know that?

Staul chuckled inside her thoughts.

> Keep going.

"The red tattoos twisting around your arms are Houndrider."

The Hidden One nodded.

Rekaré continued, chronicling each tattoo. When she was finished, the Hidden One bowed to her.

"Sesenth speaks truly. You are *benghaalph,* and are clearly qualified not only to be Sesenth's *quixnahi* but to lead my people against the colonizer threat from overseas. Kneel now, Rekaré Kinslayer, and receive my blessing."

"Just like that?"

"If you were not blessed by Staul you would not know what those tattoos meant. Only one of his beloveds would know what those marks were. And you move against Chatain."

"But you don't want to know why?"

The Hidden One shrugged. "Chatain was instrumental in the deaths of your mother and daughter. He has been trying to subvert my own for many years, from before you defeated your father and became Leader of Medvara. Do you wonder why I have so few Houndriders and Shadowwalkers left to me? Over the years I have needed to purge my followers to keep myself safe. Chatain is a danger to all Varen. He must not succeed in his goal to dominate both this world and the Gods."

"I—see." She had anticipated more of an argument.

The Hidden One's eyes twinkled. "There are those who will disagree with my choice. Firenigth, for one. But he does not see what lies ahead, and will not until it is too late. I have been waiting for you to accept your destiny for a long time, Rekaré Kinslayer. It pleases me to see it coming into being now."

"I cannot accept your rule over me."

"And that is not what I ask. This is merely a blessing, nothing more." The Hidden One extended her hand toward Rekaré, palm facing her. "But I invite you to check my intentions."

Rekaré swallowed and pressed her hand against the Hidden One's reptilian scales. She looked into the other's mind, noting what was hidden and what was open to her. She found the blessing the Hidden One intended to give her, and examined the words and intent weighting it.

It is what she says,

Staul said to Rekaré.

It will aid you.

She sent a wordless affirmation to the God, and slipped her hand free.

"I accept your blessing and your alliance," she said, and knelt.

As the Hidden One pronounced her blessing, though, Rekaré

mused upon the irony. The Saubral had been enemies with her people for years.

Chatain, you do not know what awaits you.

If she were fortunate, she would be able to forge similar alliances with the other nations of Varen—well, except for Waykemin.

And that I will leave to Katerin Leader.

Katerin, who she now served.

"We will feast tonight," the Hidden One said. "Go forth and rest until then, Rekaré Kinslayer." She lifted her hands, and the faint mutterings of the city rose about them again.

Rekaré bowed again to the Hidden One as Sesenth repeated her deep obeisance. She followed Sesenth toward a different doorway.

Firenigth intercepted them, drawing his sword. "Rekaré Kinslayer! I challenge you, as a false *benghaalph* and *quixnahi*!"

Sesenth raised her hand. "The Hidden One has spoken!"

"Then she should not object to her chosen one proving herself." Firenigth's eyes glowed red. "After all, if this one should truly be what she claims, then defeating me shouldn't be that difficult." He scowled at her. "She wears Staul's cowl, but is she really of him?"

"Firenigth," the Hidden One growled. "You presume much. She read my marks accurately."

"Ah, but did she *know* them?"

I can't let this one go. I have to prove myself here, or else risk a knife in the back as long as I'm in Saubral territory. Where there is one like him there will be more. They will be more cautious if I defeat this one.

Rekaré unsheathed her sword. "I accept."

God and Goddess, aid me!

A slow smile spread across Firenigth's lips. "You see? She accepts!"

"You did not need to do this," the Hidden One sighed.

"Better to prove myself now than to dread a hidden knife," Rekaré said. "Is it to first blood, or to the death?"

"Blood," the Hidden One said.

"Death," Firenigth growled. "I swear it by my Lord Staul."

"Then death it will be, by Staul and Dovré united!" Rekaré snapped.

"See? She even swears by the alien Goddess!" he crowed.

"The Seven Crowned Gods rule over all, even here in Saubral," she countered, circling around Sesenth, watching as Firenigth turned to face her.

What kind of fighter would he be? Bold? Cunning? Her past encounters with Shadowwalkers had been defensive. How would their dueling style differ?

"This is Staul's land, and Staul only!"

He lies,

the God whispered to her.

But neither Dovré nor I can help you.

Typical of the Gods, she thought but did not say, concentrating instead on her opponent.

Firenigth feinted and she parried. He withdrew, circling.
Cautious.

But one who felt capable of matching her in single combat. She probed his defenses and they engaged. He was a competent fighter, confident but in no hurry to press his attack.
A sneaky one.

But hadn't the Hidden One said something about him?
He does not see what lies ahead, and will not until it is too late.

Did that apply to fighting as well?

Kovi had also said Firenigth had gone on just enough raids to earn a bureaucrat's role.

A schemer. I should know how to deal with those after eleven years in Medvara.

They engaged again. This time she drew blood, slashing his shoulder.

"Do you yield?" she asked.

"Never!" He came at her wildly.

She held back, this time opening a gash across his forehead. As she expected, it bled freely, dripping into his eyes.

"Second blood. Yield."

"I will never yield to Aireii filth, no matter what your claims are to *benghaalph* and *quixnahi*!"

"I do not wish to kill you." It was a poor way to begin an alliance.

"Then you will die!" He charged at her. She evaded him.

"Do not play with him!" the Hidden One called. "You have given him many choices. Finish him, Kinslayer!"

"Even you have turned against me!" Firenigth bellowed. "You will see the error of your ways!" He wiped his eyes clear, and ran toward Rekaré recklessly with his sword extended, this time not even bothering with tactics.

He wants to die.

She stepped aside as he swung at her, then moved in close, impaling him. She pulled the sword free, then decapitated him.

Just like she had done to Gegarth, the previous Shadowwalker she had killed. Just like she had done to her father Zauril. Just like she had done a few days ago to her cousin Chiral. She knelt to wipe her sword on Firenigth's clothing, stood, sheathed it, then turned to face the Hidden One.

"My regrets," she said. "It was not my choice to kill him."

"You have done me a great favor, Lady Rekaré. Sooner or later he would have challenged me." The Hidden One rose and knelt by Firenigth's head, picking it up. "Firenigth, Firenigth my son. I wish you had chosen differently than to die at the Kinslayer's hand. But better it was her and not me." She set his head down. As she struggled to her feet, Rekaré offered her hand to help. The Hidden One looked at it, then at Rekaré. She took Rekaré's hand. Her weight was curiously light as Rekaré pulled her up.

"You must know that this makes you more than *quixnahi*, Rekaré Kinslayer," the Hidden One said. She gestured to the Shadowwalkers who still stood in the doorways. "Come forward and acknowledge your new *quixnafal*."

"*Quixnafal?*" Rekaré asked.

"You are now leader of the *quix*, my beloved Shadowwalkers."

"I—I—" What could she say to that?

The first Shadowwalker approached. He knelt, offering up his hands. Rekaré placed hers around his.

What do I do now? What do I say?

"I swear my oath to Rekaré Kinslayer as my *quixnafal*," he said. "My name is Dokenth."

"I accept your oath," she said mechanically, still disbelieving. *Is that enough? No.* "Swear that I am your *benghaalph*."

Dokenth swallowed hard. "I swear that Rekaré Kinslayer is my *benghaalph*."

"I accept your oath."

"Oh, well done," the Hidden One said softly to her as Dokenth rose and backed away.

The next Shadowwalker, this one female, approached Rekaré and knelt.

"My name is Renseth," she said in a clear, strong voice. "I swear to Rekaré Kinslayer as my *quixnafal* and *benghaalph*." Renseth continued, more quietly. "And I, too, thank you for ridding us of Firenigth. Lead us to glory, *benghaalph*!"

"I will try," Rekaré answered.

Renseth smiled and rose.

"Will you serve as Second to your *quixnafal?*" the Hidden One asked. Sesenth startled.

"I believe that position is promised to Sesenth," Rekaré said quietly. "I have vowed she will serve as my left hand."

"This will not be an issue," the Hidden One said. "Renseth will guide your *quix* in your name when you are gone from Saubral."

"Then I accept, if she will," Rekaré said.

Renseth clenched her right hand into a fist and slammed it into her chest. "I accept, and thank you for the honor." She rose and stood at Rekaré 's left.

Swearing the remaining three Shadowwalkers proceeded without further incident.

The Hidden One gestured toward Firenigth's body. "Take his body and give it to the air without ritual." She turned to Sesenth. "You will see that your *quixnahi* is properly marked?"

"I will, oh honored one."

"Good." The Hidden One straightened and faced Rekaré. "We will dine tonight and discuss your needs, once you have been properly marked with your signs of office."

"I thank you," Rekaré said. As the Hidden One turned away, she whispered to Sesenth. "So what marks will be made?"

"Two red tattoos on your cheeks, and a matching one over your brows," Sesenth answered.

"I—see."

As she followed Sesenth through Gulter's mazes, she noted that word of her victory seemed to have spread through the city already. Respectful bows replaced the disapproving stares.

You have done well, Rekaré Kinslayer,

Staul said when they stopped to drink from a fountain.

An auspicious beginning to your quest. But be
advised. Chatain also moves to consolidate
power. Empire is within your grasp.

And if I only seek vengeance and not empire?

The God did not answer.

Rekaré let out her breath slowly. She realized that not only Sesenth but six others stared at her.

"She speaks to the God," one said, disbelief tingeing his voice. "She speaks to the God!" he repeated more loudly and firmly. "The Aireii Kinslayer speaks to the God! Go, tell all who will hear of this! She speaks to the God!"

Three of the Saubral scattered into the passageways and Rekaré heard them yelling. Others pressed into the courtyard and knelt to her. She looked questioningly at Sesenth but she, too, knelt to Rekaré.

What have I done? What happens now? What am I becoming?

No God answered her.

THE END

Like this story and want to know what's coming out next, or what deals Joyce is offering on her book?

Check out Joyce's monthly newsletter at

https://joycespublishingnewsfromwideopenspaces.kit.com/ a65eaa89cd

And get a free download snippet from the Martiniere Multiverse!

BOOKS AND PUBLICATIONS

Goddess's Honor

Beyond Honor and Other Stories: Goddess's Honor Book One
Pledges of Honor: Goddess's Honor Book Two
Challenges of Honor: Goddess's Honor Book Three
Choices of Honor: Goddess's Honor Book Four
Judgment of Honor: Goddess's Honor Book Five

The Cost of Power

Return
Snippet: Outtakes from Philip Martiniere
Crucible
Snippet: The Criminal Injustice Interview
Snippet: Sibling Warfare
Redemption
Omnibus Ebook Edition

The Martiniere Legacy

First Meetings: A Martiniere Legacy Short Story
Inheritance: The Martiniere Legacy Book One
Ascendant: The Martiniere Legacy Book Two

Realization: The Martiniere Legacy Book Three

A Belated Christmas Honeymoon: A Martiniere Legacy Short Story

The Enduring Legacy: The Martiniere Legacy Book Four

People of the Martiniere Legacy

The Heritage of Michael Martiniere: A Martiniere Legacy Novel

Broken Angel: The Lost Years of Gabriel Martiniere: A Martiniere Legacy Novel

Justine Fixes Everything: Reflections on Mortality

The Martiniere Multiverse

A Different Life: What If?

A Different Life: Now. Always. Forever.

A Very Multiversal Christmas Miracle

Netwalk Sequence Author Preferred 2022 Editions

Life in the Shadows: Book One

Netwalk: Book Two

Netwalker Uprising: Book Three

Netwalk's Children: Book Four

Learning in Space: Book Five

Netwalking Space: Book Six

Bright Star Fair Witches

Becoming Solo: A Bright Star Fair Witches Novella

Non-Series Titles currently available:

Alien Savvy: A Western SF Novella

Klone's Stronghold: Reeni

Beating the Apocalypse

Bearing Witness

Fabulist and Fantastical Worlds: A Short Story Collection

Federation Cowboy

Vision of Alliance

Vella Titles:

Falcon of the Martinieres (part of *Justine Fixes Everything*)
Bearing Witness
Beating the Apocalypse
A Different Life—What If? An Alternative Martiniere Legacy Novel
Becoming Solo
A Different Life—Linda's Story: An Alternative Martiniere Legacy Novel
Federation Cowboy

Audiobooks Available:

Alien Savvy: A Western SF Novella

Released from other publishers:

"Queen of the Snows," in *Once Upon A Winter: A Folk and Fairy Tale Anthology*, edited by H. L. Macfarlane

"My Man Left Me, My Dog Hates Me, and There Goes My Truck," in *Black-Eyed Peas on New Year's Day: An Anthology of Hope*, edited by Shannon Page

"Lost Loves," in *All Worlds Wayfarer*

"The Wisdom of Robins," in *Whimsical Beasts: A Campcon Anthology*, edited by Joyce Reynolds-Ward

"The Cow at the End of the World," in *Well...It's Your Cow*, edited by Frog Jones

"To Plant or Pull Up Stakes," in *Pulling Up Stakes: A Campcon Anthology*, edited by Joyce Reynolds-Ward

"The Notice," in *Children of a Different Sky*, edited by Alma Alexander

ABOUT THE AUTHOR

The work of Joyce Reynolds-Ward includes themes of high-stakes family and political conflict, digital sentience, personal agency and control, realistic strong women, and (whenever possible) horses. She is the author of *The Netwalk Sequence* series, the *Goddess's Honor* series, *The Martiniere Legacy* series, *The People of the Martiniere Legacy* series, and the recently published *The Cost of Power* trilogy as well as standalones *Klone's Stronghold, Alien Savvy, Beating the Apocalypse,* and *Federation Cowboy.* Joyce is a Self-Published Fantasy BlogOff Semifinalist, a Writers of the Future SemiFinalist, and an Anthology Builder Finalist. She is a member of the Science Fiction and Fantasy Writers Association and a member of Soroptimists International.